Preparation

"Our neighbors have gone mad," Dmitri wrote in his journal. "They speak of the wolves as if they were the Devil. They talk of the hunt as if it is to be a holy act, the shedding of blood for the glory of God. They speak of the sheep that Nadya killed, the beast that they would have eaten for dinner willingly enough, as a defenseless innocent, a creature to be protected.

"We have lingered here too long. We should have gone west last year, or even the year before. But Marietta did not want to leave the house and I did not want to leave the farm. We were happy here. The journey seemed too hard.

"I have begun building a wagon to carry us West. I will build it of seasoned hardwood, durable enough to withstand the hardship of crossing the great desert. We must gather supplies for the long journey. It would be foolish to leave here without preparing ourselves—we would avoid the hunter's bullet only to die of starvation in the desert. I think, if I work quickly, we can leave in a month.

"Marietta says that we must not be hasty. She says that this madness will pass. Our neighbors will set a few traps. They will hunt by daylight, which offers no threat to us. And then, soon, she believes that they will come to their senses. But I remember the hunt, and I can't share her faith."

NADYA

THE WOLF CHRONICLES

PAT MURPHY

A TOM DOHERTY ASSOCIATES BOOK
New York

NADYA: THE WOLF CHRONICLES

Cover art by Michael Koelsch

A Tor Book
Published by Tom Doherty Associates, Inc.
175 Fifth Avenue
New York, N.Y. 10010

Tor Books on the World Wide Web:
http://www.tor.com

ISBN 0-812-55188-5
Library of Congress Card Catalog Number: 96-22939

First edition: November 1996
First mass market edition: September 1997

Printed in the United States of America

0 9 8 7 6 5 4 3 2 1

For Laurie, who helped me find my way to the end.
For Ellen and all the other girls who wanted to grow up and be wolves.
And for Richard, predictably, with love.

ONE

■

An American Childhood

1

Until Dmitri was a young boy, his village was in Poland. The cows, the pigs, the chickens, the men working the fields, the women washing the clothes—all of them were Polish.

Then something happened. Dmitri could see no change, but the schoolmaster told him that the village was now in Russia. The cows, the pigs, the chickens, the men and the women—all of them belonged to the tsar.

That night, Dmitri squinted at the pigs as he poured slop into their trough, but they seemed to be the same pigs as before. They had not changed. The hills around him had not moved. They were the same hills. But now they were Russian hills.

He did not understand. It seemed to him that he (and the pigs and the chickens and all the rest) did not belong to the tsar. It seemed to him that he belonged to himself.

When Dmitri was twelve, a tall black bird with long legs landed in his family's garden and stood among the cabbages and the potato plants, its crested head held high. The bird was as tall as Dmitri, and when it walked, it lifted its legs with regal grace, staring at the ground beneath its feet as if startled to find black dirt there, rather than fine carpets. When Dmitri's mother hurried from the house to chase the bird away, it took three leaping steps and then launched itself in the air, rising on powerful wings. The bird circled the garden, as if searching for something, and then flew away over the marsh. The bird was lost, Dmitri knew. He had never seen another one like it in the marsh. He felt sorry for the bird and hoped that it found its way home.

Petro Kominitsky, the schoolmaster who taught the village children three times each week, reminded Dmitri of that bird. Kominitsky was tall and thin, like the bird. In hands as soft as a woman's hands, he held a quill pen delicately and showed the schoolchildren how to write in a graceful script.

Kominitsky did not fit the village and the village did not fit him. The son of the storekeeper, he had traveled to the city and attended the university there. He had come back to teach in the village school and work in his father's store.

There was a strange and restless energy about Petro Kominitsky. Sometimes, after the children had spent the morning reciting their alphabet and working sums, he would tell them about the city and the world beyond it. He would talk about distant places: Paris and Vienna and London. And a place called America that was unimaginably far away.

People laughed at Petro Kominitsky because he had gone to the city to study at the university, and then had returned to the village to work in his father's store. Dmitri heard an old woman saying that Petro's hands were as soft as a woman's. Petro did not fit into the village life. He did not go to church with the rest of his family. He sat alone, reading books, rather than joining in conversation.

But Dmitri liked the awkward schoolmaster. He did not mind that the villagers did not like him. Many of the people who lived in the village (Dmitri thought of them as the other ones, the ones who were not his family) regarded Dmitri and his family with suspicion. Sometimes, in the village, Dmitri overheard muttered insults. Never to his face, always behind his back as he was walking away. "Little hairy one," the storekeeper would mutter. "Beast of the devil." But Petro Kominitsky always treated him like the other children, rapping his head when he didn't pay attention, nodding vaguely when he got an answer right.

Dmitri lingered after the end of the class one day, and asked Petro Kominitsky how their village had come to belong to the tsar. "It seems to me that I belong to myself," Dmitri said thoughtfully.

Kominitsky sat down at his desk, staring at Dmitri. "Speak quietly. The tsar does not like people who think like you." Dmitri frowned and stepped back, but Kominitsky was smiling suddenly, an expression that fit his face strangely. "But everyone does not think like the tsar, Dmitri, and that is good."

Dmitri did not understand all that Kominitsky told him—later, he remembered bits and pieces about the brotherhood of man, about the blood of patriots, about freedom. And more about this place called America, where every man was as good as another, where good growing land was empty and waiting for the plow.

Not long after that, the tsar's soldiers swept through town and took Petro Kominitsky away with them. The storekeeper's wife wept quietly during the Sunday service, and Ivan Levytsky, a farmer as stout and solid as the pigs he raised, took Kominitsky's place in the classroom, teaching the children their sums and their alphabet, never straying into talk of exotic places.

Dmitri was the youngest son in a family of six sons. His family lived on the edge of the village, beside marshlands that stretched eastward for three day's ride. His family grew cabbages and potatoes in the land beside their house, and worked in the landlord's fields. On Sundays, they walked to the village church.

On nights when the moon was full, his two married brothers, Wasyl and Mikail, returned to his parents' house. Then the Change came, and his mother and his father and all his brothers would run in the marsh, hunting for hares and roe deer and wild pigs.

Others from the village rarely hunted on the uncertain ground of the marsh. They did not trust it. Paths shifted and changed and the earth underfoot was treacherous. Ground that looked firm could give way beneath a person's weight; pools that looked shallow had muddy bottoms that could swallow you whole. This land belonged to wild creatures who could sniff out the solid ground.

When Dmitri was fifteen, the Change came to him, and he ran with his family. It seemed to him that the coming of the Change was like the shifting of borders. Everything was the same, and yet everything was different. He still went with his father and his brothers to tend the landlord's fields; he still worked in the family's garden; he still fed the chickens and the pigs and the cows.

On Sundays, he and his family walked the three miles to the village church. But he could feel his moods shifting with the moon, could feel an itching just under his skin that came with the new moon and increased as the moon waxed, a restlessness that sang in his blood.

He did not remember exactly when he first thought about going to America. Perhaps when he was young, listening to Petro Kominitsky tell of the freedom that waited there. As the youngest of six sons, he knew that there was little for him in the village. The small patch of land that his family owned would never support all the brothers and all their wives.

He might never have left. True, the soil was poor and the family was big and they all worked hard in the landlord's fields. But the village was his home, and it was difficult to think of leaving it behind.

The autumn that Dmitri turned eighteen, the harvest was meager. Early in October, the weather turned cold and the snows came. Not long after, someone in the village found a calf with its throat ripped out and its belly torn open. The bloody snow around the carcass was marked with wolf tracks. The calf had belonged to the village priest.

The priest went to the landlord, and the landlord knew what needed to be done. At the next full moon, the landlord went hunting. Dmitri did not fear the landlord's men, but the men brought dogs—shaggy wolfhounds, each one as heavy as a strong man. Dmitri knew these dogs and feared them: whenever he passed the landlord's house on his way to the fields, he could hear the beasts barking. The landlord had fed them on the flesh of wolves that his men had killed; Dmitri knew they recognized his smell and called out for his blood.

That night, the light of the full moon shone on the low bushes and scrub grass of the great marsh. In the distance, the dogs were baying: they had caught the scent and they were on the trail of the wolves. The men who followed the dogs cried out "Loup! Loup! Loup!", their voices matching the baying of the hounds. The wolves ran easily, their tongues out. They were following their secret paths into the marsh where they had always been safe from pursuit. No man would endanger his horse and himself by trying to ride over such dangerous terrain. The dogs might follow, but not the men.

The wind blew from the north, chasing snow before it. The air was cold, bitterly cold. The wind carried the eager barking of the dogs, and the lead wolf cast a glance back over his shoulder, his first sign of uncertainty. The land was too steady beneath his feet, rock solid rather than trembling with each footstep. The marshy ground had frozen hard enough to support horse and rider.

The lead wolf ran then and the rest of the pack followed. The dogs gave chase, their wild baying echoing across the open land. Behind them came the men, crouching low over their horses' necks and urging the animals onward over the icy ground.

The lead wolf killed one dog before the rest got him down and ripped out his throat. The dogs caught two other wolves, and the men shot four. In the moonlight, the blood was black.

In the confusion of killing, one wolf escaped. He fled in terror from the smell of blood and the thunder of the gunfire. Behind him, Dmitri could hear the harsh cries of the men, like the croacking of ravens harrying a dying animal.

Acting instinctively, he doubled back on his own trail, running toward the village, toward his own home. When dawn came, he was in his own family's shed, nestled in the loose hay near the cow's stall.

White mist rose from the marsh. He stood beside his family's house, looking out into the wild land. He was alone. His head felt light and empty. Surely this was not real. It could not be real.

He put on his clothes and he went out into the marsh, following the secret paths until he came to a place where the smell of blood was strong. Ravens rose from the carcasses of the wolves, all of them skinned and heaped on the frozen ground. Seven wolves—his mother, his father, his five brothers.

He left that day, on foot, with his possessions in a sack slung over his shoulder. He walked to the next village, where he stayed with a cousin. His cousin's wife had a sister in the next village, and her sister had an uncle in the village after that. In those days, a wandering son traveling to distant places was not so unusual, and many families, seeing in him the sons that they had sent wandering, took him in. Sometimes, a farmer would give him a ride in an ox cart; more often, he would walk. Traveling from village to village, from sister to cousin to uncle, he made his way across Europe.

As he wandered farther from home, the villagers were not so friendly, and he spent many nights in the fields or the pastures or the forests. On the night of the full moon, he hid his sack in the crotch of a tree. When the Change came, he chased down a hare in an open pasture, and the fresh meat tasted better than anything he had had since he left his home.

He found his way to a port in France, where a ship that had carried cotton from New Orleans was returning to that port with a cargo of silk fabric and window glass. The ship was short-handed and the captain was Polish. Glad to meet a man who spoke his native language, the captain offered Dmitri a berth and he worked his way to America. He was popular among the crew because he was always willing to take the night watch, prowling the deck alone while the rest of the crew slept.

From New Orleans, Dmitri traveled north, up the Mississippi River to Saint Louis, the center of the growing Rocky Mountain fur trade. For a few years, he trapped beaver on the upper Missouri, living in the company of rough men. During this time, one of the other trappers, an educated young man who had become a trapper to seek his fortune, taught Dmitri to write in English.

In the spring of 1826, Dmitri brought a load of furs down to Saint Louis. He was standing on the dock beside the overloaded keelboat, when he saw a beautiful woman on the hurricane deck of an arriving steamboat.

"I'm going to marry that woman," he told Anton, one of the French trappers who had traveled with him downriver.

His friend laughed. "That beauty? She'll have nothing to do with you."

Dmitri left Anton standing on the dock and made his way through the laborers and the traders to the steamer's gangplank. When the woman walked down the gangplank, he smiled at her, showing white teeth in a wind-burned face. He spoke low, so that only she could hear: "We are very different now, but when the full moon rises we are very much alike."

She raised her carefully plucked eyebrows and her nostrils flared as she took a deep breath, catching his scent. She returned his smile, looking him up and down. "I believe you are right," she said.

He took her hand in his and said, "You'll marry me."

"That depends on what you look like after a bath," she said.

2

In 1826, Madame Mercier, the owner and proprietor of a respectable New Orleans brothel, received a young woman named Marietta Angèle DuBois in her office. The warm breeze that blew through the open windows carried the scents of sweet spring flowers and sewage.

Madame studied the young woman. Her dark hair was piled on her head in the French style. A few wisps had escaped the knot and trailed down her neck, curling prettily against the lace of her collar. Nice touch, that—it made one wonder what she might look like with her hair down around her shoulders. And it wasn't such a far jump from that speculation to the thought of her hair spread against a white pillowcase. The gentlemen would like that. Her face was unusual: high cheekbones, delicate features. Not pretty, exactly. But passable.

"Marietta," Madame said. "A pretty name. What can you do, Marietta?"

Marietta looked up, meeting Madame's gaze with hazel-brown eyes. "I read and write in both French and English. I play the pianoforte a bit. I sing—sweetly some say. I tell fortunes with the cards."

Madame could not place Marietta's accent. She thought it might be from somewhere in the countryside, perhaps in northern France. Telling fortunes with the cards suggested Gypsy blood.

The young woman had remarkable poise. She held herself like a princess, her hands neatly folded in her lap. "That's a start," Madame said. "Is there more?"

Marietta smiled, showing even white teeth. Suddenly, she did not seem quite so refined. "I am not shy with the gentlemen."

"I see." Madame nodded. She had the right spirit. "And how is your health, child?"

"I am well. The sea air agreed with me. That, and the knowledge that I was coming to a new land."

She looked well. Her eyes were clear and bright; her face was free of pox and blemishes, a contrast to so many others, who suffered from scurvy or disease on the ships. Madame herself had been sick for half of the passage.

Nan, the black kitchen slave, brought in a tea tray and set it on the desk before Marietta. Madame fanned herself with a delicate paper fan, watching carefully as Marietta poured the tea. The young woman moved with a natural grace.

"How old are you, Marietta? Where are your parents?"

"Eighteen. My mother was a French countess. She died of the consumption. My father. . . ." She shrugged eloquently.

Madame nodded, assuming Marietta was lying. Half of her girls claimed aristocratic blood. She did not hold that against them. "Come," she said, standing and leading the way to the parlor. "Play for me. And sing."

The young woman had a delicate touch on the keys and her voice was high and sweet. Madame did not recognize the song: a country folk song about two star-crossed lovers.

Marietta cocked her head to one side as she sang, and the light from the window illuminated one half of her face, leaving the other in shadow. Madame revised her assessment. In this light, Marietta's face took on an angelic beauty.

Madame was uneasy about this young woman. But Suzette had died of a fever last month and Julienne was not well, complaining of pains in her stomach and head. And Madame guessed that Marietta would be quite popular with rich cotton traders and land speculators, vulgar men with money. They would love her sweet innocence and would long to undo that knot of hair.

"I think you will do well here," Madame said. "You will find that I take care of my girls. To start, I think. . . ." She named a salary.

Marietta continued playing, not missing a note. "Pardon me, Madame, but I thought a little more." She looked up from the keys, smiled her unladylike smile, and named a higher number.

Madame frowned. "You think well of yourself, child."

Marietta did not speak. She looked down at her hands, still smiling as she played. "Also, Madame Mercier, there will be one night each month when I cannot work."

Madame shook her head. The young woman was unreasonable. She considered dismissing her and then relented. Marietta was a pretty girl. The men would like her. "I grow soft and foolish in my old age," Madame muttered. "Very well, then." She named a figure halfway between the two.

Marietta glanced up from the keys, raised a dark eyebrow, and named a figure slightly higher than Madame's new offer.

Madame shook her head impatiently. "I am disappointed in you, child. Haggling like a fishwife." She studied Marietta, and then gave in. "Very well. As you say."

Madame had Marietta dress elegantly in white linen, like a beautiful schoolgirl rather than a prostitute. The men swarmed to her, drawn by her appearance of innocence. But beneath her refined exterior was a ferocity that surfaced unexpectedly, revealing itself in a flash of her eyes, a sudden grip on a gentleman's hand, a smile that showed too many teeth.

The customers were happy. Marietta's air of refinement attracted them; the hidden passion held them. Within a week, she was the favorite of a gambler, an American army officer, a land speculator, and a rich cotton planter. She was in constant demand.

Early in the evenings, before the customers arrived, she told the other girls' fortunes with a pack of cards that she had brought with her. The sight of the cards made Madame momentarily uneasy—fortune-telling was a low-class amusement, unsuited to the genteel surroundings of her brothel. But in the end, she dismissed the pastime as a harmless amusement, prohibiting it only when customers were present.

Of course, some of the girls were jealous of Marietta's popularity. Lisette, a sulky brunette, spoke to Madam about how noisy Marietta was. "She is very vulgar, I think," Lisette complained. "When she makes love, she yowls like a cat in heat."

Madame shrugged. Lisette had been the favorite before Marietta had arrived. "The gentlemen seem to like her."

"Her room has a funny smell. I don't think she is the sort you want here."

Madame dismissed Lisette with a wave—a jealous girl, nothing new there. But she did go to see Marietta's room. Madame demanded that the girls keep their rooms immaculate and sweet-smelling, and she would tolerate no exceptions.

Madame climbed the stairs. As she approached Marietta's room, she could hear the rustle of cards. When Madame entered, Marietta was sitting on the bed and the cards were laid out before her on the quilt that served as her bedspread.

"Ah, Marietta," Madame said. "May I come in?"

Marietta gestured to the chair. Madame settled into the chair and it creaked beneath her weight. The air was scented with flowers—there was a bouquet on the dressing table, a gift from one of Marietta's admirers. Beneath the sweet floral scent, Madame detected something else: a dark musky aroma. Not unpleasant, but rather like a heady perfume.

"What is that perfume you are wearing?" Madame asked.

Marietta shook her head. "I have no perfume."

Madame inhaled deeply. "There is something in the air."

"The flowers, perhaps," Marietta suggested.

"Perhaps," Madame said doubtfully. She was considering the cards on the bed. Each one was edged with gilt and painted with brilliant colors. The pictures showed a woman in flowing robes with her hand on the head of a lion, a couple standing beneath a winged Cupid, a man in a large hat standing before a table strewn with cups, dice, and daggers.

"I am very glad to see you, Madame," Marietta said. "I would have come to see you later today. I will not be able to work tonight."

Madame frowned and looked up from the cards. "Are you ill?"

"It is my time of the month."

"Ah," said Madame, assuming that the heavy scent was the smell of menstrual blood. "Does it give you pain?"

"A little pain." She looked down at the cards. "I cannot work."

Madame laughed. "Ah, child, we cannot stop work for every

little ache and pain. I have some tea which will make you feel better. You must work—the gentlemen expect you."

Marietta shook her head. "That is not possible, Madame. I cannot work. As I told you, I must not work for one night each month. Please understand. It is not possible."

Madame straightened her back. "Marietta, you overstep yourself." She stood, looking down at the young woman. "I expect to see you in the parlor as usual." Her voice was stern and she left without waiting for a reply.

That night, Marietta came to the parlor early in the evening, not long before sunset, but she seemed nervous, restless; her smile showed too many teeth. She lingered at the window, staring out at the setting sun.

Madame left her alone, reasoning that Marietta was young and headstrong. She was in the parlor, and that was enough for now. A short time later, just after sunset, Madame noticed that Marietta was gone. Julienne said that she had gone to her room.

After a moment's consideration, Madame decided to be gentle with the girl—at least at first. She sent Nan to Marietta's room with some soothing chamomile tea. But the slave returned with the tray, saying that the door was locked and that no one answered when she knocked.

Madame went to see for herself. The door was locked. The air in the hall was thick with the musky scent she had noticed earlier. She knocked. "Marietta, are you there? Open the door, Marietta." She listened at the door and heard snuffling, as if an animal were sniffing at the gap between the door and the floor. Though the night was warm, she felt a draft on the back of her neck. "Marietta?"

Lisette came up the stairs with a young army officer, and Madame managed a smile. Lisette's answering smile was more knowing than Madame would have liked. The couple disappeared into Lisette's room.

Madame pressed her ear to the door again. She heard a low growl and then the snuffling again. She straightened and spoke to the closed door. "Very well, Marietta. You may rest for a time, but then I expect to see you in the parlor. Do you hear me?"

No answer. She left the door and occupied herself elsewhere in the house. Marietta did not return to the parlor that evening.

The next morning, Madame went to Marietta's door and found it unlocked. The young woman sat on her bed, brushing her long dark hair as if nothing had happened.

"I cannot have such behavior in my house," Madame said to the woman.

Marietta looked up, studying Madame dispassionately. "I don't know what you mean, Madame."

"Locking your door. Refusing to answer."

"I sleep very soundly, Madame." The young woman did not seem the least bit contrite.

"You give me no choice," Madame said. "Come to my office immediately."

In her office, she paid Marietta. She stood on the porch and watched with relief as Marietta carried her small case down the muddy street toward the waterfront. The maid opened all the windows to Marietta's room, but even so it took a week for the musky odor to dissipate.

Marietta took her earnings and booked passage on a steamboat heading for Saint Louis. Hard to say what she planned to do when she got there. But on the dock, she met Dmitri, and whatever plans she had were discarded.

3

After Dmitri took a bath in the tub at the back of the barbershop, Marietta acknowledged that she did like the look of him. They married in Saint Louis, to the astonishment of Dmitri's friend Anton, and Dmitri took his leave of the trappers.

Missouri had been a state for only a few years. According to the unreliable census figures of the time, the state had a population of 66,000 (not counting Indians or Negroes) scattered over its 69,000 or so square miles. Most of those folks were clustered along the Mississippi River near Saint Louis. Only a few had ventured westward—trappers and traders and soldiers, for the most part.

Dmitri spent some of the money he had earned trapping on two oxen, a milk cow, a squealing sow and hog, half a dozen chickens, an ax, a plow, a farm wagon, and assorted other farming gear. Following the old Indian trail that the trappers had made their own, he and his bride headed westward along the Missouri River, and then followed the Osage River southward into the Ozark range.

They settled on the Osage River in the southwest portion of the state, a hilly region of creeks and few settlers. The nearest civilization was a small trading outpost.

Working together, Dmitri and Marietta felled the oak and hickory trees that covered the land. In truth, Marietta was not of aristocratic birth. She had been born on a farm to a peasant family. Restless by nature, she had left her rural home for Paris, where she had learned to play the pianoforte and charm the gentlemen. But she knew how to work hard, when the occasion demanded it. After a month on the frontier, the cotton planter who had been so taken by her soft skin and pretty playing on the pianoforte would not have recognized her. Her hands were callused and her face was brown from the sun.

Dmitri trimmed the felled trees and notched the logs so that they fit together snugly. Enlisting the assistance of the man who ran the trading post and a trapper who was passing through, he raised a cabin, a single room constructed of logs and roofed with bark. A modest home, with a packed-dirt floor, clay daubed between the logs. The fireplace was built of stone, mortared with cement made of the local limestone.

Between the tree stumps on the land that they had cleared, Marietta planted corn, beans, and squash. She hauled wood and water, hoed weeds, husked corn, churned butter, and pressed cheese. She cleaned and plucked pheasant and turkey and roasted the birds in a tin kitchen, a metal half-cylinder that reflected the heat of the fire to cook the meat. She made the cabin into a home, planting morning glories by the door.

That first year, Dmitri built a shed to shelter the milk cow, a pen for the hogs, and a coop for the chickens. He planted apple trees and a kitchen garden.

It was a fine place to live. Few settlers, good hunting. A year after they married, Nadya was born. She was a sturdy, squalling baby. When Nadya was an infant, Marietta stayed close by the cabin on the night of the Change. When the child cried, the she-wolf licked the wailing infant's face with a warm tongue, until Nadya laughed and waved her feet in the air. Often, the wolf climbed onto the bed platform. Nadya would clutch her mother's soft fur in both hands and suckle at the wolf's teat.

Nadya grew up into an independent and strong-minded child. She helped her mother gather the eggs, chop down weeds in the kitchen garden, follow the bees to find a honey tree. She learned to bring the hogs in from the forest where they ranged by rattling corn in a bucket and calling low and sweet.

Over the years, Dmitri and Marietta improved the farm, extending the cabin with a lean-to at one side and a sleeping loft for Nadya's bed, replacing the bark roof with split shingles, laying a puncheon floor over the dirt, clearing more acreage for planting.

For all their efforts at civilization, they loved the forest. Dmitri wrote about it in the journal that he kept in a leather-bound book: "The endless forest, dark and inviting, offers so many places to hide. A safe place, I think, for us and for our children."

Other settlers came to live along the river. Not too many, at first. There were a few trappers who chose to settle down. Immigrants from New England, looking for a new life. The trader who ran the trading post sold out to a New England Jew who expanded the store and added a tavern. There was so much open land, so many miles of forest, that the additional settlers did not seem to matter. There was space for everyone.

Nadya was five years old when she first realized that her family was not like other families. Dmitri and Marietta had come to town to trade for a new ax and some other necessities. Nadya was in the crossroads store, staring at the jars of candy on the high shelf behind the counter and wondering if her father might buy her a hard candy to suck on during the wagon ride home. It was late spring, and the wooden floor was warm against her bare feet.

She liked the store. The clutter of boxes and barrels intrigued her. Interesting smells clung to them: jerked beef, clarified butter, pickles, and spices. Her father leaned against the wooden counter in the back, talking with Mr. Kahn, the storekeeper, about Indian trouble up north. Two fur traders had been killed the month before. Mr. Kahn blamed all the trouble on whiskey and whiskey peddlers, and Nadya's father agreed.

Nadya's mother and Mrs. Kahn sat on a bench near shelves that held bolts of fabric and sewing notions. A three-month-old issue of *Godey's Ladies Book,* worn from handling, lay open on Mrs. Kahn's lap. Lottie Kahn, a wide-eyed three-year-old, sat at her mother's feet, staring at Nadya. One chubby hand clutched her mother's skirt. She was fascinated by the older girl, but had not yet gathered her courage to approach.

A bearded man came in the door, threw a bundle of furs onto the counter, and looked around. Nadya stared up at him with interest. He was a very shaggy man: his beard was long and unkempt; his hair needed cutting. He was wearing a buckskin coat, homespun pants, and a shirt that hadn't been changed any too recently. There hung about him—mingling with the usual man-smells of chewing tobacco, whiskey, and sweat—a strong scent of many animals. She smelled bear and deer and buffalo and beaver. But what caught her attention was the faint smell of wolf.

The man leaned against the counter, evidently content to wait for the storekeeper's attention. He glanced down at Nadya. "Hello there, young'un."

"Hello." The wolf smell came from the bundle of furs on the counter.

"You know, I've got a little sister back in New York that's not much older than you."

Nadya considered this gravely, but didn't say anything.

"What are you doing here?"

"Waiting for my papa."

"Looked like you were watching those jars of candy back there." She nodded, and the man grinned. "Thought so. Well, maybe when I trade these furs, I'll buy you a piece of candy. Would you like that?"

Nadya nodded solemnly. She watched the man untie the rope that bound the furs together and spread the furs on the counter. She could smell wolf more strongly now. Emboldened by the man's grin, she reached up and touched one of the furs, a pelt the rich color of butter.

"That's a painter," the man said. "A mountain cat." He let her stroke the soft tawny fur, then lifted it aside. "Now here's a beaver pelt. That'll make a fine hat for some gentleman in New York City."

The man lifted the beaver pelt aside, revealing a fur that gave off a warm, reassuring scent, the scent of Nadya's mother on certain nights. Nadya reached up hesitantly to stroke the fur. A layer of coarse black guard hairs lay atop an undercoat of softer silver fur.

"This 'un, I'll sell for the bounty," the man said. He lifted it off the counter and held it down where she could see the whole fur. Where the animal's head should have been, there was a mask with vacant holes in place of eyes. The black-tipped ears were shriveled; they had been pressed flat by the weight of the other furs.

Nadya stared at the empty eye-holes and took a step back, dropping her hand to her side. "Where did you get it?" she asked, suddenly wary. Until she saw the head, she had not thought about where the fur had come from.

"From a wolf bigger than you are." He shook the pelt and the fur rippled. "Saw her prowling around the edge of my camp and got her with a single shot. Right through the head."

Nadya took another step back, glaring at the man.

"What's the matter, young'un? She's dead. Can't hurt you now."

"You shouldn't have done that," she cried shrilly. "You shouldn't have shot her."

She fled across the store to hide behind her mother's long skirt. Her mother put her hand on Nadya's head. "What is it, child? What's the matter?"

"He killed her. That man." Nadya pointed across the store at the bewildered trapper, who still held the wolfskin.

"I didn't mean to scare her, missus," he said apologetically. "I was just showing her some furs."

"It's all right, Nadya," her mother said. She stooped and put her arm around Nadya's shoulders. She spoke softly. "You're safe with me. We'll go out to the wagon to wait for Papa."

"Why did he kill the wolf, Mama?"

"Hush," her mother said. "Hush now."

Her mother excused herself from her conversation, took Nadya's hand, and led her out the door. Nadya walked by her mother's side, carefully placing herself between her mother and the man who killed wolves. She would protect her mother.

"I didn't mean to scare her," he was saying.

Then they were out in the sunshine, away from the comforting and horrifying scent of the wolf fur. Nadya sat on the wagon seat and her mother explained, very softly, that the wolf the man had killed was not a person—not like Mama or Papa. That wolf was an animal, and it was not murder to kill it.

But her mother's voice trembled when she talked and she held Nadya a little too closely. Nadya knew that her mother was afraid of the man, too. When her father came out of the store, he brought a new ax, a box of supplies, and a bag of hard candy to comfort Nadya. He sat with Nadya on the wagon seat while her mother went to finish their shopping.

"He's a bad man," Nadya told her father.

"He just doesn't understand," her father said.

"Then we should tell him that he shouldn't kill wolves," Nadya said earnestly. "I'll tell him that sometimes wolves are people, too."

"No," her father said. "You can't do that."

"Why not?"

"He won't understand," her mother said. "He'll be afraid. And when men are afraid, they kill."

Nadya frowned and sucked on a hard candy, puzzled and confused.

It was a small incident. For the most part, Nadya's childhood was happy. On long winter nights, when the farmyard was dusted with snow and hickory logs burned in the fireplace, Dmitri taught Nadya to read from the *Farmer's Almanack*. They leaned over the book, huddling close to the pool of light cast by a wick burning in a cup of bear oil. Dmitri stumbled over the difficult words, but he persisted, determined that Nadya learn. Together, they sounded out the words. While they labored over the book (learning that turnips should be planted in the dark of the moon and that a silver coin, placed in a butter churn, will help the butter come), Marietta watched from the fireside, mending or knitting.

With a pen made from a wild turkey quill, Dmitri taught Nadya to write. By the wavering light, Nadya painstakingly made marks on bark that her father had peeled from the shagbark hickory tree. She learned to write her name in English. Her father could write in another alphabet as well—the alphabet he had learned when he was a boy. But he only taught her the English writing, saying that she was an American and she should write as the Americans did.

When Nadya's lessons were done, she would ask for a story.

"A story?" her father would say. "It's too late for a story." But he always smiled when he said it was too late.

"It's not too late," she would say. "There's time. Please, Papa. Just one story."

"Maybe there's time for one, Dmitri," her mother would say. Then her father would put aside the pen and the *Almanack* and he would lift his hands so that the light from the burning wick made shadows on the deerskin that stretched across the window. The shadows that Nadya's father made with his hands were magical.

"Once upon a time, there was a man," Dmitri said, and the shadows of his hands became the silhouette of a man's head—a man with a jutting chin and a big nose. "He lived in a cabin on the edge of the forest. And there was a rabbit." The shadows shifted and changed, becoming a rabbit that wiggled its nose and made Nadya giggle. "Every night the rabbit came and ate from the man's garden."

Dmitri told of how the man built a scarecrow to fool the rabbit. The rabbit ignored the scarecrow—it kept on hopping into the garden and eating all the vegetables. The man tried to keep the rabbit away by sitting in the garden all night long, but he always fell asleep. The shadow man snored noisily, and that made Nadya laugh.

"But," Nadya's father said, "on the night when the moon was full, the man changed."

Nadya watched with fascination as the shadow man shifted and became a wolf, a fierce shadow head that snapped at the air and lifted its snout to howl. The wolf chased the rabbit through the forest, growling and snapping.

"All night long, the wolf chased the rabbit and the rabbit ran from the wolf. When the moon set and the sun came up, the rabbit hid in its burrow, afraid to go near the man's garden. And the wolf became a man again."

Nadya watched the shadow wolf give way to the shadow man. Sometimes the shadow man sang a song and sometimes he howled like a wolf. Then Nadya and her mother howled, too. If they howled long and hard, the wild wolves that lived in the forest heard them and joined in.

The story was always a little different, but it always involved the shadow man and the shadow wolf. Nadya never grew tired of watching one become the other.

Of course, on nights when the moon was full, there were no lessons and no stories. In the summer, there were romps, where her mother and father, in their other form, would play tag with Nadya in the farmyard by the cabin door. In the winter, the she-wolf would cuddle Nadya, letting the child stroke her fur and snuggle against her warm belly. When Nadya was seven years old—old enough to be trusted to stay away from the fire—her mother and father went running at night, leaving her alone until morning. She was lonely then, sad that she could not go running with her parents. But her mother told her that when she grew up, she would Change when the full moon rose. And then they would run together. She had to be content with that.

Since Nadya had no brothers and sisters, she helped her mother and father in equal part: doing womanly chores with her mother and helping her father with the farming. When she was nine years old, she started helping her father plow. Her job was to ride the mule to steady it while her father rode the plow. She loved that—the aroma of the newly turned earth, the warmth of the mule beneath her, the solid shifting of the animal's muscles as it strained to pull the plow through the soil. Her father whistled and shouted to the mule, and sang folk songs in French and Polish.

In the spring, when the sap began to rise, Nadya helped tap the sugar maple trees. The aroma of the boiling syrup filled the air and she ate sticky maple sugar and hot corn cakes sweetened with maple syrup.

In the summer, the days were hot. Vegetables grew thick and green in the garden; the Indian corn grew taller than her head. At night, fireflies danced in the woodland at the edge of the fields, like sparks flying from the fire.

In the autumn, she helped with the harvest, working beside her mother and father to bring Indian corn in from the fields. Pumpkins grew in the kitchen garden—bright orange among the green leaves. And there were yellow squash and beans and all manner of good things, ready for harvest.

The summer that she was ten, her father taught her to shoot. As a target, he set a pinecone on a stump in the field. Once a week, all that summer, he took her down to the field in the early evening, and she held the rifle to her shoulder and practiced pointing it at the pinecone and pulling the trigger.

After a month of sighting on the pinecone, he let her try shooting with powder. The first time she tried, the kick of the explosion bruised her shoulder and nearly knocked her down. But she was not frightened and she tried it again, and again, until she could hit the pinecone square with every shot. She hunted squirrels in the forest near the house, aiming for the bark just below the animal's feet. The shot shattered the bark and the concussion killed the squirrel, leaving the meat untouched.

As she grew older, she and her father went hunting for larger game. At night, they hunted deer, mesmerizing the animals with a torch made from a rag soaked in bear oil and lashed to a stick. By day, they hunted turkey or bear, in season. When they went hunting, Nadya's long skirts were a hindrance, catching in the underbrush and slowing her down. Over her mother's protests and her father's laughter, she made herself a pair of trousers. After some protest, her mother let her wear the trousers when she went hunting. "There is no one here to see," her father had said. "Let the girl be comfortable."

Nadya was a good hunter—she had a better eye than her father, and she brought in most of the meat for the family table. In the fall of her twelfth year, determined to earn a rifle of her own, she hunted bears for their skins and oil and meat.

She always wore a dress to town—her mother insisted on that. One Sunday afternoon, Nadya and her father took the bear oil and skins to the store and offered them in trade for a new black-powder hunting rifle with shiny brass mountings. Mr. Kahn accepted the trade, but seemed puzzled when Nadya lifted the gun from the counter and sighted along its barrel. He frowned at Dmitri. "You're letting your daughter choose your rifle?" he murmured.

"Her rifle," Dmitri corrected. "She killed the bears. Only

seems right she should choose the rifle. After all, she's a better shot than I am."

The men who were lounging by the Franklin stove glanced up. "The girl killed eight bears?" one man asked.

"Ten," Dmitri said. "We kept the skins and meat from two for our own use."

"D'you mind if I try it?" Nadya asked Mr. Kahn.

"As you like," he said.

They stepped onto the porch of the store, with Nadya carrying the rifle easily at her side. The men from the store followed. Nadya loaded the rifle, carefully pouring a measure of black powder down the barrel, cutting a cotton patch and wrapping it around the lead ball, ramming the ball and patch down the rifle's barrel, then pouring powder into the priming pan. She looked around, searching for a target.

"You see the nail in that fence across the way," said one of the loiterers from the store. "I knew a man in Kentucky who could hit a nail like that and drive it home."

Nadya glanced at the man's grinning face. He was laughing at her, and she did not like it. She squinted at the fence across the road, where the rusty head of a nail protruded from a post. "All right," she said easily, lifted the rifle, and fired a single shot. The nail disappeared into the wood, leaving a dark hole where the bullet had struck.

"This rifle will do," Nadya said to her father. They returned to the store, leaving the loiterers staring at the fence.

4

Over the years, a small town known as Wolf Crossing grew up around the trading post and store. When Nadya was twelve, she considered going to town to be a rare adventure.

Traveling shows often visited the frontier town. Nadya watched physicians of dubious credential offer nostrums purported to cure everything from grippe to hair loss. Actors performed temperance plays that warned, at melodramatic length, of the dangers of liquor, then visited the tavern and drank their evening's earnings. Other actors, bringing high culture to the frontier, performed plays credited to Shakespeare, drawling their lines and spicing up the dull bits with extended sword battles. Tent shows exhibited all manner of exotica—from the stuffed carcass of a Plains buffalo to the head of Black Hawk, chief of the Sauk tribe, stolen from a grave and pickled in brine.

When Nadya and her family went to town on July 4, the head of the Indian was on display in a tent up near the tavern. Nadya was convinced that viewing this head was the best way to spend the penny that she had earned by selling a bucket of honey to Mr. Kahn, the storekeeper.

"Come on, Lottie. Let's go." Nadya tugged on her friend's hand.

"I don't want to see a dead Injun," Lottie said. "I'd rather buy candy."

"You can buy candy anytime," Nadya said. "And it ain't just any dead Injun. It's an Injun chief."

Lottie scuffed her bare feet in the road, raising dust. She was a year younger than Nadya, and not as eager for adventure. She looked longingly back toward her father's store. Half a dozen men sat on the front porch, whittling, chewing tobacco and spitting the juice, and talking about the Whigs and the Democrats and weather. Nadya could hear Mary Sue, Lottie's older sister, shouting at the hogs as she drove them out of the garden.

"My mama won't like it," she said, resisting Nadya's tugging.

"So don't go telling your mama." Nadya lowered her voice to a persuasive whisper. "They say he was the fiercest Injun ever. They say he scalped heaps and heaps of people."

They had reached the livery stable, and Nadya could see the tent in the patch of cleared land beside the tavern. The canvas walls of the tent were painted with scenes of wild Indians on horseback, brandishing tomahawks. Their faces were painted with crimson stripes. They didn't look anything like the Indians that used to come to visit Nadya and her family. Those Indians moved softly through the woods, appearing silently on the edge of the farmyard. They smelled of wood smoke, sweat, and forest. Her mother had always given them johnnycake to eat. They had smiled at Nadya and called her *chermechinka,* which her father told her meant "little girl" in their language. Nadya figured that the Indians on the side of the tent must have been a different and more exciting tribe than the ones that had visited her family.

"Come on," she said to Lottie. The younger girl took a few more steps, then stopped dead. Nadya could hear the man in front of the tent shouting to the crowd. The Indian whose head was on display was a Sauk chief named Ma-ka-tai-me-she-kia-kiak. The polysyllabic name rolled off the barker's tongue, exotic and enticing. "Black Hawk—that's what all that means," said the barker. "And his heart was as black as his name. Not seven years ago, he was rampaging up and down the Mississippi River, killing folks and scalping them and—"

"I'm going home," Lottie said.

"He's going to talk about the fighting," Nadya said. "Don't you want to hear—"

"No! I'm going home." Lottie jerked her hand away from Nadya and ran back to the store. Nadya watched her go, then continued down the street alone.

She reached the tent and stood at the edge of the small crowd of men and boys. The canvas flap behind the barker showed a man in full military uniform, riding on a white horse. "General Henry Atkinson rode at the head of his troops," the barker said. "He hunted down Black Hawk and lopped off his head."

The man standing in front of Nadya spit tobacco juice, then remarked to his neighbor, "That ain't so. Black Hawk got clean away. The way I hear it, he surrendered because so many of his people died."

"I was with General Atkinson on that day," the barker was saying. "And I'm not ashamed to say that it was a powerful frightening thing to be on the trail of three hundred bloodthirsty savages."

The man who had commented on Black Hawk's death squinted at the barker. "I'd wager the only Injun he's ever come close to is the one by the seegar store," he muttered.

"Seeing the head of Ma-ka-tai-me-she-kia-kiak and hearing the glorious story of the Battle of Bad Axe will cost you just a penny," the barker said. "And that penny will help me return to the West, where I can assist the settlers of Oregon in subduing the savages that threaten them every day." He lifted a corner of the flap and beckoned to the first man in the crowd. "Step up and pay your penny, brother. See the head of the fiercest Injun that ever lived."

Some men headed into the tent. The skeptical man and a few others turned away, electing to spend their money in the tavern instead. Nadya hung back, digging in the pocket of her dress for a penny, then tagged at the heels of the last man entering the small tent.

"Now where do you think you're going, young'un?" the barker asked.

Nadya held out her penny. "I got a penny."

"This ain't no place for women and children. You get along now."

Nadya gave him a steady look. "This Injun killed women and children, didn't he?"

"That's right."

"Then it only seems right that women and children should get to see him. It's only fair."

The man sighed, shrugged, then took Nadya's penny and shooed her into the tent.

The air in the tent was still and hot. Mingled with the smells of sweat, tobacco, and whiskey was something else: the tang of brine, like the smell of the pickle barrel at the store. Beneath that, the reek of something rotten. The men stood around a big jar on a table. The barker hurried to stand beside it.

"Here he is, looking just as fierce as the day that General Atkinson lopped off his head with a single swipe of the tomahawk," he said. "I remember it as if it happened just yesterday."

Nadya stared at the head floating in the jar. The face was puffy and the skin was pale.

"Looks like a mean 'un," one of the men said.

"Savages," another man said. "Thank God we've cleared them out of these parts."

The Indian's face didn't look fierce to Nadya. He looked sad—the mouth turned down, dark eyes gazed at nothing. A spot of mold was growing just above the right eye. The barker was talking about the battle at Bad Axe River, where thirteen hundred soldiers fought three hundred bloodthirsty savages. Nadya wondered a bit at that. Seemed like those soldiers weren't taking any chances. Only three hundred Indians. Seemed a little unfair. But maybe not, considering how fierce the Indians were.

"I just don't abide by this plan to ship 'em all to the Indian Territories," said a man. "No better than a pack of wild wolves. Kill 'em now, before they come after us."

The barker had taken the lid off the jar and the smell of brine and rot grew stronger. "For just a penny more, you can touch his hair," he told the crowd. "Only one penny."

The year before, when Nadya paid a penny to see a stuffed lion from Africa, she had crept close enough to lay a hand on its flea-bitten pelt. She took a step closer to the table, then hesitated. The expression on the Indian's face reminded her of her father when he was tired and disappointed.

She felt someone tug on her hair and she jumped. Tom, the blacksmith's son, snickered behind her. "Skeered he was going to scalp you?" He had slipped under the canvas while the barker was giving his spiel.

"I ain't scared of Injuns," Nadya said.

"You shouldn't even be here," Tom said. "Ain't proper."

Nadya frowned at him. He was no friend of hers. Last fall, at a corn husking, he had scared Lottie with a big corn snake that he had caught in the field. He had chased her and chased her until Nadya knocked him down, took the snake away, and let it go in the field.

Tom had grown since last fall. He wouldn't be as easy to knock down. He was acting friendly, but she didn't trust him.

"Let's go closer," he said, crowding behind her so that she had to move. The crowd had thinned out. Only a few men lingered by the jar that held the head.

Nadya was just a few feet from the table when Tom gave her a push, shoving her so that she bumped the table. The jar tumbled to the ground, spilling the head out onto the grass. Nadya stumbled and fell, landing beside the head. Chief Black Hawk's dark eyes watched her sadly. The barker shouted and Nadya scrambled for the tent flap, one step ahead of the barker and two steps behind Tom.

As soon as they were outside the tent, she turned to pursue Tom, but he was quick. She chased after him, but gave up when he circled around into his father's blacksmith shop.

She stopped in the street and straightened her dress. Her hands smelled of brine and rot where liquid from the jar had splashed her. She washed her hands in the creek that ran by the stable, but she could still smell the rot.

She wandered back to the store and found her father. That afternoon, she sat beside her father on the wagon seat as they rode from town. She looked at his face—dark on the cheeks where he needed a shave, his mouth downturned and weary. His expression reminded her of the head in the jar, and she put her arm around his waist to reassure herself that he was warm and alive.

"Papa, do Injuns have ghosts?" she asked him.

"As much as any white folks, I guess." He glanced at her. "So you went to the tent show this afternoon."

She squirmed on the hard wagon seat. No one had ever said that she could not go to the tent show, but she had known that her father would not approve. "I wanted to see the Injun chief."

"And so you did. What did you think of him?"

"He didn't seem so fierce," she said. She thought for a moment. "A man there said that we ought to kill all the Injuns, afore they kill us."

"There's folks that say people like you and me and your mama ought to be killed. There's folks who say that anyone who thinks different or acts different from the way they think or act ought to be killed. Or else treated as slaves." His voice was low and angry. "The Indians lived here before we did. They didn't go on the warpath until white folks started taking their land and poisoning them with liquor. That Chief Black Hawk—he died in jail of a broken heart after the soldiers killed his people." Her father shook his head. "People say all manner of foolish things. You best be careful not to go believing the wrong ones."

"Yes, Papa," she said.

He put a hand on her head and stroked her hair. "Don't you worry about Injun ghosts. If Black Hawk is going to haunt someone, it'll be the man who is hauling his head around in a jar, not some little girl who comes to see him."

That night, as she lay wrapped in her blanket, she dreamed of Black Hawk's head in the jar. The dark eyes were alive. As she watched him, his lips moved, as if he were trying to say something, and his eyes shifted, looking over her shoulder. She glanced behind her and saw the barker lifting a tomahawk. Under his arm, he clutched a clear glass jar large enough to hold her head. She ran from him, but her feet tangled in the canvas of the tent flap and she tripped and fell.

She woke tangled in her blanket, her heart beating fast. It took her a long time to get back to sleep again.

In her fourteenth year, Nadya noticed that the world was changing around her. It began when the rivermen started calling to her. People said that the men who steered flatboats down the river were a bad lot—drinking, fighting, and stealing when they could. But Nadya had always liked the look of them. They seemed so much at ease floating down the river, leaning back among the crates of apples and barrels of salt pork, playing the harmonica or singing songs. She had always waved at the rivermen, and they had always waved back. But in her fourteenth year, they started shouting when they waved. "Come along with us, little sweetheart!"

Then a Yankee peddler stopped at the farm to show her mother his stock of sewing notions and such. He gave Nadya a blue satin ribbon for no reason at all. He said that it would look pretty in her dark hair, and when he held it up so that she could see it, his smell changed, ever so slightly. She did not know what to say. He watched her so intently, like a hungry dog with its eye on the hoecakes. When her mother nudged her, she thanked him awkwardly. Her mother apologized for her daughter's shyness.

After dinner that night, Nadya's mother brought out her cards. She kept them wrapped in a silk scarf on the shelf with the Bible and the *Farmer's Almanack*. Nadya knew the cards well: when she was a child, she had often played with them, fingering their gilded edges and admiring the pictures of strange people in strange costumes. She would sort the cards according to suit: separating the swords, the coins, the wands, and the cups, and setting aside the special cards that did not fall into any suit. The words on these cards were written in French: *Le Diable,* The Devil; *Le Monde,* The World; *Le Mat,* The Fool.

Marietta did not read the cards very often. But when there

was a decision to be made—like whether to plant early or wait—she would lay the cards on the rough wood of the table, studying the patterns that the bright pictures made. She would shake her head over certain cards—a picture of a burning tower, a man hanging upside down—while she and Dmitri conferred in soft murmurs.

But that night, Marietta beckoned Nadya to sit beside her. "That trader," Marietta said, "you caught his eye." She unwrapped the cards and spread the silk scarf on the table, watching Nadya all the while. "What did you think of that?"

Nadya shifted uncomfortably on the wooden chair. "I didn't like the way he watched me."

Marietta shuffled the cards, her eyes still on Nadya. "He wanted you," she said. "The way a man wants a woman. It's that simple."

Nadya looked down at her hands, suddenly shy. Her mother had always talked of such things matter-of-factly, without shame.

"I'd guess that the Change will be coming to you with the next full moon," her mother said. She sat back in her chair, holding the cards loosely in her lap. "With the Change, there comes a power. Being wanted—that's part of the power. You need to understand that men will admire you, men will lust after you."

Nadya looked up at her mother's serene face. "What do I do about that?" Nadya asked.

Her mother smiled. "Don't look so worried, *chérie*. This is not a bad thing." She shuffled the cards, her eyes on Nadya. "We will read the cards for guidance." When Nadya cut the deck, her mother restacked the cards and began to lay them face up on the scarf in a cross-shaped pattern. "You are strong-minded—that's bad and good. Bad because it will lead you into trouble; good because it will keep the trouble from overwhelming you."

Nadya studied the cards. In the center of the pattern was the ten of coins, a card that pictured a happy family gathered together. The ten of coins was crossed and half-covered by *La Lune*, The Moon. On this card, two dogs howled at a frowning moon. There were other cards she recognized. In her future was the knight of swords, charging rashly forward on a gray horse. She saw *Le Diable*, a frightening figure with a man and a woman in chains at his feet; *La Mort*, a skeleton clutching a sickle; *La*

Maison Diu, a castle struck by lightning. She looked up at her mother's face.

"Ah," her mother said softly. "Perhaps this is not the best time for a reading."

"Tell me what it is, Mama."

Her mother stared at the cards. "Pain and destruction."

"When is it coming?" Nadya looked at the door, as if expecting the Devil to walk through it. "What can I do?"

"It is coming with a young man," her mother said. "He charges forward—reckless and brash—and he carries death in his hands." Her mother dealt more cards, still shaking her head. "We will try again on another day," she said at last. She swept the cards from the scarf and shuffled them together.

That night, Nadya heard her mother and father murmuring softly by the fireside. Nadya listened, but she could not make out the words.

Three nights later, the full moon shone down on the Rybak cabin. Three wolves—a grizzled male, a mature female, and a young female—romped and played in the farmyard. The Change had come.

5

Back in 1823, Mr. Hezekiah Jones attended a Methodist revival, a tent meeting that had brought in hundreds of devout Christians and an equal number of curiosity seekers from surrounding towns. Mr. Jones fell into the second category—a hard-drinking young man, he hoped to have a little fun and maybe win a few Christians over to the ways of sin.

Mr. Jones drank a great deal on Saturday night. On Sunday morning, overcome with a hangover and influenced by the persuasive sermon of a Methodist preacher, he renounced the Devil, swore that he would never again touch the demon rum, and, just incidentally, proposed to Cordelia Walker, a twenty-eight-year-old woman who had given up all hope of matrimony. Before Mr. Jones could change his mind, the preacher married the happy couple to the cheers of the crowd.

The first two vows were transitory—Mr. Jones returned to sin and drinking as soon as possible. But the new Mrs. Jones was not dismissed as easily. She was a formidable woman, not to be trifled with. Determined to save Mr. Jones's sinning soul, she made an honest man of him—a farmer, no less. Not a good farmer, but a farmer still. They emigrated to Kentucky, where he scratched out a living on a poor farm and she bore him four strapping sons. In 1842, they emigrated again, this time to Missouri, and started a farm near the town of Wolf Crossing.

Their oldest son, Rufus, was a handsome lad. In Kentucky, Mrs. Jones feared Rufus was in danger of taking up his father's godless ways. He was fond of drinking and hunting and gambling. Mrs. Jones hoped that the move to Missouri would improve the boy's outlook by removing him from evil influences.

Early in the spring of 1843, Mrs. Jones and her family attended the wedding of Zillah Shaw, daughter of a prosperous farmer. Zillah married a lanky farmboy named Samuel Prentice. Among the guests were Dmitri and Marietta Rybak and their daughter, Nadya.

The celebration was in the barn, which had been cleared of livestock for the occasion. The dirt floor had been strewn with clean straw. Rufus Jones stood by the open door with a group of men. They passed a green jug of Mr. Shaw's fine home-brewed whiskey from hand to hand. The sun was setting and Rufus's shadow stretched all the way across the open floor of the barn. The afternoon had been warm—the first spring weather—but the air was cooling quickly.

The women were clearing away the remnants of the wedding feast. Rufus could see his mother helping. His younger brothers were running around the barn floor with the other children, whooping like Indians. Four young dogs were chasing them. At the far end of the barn, a fiddler was tuning his instrument for the dance to come. The air smelled of smoke, roast venison, and manure.

Rufus took a pull on the whiskey jug to ward off the chill, then passed the jug to his father. Hezekiah took a long pull, swallowing several times before he paused for breath. "Those are almighty ugly dogs," he said, squinting his good eye at the four young hounds that romped with the children. Hezekiah had lost his other eye in a fight with an eye-gouging boatman before Rufus was born. He wore a patch over the empty socket.

"If they take after their mama, they'll be fine hunters," Mr. Shaw said. "She's as fine a bitch as ever treed a painter."

Hezekiah took another pull from the bottle, then reluctantly passed it to the next man. "That so? You do much hunting in these parts?"

Mr. Shaw nodded, taking the bait. "Not much choice in the matter. Man's got to hunt to keep the varmints out of his stock."

Rufus had heard this conversation before. By the time the bottle was empty, he guessed that his father would have turned the conversation from hunting to shooting and from shooting to who was the best shot. Soon enough, there would be talk of a shooting match with, most likely, a bottle of whiskey as the prize. Rufus was a good shot, and Hezekiah took advantage of that skill whenever he could.

Rufus made himself comfortable, leaning back against the barn wall and watching the girls primp and flutter around the fiddler, trying to look as if they didn't care that the young men were watching, as if they weren't even thinking about who would ask them to dance. Rufus liked women. In Kentucky, he had courted the sweet young daughter of a nearby farmer, taking her berry-picking in the warm days of Indian summer. They had returned happy, but with few berries to show for their efforts. He had left Kentucky just in time to avoid the consequences of that berry-picking expedition.

His mother had taught him to be polite and soft-spoken with the ladies. His father had taught him to get away with whatever he could. The combination was dangerous.

The fiddler finished his tuning and played a reel. Rufus watched as the dancers formed two lines, stamping their feet in time to the music. Light from the setting sun was fading. After the first dance, two of the older Shaw boys climbed into the rafters to light lanterns filled with bear oil. The burning wicks cast pools of yellow light.

It took a bit longer than Rufus expected for talk to turn to a shooting match. Mr. Shaw talked about a painter hunt last fall and about a wolf pack that had roved along the river the winter just past. But eventually Hezekiah brought the conversation around.

"I reckon it's the water of Kaintuck," Hezekiah said. "Don't rightly know what else it could be. It must be something that makes the hunters of that state the sharpest-eyed riflemen around."

Mr. Shaw frowned and shook his head. His cheeks and nose were ruddy from drinking. "That just ain't so, Hezekiah. Why, my own boys are sharp as any you'll find in Kentucky."

"I'd have to put that to the test before I could agree," Hezekiah said easily. "My boy Rufus is a right fine shot." He hefted the whiskey bottle, which had returned to his hand and lingered there. "Maybe a shooting match could settle the matter."

"All right, then, a shooting match," Mr. Shaw agreed. His voice was loud and a little slurred. "With a bottle of whiskey to the winner." He glanced down. Two of the young dogs were wrestling on the barn floor. "And the pick of the litter as well."

"What's the target?" Rufus asked quietly.

Mr. Shaw glanced out the barn door at the dark fields. "A candle-snuffing, I'd say. That sit well with you?"

Rufus shrugged. "One target is as good as another."

In a snuffing contest, the target was the flame of a candle. The idea was not to snuff the candle out—that would be too easy a shot. Instead, the marksman had to shoot away the snuff, the charred part of the candle's wick, without putting out the flame. When the snuff was removed, the flame would brighten. Shoot too close to the candle, and the flame would die. Shoot too far away, and you would miss the wick altogether.

"Boys!" Mr. Shaw shouted over the music of the fiddle. He stamped his feet and shouted again. "Boys, listen here!" The fiddler stopped playing in the middle of a dance. "We're having a shooting match. Mr. Jones here says that his boys from Kentucky can beat anyone from Missouri hands down. Adam, run to the house and fetch a candle. Jack! William! All the rest of you! Get your rifles."

The young men who had been dancing abandoned their partners and scattered to fetch their rifles. When Adam returned with a tallow candle, Mr. Shaw took a flaming torch from the cooking fire and led the way out into the fields. Rufus walked at his father's side. The ground was damp and the air held the scent of spring growth. The sky was overcast. Moonlight illuminated the clouds from behind, creating a silvery patch of light in the eastern sky.

Like many settlers, Mr. Shaw had cleared new land by girdling the trees—removing a strip of bark all around the trunk. Without the bark, the tree died, and the settler cut it down. In the spring, when the ground was soft, the farmer grubbed out the stumps. In Mr. Shaw's field, the stumps of girdled trees—now stripped of all their bark and pale in the torchlight—stood as a reminder of the forest that had once covered this land.

Grass had sprouted between the stumps. Beyond the field, where the uncleared forest stood, the darkness grew thicker. A chorus of crickets, singing in the field and the forest, almost drowned out the fiddle music from the barn.

Mr. Shaw led the way to the far side of the field, where a low, flat-topped stump stood on the edge of the forest. He wedged the candle into a crack in the stump and lit the wick with his torch. He gave Adam the torch. "Now you stay here, boy," he advised his son. "Call out when the snuff is long enough for shooting, then get back."

The men moved away from the stump, walking toward the barn until Mr. Shaw said, "That'll do." In the still air, the candle flame stood steady, a sliver of yellow light against the darkness of the forest.

"Three shots apiece," Hezekiah suggested, and Mr. Shaw agreed.

Jack, Mr. Shaw's oldest son, took the first shot, standing with his feet spread wide, his rifle set firmly against his shoulder. His shot went high—the distant flame flickered as the ball passed over. The chorus of crickets fell silent for a moment, and then began again, as loud as before.

Jack paused to reload. His second shot was low, cutting the wick and putting out the candle. While Adam was relighting the candle, Jack took a pull from the whiskey jug.

"Move farther away from there," Jack called to Adam when the candle was burning once again. "That damned torch is blinding me."

He took his third shot and the flame flickered and then brightened.

"Dead on!" Adam called.

Jack grinned at his father and the others. "Not bad," he said. "Who'll be next?"

One by one, the other men shot. Several missed the wick with all three shots. Two others snuffed the candle one time out of three.

Rufus did not shoot until all the others had taken their turns. Then he lifted his rifle and squinted at the candle. Though he could not see it clearly, he knew that in the blue heart of the flame, the charred portion of the wick curled in a long crescent. So far away. You might as well aim at a star.

He held his breath, steadying his rifle and sighting on the heart of the flame. His first shot was perfect: the flame brightened and he smiled as he set the rifle down and reloaded.

"Fool's luck," he said to Mr. Shaw, before Mr. Shaw could say the same to him.

He took a pull from the whiskey bottle while he waited for the candle to burn down. The men around him were quiet. In the field and woods around them, crickets sang in a relentless chorus. "Ready!" Adam called at last.

Rufus lifted his rifle to his shoulder and squeezed off the second shot. The candle flickered—a miss.

"Your luck is passing," Mr. Shaw said in a good-natured tone.

"One more shot," Hezekiah said. "Give the boy a fair chance."

Rufus reloaded and lifted his rifle for the last shot. He braced himself, setting his feet wide apart and sighting carefully. The candle flickered and brightened for the second time.

Hezekiah whooped and clapped Rufus on the back. "Fine shooting, son. Almighty fine shooting. Wouldn't you agree, Mr. Shaw?"

Hezekiah held his hand out to Mr. Shaw, but Mr. Shaw just frowned at him, shaking his head like a bull disturbed by flies. He squinted at the men around him.

"We're not quite done," Mr. Shaw said in a belligerent tone. "There's one other who ought to shoot. One other who ain't here. You just hold on. You all just wait here."

He left them standing in the field and hurried in the direction of the barn. The cloud cover had broken and the half moon cast an uncertain light over the group. Rufus looked around at the others. By the moonlight, he could see them grinning, as if at a private joke.

"Who is he getting?" Hezekiah asked Jack uneasily. "Seems like most every man came with us."

"You just wait," Jack said. "You'll see. Best shot in these parts."

A few minutes later, Rufus saw three figures emerge from the barn and come across the field. As they approached, he realized that one of them was a woman. Her dark hair was braided and the braids were tied with ribbons and coiled on her head. With her left hand, she held her skirt so that the hem did not drag in the mud. She walked with a careful, mincing step, as if she were unaccustomed to wearing shoes. Under her right arm, she carried a muzzle-loading rifle. Another man, a farmer with a broad peasant face, followed behind Mr. Shaw and the woman.

Mr. Shaw performed introductions. "Mr. Jones, this is Miss Nadya Rybak and her father, Dmitri. It seemed to me that Miss Nadya should take a turn."

"Pleased to meet you, Miss Nadya," Hezekiah said uncertainly.

She wasn't looking at him. Her eyes were on the distant candle flame.

"Now, Miss Nadya," Mr. Shaw was saying. "You see that candle over there." He explained the rules of the contest and she listened, nodding to show that she understood. Then she glanced at her father and he nodded approval.

"It's ready," Adam called from his post by the candle. In the distance, Rufus could see the bobbing torch as the boy moved to a safe distance.

"Shoot when you're ready, Miss Nadya," Mr. Shaw said.

She planted her feet wide, getting a secure footing on the rough ground. She put her rifle to her shoulder, then frowned and lowered it again. She murmured something to her father—Rufus could not make out the words—and he shrugged. She handed him the rifle and bent to unlace her shoes. That done, she pulled the shoes off and stood barefoot on the cold ground. She nodded with satisfaction and took her rifle, lifting it with greater confidence than before.

The rifle was barely to her shoulder when she squeezed off the first shot. The flame flickered and then flared brightly.

Nadya took the rifle from her shoulder and waited for the snuff to grow long enough to shoot again. The men waited in silence, looking away into the darkness. Dmitri Rybak stood at his daughter's side.

The woman glanced in Rufus's direction, catching him staring. Rather than dropping her eyes, she returned his stare. Her eyes were dark in the moonlight.

"Ready," Adam called out, and Nadya turned to face the candle. Again, she set her feet carefully and lifted the rifle smoothly to her shoulder. A faint breath of wind toyed with the wisps of hair that had escaped her braids. In the distance, the candle flame flickered and threatened to go out. She waited with the rifle at her shoulder until the flame steadied. Her second shot was as good as the first. The flame brightened and burned white.

She did not fidget as she waited for the flame to burn away the wick so that she could shoot again. She lowered the rifle and stood at ease, ignoring the men around her. The whiskey bottle passed from hand to hand to Dmitri Rybak. He took a pull, then touched Nadya's arm. She wet her lips, glanced at the candle, then accepted the bottle and drank. She handed the bottle to Rufus. Her fingers brushed his as he took the bottle—a warm touch in the cool night air.

The candle burned low and Adam called out that she could shoot again. Rufus watched her lift the rifle a third time.

Her third shot was perfect—straight through the snuff. "Good shooting," Mr. Shaw exclaimed. "Fine shooting. Well worth a jug of whiskey, Miss Nadya. To the winner!" he said, holding aloft a new jug.

The men returned to the barn in a knot of excitement and noise. Rufus walked with the others, avoiding his father. Hezekiah did not like to be disappointed and Rufus thought it just as well to stay out of his way for a time. He also wanted to get a look at Nadya Rybak in a better light.

In the barn, the tables had been cleared away and the fiddler was just starting a tune. A line of couples began forming for a reel, but Nadya was not among them. Rufus looked for her, strolling around the dance floor and peering into the shadowy corners. He tipped his hat to the group of young women who had gathered in one corner. There were some pretty girls there, but he had his mind fixed on the dark-eyed woman who was such a good shot. He made his way to the corner of the barn where the men were drinking.

"I don't see Miss Nadya," he said to Tom Williams, the son of the man who ran the blacksmith shop in town.

Tom shrugged. "I don't believe I've ever seen her dancing. I suppose she doesn't care for it."

"Have you ever tried to persuade her to change her mind? She's a handsome girl," Rufus said.

Tom looked startled. "I never thought of that. I reckon she is. But I expect that trying to change her mind is a waste of time."

"You think so? I'd wager that I could change her mind."

"You think so? I doubt it."

"How about betting two bits on the proposition? If I don't have her out there dancing by the end of the evening, you win."

Tom nodded. "I'll take you up on that."

"Then I guess I'll see if I can find her." Rufus took a gourd cup and a bottle of cider, crossed the barn to the open door, and stepped outside.

The barnyard was crowded with the farm wagons that had carried the guests to the celebration. He strolled among the wagons. On the far side of the barnyard, he saw a woman leaning against the split-rail fence, gazing into the empty field. She turned her head as he approached, and he recognized Nadya Rybak.

"How do, Miss Nadya," Rufus said. "We haven't been properly introduced. I'm Rufus Jones. My father just bought some land by the river not far from here."

"How do," she said politely.

"That was fine shooting. Congratulations."

"Thank you." Her voice was even; she did not seem particularly interested in him.

"I've never known such a pretty girl to be such a fine shot." He poured cider into the cup. "Would you care for a drink of cider? Shooting is thirsty work."

She studied his face, then accepted the cup. By her expression, he guessed that she was not used to flattery. He leaned against the railing beside her. "Mr. Shaw was pleased that you won," he said.

She shook her head. "Not at all. He was pleased that you lost. He's a stiff-necked old Yankee."

He grinned. She was plainspoken enough. "But surely you're no Yankee."

She shrugged. "We're foreigners, by his lights, and that doesn't count for much. But he'd rather lose to a foreigner than a man from Kentucky."

"Well, if I had to lose to someone, I'm happy to lose to you, Miss Nadya. Have you picked out your prize yet?"

She frowned and returned the cup to him. "Mr. Shaw gave me a bottle of whiskey."

"He also promised the pick of the litter. You can get yourself a dog."

She shook her head. "I don't care for dogs."

"Mr. Shaw makes great claims for these dogs. Fine hunters, he says. Perhaps your father. . . ."

"My father won't have a dog on the place. He likes them no better than I do."

Rufus shook his head, amazed. Just about every frontier farm had a few dogs around—to warn against intruders, to bark when varmints attacked the livestock. "I had heard you were a hunter. I'm surprised any hunter would turn down a dog."

"I hunt alone," she said. "I don't need a yapping dog to scare away the game."

He drained the cup, filled it again, and offered it to her. She took it from his hand.

"I had hoped I might have the honor of a dance," he said.

She shook her head. "I don't care to dance."

"That's kind of you. I'm sure if you elected to dance, you'd put the other girls to shame."

She looked away from him, gazing out at the open field once again. He thought he might have overdone the flattery, but then she spoke softly. "Never learned how."

"Never learned how to dance? Why, that's foolish. You move with such a natural grace. You could learn all you needed in a minute." He hesitated, then said, "I could teach you right now, if you'd like."

She glanced at his face.

"Right now," he said, setting the cider jug on the ground and balancing the cup on the fence rail. He held his arms out to her. "It won't take a minute."

"I can't," she said, standing with her back to the fence.

"Listen to the music," he said, tapping his foot in time to the fiddle tune. "Here now: I'll bow to you." He bent at the waist, grinning at her. "And you curtsy to me." She bobbed in an awkward curtsy. "Give me your hand and we'll begin."

She reached out and he took her hands in his. Her hands were small and warm, a little rough from farmwork.

"Tap your foot along with the music," he said. "That's good. Now we step forward and back. That's right. Now left hand circle." He held one hand and led her in a circle. "Right hand circle." Again, she followed obediently. "Swing your partner." He swung her, keeping time with the distant fiddle. "Very good. Promenade now." He pulled her into the promenade position and led her around a farm wagon. Her body was warm against his side.

She was a cooperative partner, moving with him easily. "You're a fine dancer," he said when the music ended.

She smiled at him for the first time. Her face was a little flushed, and a few more tendrils had escaped her braids. She looked charming. "You think so?"

"Without a doubt. You come to it naturally. Why don't you come inside and we can join the others."

She shook her head. "I don't care to."

The music started again, a slow tune in waltz time. He cocked his head to listen. "I'll teach you a dance that's all the rage in Paris," he said. "A dancing teacher who was passing through Kentucky taught it to me. Would you like to learn it?"

He smiled at her. The dancing teacher had told him that the waltz was a fine excuse to hold a girl closer than propriety would ordinarily allow. She held out her hands, and he pulled her close, slipping one arm around her waist and holding her other hand in his.

"Now step as I do. One, two three; one, two, three; one, two, three. . . ."

She was so close that he could feel the warmth of her body. Just a few thin layers of cloth separated his hand from her waist. Her face was just inches from his. He could feel his cock rising to press against his trousers.

He stopped counting and began to hum softly along with the fiddle tune. Perhaps he couldn't persuade her to dance with him in the barn. But he might persuade her to spend a little time with him alone. That would be worth losing the wager. He adjusted his hand at her waist, pulling her a little closer.

Nadya stopped in mid-step and pulled away. "I'd best be going," she said suddenly.

"In the middle of a dance?"

She took two steps back. "Yes. I think it's best." She wet her lips. "Thank you for teaching me."

"I'd be happy to continue the lesson. I wish you wouldn't run off."

She shook her head and cast a quick look over her shoulder at the barn. "I must be going." She turned away, then hesitated and turned back. "If you would like the dog Mr. Shaw promised to me, you are welcome to have it. You can tell him I said so."

She hurried away then, carrying her shoes. She did not look back. Rufus watched her go, cursing his bad luck. After a bit, he wandered back into the barn. A few moments later, Tom found him in the shadows, watching the dancers.

"No luck," Tom said. "I told you she didn't care for it."

Rufus fished in his pocket and silently paid Tom the money he owed.

6

On the day of the full moon, Nadya was in the garden, chopping at weeds with a grubbing hoe and loosening the soil for the spring planting. The work went slowly. She kept stopping to stare into the woods and think of the coming night.

On the day of the Change, the world seemed different than on other days. It looked different, felt different, sounded different, smelled different. Her blue calico dress was the same color it had been the day before, but today it looked duller, one step closer to gray. She could feel the cotton fabric, softened by many washings, slide over her skin; the cloth rubbed her nipples, making them crinkle. She could barely stand the pressure of any clothing, even the light dress, on her body.

The breeze was warm and the newly turned soil reeked of rotting leaves and grubs—rich, inviting smells. She would have preferred rolling in the green weeds to chopping them down, but the squash had to be planted, and she had promised her mother that she would till the garden.

"Hello, the house!" She heard a man's voice calling and straightened from her hoeing, grateful for the interruption. Rufus Jones rode into the farm yard on a gray horse.

Nadya hurried toward the cabin. By the time she reached the farmyard, Rufus had tied his horse to the split-rail fence and was greeting her mother politely. "Pleased to make your acquaintance, Mrs. Rybak," he was saying. "How do you do, Miss Nadya."

Nadya nodded a greeting. Rufus had been hunting and he gave her mother one of the two turkey hens that hung from his saddle. He was saying something about his father feeling a mite poorly and he thought Mrs. Rybak might have a remedy that would ease his stomach.

Nadya's mother nodded, allowing that she had some herbs that might help. She dried her hands on her apron. "I'll get them right away."

"Would you like some tea?" Nadya asked Rufus. She glanced at her mother.

"Don't you want to hurry home to bring the herbs to your father?" her mother asked. Her tone was calm, but Nadya detected an edge beneath the placid surface.

"He was sleeping when I left," Rufus said. "Surely it won't hurt to stop for a cup of tea."

"Of course not," her mother said. There was starch in her voice. "That would be lovely." She looked at Nadya thoughtfully. "Perhaps you'd best go fetch some water from the spring. Mr. Jones, come and sit down."

"Oh, I'll help Miss Nadya with the water," he said quickly.

"Don't be foolish, Mr. Jones," Nadya's mother said sharply. Then she smiled and spoke in a soothing tone. "You're our guest. Come and sit."

"I insist," Rufus said. "If Miss Nadya can show me the way to the spring, I'll carry the bucket."

"Here's the bucket." Nadya picked up the wooden bucket that stood by the door. "I'll show you the way." She started away down the path.

"Fine weather, ain't it?" Rufus said.

Nadya nodded. She had wanted to be alone with Rufus again, but now she did not know what to say. She glanced back to see her mother standing in the farmyard, her hands knotted in her apron. When Rufus glanced at her, she felt a flush of warmth on her face.

"Here—I'll carry that." He took the bucket from her hand and she felt his warm fingers brush against hers. The sensation was disturbing. When she was younger, she had walked along the top rail of the split-rail fence, balancing carefully. The feeling in her stomach reminded her of the inevitable moment when she teetered before falling. She was losing her balance, teetering on an edge that she could not even see.

He held his free hand out to her, offering to help her over a muddy patch. She hesitated. She walked this path a dozen times a day and never needed anyone's help. But she wanted to see how his touch affected the feeling in her stomach. She took his hand. The feeling in her stomach intensified: a strange fluttering, almost like hunger, but not quite.

She knew about sex. She had seen the hog fuck the sow in the mud of the barnyard and she had seen a stallion mount a mare down at the livery stable. Once, on a visit to the crossroads store, she had seen two dogs stuck together in the dirt road that ran down to the ferry. The blacksmith's dog had mounted the storekeeper's bitch. The bitch snapped and snarled and tried to run, but the dog clung to her, hugging her from behind. The two of them yelped and growled and scrabbled in the dust.

Mrs. Kahn shooed Nadya and the other girls inside just as the storekeeper threw a bucket of water over the pair. The two animals split up and ran helter-skelter in different directions. Just before the storekeeper's wife blocked her view, Nadya caught a glimpse of the dog's shiny penis, bright red between his bowed black legs.

When Nadya asked her mother about the dogs, her mother explained. She told Nadya that men fucked women, giving biological details about what goes where. Nadya had thought the whole thing quite unlikely: why would anyone do such an odd thing?

Just a month after the incident with the dogs, her friend Lottie had loaned her a book in which a young man carries off a young woman and does something scandalous to her. Unlike her mother's talk, the book lacked all details. But it made up for that lack with its breathless tone and florid language that spoke of dark passion and hot love and fevered kisses. Lottie had told her to hide the book from her mother, and so she did. She read it down by the river. When she read the book, she found herself curling up her legs and rocking to and fro. Something was happening. Her nipples grew tight and she felt a strange warmth between her legs. She did not understand why that should be.

When her father stripped for the Change, she had seen his cock and balls, hanging softly between his legs. She thought little of that, even after reading Lottie's book. She thought all the fuss about nakedness and sin and love was nonsense; it had nothing to do with her. And so the feeling that came when Rufus's hand touched hers took her by surprise. The feeling in her stomach reminded her of reading Lottie's book by the river. Something was happening.

"You're surprised to see me," Rufus said.

"That's so."

"I'd hoped you'd be glad."

She said nothing, concentrating on the feel of the cool dirt beneath her bare feet. Like walking on the fence. She did not want to fall.

"Aren't you glad?" he asked.

"I'm glad," she said. Her voice was soft and she didn't sound sure.

They had reached the spring. A small wooden shelter covered the pool and two log steps led down to the water's edge. "I'd best get the water," she said. "My feet are bare, and you don't want to get your boots wet." She took the bucket from him and went down to the bottom step, where the water lapped at her feet. She stooped to fill the bucket, holding her skirt out of the way.

"You look beautiful," he said, gazing down at her.

She straightened up, holding the bucket, and frowned at him. "You are a very strange man."

"Why do you say that?"

She stood by the cool water, studying his face. "Because you say I'm beautiful."

"You are."

She shook her head ever so slightly. Her mother was beautiful, Nadya knew that. But Nadya had studied her own face in the looking glass. It was a wide face, like her father's, and her hair was too wild to tame with braids and hairpins. She knew that she was not beautiful.

"You were the prettiest girl at the wedding."

"The best shot," she corrected.

"That, too."

She shook her head and climbed the steps. He stood on the path, blocking her way.

Lottie and other girls talked about young men and dresses and dances and getting married. Nadya had listened to the girls talk, but she had always known she was not like those girls.

When she reached the top step, she turned to tell him that he should go and talk to Lottie or one of the others, and leave her alone. Before she could speak, he kissed her. The kiss was awkward at first—lips bumping against lips. But she did not pull away, and he kissed her again, this time lifting his hand to touch her cheek. His lips were soft. His hand moved from her cheek to stroke her neck. The touch, more than the kiss, made her catch her breath.

He kissed her again, and she could feel the warmth of him through the thin calico of her dress. She could feel a trembling deep inside herself, so deep that the vibration did not reach the surface. She lifted her hand to touch his cheek, where she could feel the stubble of a beard, clean-shaven that morning. His smell changed, just as it had when they danced together at the wedding. She knew the smell of sex: a warm muskiness that clung to her mother on certain mornings. She could smell that muskiness in the air. His hand, moving downward, touched her breast, stroking gently over the fabric and coming to rest at her waist.

She stepped back. "Mama will wonder where we have been. We'd best go back."

He grinned at her, showing white teeth.

They had tea, and Nadya listened to her mother and Rufus talk about the weather, the plowing, his father's aching stomach, his family and their journey from Kentucky to Missouri. Rufus's scent overpowered the familiar smell of herbs that hung from the pegs in the wall. Rufus talked with her mother, but every now and again, Nadya caught him glancing in her direction.

When he left, Nadya waved goodbye and watched him go.

Her mother frowned at her. "You've taken a fancy to this young man, haven't you? Look at me, *chérie*. Let me see your face." Nadya looked up and her mother nodded.

"He taught me to waltz at the wedding," Nadya said. She held out her arms and took a few steps, whirling as she moved. "He put his arm around me and we danced together."

"Yes," her mother said. "What do you think that he wants?"

Nadya dropped her hands. Thinking about Rufus made her cheeks grow hot. "To kiss me, I reckon."

"To kiss you, to hug you, to run his hands over your body, to lie with you." Her mother's tone was matter-of-fact. "I have told you how it is between men and women." She stood in front of Nadya and took her hands. "And you want him to do that."

"I don't know," Nadya said. "I want. . . ." She shook her head, thinking about the warmth of Rufus's body, so close to hers. "I don't know what I want."

"There is nothing wrong with wanting a man," Nadya's mother said. "In our family, the blood has always run hot." She hesitated, studying Nadya's face. "But this man—he is not good for you. This man is dangerous."

Nadya pulled her hands away from her mother's. "What do you mean?"

"Remember the cards? A young man, fair-haired, reckless. He brings misfortune to you and to us. Remember."

"Not Rufus," Nadya said. "He won't bring misfortune."

"Listen to me, Nadya," her mother said. "You must listen. Don't go with this man."

Nadya hung her head, looking down at the porch. "I'm listening," she said sullenly.

"Do you understand?"

"I understand." Nadya understood, but she did not agree.

"That's good. Now here is Papa, coming in from the fields. Put aside your work and let us prepare for the Change."

Preparing for the Change was not so different than their regular evening chores. They simply began the work early, so that they would be ready when the sun set. Nadya's father milked the cow and fed the mule; Nadya called the hogs and chased the chickens into their coop for the night. Nadya's mother prepared a simple meal of hoecake and ham; she thought it best to change with a little food in the belly—not too much, and not too little. She put the remaining food out of reach of any varmints that might come to the unoccupied cabin and carefully banked the fire so that she could easily revive it when they returned, weary and cold from the night in the forest.

When the sun dipped near the horizon, Nadya stood on the front porch, looking into the forest. The cabin faced east and the porch was already in shadow. Nadya had pulled off her dress, hung it from a peg beside the cabin door, and waited for her parents. She shivered in the early evening air, goose bumps rising on her bare skin. She could hear her parents murmuring inside the cabin, but the words were already starting to sound like meaningless babble. She could feel the moon rising, a tugging that she felt in her belly and her crotch.

Nadya rubbed her hands over the goose bumps on her naked arms and shivered again. The sky was clear except for a few clouds hanging low in the east. Her father said something and her mother laughed. Nadya heard the rustling of clothing.

"The sun is setting," Nadya said, and she heard her mother's hand on the doorlatch.

"We are here," her mother said. Her hair was loose, falling in dark waves down her back.

Then the Change came.

You want to know how it feels, to go through the Change? It begins with warmth, as if the moonlight on your skin carried the heat of the tropical sun. But the warmth comes from within you, not from outside. You can feel your heart beating and your blood surging through your body, pounding in your veins and arteries. The moon pulls on your blood as it pulls on the ocean: you are caught in the tide, a riptide that you are powerless to resist. Your body burns with the heat and you breathe faster, moaning sometimes. There is something you want, something you need—you know that, though you cannot yet describe what that something is.

You cannot tell if this feeling is pleasure or pain. Those words do not apply. You feel a new intensity (surely it could not have felt like this on the last full moon). You feel like you might be dying or you might, at last, be coming to life. In this moment, the two seem much the same. And maybe you want to stop, you want to call out, "No, no, no, this is too much. I can't . . . , I won't. . . ." But what it is that you can't or won't do is lost in clouds and darkness, because no words come to you. Words are going away, rushing away from you, a babble that no longer has meaning or value. You are poised on the brink, on the knife's edge, at the precipice of the mountain, at the edge of the cliff, and you are staring down at a new world, a world that you never imagined existed.

And when the Change comes at last, it comes with an inexorable rush, like the rush of orgasm. You cannot control it. Your body has made its decision, and the you that thinks and talks and plans and believes that it controls so much, that you is carried along, like a straw in the river's current. The river is sweeping you away into the unknown. And there is no stopping the river, there is no turning back.

That is what the Change was like. And when it was over, Nadya stood on four legs instead of two; her body was covered with fur; her ears caught the rustling of a mouse under the porch. But all that was not important. What was important in that moment was the Change itself, the moment of shifting, the malleability of the flesh, the decision of the body.

The Change came and three wolves stood on the porch, gazing into the forest.

The wolf that had been Nadya stretched, extending her forelegs and lowering her chest to the ground so her back arched.

She yawned, opening her jaws wide with a sound like a creaking gate. When she shook herself, her fur shimmered in the moonlight. She was a gray wolf, marked with black on her back and tail and face.

She lifted her head and breathed deeply. The air was alive with scents: the odor of crushed weeds and turned earth from the field, the warm breath of livestock in the barn, the lingering aroma of cornbread left over from dinner. And there was another smell, an intriguing scent that clung to the handle of the bucket by the cabin door. She sniffed at the bucket, catching a warm man smell touched with tobacco and gunpowder. She did not know why the scent was so intriguing, but for some reason it made her whimper low in her throat.

Her father answered her whimper with a low howl. He stood in the center of the farmyard, a powerfully built gray and black wolf. Nadya's mother, a cream-colored animal marked with russet and black, leaned close to her mate, flattening her ears as she pushed her muzzle close to his, licking his face in greeting.

Among wolves, howling calls the members of the pack, bringing them together. When Dmitri extended his muzzle and howled again, Marietta joined in on a higher note. Dmitri stepped forward, and she kept pace with him, pushing her shoulder against his as their tails wagged in unison, their lips pulled back in canine grins.

Nadya left the intriguing scent and joined her parents, walking close beside her mother. Somewhere, far away, a coyote answered their howls with a yapping call. With her mother and father, Nadya raised her voice to respond. Their voices, joined in chorus, filled her with a wild joy. She was with her pack, protected by the pack. If the pack were threatened, she would fight to protect it. She felt the warmth of her mother's body beside her, smelled her mother's reassuring scent, heard the low moan of her father's voice, and it all felt right. She belonged here.

But as she passed the rail fence, she caught another whiff of the tantilizing scent in the long grass. As her father's howl trailed off, Nadya turned away, rearing up on her hind legs to sniff at the fence where Rufus had rested his hand when he tied his horse.

Her father trotted to the edge of the farmyard, where cleared land gave way to forest. He lifted his head and sampled the air, then trotted into the woods, not glancing back to see if the others followed. Marietta started after him, then looked back at Nadya. Nadya was sniffing the grass beside the fence. Marietta whimpered once, then turned to follow her mate. Nadya glanced after her mother, then set out on a different path, following the scent of Rufus and his horse.

Nadya came back to her human form on the porch of the farmhouse. The taste of blood was in her mouth. She rubbed her hand across her face, and looked at it. Flecks of dark brown dotted the skin. Dried blood. She could hear her mother in the cabin, breaking kindling to add to the fire.

Nadya blinked in the morning light, trying to remember the night. Memories of the Change faded like dreams; memories of the Change did not fit well in the human brain. The colors were wrong; the smells didn't match the human memory of smells. At best, she could recapture only fragments of the night.

She remembered sheep, bleating sheep that ran from her. She could not help but chase the clumsy creatures, so fat and foolish and warm. She cut a fat ewe from the herd and chased it along a fence, tearing at the thick fleece that covered the animal's throat. The ewe cried out, a silly bleating that made her heart beat faster, and she tore at it again, tasting blood. Dark streaks of blood colored the pale fleece. She snapped at its legs, catching one in her jaws, and the ewe stumbled. Then she was on it, bowling it over and ripping at its throat and exposed belly. Blood was warm on her muzzle, streaking her face, filling her nose with its dark scent.

She remembered a sound—the sharp crack of gunfire, the acrid scent of gunpowder, cutting through the alluring aroma of the blood. She heard shouting and more gunfire. She ran then, her fear overcoming her excitement at the kill.

Nadya sat on the porch, the taste of blood still on her lips. Her father stood in the doorway to the cabin. "Little one," he said to her. "Where did you go last night? You left us." His tone was reproachful.

Nadya hung her head. "I guess . . . I reckon I must have followed Rufus home."

Her father wet his lips, looking worried. "I smell blood. That's not good. Not good at all."

Her mother came from the cabin, carrying a basin of water, warmed on the fire. She stood on the porch, watching as Nadya splashed the warm water on her face and arms. She put her arm around Nadya's father. "She's home safe, Dmitri. That's what's important."

He shook his head. "Did they fire at you?" he asked her.

"I think so." Nadya kept her eyes on the water. The blood had colored it pale pink. "I'm sorry."

"They will come for us with guns," he said. "They will hunt us through the forest with dogs and guns."

"No, Dmitri," her mother said. "Don't be so excited. It will be all right."

"It must not happen again," he said.

Her mother rested her hand on Nadya's head. "It won't happen again. Nadya and I will see to that, won't we *chérie*?"

"It won't happen again," Nadya muttered.

Nadya's father turned away and went back into the cabin. Nadya's mother stroked her hair. "It will be all right, *chérie*. I think it will be all right." But the smell of her father's fear lingered in the air.

7

One morning, William Cooper heard the voice of God.

William Cooper was a prosperous New England farmer. A dour, taciturn man, he had married young and fathered three sons and four daughters. In the spring that he turned fifty, his wife died of a fever. She was buried in the churchyard, and William's daughter Anne, the youngest and the only one left at home, shrouded the looking glasses and pictures with white cotton cloth, as was the custom.

After his wife died, Cooper slept badly. He was bothered by sounds that he had never noticed before: the snores of his sleeping daughter in the next room, the popping and sighing of logs in the fire, the creaking of boards as the old farmhouse settled.

Night after night, he lay awake in the big featherbed in the parlor, listening as the night sounds blended to become a muttering voice. He blinked at the white-shrouded pictures, ghostly in the darkness. He strained to make out the words and sometimes he caught a few—verses from the Bible, all of them. "Amend your ways and your doings. . . ." "Repent ye, for the Kingdom of Heaven is at hand."

He accused his daughter Anne of whispering outside his door, but she denied it. "It must have been a dream, Papa," she said. She was a stolid, practical woman, little given to imaginings. "I didn't hear anything."

Cooper shook his head, suddenly filled with a strange excitement. "It's no dream," he told her. "No dream at all." And he smiled at her, happier than he had been in years. When she asked him to explain, he just smiled and shook his head, refusing to say more.

Cooper had never been a religious man. He had attended the Congregationalist church with his wife, but he had been an indifferent worshiper at best. But that evening, he sat by the fire, and read the Bible by candlelight. In his hands, the book opened of its own accord, guiding him to the verses he needed to read.

He read: "How then shall they call on him in whom they have not believed? and how shall they believe in him of whom they have not heard? and how shall they hear without a preacher? and how shall they preach, except they be sent?"

And he read: "A prophet is not without honor, but in his own country and among his own kin and in his own house."

"You're up very late, Papa," his daughter said. "You'd best get to bed." He stared at her, amazed at her audacity.

"I am reading the word of God," he said solemnly. When he opened the book again, he read aloud to her: "Now it is high time to awake out of sleep: for now is our salvation nearer than we believed."

She stared at him. "Go to bed, daughter," he said. "I will bank the fire when it is time."

She left, looking back over her shoulder at him, and he returned to his reading. By the wavering light of a tallow candle, he read about Jesus sending his Apostles to preach about the kingdom of God: "And he said unto them, Take nothing for your journey, neither staves, nor scrip, neither bread, neither money; neither have two coats apiece. And whatsoever house ye enter into, there abide, and thence depart. And whosoever will not receive you, when ye go out of that city, shake off the very dust from your feet as a testimony against them."

He thumbed through the book. "As it is written in the prophets, Behold, I send my messenger before thy face, which shall prepare thy way before thee. The voice of one crying in the wilderness, Prepare ye the way of the Lord, make straight in the desert a highway for our God. Every valley shall be exalted, and every mountain and hill shall be made low: and the crooked shall be made straight, and the rough places plain: And the glory of the Lord shall be revealed. . . ."

As he read, words echoed in his mind, repeating endlessly, like the voices of children, learning by rote. "In the wilderness," the echo said. "In the wilderness." And another echo: "The way of the Lord. The way of the Lord." The two phrases combined and recombined: "The way of the Lord in the wilderness. The Lord in the wilderness. The way of the Lord in the wilderness."

The candle guttered and he closed the book. The words continued to echo as he took off his boots and trousers and pulled a linen nightshirt over his head. "The way to the Lord is in the wilderness." The rhythm of the repeating words lulled him to sleep.

In the morning, he ate breakfast in silence and went out to the south pasture to check on the grass. It was mid-March. The winter's snow had melted, but the stone walls were dusted white with frost. He felt the cold in his bones. He was halfway to the pasture when the voice of God broke like thunder from the clear blue sky.

"Go to the wilderness," God said.

Cooper stopped walking and gazed up at the sky. A red-winged blackbird, perched on the nearby wall, flicked its tail and took flight, a black speck against the blue.

The sky was bluer than Cooper had ever seen it. The color shifted as he watched. It put him in mind of the light on a pool of water, right after a fish has risen to kiss the surface. The sky shimmered, as if ripples were passing overhead. Looking up, he feared he might fall into the sky and drown in the blue.

"Go to the wilderness," God said again, a thunderous voice that echoed in his head.

Cooper fell to his knees. He bowed his head to shield his eyes from the brilliant blue. "God be merciful to me a sinner," he cried out.

"How shall they hear without a preacher?" God said. "How shall they preach, except they be sent? Go into the wilderness and save my sinning children."

Cooper kept his eyes on the ground. "O Lord," he said. "I am not worthy."

He saw the ground split open in front of him. Flames from the pit of Hades licked at the ground, melting the frost and blackening the new shoots of grass. A ladder, each rung outlined in fire, led down into the inferno. Demons swarmed up the rungs—bat-winged demons, horned monsters, creatures twisted in body and spirit.

"Save me, Lord," Cooper shrieked, closing his eyes against the heat and the horror. "Command your poor servant."

"Go forth and preach," the Lord said.

"I will," Cooper cried. "Thy will be done."

The heat faded. When Cooper opened his eyes, the ground was whole once again. The blackbird had returned to its perch. The demons had retreated beneath the earth.

Cooper returned to his house. "Anne," he called to his daughter. "Anne, come here. Something wonderful has happened!"

He found her churning butter in the cool air of the spring house. "Anne," he said. "The Lord has called me to do his bidding. I must preach the Gospel in the wilderness." He took her hands in his. "I must leave you and go west." His face was flushed and his eyes glittered with a feverish light.

He returned to the house and began to pack a few necessities. Anne followed him. "What are you doing, Papa?" she asked. "You should sit down and rest. I'll get you a glass of cider. You've been in the sun too much."

He drank the glass of cider that she brought him, but otherwise ignored her. When she persisted in speaking to him, he began singing a hymn to drown her protests. "Jesus let thy pitying eye, call back a wandering sheep. . . ."

"Papa, you must listen."

He took two good woolen blankets and tied them into a bedroll. He pulled on a heavy deerskin coat and a flat-brimmed black hat. In his saddlebags, he packed a sturdy knife, a few candles, a paper twist filled with salt, a cloth bag filled with tea. In the parlor, he lifted a floorboard to bring out the strongbox where he kept some of the hard cash he had managed to set aside in his years of farming: six Mexican silver dollars, a handful of French and English coins.

He fetched the mule from the stable and saddled it. "I'll leave you the farm, daughter," he said. "The Lord will provide for you." Anne watched him mount.

"Where are you going, Papa?" she began.

"I have been called," he said, and turned his mule westward.

Anne watched him go. After a moment's hesitation, she returned to her butter. She was a practical woman. With her father's departure, she was a wealthy one, too. Under her care, the farm would prosper.

William Cooper was crazy, of course, but his insanity came in the form of a religious calling. He became an itinerant preacher. His sermons were filled with talk of holy visions—the pack of winged demons that pursued him through the forest, the voices of angels that sang to him, the blessed Virgin appearing to him in a forest clearing and telling him the proper trail.

He was a bit behind the times, perhaps—the last great wave of camp meetings had ended back in the 1820s, some twenty years before God hailed William Cooper from a clear blue sky. But even in the 1840s, the Methodists had their circuit riders, preachers on horseback who traveled from one frontier settlement to the next, calling the wrath of God on sinners, warning of the coming Judgment Day, and saving souls where they could. A Methodist preacher with the power of exhortation could call the Spirit of the Lord upon the Assembly, causing men and women to jerk wildly to and fro, to fall on all fours and bark like dogs, to weep and cry and shout in languages that no American could understand. The Methodists were a fiery lot in those times, doing battle both with Satan and with the Baptists (who insisted on baptism by immersion, rather than simply sprinkling).

Cooper was neither a Methodist nor a Baptist, but he had the power of exhortation. He preached and the people came to listen. Gradually, he made his way west. After months of traveling and preaching, he made his way to Missouri.

That spring was cold and wet. One rainy afternoon, Cooper rode through the forest, thoroughly miserable. Cold rain dripped from the brim of his hat and splashed onto his deerskin coat. It had been raining for hours and both his hat and coat were soaked through. His mule walked with its head down, plodding stolidly through the mud.

He was traveling through the Devil's own country. Miles of wilderness filled with beasts and Indians. The trees were so thick they shut out the light of God's sky. He missed the tidy fields of New England, fenced with stone walls. He did not like these western forests—where men grew wild, turning to drink, turning to gambling, turning to fallen women who led them down the path to Hell. Turning away from God, away from His stern and unyielding love.

Cooper peered down the trail. In the dim light from the overcast sky, he saw the trees on either side of the trail waver and shift with his movement. An oak by the trail had been scarred by the claws of a bear. As he looked, the pattern of scars flowed and shifted. A demonic face glowered at him from the trunk of the tree.

"The Lord is my light and my salvation," Cooper muttered. The branches that hung low over the trail seemed to reach for him as he passed. He closed his eyes, concentrating on his prayer. "Oh, Lord, my strength and my redeemer, hide me under the shadow of thy wings." When he opened his eyes again, the face was gone. The enemy had been banished for the moment.

"Blessed is he who puts his trust in the Lord," Cooper murmured. He pulled his scarf more tightly around his neck, hoping to stop the trickle of water that was running down his back to soak his linsey-woolsey shirt. His throat ached. The previous night's service had been invaded by a crowd of drunks, who had heckled him from the back of the cabin in which he held a meeting. Cooper had called the wrath of the Lord down on the sinners, but fighting evil with volume had strained his voice, leaving him hoarse.

"Oh, Lord, preserve my voice so that I may continue to do your good work." His head ached, a pounding pain exacerbated by the constant hammering of the rain. He felt dizzy and feverish. Thinking of his throat and future preaching, he reached into the pocket of his coat and pulled out a whiskey flask. He allowed himself the whiskey for medicinal purposes only. Now that he was a man of God, he could not be a drinking man. But he required medicinal whiskey on a regular basis. Sometimes, whiskey quieted the voices that muttered in his head, whiskey healed his throat so that he might serve the Lord by preaching another day.

The alcohol's warmth spread throughout his head and chest, easing the pain. The sun was near setting, and the weather was getting colder. Odds were good that the cold rain would turn to freezing sleet. He would be well advised to seek shelter before that happened. The nearest town, he guessed, was still many miles away.

He made camp in a clearing beside an ancient fir tree. The tree's lower branches drooped to touch the ground, forming a natural lean-to that would keep off the worst of the rain. The branches and the ground beneath them were still dry.

Cooper built a small fire and squatted beneath the sheltering branches, watching the flames lick against the damp wood. He positioned a pot filled with water among the burning sticks. The rain had let up somewhat, settling into an intermittent drizzle.

He gave thanks to the Lord for the shelter and warmth. When the water came to a boil, he made tea and laced it with whiskey from the flask. In the last settlement, a woman had asked Cooper to bless her youngest child, who was ill with the fever. To repay him, she had packed him a generous meal. He dined on bread and ham and hot tea.

The sun set, and the shadows pressed close. The clouds were so thick that the moon offered no light. Cooper built up the fire with dry branches broken from the old fir tree. He did not like the darkness. The Bible said "God is the True Light" and Cooper believed that most literally. In the darkness, he knew that the forces of Satan were strong.

For a time, he read from the Psalms by the light of the fire. When his eyes grew too tired for that, he clutched the Bible to his heart and recited what verses he could remember, whispering the words softly. " 'O God, thou knowest my foolishness; and my sins are not hid from thee. . . . For thy sake I have borne reproach; shame hath covered my face. I am become a stranger unto my brethren. . . . Deliver me out of the mire and let me not sink.' "

He wrapped himself in a damp wool blanket that smelled strongly of mule. Beneath him, the ground was littered with cones from the fir tree; they poked into his back so that he could find no comfortable position. He thought, for a moment, of his featherbed back home. Such a soft bed, packed with feathers from his own geese, plucked by his loving wife, God rest her soul. How could he have left such a soft warm bed for this barren wilderness?

Once he started thinking about his farm, he could not stop. Was Anne caring for the livestock properly? She was a careless girl; some young man might turn her head and ruin his farm. He imagined the fields gone fallow, the barns empty, the stone walls that he had built so carefully all tumbling down.

He could return to his farm, he thought then. He could turn back; it was not so far. Surely, the Lord would understand. He was an old man, his bones too brittle for this adventure. He would give generously to the church; perhaps that would be enough.

The burning wood crackled and spat as the flames licked a pitch-laden branch. The fire flared, painting the trees in shifting patterns of red and gold, like the flames of Hell. Wrapped in the damp blanket, with the fire crackling at his head, he prayed to the Lord for guidance. He clutched his Bible to him, holding it against his belly, as if the book could warm him. "O Lord, send me a sign—a sign that I am called to preach your word."

At last he dozed off. Above him, the tree branches reached out toward a hazy patch of clouds, illuminated from behind by a half moon. The fire crackled softly. An owl called, a lonely sound that made Cooper shift and mutter in his sleep.

He did not sleep easily. In his dreams, he walked alone in a barren desert. He was hungry and weary, but he kept walking. The desert was bright and hot. Beneath his feet, the sand was barren; pinnacles of bare red rock towered over him.

When he looked down, he saw a patch of darkness—his shadow, following close at his heels. But it was more than his shadow. The darkness was evil; as he watched it, the black shape flowed and changed, becoming grotesque and misshapen. It spoke to him, this darkness, this evil. "You are hungry," the shadow said in a voice no louder than a whisper. "Command that these stones be made bread."

He looked at the stones around him: great rounded lumps that reminded him of all the stones he had piled into walls around his fields. A loaf of bread would be welcome now. Surely it would not be such a sin to ask for bread.

"Just a word from you, Preacher, and the stones will be bread," the shadow whispered.

"No," Cooper croaked through a dry throat. "It is written, Man shall not live by bread alone, but by every word that proceedeth out of the mouth of God."

The shadow laughed at that, brittle laughter like the crackling of wood in a fire. "Come and look, Preacher. I have something to show you."

And suddenly Cooper stood on a pinnacle. Far away in the distance, he could see his farm: he recognized the familiar fields, the cattle grazing in the pasture, the house he had built with his own hands.

"All this I will give you," his shadow whispered, "if you will fall down and worship me."

Cooper spread his hands, reaching for the distant farm. "No," he whispered again. The word scratched his throat so that he could barely speak. "For it is written, thou shalt worship the Lord thy God, and only him shalt thou serve."

The shadow shook its dark head, still laughing softly. "Go home, old man," the shadow whispered. "Your God has no business here."

Cooper's heart ached as he looked at his distant farm. The shadow that began at his feet was spreading across the land, enveloping the New England town far below. The world was growing black around him.

"Get thee behind me, Satan!" he cried, the words rasping in his throat. "The Spirit of the Lord is upon me. He hath anointed me to preach the gospel to the poor; he hath sent me to preach repentance to the wicked. The kingdom of heaven is at hand."

The shadow let out a great wailing cry, throwing up its hands in despair. Cooper watched the blackness retreat from the green land below.

Cooper woke. His ears still rang with Satan's wild howl. The sky had cleared and the light of the half moon filtered through the branches to shine in his face. He rubbed his face, and his hand came away wet with sweat. When he lifted his head to peer into the clearing, the trees shifted dizzily. Nearby, the mule stood with its head up, staring toward the trees. The fire had burned low, but the embers still glowed.

Cooper saw something moving in the shadows, a gray shape that was as ill-defined as a patch of moonlight. He blinked and the shape became clear: Satan crouched in the shadows, his eyes glowing red. The Devil had taken the form of a wolf, a ravening beast of the forest. The beast's eyes glowed red in the darkness.

Cooper froze, staring at the beast. The wolf watched him with eyes that seemed nearly human. "Satan," Cooper said, his voice low and hoarse. The wolf cocked its ears, listening. Cooper saw another movement: more wolves, hanging back in the shadows, avoiding the circle of firelight. "Satan and his demons. You have come for me."

The Devil wolf sat motionless, its attention on Cooper. One of the demons made a sound low in its throat.

"I am protected by our Lord Jesus, and I order you to return to the pit from whence you came," Cooper cried.

The wolves did not move.

"Help me, Lord," Cooper prayed. He threw back the blanket. The branches of the fir tree snatched at him like claws, but he ducked beneath them and stood in the open. In one hand he clutched his Bible; with the other, he snatched a branch from the embers of the fire. "Get behind me, Satan," he wailed. "Jesus is my protector. Jesus is the Light and the Life."

A lump of pitch in one of the logs on the fire caught, popping suddenly and flaring with a bright yellow light just as Cooper lifted his Bible high over his head and waved the burning branch. His torch brushed against the fir tree, setting a dead branch alight. "Get back, demons of Hell."

The wolves grinned at Cooper, then slipped silently away into the shadows. Cooper stepped back and fell to his knees. The flames spread through the dry lower branches of the fir tree. He looked up at the blazing tree. As clearly as anything, as clearly as he had seen the demons in the forest, he saw a great angel standing in the flames. In one hand, the angel held a Bible; in the other, a flaming sword. "Go forth and preach," the angel said. "Tell the people to clear the wilderness and hunt the Devil down, hunt him down and kill him so that they might be saved. Do this in the name of the Lord."

Cooper bowed his head, shielding his face from the heat of the fire. "O Lord," he prayed. "I am not worthy."

His right hand ached—the torch had burned him before he dropped it—but he dismissed the pain as unimportant. He had been given a sign by the Lord. He had done battle with the Devil and emerged triumphant. He would carry the word of God to the sinners of the frontier, telling them to kill the Devil in the forest, to subdue the Devil's country and take it for their own.

When the fire in the fir tree burned low, he took his second wool blanket from the back of the mule, wrapped himself in it, and slept soundly, secure in the protection of the Lord.

8

Just two weeks later, Mrs. Kahn had a quilting bee to make a new quilt for Mary Sue, who was engaged to be married to Judd Collins. Nadya's mother woke that morning feeling poorly—she had a touch of the grippe—and so Nadya went alone, riding the mule the five miles to town.

Lottie greeted Nadya in the yard. "Nadya," she called. "I'm so glad you're here. They've been teasing me so." She tucked her hand companionably into the crook of Nadya's arm. "They've been teasing me about when I'll be getting married."

At age sixteen, Lottie was a rosy-cheeked young woman with blond hair that invariably escaped her ribbons and pins. Wisps of hair curled at the nape of her neck. The youngest of three sisters, she came in for more than her share of teasing.

"Didn't your mother come?" she asked Nadya.

"She's feeling poorly," Nadya said. "I came by myself."

"You're so brave," Lottie said. "I wouldn't want to come so

far by myself. Mrs. Jones has been talking about the wolves that killed their sheep. And I'd worry about Indians."

Nadya shrugged. Though there had been no Indian trouble for more than a decade and no wolf had ever attacked a person to Nadya's recollection, Lottie feared the forest.

"There'll be a dance at Mary Sue's wedding," Lottie said. Lottie lowered her voice. "I asked Mary Sue to invite Silas Whitman. I danced with him at Zillah's wedding. And Mary Sue told Mama and now they're all teasing me. You won't tease me, will you?"

Nadya shook her head. She never had to say much around Lottie; Lottie did the talking for both of them.

"Is there anyone you're sweet on, Nadya?"

"Rufus Jones came visiting a few days back," Nadya admitted softly.

"He came visiting?" Lottie's eyes widened with excitement. "Oh, Nadya, he didn't."

Nadya nodded. "He sure did."

Lottie wet her lips. "Mrs. Jones is here, helping with the quilting." She made a face. "She doesn't approve of dancing at weddings. I don't think she likes anyone to have any fun."

"Nadya!" Mrs. Kahn called from the doorway. "How nice to see you. Isn't your mother with you?"

"My mama was feeling poorly," Nadya said softly. "She told me to give you her love."

"You came all this way alone?" Mrs. Kahn shook her head and clicked her tongue. "My goodness, this is no time for a girl to be gallivanting about alone. Now you come on in and sit down here."

The Kahns had a fine house, with four separate rooms and a puncheon floor in the parlor. Mrs. Kahn had a dozen store-bought chairs and a mantelpiece clock. There was a looking glass on the parlor wall and the puncheon floor was covered with a real machine-woven carpet, not a rag rug.

The quilt frame stretched the width of the parlor, leaving just enough space at the sides for women to sit beside it. The room was already crowded: Mrs. Shaw and her daughter Zillah sat on one side of the quilt, Mrs. Whitman and her daughters sat on the other. Mrs. Jones sat at the far end of the quilt frame, enthroned in one of Mrs. Kahn's best chairs. Mary Sue sat beside her. Lottie sat on a stool at one corner and Nadya sat between her and Mrs. Kahn.

The quilt, an intricate design of bright calico diamonds, was stretched on the frame. Nadya threaded a needle and began stitching the brightly colored patchwork to the padded lining.

"Nadya rode from her house alone," Mrs. Kahn announced to the others.

"Oh, dear," Mrs. Whitman murmured. "Hadn't you heard about the wolves?" The Whitmans had moved to Missouri from Connecticut just a year before, and Mrs. Whitman was still very nervous about wild animals and Indians.

Nadya shook her head. "What about wolves?"

Mrs. Whitman clapped her hands. "Wolves attacked the Jones farm! Mrs. Jones, you must tell the child."

Mrs. Jones looked up from her stitching and smiled grimly. She was a matronly woman who wore a silver cross on the bosom of her dark calico dress. "I woke in the night to sound of our sheep, bleating in terror. A pack of wolves had attacked our flock. Ravening beasts from the depths of the forest dragging down the innocent lambs. Rufus chased them away with a shot, but not before the wolves had killed our fattest ewe." She shook her head. "The poor defenseless creature never had a chance."

Nadya ducked her head and kept her eyes on her stitching.

"Oh, you must have been so frightened," Mrs. Whitman said. "When I hear wolves howling, the sound sends chills up my spine. It's as if the Devil himself were out there, crying for blood."

"I put my faith in the Lord," Mrs. Jones said staunchly. "The Devil has no power over a true Christian."

Nadya neatly stitched around a red calico diamond. It seemed to her that rifles would do a better job of driving a wolf away than Mrs. Jones's prayers, but she did not think it would be wise to mention that.

"So you can see that this is no time for you to be wandering about by yourself," Mrs. Kahn said to Nadya. "I'll have one of the boys escort you home."

"I heard that there was a preacher downriver in White's Landing a few days back," Mrs. Shaw said, changing the subject. "Reverend William Cooper is his name. They say he can exhort the bark off a tree. He'll be here next Sunday."

"I don't know if Mr. Shaw will come to hear a preacher," Mrs. Shaw murmured. The last preacher to visit the community had been a Baptist, traveling by flatboat. He held a Sunday service on the riverside and dunked half a dozen farmers. Mr. Shaw's dunking had given him a fierce case of the grippe.

Mrs. Jones straightened her back, looking even more formidable. "It's our Christian duty to attend this meeting," she said. "I will bring all my boys."

The mention of Mrs. Jones's boys brought the conversation back to Mary Sue's marriage. As they worked, the women talked about the dress Mary Sue would wear and about the latest fashions in *Godey's Ladies Book*. Mary Sue talked about all the people who would be coming to the wedding and the dance. They talked about the weather and the crops, the bee tree that Mrs. Whitman had found a month before, chatting amiably until teatime. After eating, they returned to their work on the quilt.

"Take smaller stitches, Lottie," Mrs. Kahn admonished her daughter. "Look at Nadya's stitches. See how small and tight they are."

Nadya glanced up at her friend with a sympathetic expression. Her own hands were tired from the hours of careful work.

"Maybe Lottie and Nadya should fetch some water for another pot of tea," Mrs. Shaw suggested kindly. "I'll finish up that corner."

Lottie and Nadya wasted no time hurrying out of the house. They took two buckets from beside the door and strolled down to the spring. "So now that you know about the wolves, aren't you scared about riding around alone?" Lottie asked.

"Nope," Nadya said. "A wolf ain't going to bother with me."

Lottie shook her head. "You'd best be careful, Nadya. One of my brothers will ride home with you."

Nadya frowned. "What's your brother going to do that I couldn't do myself?"

"Well, he'd shoot any wolf that came after you."

"So? I'm a better shot than any of your brothers. I could shoot a wolf myself, if it came to that."

Lottie shook her head at Nadya's audacity. "I'd be so scared."

Nadya shrugged. "I've shot deer. I've shot bear. I can take care of myself."

"I guess so," Lottie said doubtfully. Then she brightened, changing the subject. "Do you reckon that Rufus will come to fetch his mother?"

Nadya shrugged. "I reckon so." She had wondered that herself. The thought of Rufus alarmed her more than all the talk of wolves. She looked down at the path.

"When he came visiting, what happened?" Lottie asked.

"He talked to my mama for a while about herbs for Mr. Jones. And he came with me to the spring to fetch water."

Lottie stopped and stared at Nadya. "Nadya, you're blushing. I've never seen you blush before."

Nadya scuffed her bare foot in the dust.

"What happened? Did he hold your hand? Did he kiss you?"

Nadya nodded. "He held my hand. And then he kissed me."

"Oh, Nadya. Was it like in the book? Did you swoon in his arms?"

"It's more like standing on top of the barn roof, wondering if you're going to fall."

"I've never done that," Lottie said.

"Or standing on the bluff over the river, looking at the current below. That current could sweep you away and you'd never get back again." Nadya shook her head. "Don't know that I like it."

"It's so exciting, Nadya. I hope that Silas Whitman comes visiting me. What did you say to him?"

"I hardly talked at all," Nadya confessed. "I didn't know what to say."

"That's all right," Lottie said. "My sister Mary Sue says that you don't have to talk much. I asked her, and she said that all you have to do when you're sitting with a man is to tell him how wonderful he is, and that's enough. Like this." They had reached the spring. Lottie set down her bucket and took Nadya's hand in hers. "Oh, Rufus—I feel so safe with you here. You're so strong and brave."

Nadya frowned at her. "That's silly, Lottie. He doesn't make me feel safe."

"But you could say he did, couldn't you?" Lottie picked up her bucket and dipped it in the spring. "Mary Sue says that men like to hear things like that."

Nadya filled her bucket, considering what Lottie had said. She had nothing against lying, but this seemed like a foolish thing to lie about. "I don't know why he would make me feel safe," Nadya said. "I can shoot as well as he can. Maybe a little better. Seems like he ought to tell me that I make him feel safe."

"Oh, Nadya, don't you go around saying things like that. He tells you that you're pretty and you tell him that he's strong. That's what Mary Sue says." Lottie spoke with the superior wisdom of a girl who had older sisters.

"My mama says he's dangerous," Nadya said.

"How exciting!" Lottie danced in a little circle. "I don't see how you can be so calm about it. If it was me, I'd be beside myself."

"We'd best get back with the water," Nadya said.

As they walked back toward the house, Lottie did most of the talking. "I can help you fix your hair for Mary Sue's wedding. We can put it up like the picture I saw in *Godey's Ladies Book*. You'll look so fine. But you have to promise that you won't get into a shooting match or anything like that."

Nadya walked at Lottie's side. Her friend's excitement made her uneasy. She was not sure how she felt about Rufus, but Lottie seemed so certain that she should be happy.

They returned to the cabin and built up the fire to boil water for tea. The quilt was almost done—all that remained was the edging, and Lottie and Mary Sue and Mrs. Kahn would manage that.

Lottie had just made a pot of tea when the dogs began barking outside. "Hello!" A man's voice called from the farmyard. "Hello, ladies!"

Mr. Whitman had come to escort Mrs. Whitman and her daughters home. He had a cup of tea with the women, and while they were drinking it, Mr. Kahn and his sons returned from fishing, carrying a string of catfish. Then Rufus Jones and his brother Moses appeared in the doorway. Rufus took off his hat and smiled at all the women. It seemed to Nadya that his eyes lingered on her.

Mrs. Kahn insisted that Nadya accompany Mrs. Jones and her sons to the fork in the trail that led to the Rybak house. Then Rufus would escort Nadya to her door. "We just can't be too careful," Mrs. Kahn said.

"I'm fine on my own," Nadya protested, but Mrs. Jones hushed her with a wave of a hand.

"Of course you will come with us. I'll have no more said about it."

Nadya rode with Mrs. Jones in the farm wagon for the first few miles. Her mule was tied on behind the wagon. As they bumped over the rough trail, Mrs. Jones lectured Nadya on the dangers of wandering through the forest alone. Nadya remained silent, watching Rufus's back. He sat on the driver's seat, eyes on the trail ahead.

At the fork in the road, Moses took the reins. Rufus swung down from the driver's seat and untied Nadya's mule from the back of the wagon. Nadya jumped down from the wagon before he could help her, not wanting to touch his hand.

"You hurry home, Rufus," Mrs. Jones said to her son.

Rufus touched his hat to his mother and waved as the horse pulled the wagon down the main trail.

"It's a pleasure to have your company again so soon," Rufus said. The wagon reached a bend in the trail taking his mother out of sight. Rufus reached out and took Nadya's hand. "I had hoped I might see you today."

"I was glad to see you, too," Nadya said. She wasn't certain of the truth of her words until after she said them. He squeezed her hand.

"Come on," he said, and they started in the direction of the Rybak farm, leading the mule.

The trail followed the river, more or less. Sometimes, it ran alongside the water, and sometimes it snaked between the trees, avoiding the brambles and thickets at the river's edge.

Nadya walked silently at his side. It was strange, having his hand in hers. Overhead, squirrels chattered and barked at them.

"Here—stop a bit," he said. He let go of her hand and stepped to where a dogwood tree was blooming. He picked a few of the pale blossoms and returned to her side. "These would look nice in your hair," he said, and reached up to tuck the flowers behind her ear. He stepped back and looked at her. "It suits you," he said. "You look very pretty."

She returned his stare, still silent.

"You're such a quiet one," he said. "Don't you like flowers?"

"I like flowers."

He hesitated. "I know a place not far from here, down by the river, where there's a beautiful patch of flowers. Would you like to see it?"

His scent had changed—she could smell the muskiness of sex. "All right," she said. "I'd like to."

He took her hand again, holding it tighter than before, and led her off the main trail, along a deer path that led through the trees and downward toward the river. Partway down, out of sight of the trail, he tied the mule to a tree.

The path led to a secluded hollow where the grass was already thick and green. A redbud tree bloomed on the riverbank, its flowers brilliant against the spring greenery. He held her hand and led her to where the sheltering branch of a willow blocked the view of the river. The tree formed a great room, carpeted with ferns and perfumed with the fragrance of flowers and plants.

"I found this when I was hunting," he said. "It's a beautiful place, isn't it?" He looked down at her. "I hoped you would come here with me." Then he reached out and put his arms around her. She could feel the warmth of his skin through her dress; she could smell his sweat—a complex musky smell mingled with the aroma of tobacco. She tilted her head to look up into his face and he kissed her as he had at the spring.

She sensed something waiting beneath the surface, like the currents that boiled in the river. There was a mystery here, something that went beyond the farm animals mating in the barnyard. She had listened to the cats yowling at night. The female in heat made a low moaning sound that contained both pleading and threat. She understood that sound now.

"Here," he said, releasing her. "Let's sit in the grass. That would be fine." He led her to a place where the grass was soft. She sat there, her feet pulled up under her dress and her arms wrapped around her knees. He sat beside her and put his arm around her shoulders.

"I should have known you would come here with me," he said then. "You aren't like the other girls."

She nodded. She knew that was true. He kissed her lightly. His arm dropped from her shoudler to her waist. His other hand caressed her thigh through the fabric of her dress and her petticoat. He lifted his eyes to her face. "I love you, Nadya." His hand continued to stroke her thigh.

"My mama says that you're dangerous," she said.

"Your mama doesn't like you playing with the boys, but I think you like me." He kissed her again. "Don't you believe that I love you, Nadya?"

She ignored the question. "Your mother told me about the wolf that killed your sheep the other night."

"Ah, sweet Nadya—are you afraid of wolves?" He tightened the arm that encircled her shoulders. "I'll keep you safe. I'll kill any wolf that comes near us."

"No!" she said, starting to pull away. "You can't."

"What is it, Nadya?" He reached out and held her tighter. "What is it?"

"You can't kill wolves," she said. "You've got to promise me that."

"Why?"

"I can't say. But you must promise."

He laughed. "Does it worry you that I hunt for wolves? Well then, I won't go hunting for wolves if that makes you unhappy, I promise." His hand resumed its movement on her thigh. "Now don't you believe that I love you, Nadya?"

Her body believed him. When he kissed her, she responded. She felt his hand on her thigh, lifting her dress so that he could stroke the bare skin. He kept kissing her, giving her no chance to answer his question, but she did not mind that. There was a warmth in her body, a kind of tingling that felt like the coming of the Change, only different. His body pressed against hers, pushing her back on the grass. One of his hands fumbled at the buttons of her dress; the other slid higher between her thighs. She was not wearing any underwear, and his hand explored the warmth between her legs. She made a sound—almost a growl like the cats in the barn—and he pressed his fingers harder against her.

"Oh, Nadya, I can't stop myself." He was on top of her now, fumbling with the buttons of his trousers. His hand was rubbing her nipples, squeezing them gently. The tingling was growing greater, spreading through her body. She reached down and touched his cock, and he moaned, pressing against her hand.

Rufus pushed his leg between her thighs, spreading her legs

apart. The movement of his leg against her crotch made her squirm as the tingling grew stronger. It was frightening, this feeling, but she welcomed it at the same time. She wanted something that she could not name.

Abruptly, he shoved his cock between her thighs and thrust into her. She cried out, startled. There was a sensation of tearing and wetness and a sudden pain that mingled with the warmth and tingling. He thrust again and then came quickly, collapsing against her with a great moan. She moved her hips against him, trying to shift him so that the tingling sensation would return, but he did not move, lying atop her like a dead man. "Oh," he moaned, "Oh, Nadya."

He rolled off her and lay in the grass, staring up at the sky. His cock glistened in the late afternoon sunlight. Streaked with semen and blood, it had started to droop. She reached between her own legs, and her fingers came away touched with blood. But even so, there was still pleasure in her own touch.

He looked over at her, propping himself up on one elbow. The top of her dress gaped open and her nipples were crinkled and brown in the sun. Her skirt was bunched around her waist. He reached over and tugged on her dress, pulling the fabric so that it covered her breasts. "You'd best cover yourself," he said.

"Why?"

He shook his head, as if she should not have asked and frowned. As she watched, he tucked his cock inside his trousers and started to button them.

She put her hand on his to stop him. "No," she said. Her dress gaped when she moved, exposing her breasts once again. She slipped her hand beneath his and into his trousers. He made a sound, the beginning of a protest, but it died in his throat. His cock was warm in her hand; the skin so soft and smooth. She slid her hand lower, cupping his balls and feeling his rough pubic hair against her fingers. She kept one hand on his cock, the other between her own legs, teasing the slippery folds, pressing into her body.

Rufus moaned and his eyes half closed. He put one hand on her breast and started to move toward her, as if to roll on top of her again.

"No," she said. "Not that way." She pushed him so that he

lay flat on his back. Before he could move, she threw a leg over his and straddled him. His cock was erect now, and she rubbed it against her crotch, directing its movement with her hand.

With her free hand, she lifted Rufus's hand to her breast, relishing the feel of his rough skin against her nipple. His eyes were open now; he looked surprised, a little confused. She rubbed herself up and down on his cock, then lifted herself and slipped his cock inside her. With her hand, she continued to rub the hard knot of flesh in the midst of the folds where the tingling seemed to center. She rocked up and down, feeling his cock slip in and out with each movement. His hand rubbed against her nipple and she growled, a sound that rumbled from her throat without her thought or will. She squeezed her eyes closed, shutting out the brightness of the sunlight that filtered through the willow leaves. She bent so that her breasts rubbed against his chest and she nipped at his shoulder, rocking back and forth faster now, still faster.

She arched her back to change the position of his cock inside her, and the pleasure was so intense it was nearly pain. She felt his cock inside her, squeezed by the spasms of her muscles. A great wave pulsed within her, beginning between her legs and spreading outward. Pleasure, urgency, darkness and warmth—a confusion of sensations left her gasping and limp.

"Ah," she said. "Ah, Rufus." She opened her eyes then, and looked down at him, smiling fondly.

His eyes were open and he was watching her. He wasn't smiling; she could not read his expression. His cock was growing soft within her, so she slipped off him and lay beside him in the grass, where she could watch his face. He looked up at the sky.

"What are you thinking, Rufus?" she asked him.

He kept looking at the sky. "You're not like the other girls, Nadya."

She smiled. "That's so. You already told me that."

"It's not proper. You shouldn't. . . ." He hesitated. "You oughtn't act like that."

"Like what?"

He shook his head and frowned at her. "Girls don't act like that. You're very bold."

She continued to smile. "And so are you."

He reached out and tugged her dress down so that it covered her. "We'd best be getting home."

She watched him sit up and hurriedly button his trousers and tuck in his shirt. He did not look at her again. She made no move to dress herself, just studied him, trying to understand his expression. He smelled of sex and anger and fear. She did not understand the anger or the fear. What had frightened him?

He glanced down at her. "Button yourself," he said roughly. "Cover yourself and act decent."

She sat up then, pulling her skirt down to cover her legs and slowly buttoning her dress.

"Come along," he said, and led the way back up to where the mule was tied. He did not take her hand. He accompanied her home, but did not linger to have tea or talk with her parents, leaving her at the doorstep and hurrying away into the forest as if he were suddenly afraid of her.

9

In addition to his daily record of business at the store, Abraham Kahn kept a journal in which he noted unusual events in the town of Wolf Crossing. When a drunken riverman drowned in the river, he remarked, "Half-blood barger goes to his reward, helped by Rum and the River." When a very large wagon train heading west passed through, he wrote: "Another pack of fools, heading Westward to Oblivion." In April, when William Cooper came to town to preach the Gospel of the Lord, Kahn wrote: "Fire and Brimstone by the river—Wm. Cooper preaches we should hunt wolves for the Glory of the Lord. The Lord will get the Glory; I'll buy the skins."

On the Saturday morning that Cooper preached, Nadya and her family came to town. The mule had thrown a shoe and her father was taking him to the blacksmith.

Nadya and her family arrived in town late in the morning. The benches in front of the general store were crowded with loafing men: trappers, come to town to trade and drink; a rough-looking crew from the barge that was tied at the crossing; a few farmers.

Nadya saw Mr. Jones among them but looked for Rufus in vain. A green jug was passing from hand to hand, and Nadya could smell the sharp scent of chewing tobacco.

Nadya's father pulled the farm wagon to the side of the dirt street. He stopped by the bench to chat with the men, while Nadya and her mother went into the store.

Abraham Kahn was counting out nutmegs and cinnamon sticks for Mrs. Walker, and the spices perfumed the air. There were traps displayed on the wall behind him, the great metal jaws clenched tightly closed. Nadya knew those traps—her father had warned her of them many times.

Mrs. Kahn was helping Mrs. Jones, who had just purchased a length of plain red calico for new shirts for her sons. "Those boys are almighty rough on clothes," she was saying to Mrs. Kahn. "I pity the girl that marries Rufus. She'll be sewing her fingers to the bone just to keep him in shirts."

Mrs. Kahn looked up and greeted Nadya and her mother. "Morning, Mrs. Rybak, Miss Nadya. How are you today?"

Mrs. Jones studied the pair of them. "Morning, Mrs. Rybak," Mrs. Jones said. "How nice to see you again. Did Nadya tell you that the tea you sent was a great help to Mr. Jones?"

"I'm pleased to hear it, Mrs. Jones." Nadya watched in silence. She knew that her mother did not care for Mrs. Jones, but she smiled as if Mrs. Jones were a friend. "It is really the simplest thing to make. If you like, I can show you the herbs that I use."

"Mr. Jones won't be needing the remedy again. He told me that very morning that he had sworn off the demon whiskey and would drink only healthful beverages from now on."

Nadya wondered at that. She was certain that Mr. Jones had been among the loiterers on the porch. In her experience, a jug being passed on the porch of a store rarely contained healthful beverages. But she held her tongue and listened while her mother murmured polite congratulations.

"I do hope that you and your family will be attending the services by the river this afternoon," Mrs. Jones said. "A preacher of fine repute has come to speak to us of the ways of sin. My family will be there."

"And what denomination is the preacher?" Nadya's mother asked. Nadya knew this was simply politeness. If the preacher were a Baptist, Nadya's mother would claim to be strictly Methodist. If he were a Methodist, she might declare herself a Baptist. One way or the other, she would politely evade the preaching.

"He is a man of God," Mrs. Jones declared. "I don't know more than that. But that is all I need to know. All Christians are brothers under the skin."

Nadya's mother nodded thoughtfully. "Thank you so much for telling us about it. Perhaps we will see you there."

Mrs. Jones took the calico that Mrs. Kahn had folded neatly. "Now I must be going, to tell others that we are blessed with a preacher today. Perhaps some of those who prefer dancing to praying will come and see the evil of their ways. I will see you by the river." She left the store without looking back.

Nadya's mother and Mrs. Kahn exchanged glances. "She's enough to give being a Christian a bad name," Mrs. Kahn murmured, and Nadya's mother laughed.

"I hear that she scolded Mrs. Shaw for allowing dancing and drinking at the wedding," Nadya's mother said softly.

"I hear the same. But Mr. Jones and his sons were drinking and dancing with the rest of them."

Nadya's mother smiled and shrugged. "Ah, but you heard what Mrs. Jones said. Mr. Jones has declared he will only drink healthful beverages."

Mrs. Kahn laughed. "Ah, but whiskey can be medicinal, and surely that's a healthful thing."

"And dancing is fine exercise, and that is needed for health as well," Nadya's mother replied.

"Of course," Mrs. Kahn said. "I should have thought of that myself. And all Mr. Jones's gasconading about what fine shots his boys are, that's exercise for the lungs."

The women laughed softly.

"And so what is it that brings you to town?" Mrs. Kahn asked.

"Nadya thought she'd sew a new dress to wear to Mary Sue's wedding, so we have come for calico."

"A new dress?" Mrs. Kahn smiled at Nadya. "Miss Nadya, you're not buying black powder and lead shot? You're becoming a lady."

Nadya blushed and looked down at her feet.

"Here now, Nadya, I have some lovely cloth to choose from." Mrs. Kahn pulled bolt after bolt from the shelves, placing them on the table for Nadya's examination. Nadya favored a length of fine dark blue cloth, patterned with tiny red roses.

"The color compliments your complexion," Mrs. Kahn said. "And it won't show the dirt."

Nadya's mother fingered the cloth, testing the weave. "It seems quite sturdy," she said.

"Oh, it will wear well, I'm sure of that."

While Mrs. Kahn was cutting and folding the cloth, Lottie came into the store from the back. The mothers remained in the store, chatting about home remedies and recipes, but Nadya and Lottie escaped to the outside.

Nadya's father was sitting on the porch. The two young women lingered for a moment, to see if the men were talking about anything interesting. Mr. Walker was holding a penny paper that had just come in from Philadelphia. "It's a brand-new party for new times," he was saying. "Call themselves the Native Americans. They have no use for Papists, and I'll go along with that. Take those Irishmen, fresh off the boat. You can scarcely understand a word that comes out of their mouths." He slapped the paper against his thigh. "Keep America for Americans. That's what I say."

"Keep America for the Americans," Nadya's father said slowly, repeating the words as if he had not heard them right. His Polish accent grew thicker, as it always did when he was upset. "Twenty years, I have been in this country. I would guess that I am an American. But these people would say I'm not." Mr. Walker started to interrupt, but Nadya's father kept going. "America is for all types of men from all different countries. That's what makes this country strong."

"Next thing you know, you'll be saying we should set free the slaves," Mr. Jones said.

"Come on," Lottie whispered to Nadya. "They're just talking politics. Let's go." They walked down the dusty street, and Lottie companionably linked her arm in Nadya's.

"Do you want to go down to the river?" Lottie asked. "Mrs. Jones said there'd be a preacher talking about God."

"I don't know," Nadya said, looking doubtful. "I'd better ask my mama."

"Oh, come on. Let's just go. Your mama will be glad you are hearing the word of God. Besides, maybe Rufus and Silas will be there."

"All right," Nadya said. "I'll go."

Arm in arm, they strolled to the river crossing. They could hear singing in the distance, and as they grew closer, they could make out someone shouting the words to each line, followed by muddled singing. The tune was familiar, a popular song modified to match a holier set of words.

They followed the sound to the riverbank, where a small hollow created a natural amphitheater. The preacher stood above the crowd, on the broad stump of an oak tree. A group of farmers and folks from town stood near the stump, watching the preacher with anticipation and doing their best to sing the hymn. Mrs. Jones was in the front of the group, her raised hand beating the rhythm of the hymn in the air, like a dutiful singing teacher. Her voice rang above the others, a sturdy contralto that made up in volume what it lacked in grace. " 'He comes! He comes! The Judge severe! The Seventh Trumpet speaks him near. His lightnings flash; his thunders roll. How welcome to the faithful soul.' " Nadya didn't see Rufus anywhere.

On the far side of the hollow there was a clump of rivermen. They weren't singing. Rather, they chewed tobacco and watched the preacher in silence.

The hymn droned to a close, Mrs. Jones singing the last line as a determined solo. The preacher lifted his Bible and read in a sonorous voice. " 'Serve the Lord with gladness: come before His presence with singing. Know ye that the Lord He is God: it is He that hath made us; we are His people and the sheep of His pasture.' "

Nadya frowned at that—she did not think much of sheep and she would rather not be called one. But no one else in the crowd seemed to mind.

The preacher closed the book with a snap and looked at the people gathered around him. "Brothers and sisters," he said to them. "We are the people of the Lord, we are His sheep. But I see many sheep that have strayed from the flock, lambs that are in danger from the wolves of Satan that linger outside the pasture gate. I see men who gamble, and men who curse and take the name of their Lord in vain, and men who lie and cheat and steal. I see women who wear gaudy clothing, women who are proud of their outward show, caring not for their inner beauty. I see men who are idle and women who are foolish. How many of you are ready to meet your Lord, to face his Judgment? How many of you could hold your heads up and walk through the pasture gates into Heaven?" He looked out at the crowd, and a man in the front row spat a stream of tobacco juice over the riverbank.

"Brothers and Sisters," the preacher said. "I was a sinner, too. Listen to me, Brothers and Sisters, for I was once like you. And then I found the love of the Lord."

"I'd sooner have the love of a good woman," called out one of the rivermen in the back, and his companions laughed.

"That way lies the path to Hell," the preacher shouted back.

"That way lies the path to glory," called the man, and again his friends laughed, slapping him on the back. "Have you ever walked that path, Preacher?"

"I walk the path of the Lord," the preacher said. "I follow the word of the Lord. You must listen to me." He brandished his Bible over his head, swayed as if he were about to fall from the stump, and he steadied himself. His eyes were blinking furiously. "You must listen," he cried, but Nadya could barely hear his voice over the catcalls of the rivermen.

"Listen," the preacher shouted. Then he tilted back his head and howled, a piercing wail that cut through the laughter of the hecklers. Mrs. Jones took a step back, startled by the howl, her hands clasped together as if in prayer. The preacher tilted back his head and howled again. When he stopped, the crowd was silent, watching him to see what would happen next.

"I hear you howling like the beasts you are," he snarled at the rivermen. "I hear you and the Lord hears you, and he judges you, as I am not fit to judge."

"Why have you come to this barren wilderness, Brothers and Sisters? Why have you come to this howling land, where wild beasts shriek in the night, where savage Indians lurk in the darkness? Why have you come here, forsaking your comfortable lives in the East?" He waited a moment, then filled the silence with a shout. "You have come here at the command of the Lord!"

"Not likely," yelled a riverman, but the preacher lifted his hands up over his head, waving his Bible as if it were a club.

"The Good Book commands us to be fruitful and multiply, to replenish the earth and subdue it," the preacher cried. "Our Lord commands us to have dominion over every living thing that moveth on the face of the earth. The Lord asks this of us, he sends us into the wilderness to claim it for his own. You have come to take this land for the Lord. Clear the land and plant your crops and raise your families."

"Amen!" called a farmer who stood near Nadya. "Amen!"

"This land, this wild and desolate land—it can strike despair into a man's heart." The preacher's voice dropped. "I know it, Brothers and Sisters, for my own heart has been laid low by loneliness and fear. My own heart has ached for the comforts of civilization." He lowered his hands, bringing his Bible to his chest. "Just a few nights ago, Brothers and Sisters, when I lay shivering in the cold and the rain, I thought of turning my back on this land. I thought of returning to my home in Connecticut, of seeking an easier life, a life where a man can eat a fine dinner and sleep in a warm bed." His head was bowed and his tone was that of a man confiding his secret thoughts. "And I prayed to the Lord to send me a sign. Tell me what to do, oh Lord. Help me find the way."

He lifted his head. "In the darkness, wolves howled—a dreadful howling, like the shrieking of the souls burning in Hell, doomed for all eternity to be wrapped in sheets of fire and brimstone."

Nadya glanced at Lottie, who was listening with rapt attention. "I always thought the wolves sounded nice," she murmured to Lottie. "Like singing."

"Hush," Lottie said. "I'm listening."

"You have heard the beasts, Brothers and Sisters, I know you have heard them," the preacher said. "Damned souls, spawn of Satan—they howl their anguish at the sky and turn, in anger, on the righteous children of the Lord. Imagine this sound—but imagine it near to you, as near to you as I am standing. The beasts were all around me, shrieking in anger and calling for blood."

Half a dozen stragglers joined the crowd, attracted by the howling and shouting.

"I lifted my head from my prayer, Brothers and Sisters, and I saw the eyes of wolves—great yellow eyes that flashed in the firelight, the eyes of devils glaring from the darkness. Demons from Hell, clad in the guise of wolves. Each as big as a man, grinning at me, showing their teeth and snarling."

Mrs. Jones fell to her knees, clasping her hands in prayer. "Save us, Lord, from the demons of Satan," she wailed.

"What did I do, Brothers and Sisters?" the preacher was saying. "What could I do against the demons of Satan?" He lifted his Bible, to remind them of its presence. "I trusted in the power of the Lord."

A chorus of fervent "Amens" drowned out the hooting of the hecklers.

"Here it is, Brothers and Sisters, here is my weapon—the word of the Lord. I lifted this Holy Book so that the beasts could see it, could tremble before the truth of the Lord. And I called out to the Lord. I called to him: 'May the spirit come down, may it come like a fire, may it come in streams of fire, may the fire of the Lord come down and free the earth of this pestilence.' "

Three women at the front of the crowd knelt together, rocking back and forth in time with the preacher's words. Whenever he paused for breath, they chorused, "Amen." The men in the front were shifting from foot to foot, swaying with the kneeling women.

"The very air around me trembled," the preacher said. "I felt the power, the power, the power of sanctification. In the light of the burning fire, I saw a great figure—an angel standing in the flame with a sword that was also a flame." He spoke with unshakable confidence, lifting his hand as if to show the Lord's angel to anyone who could see.

"The angel lifted his sword, holding it high so that it blazed and lit the forest all around, bringing the glory of God to the darkness. And the demons fled, banished into the darkness.

"I stood in the darkness before the angel and I heard the angel speak to me. 'Take this land for the Lord,' the angel said to me. 'Drive the Devil from this wilderness.' "

"Praise the Lord," Mrs. Jones shouted, and the others took up the words. "Praise the Lord!"

The preacher raised his voice, thundering over the moaning

and shouting. "Take this land, Brothers and Sisters! Drive out the Devil! Kill the spawn of Satan. Drive them from this fair land that it may belong to the Lord."

"Drive out the Devil!" Mrs. Jones cried. "Drive him out!"

The preacher glared at the crowd, sweeping Nadya and Lottie with his gaze. "Listen to the message of the angel of God," he cried. "There are some among you who have not accepted the power of the Lord. They think that they can make peace with the Devil. I tell these sinners that Hell stands ready to receive them. Hell opens its yawning mouth to receive them. Repent, or you will spend your eternity burning in the pit. Repent!"

Two women in the front row had been taken by the Holy Spirit—they lay on the ground, jerking and moaning uncontrollably. Others were falling to their knees, calling out to the Lord to save them.

"There is no peace with the Devil! There is no concord between the wolf and the lamb. Let us pray, Brothers and Sisters, let us pray that the spirit of fire will come to us and set us ablaze with the glory of the Lord." He bowed his head, lowering his voice. "Let us pray that we triumph over the Devil, that we take this land for the Lord. Let us bring civilization to this howling wilderness. Pray with me, Brothers and Sisters. Pray with me and bring the power of the Lord to this land."

He bowed his head, for a moment, then began a hymn, a sweet slow song that asked Jesus to watch over the wandering sheep. Nadya watched as the preacher walked among the men and women who knelt on the grassy ground. He laid a hand on one woman's head, patted another man on the shoulder. The two women who had been taken by the Spirit lay in the grass, resting quietly now.

"Come on," Lottie said. "Let's go and get him to bless us."

"I don't want to," Nadya said, hanging back.

Lottie glanced at her. "What's the matter? Come on." She looked back toward the preacher. "There's Silas. We can go talk to him."

Nadya shook her head. "I have to go find my mama," she said. "She won't know where I am." She was trembling. She turned away from her friend, hurrying up the slope to the store.

On her way back to the store, Nadya met her father. "Papa,"

she said. "The preacher said that wolves are demons of Satan. He said that we should kill all the wolves."

She thought he might be angry—angry with the people for talking of hunting, angry with her for killing the sheep at the Jones farm—but he just looked at her sadly and took her hand. "We'd best be going home, Nadya. This is no place for us just now."

Our neighbors have gone mad," Dmitri wrote in his journal. "They speak of the wolves as if they were the Devil. They talk of the hunt as if it is to be a holy act, the shedding of blood for the glory of God. They speak of the sheep that Nadya killed, the beast that they would have eaten for dinner willingly enough, as a defenseless innocent, a creature to be protected.

"We have lingered here too long. We should have gone west last year, or even the year before. But Marietta did not want to leave the house and I did not want to leave the farm. We were happy here. The journey seemed too hard.

"I have begun building a wagon to carry us West. I will build it of seasoned hardwood, durable enough to withstand the hardship of crossing the great desert. We must gather supplies for the long journey. It would be foolish to leave here without preparing ourselves—we would avoid the hunter's bullet only to die of starvation in the desert. I think, if I work quickly, we can leave in a month.

"Marietta says that we must not be hasty. She says that this madness will pass. Our neighbors will set a few traps. They will hunt by daylight, which offers no threat to us. And then, soon, she believes that they will come to their senses. But I remember the hunt, and I can't share her faith."

10

Midway through the next week, Hezekiah Jones stopped by the Rybak farm. "Hello," he called out. "Hello, neighbor."

Dmitri was trimming and smoothing a length of oak to make

a spare axle for the wagon that would carry them westward. He had spent the morning reinforcing the wagonbed with oak planks. Dmitri glanced up from his work when Jones rode into the farmyard, reined in his horse, and swung down from the saddle.

"What's all this? You emigrating?" Jones asked, staring at the wagon.

"Soon as we can," Dmitri said.

Jones considered the wagon, then glanced around the farmyard. "I hadn't heard tell that your farm was for sale."

"You're hearing it now," Dmitri said. The man stank of unwashed clothing, chewing tobacco, and alcohol—hard cider, by the smell. "Too crowded here. Time to move on."

Jones nodded and thoughtfully shifted the wad of chewing tobacco that was tucked in his lip. "Reasonable piece of land. Maybe I'll make you an offer. You in a hurry to sell?"

Dmitri studied Jones's face. "Two dollars an acre. Hard currency."

Jones shifted the wad of tobacco again and spat a stream of brown juice. "Ain't easy to come by so much hard currency."

"Ain't easy to be a farmer," Dmitri said.

"I might manage a dollar an acre."

Dmitri continued smoothing the oak shaft. Jones knew that a dollar an acre was an absurd price. Two dollars an acre for cleared land was already a bargain. Dmitri would need the hard currency once they reached California. He would sell for less only if he had to. "I reckon I'll wait until someone with a better understanding of the value of land comes along," he said slowly.

"Suit yourself," Jones said easily. "Suit yourself. I came to invite you for some hunting Saturday next. Me and my boys gonna kill the varmints that killed my sheep. Some other folks will be joining us. We'll be gathering at the saloon. Thought you might like to come along." Jones grinned, showing crooked, tobacco-stained teeth. "A little whiskey and a little hunting. And the preacher's coming along to give us his blessing. A fine sporting afternoon."

The full moon was Sunday night. Saturday's hunt offered no danger to Dmitri's family. He looked up from the axle. "Strange thing, Mr. Jones," he said. "We never had no wolf trouble round here before. Maybe you should keep better watch on those sheep of yours."

Jones's smile faltered. "What's that?" he said.

"Never had any trouble with wolves," Dmitri said. "They never bothered my stock. Maybe you'd be better off bringing your sheep in at night."

Jones scowled. "What's that you're saying? You saying we shouldn't hunt those varmints?"

"Don't see that you have any call to," Dmitri said. "Don't see the need."

"You saying you won't go hunting?"

"I'm saying I'll have nothing to do with your sporting day. Won't slaughter animals that never did me no harm. Won't sell my land for less than it's worth." Dmitri was a patient man, slow to anger. But the full moon was near, and this man threatened his family so casually, so confidently, insolently chewing his tobacco and eyeing Dmitri's land. Dmitri shifted his weight, setting his feet wide apart. He hefted the axle in his hands, holding the heavy shaft so that he could swing it as a club. He bared his teeth in a ferocious grin. "I'd suggest you get yourself off my land. You'd best hurry."

Jones eyed the axle and hurried to mount his horse. He jerked on the reins and kicked the horse savagely. Dmitri returned to his work, relieved that the hunt would be on Saturday. They were safe for this full moon.

Over dinner that night, Nadya's father told Nadya and her mother about the coming hunt. The sun was near setting. Its light shone through the open windows. There was no other light; Marietta was saving oil for the journey. "Jones and all his sons will go hunting for wolves this Saturday," he told them.

Nadya shook her head. "That can't be so," she said. "Rufus said that he wouldn't hunt wolves."

Dmitri studied his daughter's face. "When did he do that?"

Nadya would not meet his eyes. "When I asked him," she said. Her voice had an edge to it, a slight tremor of contained emotion. "He promised he wouldn't."

"When was that? When did you ask him?"

"When he brought me home from the quilting," she said. Still, she would not meet his eyes.

"Look at me, Nadya," he said angrily. "Why won't you look at me?"

"She's upset, Dmitri," Marietta said softly.

He looked at his wife. "What do you know about this?"

Nadya stood up and headed for the cabin door.

"Where are you going, Nadya?" Dmitri asked, shocked at her behavior.

"I'd best check to see that the chickens are locked up for the night," she said, and rushed away.

Dmitri turned to his wife, shaking his head. "What is all this about?" He was bewildered by his daughter's tears.

Marietta took his hand in both of hers. "She can't hear you. She can only hear the roar of the blood rushing in her ears. She is growing up." She lifted her eyes to meet his. "Do you remember how hard that was?"

"That boy and his family—they're no friends to us. The father is a drunkard; the mother is a zealot. The son is a gambler. He means her no good."

"I know that," Marietta said. "I read the cards. I told her that she should not love this boy. I told her to take care. Might as well tell the river not to flow downhill." She released his hand. "What else can we do? Lock our daughter up? Deny her nature?" She shook her head. "We must hurry to build the wagon and prepare for our journey. She will be very sad when we go, but on the trail to Oregon, she will forget him." She smiled at her husband. "Be happy that we have time to prepare. She will survive the pain of heartbreak as we all have before her."

Dmitri shook his head slowly. He pushed himself away from the table and went to the door. By the light of the moon, he could see Nadya standing at the edge of the forest, leaning against the fence. He went to stand at her side.

"Hello, Nadya," he said softly.

"Hello, Papa."

The moonlight was bright enough to cast shadows.

"Do you remember," Dmitri asked, "when I used to tell you stories with shadows?"

"I remember," Nadya said softly. She kept her face turned away so that he could not see her eyes.

"They were lies, those stories," Dmitri said. He hesitated,

wishing that he could see her face. "In my stories, the wolf always wins. That's a lie."

"But the wolf could win, Papa. Don't you think? I think the wolf could win."

"The hunters win, Nadya. They always have and they always will."

Nadya turned to face him then. Her jaw was set and her expression was stubborn. "Rufus won't let them go hunting," she said. "He said he wouldn't hunt wolves."

Dmitri hesitated. "I'm not the only one who lies."

She turned her face to the forest again.

"The Oregon Territory is a beautiful land," he said. "Acres and acres of rich land, with never a person nearby. We'll be emigrating as soon as the wagon's done."

She didn't answer.

"We'll be happy there. Far from all the hunters and fools. Are you listening to me?"

She didn't answer.

At last, he sighed heavily. "Come inside when you get cold," he told her, and stamped back into the warmth of the cabin. When she came back inside to sit by the fire, he ignored her, talking with Marietta about the things they would need for the trip, telling her about the route that they would follow. Nadya climbed the ladder to her loft bed and lay down to sleep, but he kept up the cheerful conversation, knowing that she could hear him, hoping that she would listen to reason.

All would have been well, had it not been for the rain. The rain brought bad luck.

Nadya woke on Saturday to the sound of raindrops rattling against the greased paper windows. A thunderstorm had swept in during the night. The wind shook the branches of the trees and the rain hammered down, filling the ditches and gullies to overflowing.

Her parents tried to act as if nothing were wrong. They went about their work, as if this day were like any other. But Nadya could smell the tension in the air. It rained all night. No one would go hunting in such a downpour.

Sunday morning dawned wet and cold. In the morning, Nadya watched the sky and prayed that the rain would continue. But early in the afternoon, the rain became a drizzle. Water dripped from the branches of the trees, but the sky was clearing.

Nadya sat on the porch, mending a tear in her father's second-best pair of trousers. Through the half-open door, she listened to the murmur of her parent's voices inside the cabin.

"Surely they wouldn't begin a hunt so late in the day," her mother said.

"Depends on how much they've been drinking," her father's voice rumbled. "Depends on how foolish they feel. From what little I've seen of Rufus and Hezekiah Jones, I would guess that they're foolish enough."

Nadya set the mending in her lap. He was wrong about Rufus. He had to be.

"We'd best put some space between ourselves and the town before the moon rises," her father said.

"We can't pack the wagon quickly enough," her mother said. "We haven't time."

"We'll leave the wagon and save our skins. We have no choice."

Nadya knew there would be no hunt. Her father wouldn't believe her, but she knew that Rufus would stop them. He wouldn't allow it. He had said so, down by the river.

But even as she thought about Rufus, she felt uneasy. It would be difficult for him to persuade the others. He might need her help. While her parents argued, she slipped away to the barn, saddled the mule, and headed for town.

When Nadya was eight, her father had built their barn from rough-hewn logs. Neighbors had helped raise the walls and the ridge beam, leaving her father to complete the structure. Nadya's father told her not to climb on the newly erected frame. "It's dangerous," he had said. "You'll fall."

The next day, when her father was out of sight, she climbed to the top of the barn and walked the length of the roof's ridgebeam. She started with confidence, arms extended like a tightrope walker's. She was halfway across when she looked down at the ground far below. In that moment, she swayed, feeling suddenly dizzy. Just before she recovered her balance, she imagined what it would be like to fall, arms flailing at the beam and missing, body tumbling to break on the ground below. Her legs trembled and she could feel her heart pounding. And then, despite the panic, she continued to the far end of the beam.

As she rode the mule into town, she felt as she had when she stood on the ridgebeam. Defiant and frightened. The ground lay far below her, and she did not dare look down.

She found Rufus in the tavern, playing cards. She recognized the other men at the table, all of them neighbors: Hezekiah Jones, Tom Williams, Mr. Shaw, Mr. Whitman. Their faces looked unfamiliar in the dim light of the tavern, skin slack with drink, eyes rimmed with red.

Mr. Shaw frowned at her. "What are you doing here?" he asked her. "This is no place for a young lady."

"I came to talk to Rufus." Her voice was strained. The smell of the tavern—tobacco spit, whiskey, and sweat—made her feel sick.

"Does your papa know you're here?" Mr. Shaw said. "I don't think it's proper. . . ."

Rufus looked up from his cards and stared at her. She could not read his expression. He tossed his cards facedown on the table and pushed back his chair. When he stood, he swayed, unsteady on his feet. "How do, Miss Nadya," he said, his words a little slurred. "I'd be pleased to talk with you. Let's leave these fellas behind."

He took her arm and led her toward the door. Behind her, Nadya heard Tom Williams's voice, but she could not make out the words. All the men laughed—an unfriendly sound containing no merriment.

Outside, the day was clearing. The clouds that had covered the sun had dissipated. Muddy puddles filled the ruts of the dirt track that ran past the tavern's front porch. The livery stable and store had been washed clean; the white façades glistened in the late afternoon sunshine. The street was deserted.

"Rufus," she said. "I had to talk to you."

"Darling, I've been thinking about you, too," he said. He put his arms around her and started to pull her into an embrace. He reeked of whiskey. "We'll go to the hayloft in the livery stable. No one will bother us there."

She pulled back, shaking his arms off her. "My father said that you were going hunting for wolves."

He frowned. "We have time. They won't go hunting without me." He reached out and took hold of her hand. "I've missed you, Nadya."

"You're going hunting?" she asked. The air seemed suddenly colder. She could feel a trembling that began deep inside her. It had not yet reached the surface.

"Not yet. I tell you, we have time." With his free hand, he fumbled at the buttons on the front of her dress. His fingers were clumsy and the buttons did not cooperate.

"You promised," Nadya said, taking a step back away from him. "You promised you wouldn't hunt wolves."

He stared at her, then burst out laughing. "Not hunt wolves? That's the most damn-fool idea I've ever heard."

"You said you wouldn't," she said.

"Never said anything like it," he protested.

"Down by the river," she said. "You promised me you wouldn't hunt wolves."

He was looking at her with the same expression he had worn when she climbed on top of him to satisfy her desire. He was astounded and bewildered and disapproving. "What do those varmints matter to you? Come on, now." He tried to pull her to him. She jerked her wrist away.

"You mustn't kill wolves," she said. "You can't."

He glared at her then. "Don't you tell me what I can't do." His voice had lost its wheedling tone. "Just because we've had a little fun together doesn't mean you can tell me what to do. I'll kill every wolf in the county, if I like."

"But you said—"

"You're a crazy one," he told her. "You don't act like a normal woman. I didn't say nothing about wolves."

"My mother warned me," Nadya said. The trembling had reached the surface. She was cold, very cold, and she could not stop shaking. "She told me that you were dangerous. I should have listened."

She turned away, walking toward the mule that was tied at the hitching post.

"Hold on there," he said. He grabbed her shoulder. As she

turned to face him, she lifted an elbow and caught him with a clout on the side of the head. He stumbled and fell.

"Leave me be," she said. "Just leave me be."

She mounted the mule and kicked the beast into a trot. When she was halfway down the street, she glanced back and saw Rufus struggling to his feet.

"The weather's clear," he shouted—to the men in the saloon, to Nadya's retreating back. "Let's go hunting. Let's kill some wolves!"

She kicked the mule again. The sun was already low in the sky. She could feel the pull of the full moon—a sensation in her belly and her crotch. For the first time, she feared the Change.

The ride home was long and she felt sick to her stomach, sick at heart. As she came into the farmyard, she saw her mother, waiting for her on the porch.

Nadya swung off the mule and ran into her mother's arms. "I saw Rufus," she said. "I saw him and the other men and. . . ." Then she wept, unable to stop the tears.

Her father put his hand on her shoulder. "Come," he said. "There is little time left."

They had only gotten as far as the riverbank when the moon rose.

William Cooper came to the tavern and said a prayer before the hunt began. It was clear from his expression that he disapproved of drinking and gambling. But Rufus guessed that he disapproved of wolves more.

"May the All Mighty God give us the strength to overcome the forces of darkness," the preacher prayed. "We come in your name, to do away with the beasts of waste and desolation that devour your innocent creatures. We call on you to bless our bullets and guide our aim."

The prayer droned on, and Rufus kept his head bowed. He was thinking of Nadya—still angry that she had pulled away, that she had demanded that he stop the hunt. She was crazy, that was clear. A pretty girl, but crazy. There were many other pretty girls in town.

When Cooper finally wound down, Rufus murmured

"Amen" with the others. They toasted the preacher a few times. Then there was another delay when the preacher had insisted on coming along. They finally got under way just before sunset. It didn't matter, Rufus figured. The full moon would provide the light they needed. They were all accustomed to night hunting.

The air was crisp and cool but the glow of the whiskey kept Rufus warm. The drizzle had let up, though the leaves still glistened wetly. The hounds set out, and the men followed on horseback. They took the trail north along the river, where Rufus had spotted wolf sign, now and again.

The sun set and the full moon rose. In the moonlight, colors had faded from the forest: the world was black and white with shades of silver-gray.

At the turnoff that led to the Rybak farm, the hounds found a scent, and they gave voice, a deep musical baying that echoed across the valley. Rufus's horse ran ahead of the others, surefooted even in the darkness. Behind him, he could hear Cooper calling for the Lord's assistance in this hunt against the demons of Satan.

Rufus had never believed in demons, despite his mother's preaching. But he liked hunting and he favored the darkness. Darkness and blood and excitement.

The hounds headed north, first away from the river, then doubling back so they crossed their own path. There they milled about, momentarily confused, then picked the scent up again and followed it down along the water. The river was at flood. The muddy waters swirled around the bases of oak trees that normally stood high on the bank.

By the river, the dogs lost the trail. They cast about frantically, running up and down the riverbank and sniffing the muddy ground. They caught the scent again and coursed along the bank, heading south now. Then around a great circle and heading north.

Rufus was in the lead when the hounds' baying grew more frantic. He spurred his tired horse. He came out of the trees and saw three wolves, trapped by the dogs on a jutting cliff, where the river had eaten away the bank. The animals stood with their backs to the edge, holding off the dogs. As Rufus approached, the biggest wolf rushed the hounds, snapping and snarling.

Rufus waited until the animal broke clear of the pack of hounds and then squeezed off a shot. The wolf tumbled, somersaulting forward as his front legs went out from under him. Half of the dog pack attacked the fallen wolf; the rest took off after the other two. Rufus reined in his horse and reloaded. Then he spurred his horse, leaving the fallen animal to the men who followed.

He caught up with the pack of hounds. A short distance away, he could see the two wolves bounding away, just ahead of the hounds. The moonlight shone on the lead animal's gray fur. He aimed and fired: good shot; the animal fell. One wolf remaining.

It ran toward the river's edge. He could see it clearly, and he struggled to reload, but his horse shied. He fumbled with the rifle. Too late: the animal reached the edge one leap ahead of the running hounds and launched itself over the cliff. The dogs milled in a pack on the river's edge, yelping and snarling. Below, where the river ran like liquid silver, he could see a dark head, the wolf struggling in the current. He did not waste powder firing at the distant animal, but used the butt of his rifle to club the dogs away from the body of the fallen female.

By the time the other men arrived, the swimming wolf had been carried south by the current. The others built a fire, while Rufus skinned the two carcasses. The two wolves were in fine condition, fat and healthy, with thick fur.

He slit the skin along the female's belly and peeled back the fur, working carefully to avoid spoiling the skin. Kahn would trade whiskey for the furs. The air was cold, and the animal's blood was warm on his hands. Steam rose from the body in the night air.

The preacher was the last to arrive. He stood by the fire with the others and called for a prayer of thanks. Rufus continued skinning the wolf while the preacher thanked God for their salvation.

After the prayer, he went to work on the male wolf. He could hear the men around the fire talking about the wolf that got away. "It'll drown, sure enough," he heard one man say. The male's body had cooled and his hands were icy by the time he was done. He bundled the furs and strapped them behind his saddle, then went to the fire to warm his hands and share the whiskey bottle that was making its way around the circle. Someone was telling a story about another hunt where they had killed four wolves, and someone else told of wolf hunting on the plains.

The moon set and they finished the bottle. Rufus tied the wolfskins behind his saddle, patting his horse when it shied away from the scent. The day was dawning, gray and dim.

Rufus parted company with the others at the turnoff that led to the Rybak farm and his own family's farm.

Nadya woke to find herself lying by the river at a bend where the current had created a narrow gravel beach. She was naked. Her skin was marked with bruises, streaked with river silt and blood. During the long chase, brambles had slashed her. The dogs had snapped at her feet and legs, leaving bloody gashes behind.

She sat up and hugged her knees for warmth. Early morning: the sun was barely above the horizon. Pale mist rose from the river, shifting and flowing like the water itself. From years of hunting the area, she recognized this stretch of river. She was just a mile or so downstream of the farm.

Her memories were blurred: darkness, panic, pain. Running—she remembered running among the trees, terrified by the baying of the hounds. And shouting—she remembered men's voices, shouting and singing and laughing like devils. Her body remembered the tugging of the river's currents, dragging her this way and that. Her muscles ached—she had fought the current, paddling desperately for this small beach.

She shivered. Where were her parents? That, she did not remember. Perhaps they had been carried further downstream. If that were the case, they would meet her at the farm. Surely, if she found her way to the farm, they would be there.

She clambered up the bank. She was used to going barefoot, but the brambles growing by the river scratched her bare skin and snagged in her hair. Under the oak trees at the top of the bank, the going was easier: last autumn's leaves, now damp and half rotted, were soft underfoot. She forced her tired muscles into a trot, telling herself that she would see her mother and father as soon as she reached the cabin. Of course, they would have to be at the cabin.

She was almost to the cabin when she heard a man shout. She did not recognize the voice exactly. At least, recognition did not penetrate the strange haze that occupied her mind, a peculiar cloudiness, as if her head were filled with river mist that ebbed and swirled. But the voice sounded familiar—that voice had called out to the hounds the night before, urging them on. The voice called to her again, and she ran faster, ducking through the trees, ignoring the brush that scratched her legs.

"Mama!" she called as she ran toward the cabin. "Mama! Papa!" She pushed the cabin door open. The room was empty, but she snatched her father's rifle from its place beside the door and the powder horn from the peg on the wall. She loaded the rifle quickly, her hands trembling in the cold. She spilled the black powder, but did not stop until she had rammed the bullet into place.

Still naked, she held the loaded rifle. With one foot, she kicked open the cabin door.

She smelled blood. Dried blood, mingled with the scent of wolf fur. She recognized the man on the horse—vaguely, dimly, through the river mist that filled her head—recognized him by his smell. His name didn't come to her—names were not really important yet. Someday soon, maybe they would be, but just then, names had not yet returned to her.

But his smell—that she knew. It was the smell of passion and the smell of death. Gunpowder and blood and river water and dogs baying as they rushed through the night, chasing wild things that ran and ran and ran. The smell told her what to do, even before she saw the two bundles of gray fur, tied to the saddle behind him.

"Nadya," the man said, and she lifted the rifle and shot him, point-blank, not thinking, not thinking at all.

His horse shied at the sound, and shied again at the sudden limpness of the man in the saddle. The man slumped then fell, sliding gracelessly to the ground. The smell of fresh blood joined the smell of dried blood, and a brilliant red stain spread across the back of the man's shirt where the bullet had left his body. The horse backed away from the body at its feet.

Nadya let the body lie in the dirt. She spoke soothingly to the horse, murmuring in French the endearments with which her mother had once comforted her. She tied the horse to the split-rail fence and returned to the cabin. She walked past the body, but did not look at it.

She stirred up the embers and built a fire. She did not think. She built a fire and heated water for tea. She washed herself, using a rag and warm water to wipe away the dirt and blood. Even when she put on her hunting trousers and a warm shirt, she could not stop shivering. The cold came from deep inside her.

The water boiled and she made tea, carefully measuring the dried leaves into the pot. Her mother liked her tea just so—Nadya was careful to make it properly, and she sat by the fire to drink it. She caught herself listening for the sound of her parents' footsteps. Her mind shied away from the memory of the two bundles of fur on the back of the horse. She had another cup of tea.

Then she took the shovel and went to a place in the woods where the ground was soft. The horse carried the man's body and she talked soothingly to the animal as they walked.

She buried the two bundles of fur side by side in a single grave. She stood by the grave for a time, unable to pray. "I'm sorry," she said at last. "I'm sorry. I shouldn't have. . . . I didn't mean. . . ." But the words stopped. She bowed her head and stood silent again. "Papa," she said at last. "There was nothing wrong with your stories. They weren't lies. The wolf can win. Just not here. Not now. But somewhere, the wolf can win."

Some distance away, she buried the body of the man who had killed her parents. Rufus's body. The name had returned to her with the memory of love and betrayal. But she said nothing over his grave. She had nothing to say to him.

She took care to conceal the graves, strewing the fresh-dug soil with a layer of leaves. Then she packed a few things: gunpowder, salt, tea, a pot in which to boil water, two blankets, her hunting knife, a hatchet, a pistol. Necessities only, dictated by a tiny part of her brain where the river mist had lifted.

She closed the door on her way out of the cabin. She lifted the rail that kept the pigs in their pen, opened the gate that kept the mule in its stable. Then she tied her small bundle behind the saddle, mounted, and turned the horse west.

TWO

■

Traveling West

II

Elizabeth Metcalf stood on a wooden sidewalk in Independence, Missouri, her hands clasped in front of her, her sunbonnet tied firmly beneath her chin. She wore a traveling dress of dark blue linen, a sensible color that would hide the stains that were inevitable along the trail.

Edward, the young man her father had hired to help them on their way to California, was swearing at the oxen. The wagon was stuck in one of the many mud holes that pitted the dirt track that served as the town's main street, and the oxen were straining to pull it out. As Elizabeth watched, the lead ox slacked off and the wagon rocked back into the hole. The right rear wheel settled into the mud up to the hub. The language that Edward used was not fit for the ears of a lady, and Elizabeth did her best not to listen.

It had been almost a year since Papa had decided that he would travel to join his brother Joseph in California. He had read and reread the letter in which Joseph told of the opportunities of this new land. Inspired by his brother's glowing description of California, he had made plans: he would bring a library over the mountains and a printing press so that he could print new books when he arrived. "It's a new land, Elizabeth," he told her. "A place for new ways of thinking, not mired in the old ways, like this place."

From the congressional printing office, Papa obtained a copy of John Frémont's report of his expeditions to Oregon and California, with its map and drawings. From publishers in Boston, New York, and Philadelphia, he gathered other books about the

West. Together, Elizabeth and her papa read traders' accounts of life on the Santa Fe Trail, descriptions by soldiers who had toured the savage Pawnee villages, reports from emigrants traveling overland. All winter long, they had read of the West.

Sometimes, it seemed to Elizabeth that she and Papa were reading different books. Papa talked of the abundance of game, the fascinating habits of the Indians along the trail, the beauty of the prairie flowers in bloom. Elizabeth took note of the dangers—wagons capsized in river crossings, tents blown over in violent storms, stock stampeded, travelers exhausted and sick with fever.

After reading the books, Elizabeth packed carefully for the trip. While Papa filled his trunks with books and located a cast-iron hand press that would fit in the wagon, Elizabeth put together a kit of medicines, ordered sturdy boots for herself and Papa, bought gaudy ribbons and trinkets that they might trade with the savages. She had to shop carefully—their funds were limited—but she was used to being frugal.

Despite all her reading and planning, the endeavor had not seemed real until now. Papa had described it as an adventure, and she had thought of it as something unavoidable—one of Papa's plans that was impossible to escape. Now, standing alone on the wooden sidewalk, she felt uprooted and lost.

Independence, the easternmost end of the Santa Fe Trail and a jumping-off place for the westward migration, was a rough town, a sharp contrast to Elizabeth's hometown of Springfield, Illinois. Early that morning, a spring rain had washed the dust from the air, leaving behind the native stinks of manure, sweat, chewing tobacco, black powder, and tar. Elizabeth could smell cheap perfume from the building behind her, mingling with the odor of burned hair and hooves from the blacksmith shop across the street.

A mountain man rode by the wagon, touching his hand to the brim of his slouch hat as he passed Elizabeth. At the knees, his buckskin trousers were black and shiny with wear; in place of a shirt, he wore a strange garment sewn of furs, some of them with the paws and tails still intact. Elizabeth could not identify all of the animals that had contributed to his clothing, but she noted a wolf tail dangling from one shoulder and the tiny claws of a weasel hanging from the back. A rank smell of sweat and wet fur drifted to Elizabeth as he passed. A short distance down the street, the man dismounted at a saloon door and disappeared inside.

The town was crowded with establishments whose purpose was to separate bullwhackers from the Mexican silver that they had earned on the Santa Fe Trail and mountain men from their trapping revenues. From where she stood, Elizabeth could count four saloons. A wooden sign painted with a grinning skull hung in front of the one that the mountain man had entered. The death's-head advertised the town's specialty drink: skull varnish, a sweet and deadly mixture of dark molasses and the milky whiskey peculiar to Missouri.

Elizabeth heard a sound overhead and looked up. A young woman in a low-cut dress had thrown open the shutters of a second-story window. She leaned out to watch the men in the street below. Her cheeks were bright with rouge and her lips were an unnatural red. She saw Elizabeth looking up at her and her bright red lips parted in a smile. "Have fun in California, ducky," she called. "Lord knows, we'll all be having fun here."

Elizabeth looked away, feeling her face growing hot. Surely life on the trail could be no worse than life in Independence. They had spent the previous night in a hotel of sorts—her father had insisted that they take advantage of their last opportunity to spend the night under a real roof. One wall of her room had been nothing more than a calico curtain that billowed and swayed with passing breezes. The hotel was connected to a saloon and Elizabeth had lain awake, listening to the slap of cards as some fool of a bullwhacker lost his money to a Missouri gambler. She drifted off to sleep, but gunshots in the street outside had wakened her. She had thrown a shawl over her nightgown and poked her head through the curtain.

"Go back to bed, missy," said the tavernkeeper as he hurried down the corridor. "The boys are just having some fun."

After that, she remained in bed, uneasy and frightened, until morning. She did not think much of the sort of fun they favored in Independence.

"Giddap, you mangy godforsaken beast," Edward shouted to the lead ox. "Giddap there." He snapped his whip against the animal's flank and the oxen leaned into the yoke, pulling hard.

When the beasts began to slack off, Edward flicked his whip again. Finally, the wagon lurched forward, its wheel rocking out of the mud hole.

"Good pulling, Bill Sikes!" Papa called cheerfully. He trotted up beside the wagon on his bay mare. "Good pulling, Fagin, you old villain!" He beamed at Edward, who continued scowling and snapped the whip again. Papa had named the six oxen of their team after characters in *Oliver Twist,* his favorite book. The largest ox was the ill-tempered Bill Sikes. The second-largest was Fagin, who frequently tried to slack off when the others pulled. Then there was Mr. Bumble, the Artful Dodger, Charlie Bates, and the smallest of the lot, Oliver. Sweet Nancy, the milk cow, was tied to the back of the wagon and followed along behind. Papa's mare was named Nell, after the little girl in *The Old Curiosity Shop,* there being no other young ladies in *Oliver Twist* worth mentioning.

The wagon rolled forward, leaving the pothole behind. "Whoa!" Edward called, and the oxen shambled to a stop. Elizabeth stepped carefully toward the wagon, avoiding the worst puddles. Her boots were already scuffed and caked with mud. She stepped up to the hub of the wheel and then to the wagon seat. As soon as she was settled, Edward cracked his whip again, shouted that he'd twist Fagin's tail clean off if the flea-bitten beast slacked again, and the wagon jerked forward.

"I've found a fine company for us to join," Papa said, riding alongside the wagon. "I think it will all work out very well. I—"

"Hello, Grampa!" the woman in the window called. "Why don't you stop by for a little fun?"

Papa lifted a hand and waved, smiling pleasantly. "No time, ma'am. We're off to California. Goodbye."

"I'll be glad to be on the trail," Elizabeth said.

"Oh, yes," her father agreed. "Quite so. Out to—what did Irving say?—to the 'fertile and verdant wastes, where there is neither the log house of the white man nor the wigwam of the Indian.' " Her father, also kept awake by the sounds of the saloon, had spent the evening rereading Washington Irving's *Tour of the Prairies.* He had quoted from it several times that morning already.

"Tell me about the company, Papa," Elizabeth asked.

"Three wagons, driven by strong men with their families," he said. "All bound for California."

It was late in the season. The books Elizabeth had read all advised emigrants to set out just a few weeks after the first spring rains fell, when the prairie grass was thick and there was plenty of grazing for the oxen. Set out too early, and you had to carry grain to sustain your livestock. Set out too late, and you ran the risk of encountering winter storms in the California mountains.

They were late. A series of mishaps had delayed their departure from Illinois: selling the farm had taken longer than Papa had expected; one of the oxen had fallen sick and they had to replace him; the mare had thrown a shoe. All the problems had been minor, but each one had caused delays. By the time that they reached Independence, all the larger wagon trains had set out. But the farm was sold, all their possessions were in the wagon. There was no turning back.

"Tell me about the people," Elizabeth asked. "What are they like?"

"Not well read," her father admitted. "I don't think they care much for reading. But stouthearted and true. A fine company, I'm sure."

Elizabeth regarded him doubtfully. Her father, she felt, was not always the best judge of character. He tended to be optimistic to the point of blindness.

"Don't you give me that sour look. It will all work out just fine," he assured her.

He had said the same thing two years before, when he decided to join a partner in the pork business. The plan had been to buy up fat hogs and ship them down the Mississippi by flatboat for sale in New Orleans. Elizabeth and her father had waved goodbye to his partner and their hogs as he headed south on the river. They had never heard from the man again.

"A stouthearted company," he repeated. "Salt of the earth."

The company they joined was from Kentucky—a group of neighbors and relatives who had decided to pull up stakes and travel together. Peter Akin, a barrel-chested man with grizzled hair, was the patriarch of the group.

"Pleased to meet you, Miss Elizabeth," he said, engulfing her hand in his. "We're glad you folks can join us. We can always use two more men with rifles in Injun country." He released Elizabeth's hand and clapped her father on the back.

Elizabeth glanced around at the camp, where Akin's company had been settled for the past two days. There were half a dozen children of various ages, grimy faced and barefoot, playing in the dirt near the wagons. The other men were lounging in the shade, whittling and chewing tobacco. Two women huddled over a smoky fire, cooking biscuits. Every now and again, one of the women would call out to the children.

"Now that you've joined up, we'd best get moving. It's early yet," Peter Akin said.

"There's a fair camp about ten miles on," Edward suggested. As a bullwhacker with a wagon train to Santa Fe, he had traveled the first part of the trail, where the trail to California and the Santa Fe Trail ran together.

With that, they agreed. Peter Akin roused the men who were whittling; the women rounded up the children. Elizabeth stood by the wagon, watching the preparations. Her own gear was packed and she thought she would only be in the way if she offered to help. The moment of idleness gave her the opportunity to study her new traveling companions.

Peter Akin seemed like a solid farmer. Not well read, her father had said. Elizabeth would guess that he could not read at all. But he seemed to be a confident man, shouting orders to the others as they yoked the oxen.

The three wagons of Akin's party were larger than her father's. Papa, following the advice offered in his books, had selected a well-built light wagon and had it reinforced for the rough journey. The bed was constructed of oak, well seasoned so that it would not crack in the desert air, and sealed with tar so it could float across a river like a boat, if need be. The wooden axles were liberally coated with bear grease, so that the wheels would turn smoothly. In the warmth of the morning sunshine, the wagon—and the grease bucket that hung from its side—gave off a pungent smell of tar and bear grease and dust.

With a great deal of hollering and cracking of whips, the wagons set forth. Akin's wagon led the way, and Elizabeth's wagon brought up the rear. They followed the wagon ruts that led away from Independence, heading west.

On that first day, they followed the Santa Fe Trail, well worn by the massive mule-drawn wagons that carried trade goods to Mexico. Elizabeth glanced back only once, taking a last look at the distant smoke of Independence. Then she looked forward, out into the open prairie. The gently rolling land was green with new grass and blooming with wild flowers. The bell that hung around Sweet Nancy's neck clanged in a regular rhythm as the milk cow patiently followed the wagon.

Elizabeth rode for the first hour. Then, tired of the wagon's jolting, she slipped down from the seat and walked, easily keeping pace with the slow-moving oxen. As she walked, she gathered wild flowers—a bright bouquet of mountain pink, a handful of purple larkspur.

"Hallo!" a woman called from the back of Peter Akin's wagon. "You must be Miss Elizabeth. I'm Molly Akin. You kin call me Molly."

Molly sat in a sort of throne, constructed of blankets and trunks and positioned to give her a view out the back of the wagon. She held a baby in her arms and a dirty-faced toddler clung to her knee. Her bonnet was pushed back on her head and her hair was escaping her bun, gray-brown wisps curling around her face. "The young'uns want to come and walk with you."

As Elizabeth watched, three boys and a girl spilled from the back of the wagon. The boys ranged from seven to ten years old—they were uniformly dark-haired and loud. The girl was about nine years old. She came to walk at Elizabeth's side.

"I'm Jenny," she told Elizabeth. "Them's my brothers—Matthew, Mark, and Luke. What're you picking weeds for?"

"They're pretty," Elizabeth said. "Maybe you should pick some for your mother."

Jenny eyed the bouquet dubiously, then shrugged. "She wouldn't know what to do with 'em. But I reckon I'll walk with you and watch for Injuns."

"What will you do if you see one?"

She shrugged again. Her face was dirty and her hair needed combing. "My pa says he'll shoot the first Injun that gets in his way," she offered.

"But some Indians are friendly," Elizabeth said. "You want to watch out for Pawnees—they're a murderous lot. But along here, we'll likely meet Osages and they're friendly enough."

Jenny squinted at the sun. "Maybe so," she said. "But what if you meet some Injuns and you think they're friendly and they're not?" She shook her head. "Then I reckon you'll be in trouble."

"Suppose they're friendly and you shoot one," Elizabeth said. "Won't you be in trouble then?"

Jenny frowned. "I reckon you might." She shook her head. "Maybe we can talk to 'em first and find out. Then we can shoot 'em."

Elizabeth decided to be satisfied with that limited success. Jenny helped her gather flowers. They passed a grave by the side of the trail. The wooden cross was weathered and Elizabeth could not read the name painted in tar on the crosspiece. The sight of the grave brought to mind all the ways a person could die on the trail—a fever or sickness, an accidental shooting, an Indian attack. Elizabeth shivered despite the warmth of the day and left her bouquet at the foot of the cross.

It was sunny all that first day—brave and hopeful weather. They camped at a small creek just eight miles from Independence. Just eight miles, but it might as well have been a hundred. It felt so strange, camping there in the open, without a sign of human habitation. A few trees, right by the creek, and the prairie all around.

When the wagons stopped, Molly Akin called to Elizabeth, inviting her for a cup of tea. "Hallo, Miss Elizabeth. Come and sit," she said.

Molly sent the children searching for wood to burn while the men were hobbling the horses and tethering the oxen. While waiting for the water to boil, Molly quizzed Elizabeth about her life. "I must say, I'm surprised that a handsome woman like yourself is traveling west without a husband. 'Course, I hear a woman can have her pick of men in California. She can be treated like a queen, they say."

Elizabeth kept her eyes on the fire. "I've never met a man who can compare to my papa," she said. "And I promised my mother, on her dying day, that I'd care for Papa. And so I have."

"That's real nice," Molly said, patting Elizabeth's hand familiarly. "But I reckon that somewhere in California, there's a man that can turn your head."

"Perhaps that's so," Elizabeth allowed, not wanting to argue on so short an acquaintance. "But I plan to pursue a career as a schoolteacher in the West."

"A schoolmarm?" Molly shook her head. "I don't see the use of schooling, myself. Peter never learned to read nor write a lick, and he's the finest man I know."

Elizabeth smiled uneasily.

Over hot tea, Molly introduced Elizabeth to half a dozen men, all of whom seemed to be brothers or cousins to Peter Akin or Molly, and to three other women, wives of the brothers or cousins. The men all seemed much like Peter Akin—sturdy and confident. The women, much like Molly—a bit worn and faded.

After a time, Elizabeth returned to her own wagon for provisions. Over the fire, she cooked bacon and corn bread. "It's like a picnic," she told her father, while she and Papa and Edward ate under the open sky. After they ate, Edward showed her how to scour the cast-iron frying pan with prairie grasses and sand.

When the first stars came out, Papa and Edward camped out under the stars and Elizabeth made her bed in the back of the wagon. The canvas cover made a cozy room that smelled of her cooking spices and Papa's tobacco. The moonlight illuminated the canvas from outside. She had sewn patch pockets on the inside of the canvas wagon cover—one for Papa's pipe, another for her combs, a half a dozen for small necessities. In the moonlight, the pockets formed patterns of shadow.

She fell asleep to the yapping of distant coyotes. A lonely sound, she thought, but an improvement over the slap of cards and the rattle of dice.

The first two weeks were easy traveling. The oxen learned to pull in unison and Edward finally took to calling them by their proper names. The weather was fine and clear.

Some forty miles west of Independence, they turned north, leaving behind the worn ruts of the Santa Fe Trail for the smaller track made by emigrant wagons heading for Oregon and California. They crossed the Kaw River without mishap, paying three dollars a wagon for the ferry. The Big Blue River was low enough to ford, and they crossed that on a sunny day. Their wagon was so well caulked that not a drop of water leaked through the bed.

Though all seemed placid, Elizabeth felt a division between her party and their fellow travelers. By all accounts, the best way to travel with oxen was to wake early and set forth at dawn. During the hottest hours of the day, you stopped to let the beasts rest and graze. Then after your midday break you resumed your journey until early evening.

But Peter Akin and his clan did not like to rise before the sun. Despite Edward's cries of "Catch up! Catch up!"—the traditional shout for rousing a camp at dawn—the wagon train never got underway early. To make up time, Peter insisted on driving through the heat of the day, allowing the oxen little time to rest and feed. When Edward suggested that the group stop for a day to rest the oxen, Peter dismissed the notion. "Can't take the time," he said. "We're late in the season already."

More than once, Elizabeth overheard Edward talking seriously with her father. "They'll wear the oxen out by the time we reach Fort Laramie," Edward told her father. "It's just no good."

Her father spoke to Peter about the matter, but nothing ever changed.

It was so late in the season, they had to stick with this wagon train, for the odds of another coming along after were slim. And they did not want to travel alone. All the books advised traveling in a group for protection against Indian attack.

But always there were arguments. Where the wagon ruts led down a small rise, Edward recommended locking the wheels to act as brakes. Peter laughed at him, saying there was no need. But of course, a wagon escaped and overturned. It was a miracle, Elizabeth thought, that no one was killed. They had to wait while the wagon was set upright and its contents were gathered from where they had scattered over the prairie grass.

Still, there were pleasant times. Elizabeth enjoyed walking with Jenny each day. They gathered flowers together and left them by the graves that were all too common along the trail. Once, Elizabeth wove a daisy wreath for Jenny's hair, and the girl wore it until the flowers drooped and lost their petals. Each morning, Jenny came to Elizabeth's wagon to eat breakfast. On the second day, Elizabeth insisted on washing the girl's face and combing the tangles from her hair. Jenny protested, but after that day she always stopped by in the morning to have Elizabeth comb and braid her thick dark hair. In the late afternoon, when they had stopped for the day, she read to the girl from *Oliver Twist.*

They had been traveling for almost a month when they reached the Platte River, a slow-moving current of muddy water that marked the way westward. There Peter Akin was content to rest for a day. That evening, he and his cousins brought out a jug of whiskey and stayed up late, drinking and laughing. Long after Elizabeth had retired to her bed, she heard the men around the campfire.

The next day, Elizabeth woke to the sound of a blustering wind and rain rattling on the canvas wagon cover. "Hallo, Elizabeth," she heard Jenny call, and the girl climbed into the back of the wagon. Her hair was wet and water drops glittered on her wool coat.

"Pa's not happy this morning," Jenny told Elizabeth. "Too much whiskey last night. I reckon we won't travel far today."

They were late getting started and then it was slow going. Peter Akin's wagon was the first to bog down in the mud. Akin whipped his team and swore. Though the oxen strained at their yokes, the mud held the wheels firm. To free the big wagon, Papa and Edward had to hitch their team to Akin's team. Molly stood in the rain, holding the baby, while the men labored to rock the wheels free. The same process was repeated three times that day, as the big wagons bogged down, one by one. Elizabeth's papa's wagon was light enough that the team could pull it through the muck, but Papa had to keep stopping to help free the clumsier vehicles.

By noon, Edward and Papa were soaked to the skin. When they came into the shelter of the wagon for the noon meal, Papa's lips were blue with the cold and he could not stop shivering. Elizabeth gave them both brandy from the medicinal stores, hoping to warm them. Since there was no way to start a fire in the downpour, she fed them cold biscuits and ham and dried fruit and wrapped them in wool blankets against the chill. Papa had finally stopped shivering when she heard Peter Akin's voice at the back of the wagon.

"Time to get moving," he called. "Time to head out."

She looked out through the back flap. Akin stood in the downpour, his hat dripping water. The wagon ruts behind him were filled with water. "Perhaps we should stop for the afternoon, Mr. Akin," she said. "It hardly seems prudent to continue in this downpour. Tomorrow, the sky may clear."

He looked at her as if she had no right to speak of what might happen. "It might let up or it might rain harder," he growled. "We've got to move on. It's late in the season. We should be farther along by now."

He turned away, starting for one of the other wagons.

"But Mr. Akin," Elizabeth called. "This is unhealthy weather. My father needs a bit longer to rest and dry himself."

He did not turn back. Perhaps he hadn't heard.

When she turned back into the wagon, Papa was already pulling on his wet coat. "If he'd stir himself early in the morning and move when he should, we'd be farther along," Edward was saying in a low furious tone. "If the oxen were rested they could pull his wagons through the mud. He's a fool, I say."

"Perhaps we should wait a bit," Elizabeth said. "Let them go ahead. We can catch up easily enough the first time they bog down. And they can't get far without our oxen to pull them from the mire."

"Now, now," Papa said. "Edward, Elizabeth—that's not very Christian of you. We must help each other along. I don't begrudge a little assistance now and again. They would do the same for us."

Elizabeth bowed her head, ashamed of her angry words.

They made scarcely four miles that day, by Elizabeth's guess. And they spent a miserable night huddled in the wagon—unable to build a fire to warm themselves or cook hot food.

The next day, Edward fell ill, a fever brought on by the chill. That day, he rode in the back of the wagon. The rain continued, settling into a steady drizzle that soaked through even the thickest wool. Papa drove the team in the rain, while Elizabeth watched over the sick man. The fever was bad—he tossed in his bed and moaned each time the wagon jounced over a rut. When they stopped at noon, Elizabeth sat with him, but most of the time he didn't even seem to notice she was there. She gave him water to drink, and hot tea, and she dosed him from her medicine kit. But the fever continued, unabated.

That night, bundled in blankets and shivering to the end, Edward died. In the morning, Elizabeth's father rose early and dug a grave in the muddy ground. They buried Edward beside the Platte. Jenny helped Elizabeth pile stones on the grave to keep off the wolves.

They traveled that day, and again Elizabeth's father drove the team. When they stopped for the noon meal, he complained of a pain in his stomach. The next morning, he had the fever—his hands shook as he held a cup of tea. He would not eat breakfast, no matter how much Elizabeth urged him. His face was pale and damp with sweat and his usual good humor had left him.

Elizabeth put him to bed in the back of the wagon, wrapped in a quilt with a cup of hot tea at his side. She went to talk to Peter Akin.

She found him at the fire with Molly, finishing his breakfast. "My papa has the fever," she said. "He's too ill to travel. We must stop for a day so that he can rest."

Peter spat into the fire, avoiding her eyes. "I don't reckon we can spare a day just now. It being so late in the season, I reckon we just have to keep moving."

He didn't say it, but Elizabeth knew he feared contagion. There had been epidemics on the trail—cholera, typhus, and other unnamed fevers that spread from wagon to wagon and killed more travelers than the Pawnees ever scalped.

"It's just a chill," Elizabeth said. "One day's rest, and I'm sure he'll be well enough to travel."

Peter turned away without speaking.

"You just hurry along when he's well," Molly said from her seat by the fire. "You follow the river and catch us when we take a day to rest." She looked up at Elizabeth with sympathy.

Jenny came from the wagon and stood at Elizabeth's side. The girl hadn't come to the wagon that morning, and Elizabeth suspected that Molly had forbidden her to go near the sickbed.

"Maybe I should stay with Elizabeth," Jenny said softly. "Just to help a bit. We'll catch up soon enough."

Molly shook her head at her daughter. "You'll do no such

thing. You'll stay with me, and that's that." She glanced at Elizabeth. "Elizabeth and her papa can take care of themselves. Lord willing, they'll be back with us soon enough."

"Lord willing," Elizabeth repeated with a bitter edge in her voice.

Giddap! Giddap now." Peter Akin cracked the whip overhead and the oxen leaned into their yokes. The first wagon creaked and jerked forward.

Elizabeth stood beside the wagon and watched the others pull away. After two days of rain, the weather had cleared; the sky was pale blue overhead, an endless ocean of sky. A person could drown in it. The tall prairie grass glistened in the pale morning light. The Platte River traced a meandering line across the open grassland.

"Come along as soon as your papa is well," Molly called from her throne in the back of the wagon. "You hurry after us." Jenny sat beside her mother. Molly's hand was on the girl's shoulder, as if to restrain her from leaping out the back of the wagon.

Elizabeth lifted her hand and waved to Jenny. She turned away then, not wanting to watch the wagons grow tiny in the distance. Surely Papa would get well very soon.

The air inside the wagon was heavy with the scent of cayenne pepper. That morning, while the others prepared their wagons to leave, she had made a flannel poultice of pepper. Her book of home remedies said that the poultice would help bring down the fever, but all that it had done was make her sneeze and perfume the air with spice.

Papa lay still and pale in the bed. When Elizabeth took his hand, it was clammy with cold sweat. His eyelids fluttered when she touched him. "Can you take some tea?" she asked him.

"I'll try." With an effort, he lifted his head. "Have the others gone on?"

"They call themselves Christians, but they could not wait a day for us," she said, unable to control her anger.

"Ah, Liz—be charitable. We'll pass them on the trail as soon as I'm well. We'll get to California months before them." He managed a weak smile. "That's what we'll do."

She busied herself with the little things that she could do to make him more comfortable—rolling up the canvas sides of the wagon to let a breeze pass through, replenishing his poultice, brewing strong blackberry leaf tea, which Molly had advised her was good for the diarrhea that accompanied the fever. When there was nothing left to do, she sat by the bed and read to him from Dickens. For a time, he fell into a feverish sleep, moaning and tossing as he dozed.

That night, she stayed up late, sitting on a trunk beside the bed and holding Papa's hand. She was exhausted—she had had little sleep since Edward had fallen ill, and when she had slept her rest had been disturbed by dark and terrifying dreams that she could not recall when she awoke. Though she was weary, she could not bring herself to lie down.

Through the thin canvas walls of the wagon cover, she heard the sounds of the prairie: the mournful cry of a bird; the screech of a night hawk on the hunt; the yipping and howling of a pack of coyotes. She pulled her shawl more tightly around her shoulders and leaned forward to tuck the quilt around Papa. He moaned and shifted in his sleep. His breathing was labored and irregular, each new breath an effort.

She held his hand and listened to the whisper of his breath coming and going. She willed him to keep breathing, praying to Jesus and Mary to help him, to keep him with her. It seemed to her that he would keep breathing only as long as she continued the struggle with him, as long as she kept praying.

In the morning, dawn light shining through the canvas of the wagon woke her. Papa's hand was cold in hers. He lay quiet and silent; his breathing had stopped in the night. She wept then, reaching out to embrace him, burying her face in the quilt to muffle her sobs. His skin, when she touched him, was cold and stiff. She backed away, not knowing what to do.

She climbed from the wagon, staring around her wildly. The wind blew across the open prairie, making the grass whisper and sway. In all directions, there was only the grass: not a wagon, not a person, not even a tree standing above the flatness. The bell on the milk cow's neck rang softly as she moved her head, searching for the best grass. Elizabeth was alone in the wilderness, and there was no one to help her.

She sat in the prairie grass and cried. Twenty-three years old and suddenly alone in the world. What else was there to do? The grass whispered around her. After a time, her tears ran dry and her pain and panic gave way to a kind of numbness.

Elizabeth closed Papa's eyes and washed his poor pale face with a cloth, wet with river water. She wrapped him in her best quilt, his favorite quilt, a Flying Star pattern of brilliant blue triangles on a background of white. He had always said that the blue matched her eyes.

She took the shovel from the wagon and went to the river bluff to dig a grave. She dug the grave as deep as she could, though the soil was hard and her hands blistered. She tried not to think of the graves along the trail where wolves had dug up the bodies. The sun was low in the sky when she finished.

It took all her strength to drag Papa's body from the wagon and to the grave. She buried him, trying not to think of him as Papa. Her papa was in heaven—this was only the body he had left behind.

Alone in the prairie, she wept and read from the Bible, Papa's Bible, now her own. " 'The Lord is my shepherd; I shall not want. . . .' " The wind from the prairie played with her dress and flirted with her hair. " 'Surely goodness and mercy shall follow me all the days of my life: and I will dwell in the house of the Lord forever. Amen.' "

With blistered hands, she shoveled dirt into the grave, tamping it down to make it more difficult for wolves to dig up. She spent the afternoon carrying rocks to the mound, covering the dirt with stones. From two wooden slats, pried loose from a packing box, she fashioned a cross.

It was late afternoon when she was done. She stood by the grave for a moment, thinking about what to do. She could not return to Illinois—the farm was sold and all the money spent on preparations for the journey. There was nothing for her there.

She had no choice. She would go on to California where her uncle and his family were living. They would take her in, and she could work as a schoolteacher. She wasn't helpless. She had watched Edward and Papa yoke the oxen and drive them. Surely she could manage that. Tomorrow, she would try.

She went to the river and washed her face and hands. She gave a ration of grain to each ox and to Papa's bay mare. Bill Sikes, the lead ox, was tethered; the other oxen stayed close by. The mare was tied to a wagon wheel by a long rope, giving her the freedom to wander and graze.

Elizabeth made a small meal of dried beef and biscuits from the day before, washed down with lemonade made with lemon syrup and river water. She was not hungry—she felt hollow and empty, but she wasn't hungry. Still, she knew that she needed to eat. Finally, exhausted, she put on her nightgown and lay down in the wagon. But she could not sleep.

The full moon rose. Its light shone through the canvas top of the wagon, filling the small space with shadows. She was afraid, lying there alone. Somewhere in the distance, she heard wolves howling and she shivered, thinking of wolves digging up Papa's grave, thinking of Indians prowling outside the wagon, creeping closer and closer.

At last, she got out of bed and lit a candle. By candlelight, she sat in the wagon and read from the Bible, searching for comfort.

12

After leaving Wolf Crossing, Nadya avoided settlements. That first night on the trail, as she sat by her campfire, she took out her hunting knife, sawed off her long braid, and threw it on the fire. When the hair burned, the acrid smoke brought tears to her eyes.

The next day, she rode west, always west. She wore trousers and kept Papa's hat pulled low over her eyes. If anyone wondered where the Rybak family had gone, if they wondered what had happened to Nadya Rybak, if they wondered how Rufus had died, they would come looking for a young woman, traveling with her parents. No one would be looking for a young man, traveling alone.

After a few days, she left the Missouri woodlands behind. The prairie lands of Kansas were flat and open: no trees; no hills; just an endless sky. She talked sometimes as she rode. Not to herself, but to her mother. She said that she was sorry, that she should have listened, that the cards had warned her. The wind, when it blew through the tall grass, whispered in her mother's voice. Nadya wept sometimes, and the wind caught her tears and carried them away to water the prairie grass.

The horse, Rufus's gray gelding, kept up a steady pace. Each day, she rode until she was exhausted, but even then she did not sleep well. She lay awake at night, wrapped in a blanket and staring up at the stars that dotted the vast sky.

She ate whatever she killed—jackrabbits and wild prairie chickens and once a pronghorn antelope. She did not care much for food, and she ate what she needed to live, nothing more. After a time, her trail joined the emigrant trail that ran alongside the Platte River and she followed the ruts left by emigrant wagons heading west.

Sometimes, she made camp where other travelers had camped. She could smell their leavings. Bear grease dripping from wagon wheels. Corn bread and whiskey. Used tea leaves, dumped in the prairie grass. Familiar scents that reminded her of home.

She gained on the emigrants, day by day. They were traveling slowly in ox-drawn wagons; she made better time. At night, as she gazed up at the stars, she thought about catching up to the emigrants. Perhaps she could travel with them for a time. Sometimes, she thought she would welcome human company.

But then she would remember her last experience of human company. She remembered the baying of hounds and the shouting of the men on her trail, pursuing her. She remembered the wolfskins strapped behind Rufus's saddle. And she knew that she wanted no company. When she saw the wagon train in the distance, she would leave the trail and make her way around the emigrants, not even stopping to exchange greetings. She wanted nothing to do with other travelers on the trail.

On the afternoon of the Change, she stopped well before sunset and made camp by the Platte River. After building a fire, she roasted and ate a prairie hen that she had shot. She tethered her horse securely in a patch of lush prairie grass and stowed her saddlebags nearby. The moon was still below the horizon, but she could feel its pull in her belly, in her groin.

Alone on the prairie, with the emptiness of the grassland around her, she undressed, folding her clothing and putting it in her saddlebags to keep it from the dew. So strange, so lonely, to be waiting for the Change with no one else nearby. Always before, her parents had been with her.

She stood naked in the tall prairie grass. The wind ruffled her short, unruly hair, and she pushed it back from her face. She faced the east, looking toward the rising moon. The sun set behind her and her long shadow stretched away into the empty land. She felt as cold and as empty as the land around her.

In the distance she heard a wolf howl, a low note that was joined, after a moment, by another wolf. A third wolf joined in, then a fourth and a fifth. Somewhere nearby, a pack was gathering together and announcing their claim on this land. This patch of prairie was their territory, their place.

The first light of the full moon burned on Nadya's skin. She closed her eyes and opened her arms to the moonlight. She Changed, and a gray wolf stood by the grazing horse, gazing eastward in the moonlight.

The past, which had concerned her so much as she made her way across the prairie, faded with the Change; the future became irrelevant. Those other times—that faded past, that irrelevant future—those times did not exist. What mattered was this single moment, this now.

The warm air was rich with scents. She lifted her head and breathed deeply, catching smells that had eluded her before. Somewhere, not too far, there were other wolves.

She followed her nose to find the pack's scent markings on a nearby boulder. This unobtrusive gray rock had been marked by each member of the pack in turn. She investigated the smells thoroughly. The wolves had been here recently—maybe a few hours back. Two males and three females. One of the females, by the smell, had pups; Nadya could smell traces of nursing milk where the wolf had rested in the grass. She left her own scent mark on the boulder and continued on her way.

The wolves howled again. They were speaking to her, but not in the structured, controlled fashion of human words and sentences. The howling went straight to her heart and her belly and her groin with a visceral pull. She could not ignore this call, any more than she could stop her heart from beating. The message was one of longing and one of threat. We are here, this is our land, our place. Do you hear us? We are here. This is ours.

Thought and action were the same; there was no gap between them. She was thinking about going to the wolves and she was trotting toward them, moving across the prairie with a steady loping pace that she could maintain for hours without tiring. She headed away from the river, following the scent of wolves in the grass.

She had been traveling for half an hour when she saw the pack in the distance. Half a dozen wolves had gathered on a small rise. On the wind, she caught a milky scent—this was a den site with young pups. She slowed her pace, drawn to the wolves but feeling suddenly anxious. Her heart was pounding quickly, and she resisted the urge to run.

In the Missouri woods, in the company of her own family, she had never met another pack. More than once, they had found the scent markings of other wolves in their nocturnal wanderings, but her father had always led his family away from those animals, avoiding an encounter with another pack.

Nadya was upwind of the pack and they had not noticed her yet. She hesitated, gazing at the distant animals. The hair on her neck and back was bristling, an involuntary response to the nearness of these strange wolves. One of the wolves caught sight of her and barked, a breathy sound that turned into a low, hoarse howl, alerting the pack to the presence of a stranger. All the wolves turned to face Nadya, fixing her with intense stares.

Nadya whined low in her throat, flattening her ears, tucking her tail between her legs, and lowering her head submissively. Part of her wanted to run away, but she was drawn to the pack by her loneliness and her need for companionship. At the same time, she was afraid, knowing that she did not belong here.

It is difficult to apply human words to situations that have no words. Encounters among wolves are not discussions, not quarrels, not arguments. But a conversation takes place, a dialogue of movements and gestures. There are no words, but much is communicated by the position of the ears, the attitude of the tail, the angle of the head. Much is expressed by pulling back the lips to show the teeth, by staring fixedly, by growling low in the throat.

A wolf pack is a complex social hierarchy in which each animal knows its position. The central question in any conversation among wolves is simple: who is dominant? who has the power? The dominant wolf is not always the strongest animal. Sometimes, dominance is a matter of attitude, of personality and intelligence. But always the question of dominance is at the heart of any interaction.

In an established pack, relationships are clear and well defined. As puppies, packmates wrestle and fight in ritualized combat, establishing the social order. As adults, the wolves in the pack are always testing one another, jockeying for better positions in the hierarchy. But though they challenge one another constantly, each wolf knows its place, knows who is dominant and who must submit.

That's how it is in an established pack. But when a strange wolf meets that pack, power relationships are not clear. The outsider is a threat to the established social order, a competitor for the resources on which the pack depends, a trespasser on the pack's territory. Nadya was all of those things—and a threat to the pack's young pups as well. In this situation, the rules of ritualized combat did not apply. The wolves of this pack would protect their own by injuring or killing the outsider.

The alpha female, the mother of the pups in the den, was the first to rush Nadya, lunging toward her and biting at her forelegs. Nadya reared back on her hind legs, snatching her legs away from the snapping jaws. The other wolf reared back as well, snarling and biting savagely at Nadya's neck. Nadya parried the wolf's open jaws with her teeth, matching bite for bite while backing away, giving ground before the fierce attack. The wolf got a grip on the thick fur at Nadya's neck and shook her head like a terrier with a rat, trying to tear the skin. Nadya caught the alpha female's ear in her teeth, tasting blood and preventing the animal from shaking her head again. The wolf lost her grip on Nadya's neck, and Nadya wrestled her to the ground.

If the alpha female had been alone, Nadya might have won the fight. But as Nadya wrestled the alpha female to the ground, the rest of the pack closed in, mobbing her from all sides, tearing at her face, snapping at her legs, biting at her unprotected back. She was borne down beneath half a dozen snarling wolves.

She felt jaws closing on her foreleg, jaws tearing at her lip, jaws ripping at her ear.

She had to get away. Thought became action and she was wriggling out from beneath them, bucking them off, snapping and snarling and threatening. Then she was on her feet and running—a panicked desperate flight away from the den, away from the wolves. The pack chased her through the prairie grass, but she outpaced them, her legs pumping, her breath coming fast, her heart pumping.

She did not know how long they chased her. A mile perhaps, then the pack members abandoned the chase, one by one. She was alone again, running across the prairie in the moonlight, running though no one pursued her. Running to escape the scent of the wolves, the scent of home, the scent of sorrow.

At last, she collapsed in the grass, breathing hard. Her lip was torn where a wolf had grabbed it. Her forelegs and back were bloody where hard bites had broken the skin. She was bruised from falling beneath the pack of wolves and weary from running.

For a time, she lay in the grass and licked her wounds, cleaning her fur of blood and soothing the cuts with her tongue. As she rested, her heart slowed to a steady beat.

In the distance, a wolf howled. It was the alpha female, calling the others back to her. Nadya lay still, listening as the other wolves joined in, singing in the night. This is our place, they said. You do not belong here.

Nadya sampled the wind. She could not smell the pack—she was far from the den now. The wind had shifted and she caught the scent of wood smoke and oxen. She stood, lifting her head and breathing deeply. Intriguing smells: lye soap and cayenne pepper, wheat flour and salted pork, cornmeal and spices.

She stood and shook herself, then followed the wind, drifting toward the human smells. A canvas-topped wagon stood by the river. A bay mare was tied to the wagon's wheel, asleep on her feet, by the look of it. Six oxen grazed nearby, tethered in the tall grass. The grazing oxen glanced at Nadya, then ignored her, understanding from her actions that she was not hunting just now. Not far from where the oxen grazed, Nadya found a mound of earth, a grave, newly dug.

She drifted closer to the wagon. The ashes in the fire pit were cold, but the smell of biscuits lingered. And other smells: a woman, alone. A flame flickered inside the wagon, illuminating the canvas from within.

The human part of Nadya, a tiny corner of her mind, thought it odd to see a lone wagon. Emigrants traveled in groups for protection against Indian attack.

Curious, drawn by the smell of the woman, Nadya approached the wagon slowly, until she stood right behind it, breathing deeply of the scents. She heard paper rustling inside the wagon. The woman was reading by the light of a tallow candle. The scent of burning tallow touched the human part of Nadya, reminding her of winter nights in the cabin in Missouri. She stood by the wagon for a moment, forgetting her pains, feeling warm and happy.

A night hawk called overhead and the horse woke, startled by the sound. The mare snorted and shifted her feet restlessly. Catching sight of Nadya, she snorted again and reared up, tugging on the wagon wheel and rocking the wagon, just a little.

Nadya slipped away from the spooked horse, quietly putting distance between herself and the wagon. She was moving away when the woman flung the back flap of the wagon open. The woman's eyes were wild; she stank of fear. She clutched a pistol awkwardly in both hands. Her white nightgown flapped in the breeze. The horse, terrified by this sudden apparition, reared again, whinnying in fear.

Nadya was just starting to run when she heard the explosion of the pistol. Then the oxen were running with her, the lead ox having lunged forward and ripped up his tether. His bell rang furiously as he ran, and the other oxen followed him, stampeding away from the frightening noise, the flapping white thing that pursued them and called out in a human voice. "Whoa! Wait! Bill Sikes! Fagin! Oliver! Whoa!"

The voice faded behind Nadya as she ran, outpacing the oxen. For the second time that night, she ran away through the tall grass, her heart pounding with fear. This time, she ran back to her own camp, where the gray gelding grazed by the riverside. She lay down beside her saddlebags and bedroll, reassured by the familiar smells. She curled up and finally, exhausted from running and fear, slept for a time.

When she woke, the moon was low in the western sky. In the east, she could see the first light of dawn. She stood to greet the sun and the morning light touched her gray fur with color, warming her after the long night.

What is it like, returning to humanity after a night on the wild side? It's like waking from a dream of passion alone in your bed. You remember holding someone in your arms, but that someone is gone.

It's like pulling on a pair of old shoes that don't quite fit anymore. Too tight, too confining. As the sun rises and the moon sets, the scents that fill your world begin to fade. And words return to you, words and thoughts that seem so important when you are human. But in that moment, when you are coming back, words seem trivial and foolish, the gruntings of an ape shaping sounds around an idea.

In the moment that you return to yourself, you know that words are all too often lies. Even when you try to make them true, words are incomplete. There are no words for the night you have lived, for the scents no human can smell, for the sounds that humans can't hear. No words for the fears and longings that have touched you and left you changed.

But words come back to you. And with the words come memories of the past and worries for the future, filling your mind so that the world of now is diminished, squeezed smaller and smaller so that there's scarcely any room for it at all.

Nadya stretched in the sunlight. Her body, now changed, no longer bore the bites and bruises of the night before, but the memory of those pains lingered. She was alone, and that was hard. It was always hard returning to her human form, but it had been easier when her mother and father were with her.

She bathed in the river, immersing herself in the warm murky water and scrubbing with the bar of lye soap she had carried in her saddlebag. The smell of the soap reminded her of the wagon she had visited in the night. Fragments of memory: a wild-eyed woman, running in the moonlight; a pistol shot; a desperate voice calling to the oxen, calling them back. Why would a woman be out on the prairie alone? And what would she do without her oxen, without her horse?

Nadya left the river and dried herself on her shirt, then pulled on her clothes. She was weary from the Change, but memories of the previous night made her restless, unable to sleep. She saddled her horse and went looking for the oxen that had stampeded in the night.

13

Elizabeth woke late in the morning. For a moment, lying in her bed, she blinked up at the canvas wagon top, confused and disoriented. Perhaps she had dreamed it all—the terror in the night, the wolf, the stampeding oxen.

No. Papa's pistol lay on the trunk beside the bed. Her eyes were sore; she had cried herself to sleep. She remembered the sound of Bill Sike's bell, ringing furiously as the animal ran.

She got out of bed and pushed back the canvas flap at the back of the wagon. The morning sunlight shone brightly on the prairie grass. A beautiful sunny day in an empty world. The oxen were gone; the mare was gone. Without the oxen to pull the wagon, without the mare to ride, she could not travel. She would die on the prairie, alone and helpless.

She let the flap drop closed. Slowly, she dressed, feeling strangely numb. She stepped out of the wagon and went to the river where she washed her face and hands. Then she sat by the ashes of last night's fire, brushing her hair and braiding it neatly. There seemed to be nothing else to do. Perhaps the Lord would take mercy on her. Perhaps the mare would return of her own accord. Perhaps another wagon train would pass by. She knew it was unlikely, so late in the season, but it could happen.

She built a small fire and made breakfast. Despite all that had happened, she was hungry, and that was one problem she could solve. She made a batch of biscuits and baked them in her Dutch oven. Just as she was taking them off the fire, she heard a sound: the distant ringing of a bell. She thought for a moment that it was her imagination. Then she heard singing, and she stood up, staring in the direction of the voice. The tune, a rollicking melody, was not familiar; the words were not in English or French. She did not recognize the language.

A figure on a horse rode along the riverbank toward her. The stranger led the runaway mare and Bill Sikes. The other oxen and the milk cow followed placidly.

"Hello," Elizabeth called. "Oh, hello!" She clasped her hands together, thanking the Lord for his mercy. Perhaps this man was a scout for another wagon train, she thought.

The man stopped singing as he approached, reined in his horse, and swung out of the saddle. He wore deerskin trousers, a red flannel shirt, and a broad-brimmed black hat. Elizabeth could see a pistol at his belt; a rifle was lashed to his saddle. There were outlaws on the plains—Indians and half-breeds and men who had lived among the Indians for so long they could scarcely be called civilized. She hesitated for a moment, staring at the man.

"Hello," she said again, and the stranger pushed back his hat. He was just a boy. Though the face beneath the hat was tanned by the sun, the chin was beardless and the features were delicate. Almost feminine, Elizabeth thought. He was not a big lad—just Elizabeth's height. No more than nineteen years old, she guessed.

"It is so wonderful to see another living soul," she said. "I'm Elizabeth Metcalf. Thank you for bringing back my oxen."

He studied her face for a moment, but did not speak. After a moment's hesitation, he tugged his hat from his head, revealing raggedly cropped hair.

"Pleased to meet you," he mumbled. His eyes were on the ground. She almost smiled then—he was so awkward and shy. "You can call me Nat."

"Is that short for Nathan?" she asked.

He nodded, still looking at the ground. "Is your wagon train far from here?" she asked eagerly. "I wonder if I might join it. I'm all alone here." Her voice faltered.

He looked up then and met her eyes. "I'm not with a wagon train. I'm traveling alone. I found your animals wandering, and so I brought them back." He spoke softly and his words had a faint accent that Elizabeth could not identify.

"Alone?" Elizabeth's voice faltered. "I thought. . . . I expected. . . . I hoped you were with a wagon train." She stopped, gathering herself. Even without a wagon train, he could help her.

Surely the Lord had sent him to help her. "My father died yesterday." Her voice broke, but she did not cry. This was not the time for tears.

Nat nodded, his face unreadable.

"Where are you going?" she asked.

"Oregon."

"I'm going to California," Elizabeth said. "My uncle lives there." She hesitated again, studying Nat's face. "Our trails are the same for a while. Perhaps we could travel together."

Nat glanced at the wagon and the oxen. "You travel slow," he commented.

"Maybe you could travel with me for a little while," she said. "Until we catch up with the wagon train that left us behind. Please. You have to help me."

Nat frowned, obviously reluctant.

"Come," she said, "have a cup of tea with me. And some biscuits, I've just baked biscuits. At least you can do that."

Nat's parents had died in Missouri, not so long ago. He told her that much. He sat by the fire, staring down into his cup of tea, clearly reluctant to talk much about them, about himself.

Elizabeth guessed at his story: a sickness, perhaps; a failing farm; a shy boy with no relatives to call on. He said little; her imagination filled in the gaps. It was a common enough story. No need to drag it from him.

He had decided to travel West, to Oregon. He hadn't liked any of the wagon trains he saw, and so he set out on his own. "I'm a good hunter," he said. "It's easier traveling alone."

"Aren't you afraid of Indians?"

He shrugged. "There's a lot of space out here. Not so many Indians."

"It's lonely," she said.

"Sometimes," he admitted, glancing up from his tea. His eyes were golden, the color of ripe wheat.

"It would be better traveling together," she said bravely.

"I'm used to traveling alone." Then he looked up and met her eyes.

For all his brave words, she could see that he was lonely.

"Please," she said. And she reached out and took his hand in both of hers. "I heard the wolves howling last night, and I was so afraid. Please travel with me for a time. Until I catch up with the wagon train. Then you can go on alone, if you like."

He hesitated, then nodded at last. "I reckon I could do that."

"Thank you," she said. "Oh, thank you."

He glanced at the sun, still low in the eastern sky, then looked around at the oxen. "I suppose we'd best be moving," he said. "We can make some miles today."

Elizabeth packed the wagon, stowing her belongings for the jostling of the trail. As she packed, Elizabeth heard Nat talking softly to the oxen in a language she couldn't understand—French, perhaps. When Bill Sikes tossed his head and turned away from the yoke, Nat spoke in another language—a few short words that sounded like a curse.

"What did you say to him?" Elizabeth asked Nat.

"I told him if he was good, he'd get nice grass to eat, and if he was bad, I'd twist his tail."

"I'd like to say a prayer at my papa's grave," she said.

Nat shrugged, but said nothing.

"Would you like to join me?" she asked gently.

"I reckon not."

Elizabeth frowned. "Aren't you a good Christian, Nat?"

"I reckon I'm good. But I don't reckon I'm a Christian." His scowl deepened. "I don't care much for Christians, these days."

"But if you don't care for Christians, that leaves you with gamblers and thieves."

Nat regarded her steadily. "The folks who left you here alone with your papa—were they Christians?"

"They professed to be."

Nat nodded. "And they left you here to fend for yourself if you could. Doesn't seem like a good thing to do."

"Well, I suppose not all Christians are as good as they could be."

"And not all folks who aren't Christians are as bad as they could be," Nat said. "Some aren't bad at all."

"I suppose that's so."

"You say your prayer and we'll get along," Nat said.

Elizabeth said a silent prayer at Papa's grave. It was hard, leaving him here. She would never find this spot again, out here in the middle of the prairie. Nat stood by his horse, watching without comment. His face was sorrowful. Old sorrow, Elizabeth thought, memories of graves that he had left behind.

When Elizabeth looked up, he mounted his horse. She realized then that he expected her to drive the oxen.

"I've never driven the oxen before," she told him. "Papa or Edward always did that."

He shrugged, looking down at her from the back of his horse. "I reckon there's a first time for everything," he said. "You might as well try."

She took the whip from the wagon seat and flicked it out, doing her best to imitate Edward's smooth motion. The lash arced languidly through the air without a sound.

"Use your whole arm, not just your wrist," Nat suggested. "Here." He leaned down from the horse and took the whip from her. With a snap of his arm, he sent it rippling through the air to crack—not as sharply as Edward had cracked it, but loudly nonetheless. The oxen lifted their heads and took notice.

He handed the whip back to Elizabeth. She tried it and got a feeble snap.

"You'll get it with practice," Nat said. "Let's get them moving."

"Giddap!" Elizabeth shouted, but the oxen didn't move. She raised her voice. "Giddap!" Oliver lifted his head and shuffled his feet, but the others did not move. "Giddap, Sikes!" she shouted. "Giddap, Fagin. Giddap there!" She cracked the whip and the end of the lash fell lightly on Sikes's flank. The ox reluctantly leaned into the yoke. "Move, Sikes. Get a move on." She snapped the whip again, trying to use her whole arm. By chance, the lash tickled Sikes's flank again, and the ox moved slowly forward, leading the team after.

It took constant shouting and attention to keep the oxen moving. Nat rode alongside her for a time, then rode ahead. After a bit, Elizabeth lost sight of him.

The trail beside the river was unmistakable: ruts had been worn in the grass by hundreds of wagons before her. The wind made the prairie grasses shift and billow. For miles and miles ahead, she could see nothing but more prairie. All around her, insects cried in the grass, a constant trilling that rose and fell in waves.

Once, she startled a herd of pronghorn antelope that had been drinking at the river. The graceful creatures bounded away, stopping at a safe distance to look back and study the ungainly oxen and the wagon they pulled. Once, the wagon passed a prairie-dog town: the curious animals sat up on their haunches, peering cautiously toward Elizabeth. One barked a warning to the others and they all vanished down their holes.

Always a little frightened, always a little lonely, Elizabeth watched for Indians. No sign of Nat. She did not stop to eat a noon meal: she chewed on dried beef and johnnycake left over from dinner. She worried about Nat. Surely he wouldn't leave her. He was young, but he carried a rifle with confidence and he offered some protection.

Late in the day, she saw him on the trail ahead. He lifted his hand in a casual wave and rode up beside the wagon. "Dinner for tonight," he said matter-of-factly, waving at the sage hen that dangled from his saddle. "There's a place to make camp not far ahead."

She smiled at him, relieved and unwilling to let him know that she had worried.

She cooked a fine dinner that night—roast sage hen, johnnycake with honey, and stewed dried apples for dessert.

"With luck, we'll catch the wagon train soon," Elizabeth said. "Peter Akin said he would take a day to rest the oxen."

Nat nodded, but didn't comment.

That night, Elizabeth did not lie awake. Her right arm ached from wielding the whip. She was tired, bone tired.

She could hear Nat's movements as he put another buffalo chip on the fire, laid out his bedroll, checked on the horses. Prairie wolves howled in the distance. She thanked the good Lord for sending Nathan to help her. An unlikely savior, but a savior nonetheless.

14

Nadya lay by the fire, listening to the distant wolves. She re-sisted the urge to return their call. Elizabeth was skittish and fearful, and Nadya did not want to disturb her rest.

Nadya closed her eyes, thinking about Elizabeth. When Nadya rode up with the oxen, she had intended to return the animals and travel on alone. That was what she told herself.

Then she talked to Elizabeth, a tall woman with dark hair and deep blue eyes. Talking to her in the morning sunlight, Nadya could remember seeing Elizabeth running frightened in the darkness. "Perhaps we could travel together," Elizabeth had said. Lurking beneath Elizabeth's serenity, barely concealed, Nadya could see the fear. Fear of the prairie, fear of the wolves, fear of all the dangers on the trail.

Nadya had declined the offer of companionship, preferring to be alone. And then Elizabeth reached out and took her hand. She remembered the touch of Elizabeth's hand on hers, cool smooth skin on her dry callused hand. After the weeks of traveling alone, after the night of fear and flight, the touch of Elizabeth's hand was like a benediction, a blessing.

In that moment, when Elizabeth touched her, Nadya forgave this tall, blue-eyed woman for fearing the wolves in the night. "Please travel with me for a time," Elizabeth had pleaded. "Until I catch up with the wagon train." In that moment, Nadya had known that she would help Elizabeth for as long as she needed help.

Nadya could not leave this woman. Elizabeth gave her tea that tasted like the tea Nadya's mother brewed. Sweet and hot and served in a china cup. Elizabeth served her biscuits, hot biscuits that smelled of home. Elizabeth touched her hand—no one had touched her since she left her parent's cabin—and the warmth of skin on skin held her.

Nadya closed her eyes and the music of distant howling lulled her to sleep.

* * *

They got an early start the next day. In the eastern sky, the rising sun touched wispy clouds with pink and orange. It was a warm day, likely to get warmer. In the low bushes by the river, a meadowlark warbled, high and sweet.

Elizabeth made a fire and heated water for tea; she warmed the leftover johnnycake by the fire and they ate breakfast. "Did you sleep well?" Elizabeth asked Nadya.

Nadya looked up from her tea. So strange to have another person to talk with. "Well enough," she said.

"I heard wolves howling," Elizabeth said. "I worried a bit." Dark blue eyes, a little anxious.

"Don't worry about that," Nadya said, frowning a little. "Don't worry about wolves."

Nadya took the oxen to the river for water, while Elizabeth packed the wagon. Together, they yoked the oxen. Elizabeth told her the oxen's names—the strangest names for oxen that Nadya had ever heard.

"Fagin? Artful Dodger? What kind of names are those?"

"They're characters in Dickens," Elizabeth explained, obviously surprised that Nadya didn't know.

"Dickens?" Nadya shook her head. "Like 'go to the dickens'?"

"No, no. The author, Charles Dickens."

Nadya frowned and shook her head.

"He wrote a book called *Oliver Twist* about a poor orphan named Oliver and how he made his way in the world."

"Seem like highfalutin names for oxen," Nadya observed.

"Maybe so," Elizabeth admitted.

But no matter how highfalutin their names, the oxen acted like all other oxen: stubborn when it came to the yoke. When Bill Sikes tossed his head and fought the yoke, Elizabeth slipped and fell, but she scrambled back to her feet and tried again. She was ineffectual, but willing to work. She would learn, Nadya thought.

Elizabeth walked alongside the wagon, driving the oxen, and Nadya rode ahead, allegedly to look for the wagon train that had left Elizabeth behind, but actually because she preferred to ride alone, looking out over the swaying grasses. She promised that she would return to the wagon when the sun was high, to join Elizabeth for the noon meal.

She was a few miles ahead of the wagon, riding a short distance away from the wagon trail, when she caught the scent of humans and horses. The prairie grass had begun to spring back, but she could see evidence that a party on horseback had passed that way.

She dismounted and examined the ground. There were hoofprints of unshod horses—maybe Indian ponies. A dozen or so. And along with them, the hoof prints of settlers' horses—larger animals that had been shod. The hoof prints were heading away from the river. They were at least a day old—the grass was still recovering. Not a hunting party—they were heading away from the buffalo trails.

Wary, she headed back to the trail and met the wagon. She did not mention the Indian sign to Elizabeth, but she rode alongside the wagon, keeping her rifle ready.

The sun was high when she caught the scent of wood smoke on the breeze. Far ahead, she saw something white in the sun—the arched canvas of a wagon.

"Look there," Nadya said. She pointed to the distant wagon, standing motionless in the sun.

"It's the wagon train," Elizabeth said. "We've caught up."

Nadya sat still, staring at the wagon. Near it were two other blackened shapes, each about the size of the wagon. She watched for movement—for people or animals. Nothing. The smell of ashes was strong.

"The wagons have been burned," Nadya said. "And I don't see any people about. You'd best stay here. I'll go and see—"

"No. Don't leave." Elizabeth shook her head. She scrambled up into the wagon and emerged with a pistol, which she clutched awkwardly. "It would be better to stay together."

Nadya hesitated, then shrugged. The Indian trail had been at least a day old. The smell of ashes was muted, damped down by an evening of dew. Indians were not likely to have lingered. "All right."

Elizabeth flicked the whip and clicked her tongue to the oxen. The beasts pulled and the wagon jerked forward.

As they approached, two buzzards flew up from the trail, flapping heavily. Nadya could smell blood, mixed with the scent of smoke. A man's body lay facedown beside the trail. His homespun shirt was stained red-brown where arrows had pierced him. The arrows were gone, reclaimed by the Indians. His torn shirt flapped in the wind, revealing blackened wounds and the work of hungry buzzards.

A cloud of flies rose from the body as Nadya dismounted and approached. She could see a trail of ants climbing up the man's side and disappearing into a tear in the shirt. She did not look too closely at what they carried away. Kneeling beside the body, she turned it over. By the smell, she guessed that he had been dead for a day or more.

She glanced up at Elizabeth. "Do you know him?"

Elizabeth's face was pale. "Peter Akin," Elizabeth said. "He always said. . . he used to say that he would kill some wild Indians when he got out West."

Nadya nodded. "Maybe he thought he could kill an Indian and pay nothing for it," she said. She stared down at the man. Kill an Indian; kill a wolf; kill anything you didn't like, anyone who got in your way. "Well, he was wrong." She glanced up at Elizabeth. "I saw signs that a group of Indians, herding horses, passed near the trail a day ago. Most likely, they're long gone."

Nadya glanced toward the burned wagons. "You stay here," she said. "I'll see if anyone's left alive."

This time, Elizabeth did not argue. She gripped her pistol in both hands and her knuckles were white. Her hands were trembling, but she nodded.

Nadya rode toward the wagons. They had been circled; in the center of the circle were the remnants of a campfire, long since out. Clearly, the emigrants had been camped when the Indians came upon them.

Buzzards lifted their heads to glare at Nadya as she approached. "Get," she shouted. "Go on, get!" She urged her horse toward the birds and they took reluctant flight. More dead: four other men, positioned by the wagons; three women and four children, cowering together by the only wagon that had not burned. The reek of ashes and blood filled the air. There was no sound except wind in the prairie grass and the croaking of crows that perched on the charred hoops of a burned wagon.

Boxes and trunks had been tossed about and broken, their contents strewn in the grass. She looked down and saw the photograph of a woman, gazing up at her from behind cracked glass. There were white goose feathers caught in the blades of grass, floating on the wind. A tattered calico bag—once a featherbed, now empty—lay crumpled on the ground.

One of the women lay facedown. A breeze caught her skirt and Nadya's horse shied away from the flapping cloth. "Whoa!" Nadya called, tugging angrily at the reins. "Easy now."

She felt a knot in her stomach: a mix of fear and anger. Fear of death, of destruction. Anger at the Indians—but more than that. She was angry at the emigrants who had brought this upon themselves, at the dead man, who thought that Indians and, no doubt, wolves, should be shot on sight.

She peered through the canvas flap at the back of the unburned wagon. Here, too, boxes and bags were scattered. A bag of flour had burst open, and the wind had dusted the wreckage with white. Flour had drifted against the trunks, settled into the folds of a rumpled blanket.

There were footprints in the flour—small feet heading toward the front of the wagon. Nadya sniffed the air and caught a human scent. She heard a sound—a tiny rustling, like a prairie mouse in a cupboard. She turned toward the sound. A pair of dark eyes glittered in the shadow behind a box.

"Come on out," she said roughly, her tone colored by the anger and fear that knotted her stomach. "Whoever you are, come out."

A girl squeezed from behind the box. Her face was dirty, except where tears had washed it clean. She was holding a pistol, leveled at Nadya.

"Hey, young'un. I'm not going to hurt you," Nadya said.

The girl didn't speak.

"What's your name?"

She did not lower the gun. "Jenny," she said.

"Do you know Elizabeth?" Nadya asked her. "She's outside."

The girl's expression changed, becoming a shade less desperate.

"I'll get her," Nadya said.

Nadya brought Elizabeth to the wagon and Jenny ran into her arms. Together, they sat in Elizabeth's wagon and Jenny told about what had happened to the wagon train. The Indians had come to the camp, asking for food. Peter Akin had refused them any gifts, and they had grown insistent. Then one of Peter's cousins saw the leather strap of a bridle dangling beneath an Indian's blanket: the Indian had stolen the bridle from his wagon. The cousin snatched the bridle back.

"Then Pa shot the Injun," Jenny said. "And I hid in the back of the wagon. There was a lot of shooting. Then everyone was dead." Her voice trembled.

Elizabeth's face was pale and set. Her arms were locked around Jenny, holding the girl, protecting her.

"We'd best be going," Nadya said softly. "This is no place to stay. The Indians could be back."

"I wonder. . . ." Elizabeth stopped, and began again, speaking tentatively. "I think we should give them a Christian burial."

Nadya squinted at the wagon train. The idea of lingering in this place of death chilled her. The Indians were not likely to return, but even so, the spot seemed cursed.

"We can't stay here," Nadya said. "We have to move on. Let it be."

Elizabeth hesitated, frowning. "The buzzards will eat them," she murmured. "And the wolves. . . ." Her face was wet with tears.

"The wolves won't touch them," Nadya said. It turned her stomach to think of it. "And as for the buzzards—it's natural enough. The birds will eat the flesh and the ants will clean the bones. We have to go."

"Say a prayer with me." Elizabeth bowed her head. "Dear Lord, please bless all the good people of this wagon train and gather them to your bosom and protect them and keep them from harm. And keep us safe from the savages who live in these wild lands." Her voice faltered. "And guide us to California. Amen."

Jenny echoed, "Amen."

"Let's be on our way," Nadya said. She clicked her tongue to the oxen, urging them forward.

Nadya rode ahead of the wagon, always in sight but far enough away to make conversation impossible. She did not want to talk about the emigrants and the Indians. The death and destruction had left her saddened, angry, and confused. She kept seeing the gaze of the woman in the photograph.

Elizabeth did not call for a rest at noon and Nadya did not suggest it. Though the oxen grew weary, they kept traveling, eager to put distance between themselves and the wreckage of the wagon train.

That evening, they made camp in a bend of the river. The water protected them on two sides, but there were no trees or other shelter. Nadya felt exposed, visible to any marauding Pawnees that lingered nearby. The Indians had left, she was reasonably certain of that, but even that did not soothe her nerves. The memory of Peter Akin's arrow-riddled body remained with her. As she watered the horses and oxen, she found herself scanning the horizon and testing the breeze, searching for any sign that something might be amiss. Her pistol was holstered at her belt, and she kept her rifle at her side. She was tense, on edge.

She tethered the oxen near the wagon, and returned to where Elizabeth was building a fire in a shallow depression. She was arranging three large rocks to form a sort of tripod on which the cast-iron pan could rest. Jenny was gathering what fuel she could find. There was no wood on the open prairie, but there were other things to burn. Dried buffalo droppings and knots of dry prairie grass burned with a hot odorless flame.

Nadya squatted by the fireplace, watching Elizabeth work.

"Where's your pistol?" Nadya asked suddenly. She had assumed that Elizabeth would keep the weapon handy, an obvious precaution.

Elizabeth looked up, startled by Nadya's tone. "In the wagon," she said. "Just inside, by the wagon seat."

Nadya frowned at her. "Why don't you have it with you? That's quite a ways to run, with an Injun after you."

Elizabeth glanced toward the wagon. "I suppose you're right. I didn't think about it."

"The people in your wagon train didn't think," Nadya said sharply. "There's no room out here for people who don't think. You need to keep your pistol primed and at your side. Bring it here—along with any other rifles you've got."

Elizabeth bit her lip and started toward the wagon. She returned with the pistol in one hand and a rifle tucked under one arm. Nadya noticed that she carried the rifle like a piece of firewood, clutching it awkwardly beneath her arm. The pistol drooped in her hand.

"You don't know how to shoot, do you?" Nadya asked.

"Papa didn't think it was right for a lady. And he and Edward were here to protect me." She stooped, put the weapons on the ground, and then stood and looked up at Nadya, biting her lip. Her face was pale. "And I don't see the need to . . . to bully me and shout about it."

Startled, Nadya spoke softly. "I didn't mean to bully you."

Elizabeth turned away and knelt by the fireplace. She pushed angrily at one of the rocks, shifting it into a better spot. "I don't know how to shoot," she said, not looking up at Nadya. "I fired the pistol just one time—at a wolf that was prowling by the oxen."

Elizabeth stopped rearranging the rocks and looked up. Her face was wet with tears. "I don't know what to do. I'm so afraid."

"There now," Nadya said, putting her arm around Elizabeth's shoulders and making the same sort of noises she would make to soothe a spooked horse. "Easy now."

"I don't know how to shoot. And you were so angry," Elizabeth said. "So angry that I was afraid you'd leave us."

"I'll show you how to shoot. Just take it easy now." She rubbed Elizabeth's shoulders. "I'll show you how tonight."

Elizabeth rubbed her sleeve across her face, leaving a streak of dirt behind. Nadya saw Jenny returning with a handful of buffalo chips and felt Elizabeth straighten her back. Nadya stood up hastily. "Hello, Jenny," she said. "I'm going to teach Elizabeth to shoot."

Jenny carried an armload of buffalo chips to the fireplace and set them down. "To shoot?" she said, staring at Nadya.

"That's right. I learned to shoot when I was younger than you. If we need to defend ourselves, I don't want to be the only one who knows how to pull a trigger. Before I'm done, you'll both be loading and shooting like Texas Rangers."

15

Jenny sat and watched Nat load the rifle and listened to him talk. Jenny knew how to be very still and quiet—a handy skill in a large family. If you sat still and quiet, people forgot you were there sometimes, and that could be good. When Pa was drinking or Ma was angry, it was just as well to be forgotten. She sat quietly and watched and listened.

"I wouldn't trust my life to the pistol," Nat was saying. "It's unreliable at best—won't fire when you need it. And even when it does fire, you can't hit anything that ain't in spitting range. You point it in the general direction of whatever you want to hit, then wait until you're real close. You only get one chance, then you have to reload, so you better make sure. Now this musketoon's a bit better. The barrel's rifled so if you're good and if you're lucky, you could hit a deer at a hundred—maybe a hundred fifty paces." Nat shrugged. "My rifle—that's a Hawken rifle—will do better than that. But even so, this 'un's better than the pistol."

Jenny glanced at Elizabeth. She had her hands folded in her lap, watching Nat and listening intently.

"Now I'm going to show you how to load. Pay attention here." Nat glanced at Jenny and she nodded, to show she was paying attention. "Start with one measure of powder," he said, pouring black powder from his powder horn into a cup that had been carved from a deer antler. Jenny watched as he poured the powder from the cup into the barrel of the musket. "Now you need a ball and a patch." Nat took a lead ball from the pouch at his side and slapped it onto a strip of cotton. With his knife, he cut the cloth strip so that the ball sat on a small square of cloth. He pushed ball and patch into the barrel of the musket. "Use your short starter to get the ball on its way," he said, taking a rod attached to a brass knob and shoving the rod into the barrel. "Then use the ramrod to take it all the way home." He pushed the ramrod down the musket's barrel. "Now she's loaded, and you've got to prime her. You pull back on this here."

"What's that called?" Elizabeth asked.

Nat stopped and smiled, just a little. "I don't reckon its name matters much. It'll work fine even if you don't call it by name."

"I'll remember better if I know the name," Elizabeth said. Her voice was steady, but it held a stubborn note.

Nat's smile grew broader and he nodded. "All right, then, it's called a frisson. Now you pull this here halfway back—this is called the cock and what you're doing is cocking the musket. Put priming powder into the pan till it's 'bout half full. Now put the frisson down. And it's ready to fire."

He looked at Jenny and she nodded solemnly. She had watched her father and her brothers shoot their rifles, but her mother hadn't known how to shoot the rifle. Neither had her sisters. Women didn't shoot rifles. It seemed strange that Nat didn't know that.

"Now there's my target—that rock over yonder." He pointed at a small rock that he'd set atop a distant boulder. "To fire, I pull back the cock all the way." He did so. "I put the gun to my shoulder and I hold it steady. And then I squeeze the trigger."

There was a flash of light in the priming pan and a tremendous explosion, accompanied by a cloud of white smoke. Jenny jumped back at the sound, covering her ears. When she looked to see what had happened to the distant rock, it had disappeared.

"Blasted it out of there," he said with satisfaction. "All right, your turn." He held the musket out to Elizabeth, who looked at it as if it were a snake that might bite her. "Take it now," he said. "And load it."

Elizabeth did not move. "I've never done such a thing before," she said, her voice uneasy. "I don't know if I. . . ."

"Have you ever crossed the prairie before?" Nat asked, his voice was soft and even.

"Well, no, of course I haven't."

"Have you ever protected yourself from Indians before?"

"Why, no," Elizabeth said, with just a hint of anger in her voice. "You know I haven't."

"Well, when you try new things, you have to learn new ways." He still held out the musket. Reluctantly, Elizabeth took it by the stock. "Now you load it, and Jenny, you put that rock back in place."

Jenny ran and found the rock on the far side of the boulder. Its smooth surface was chipped and hot where the bullet had struck the stone. Touching that chipped surface, she felt a little frightened, as if the stone itself now held some sort of power and significance.

When she returned to her companions, Nat was showing Elizabeth how to hold the musket. "Brace it against your shoulder—like this. She'll kick like a mule when you pull the trigger, and if you don't hold it tight against you, the stock will slam into your shoulder." Jenny watched as Nat adjusted Elizabeth's hands, so that she gripped the rifle firmly. "Just hold it for a moment. Get used to having it in your hands. And point it at that rock over there."

Elizabeth frowned in concentration.

"I want you to knock it right off the boulder," Nat said. He moved so that he was standing close behind her. "Hold your musket steady." He put his hands on Elizabeth's, positioning the rifle and helping her steady it. "Good. Hold it." He moved his hands away, and she stood stiffly with the rifle at her shoulder. "Now squeeze the trigger."

Elizabeth squeezed the trigger. The explosion was loud, but Jenny was ready for it this time, and she kept her eyes on the distant rock. It remained where it was. Then Elizabeth was coughing, lowering the rifle and stepping away from the cloud of white smoke.

"That was fine," Nat said, taking the rifle from her hands. "But next time, don't jump when you hear the blast."

"It's a waste of powder," Elizabeth said. She was frowning, looking close to tears. "I didn't come anywhere close to hitting that rock."

Nat nodded. "Nope. You didn't come near it."

Her voice trembled. "Then why should I. . . ."

"When you learned how to read, did you start out with that book you told me about, that Dickens fellow?" Nat asked.

She shook her head without speaking.

"Where did you start?" Nat's voice was softer.

"I started with *McGuffy's First Reader,*" she said.

"So you start one place and you end up somewhere else," Nat

said. "Same with shooting. That's how it works." He patted her on the shoulder awkwardly. "You did fine for your first time. Tomorrow, you can try again. Now it's Jenny's turn."

Jenny was startled when he looked at her. She had thought that they both would have forgotten her by now. Nat studied her, and it seemed to Jenny that he knew what she was thinking. He handed her the rifle and she took it automatically.

"Jenny's too young to learn such a thing," Elizabeth began. "I don't think. . . ."

Nat kept watching Jenny. "What do you think, Jenny? Do you want to know how to shoot?"

Jenny looked down at the rifle and then back at Nat. She thought about the power that she had felt in the stone and imagined that power in her own hands. When the Indians had attacked the wagons, she had heard the guns going off, she had smelled the smoke of the black powder. But she had huddled in the wagon, frightened but unable to do anything.

"Yes," she said very softly. "I'd like to learn." She glanced at Elizabeth. "I think it would be a good idea. In case the Indians come back."

"Load it," Nat said. "Just like I did."

She held the rifle carefully, barrel pointed toward the sky, and gingerly measured black powder into the barrel. She looked up, and Nat nodded. "Go on." Jenny continued: cotton patch, lead ball, all rammed home; frisson back and cock pulled halfway back, priming powder into the pan.

"Well done," Nat said. "Now knock that rock off of there."

Jenny stood up slowly and lifted the rifle to her shoulder. The rock seemed very far away. "Set your feet wide apart," Nat said. "Stand steady, like a rock." He stood close behind her. She could feel the warmth of his hands through her dress as he adjusted the position of the stock against her shoulder. His hands were rough with calluses. He held her hands, his head looking over her shoulder, his breath warm on her neck. "You've got it. Now squeeze the trigger."

The powder in the pan exploded in a flash of flame and a blast of sound. The stock of the rifle slammed hard against her shoulder. The rock jumped and disappeared behind the boulder.

Her ears were ringing and her shoulder throbbed. She was

dazed and she felt like crying. But the rock was gone.

Nat clapped her on the back. "Fine shooting," Nat said. "You held steady. Good job."

Elizabeth stepped to her side and laid a hand on Jenny's head. "Are you all right?" she asked.

Jenny nodded. Yes, it seemed to her that she was all right. Her shoulder ached and her hands were trembling as Nat took the musket from her. But it seemed to her that the trembling came from a power deep inside of her.

"We'll try again tomorrow," Nat said. "With practice, you'll be able to load faster, shoot better. Like this."

Jenny watched as he loaded the rifle again, his hands racing through the steps. "Always make your first shot count," he told them as he worked. "Takes time to reload, and you may not have time. Here now." Rifle loaded, he reached down and picked a stone from the ground. "Toss this as high as you can."

Jenny took the stone. It was about as big around as a silver dollar. She threw it as hard as she could so that it flew high into the air, a speck of gray against the royal blue of the dusk sky. Nat raised the rifle and fired. The stone shattered in the air.

"You'll be doing that, by the time we get to California," Nat said with satisfaction.

At dinner, Jenny sat between Nat and Elizabeth, watching the last of the cooking fire burn down. Buffalo chips and prairie grass burned quickly and left no coals behind.

Nat was leaning back on his hands, looking up at the sky. Dusk had faded to darkness and the first stars, a few bright points, had appeared overhead. In the east, the moon was rising. A few days past full, it cast a silver light over the open land. There were no colors in this moonlit world—the prairie grass was as gray as the hair on an old man's head; the wagon top was white; the bed and running gear were black; the Platte was a ribbon of silver.

From the river, Jenny could hear the sweet high chirping of young frogs—the spring peepers that scattered before her when she went to the river to get water. It seemed so quiet, there in the camp with only her and Elizabeth and Nat. So quiet, with all her family gone. It had never been so quiet around their camp. Pa would have been talking and joking with the other men; one of the children would have been crying—down with the colic or some such; Ma would have been chatting with a cousin or scolding one of her brothers.

From overhead, she heard the cry of a night hawk, hunting for its dinner. In the distance, a wolf howled—a long thin wail that was joined, after a moment, by a chorus of others.

Elizabeth shivered. Though the night was warm, she drew her shawl around her shoulders. "I hate that sound. It sends chills up my spine." She looked at Jenny and smiled. "After we know how to shoot, those varmints better not come around here at night. Not if they know what's good for them."

Jenny saw Nat glance at Elizabeth with a strange expression on his face. The moonlight reflected from his eyes. In that moment, he looked like a painter or a coon, caught in the glow of torchlight. "Why do you hate them?" he asked. His voice was flat and even.

Elizabeth turned to look at him, obviously startled at his tone. "I don't know what you mean, exactly," she stammered. "They frighten me."

"They belong here," Nat said. "What have they ever done to you, that you want to kill them?" His voice was very soft. Jenny could not read his expression in the moonlight, but she knew that he was tense by the set of his shoulders, the angle of his head.

Jenny pulled her legs in close to her body, wrapping her arms around them and making herself very small. She would sit very still and no one would ask her what she thought about any of this.

"The night that the oxen stampeded—it was a wolf that frightened them," Elizabeth said, her voice unsteady.

Nat shook his head. "It was the sound of a pistol shot that made the oxen stampede. Not the wolf. Don't blame the wolves for your foolishness." He turned his face away, looking out over the open prairie. "Maybe I'm doing wrong by teaching you to shoot. Don't know who or what you'll kill."

A wolf howled and again a chorus answered.

"Listen to them," Nat demanded. "What do you hear?"

"I don't know." Elizabeth's voice was shaky. "Wolves, out

in the darkness. What's wrong, Nat? You're frightening me."

"Why do you want to kill them? Listen and tell me," Nat insisted.

"I hear dangerous animals, wild beasts. They'll attack us, kill the oxen."

"You're not listening to the wolves. You're listening to one of those books of yours, to what other people say." Nat spoke quickly, a burst of angry words. "You're afraid of the darkness, so you want to kill the wolves that live in the darkness. The men in the wagon train were afraid of the Indians, so they wanted to kill the Indians. I've known people like those men. They say 'The only good Indian is a dead Indian. The only good wolf is a dead wolf. This black man—he should be my slave.'

"People like that say 'I will push you away and take your land, and if you fight back then I'll say you are a savage and a beast and I'll kill you.' People like that, they never stop and listen."

Nat sat still for a moment. "Listen carefully. Here now." He tilted back his head and let loose a howl that made the hair stand up on the back of Jenny's neck. His voice rose, expanding to fill the wilderness that surrounded them. The world was empty and they were alone, all alone in the great darkness. A moment of silence, then the distant wolves responded with their plaintive chorus.

"Can't you hear what they are saying?" Nat asked. "Can't you hear it?"

"They're saying it's awful lonely," Jenny said. She hadn't meant to say anything, but she couldn't help herself. The words were out before she could stop them. "Way out there in the darkness. They're out there and they're lonely and they can't come in."

Nat turned to look at her. Jenny could see only the glitter of his eyes in the moonlight. "Yes, it's lonely," he said. "But when one wolf in the pack calls, another one answers. And they say, 'You're not alone. We're here. The world isn't empty.' They are calling the moon up from where she sleeps below the horizon. They are calling to the buffalo—the buffalo know the wolves and the wolves know the buffalo. They speak to each other and they understand each other. The buffalo know that the wolves will hunt them, and that is always how it has been."

"But it's so sad, out there in the dark," Jenny said. "So sad."

Nat shrugged. "A little sad, sometimes. But the darkness belongs to them. The darkness and the moonlight. This is their world. Sometimes, they catch the scent of a fire, and they come to see what new thing has come into their world. Sometimes they watch wagons drawn by great dull oxen lumber across their land, wearing away the grass and leaving a trail behind. They are curious about the new creatures who come to their land." He looked at Elizabeth. "But that's no reason to shoot them. No reason at all. That's no reason to be afraid of them. The wolves do you no harm. Let them be."

His voice was calmer now. He kept on looking at Elizabeth. "I'll teach you to shoot, but you mustn't shoot wolves."

"I won't," Elizabeth said. "I didn't mean to. . . . I won't shoot wolves."

"I won't shoot wolves, either," Jenny said.

Nat put his arm around her shoulders and hugged her gently. "I know you won't. I know."

Jenny sat in silence, glad of the warmth of Nat's arm around her shoulders. The wolves had fallen silent, and the sound of the frogs from the river was loud.

"I think it's time to go to bed," Elizabeth said at last. "We'll be up early."

In the wagon, Jenny lay awake for a time, listening to Elizabeth breathe. Elizabeth had made her a cozy bed of quilts between two trunks. She had always slept with her little sister, a warm body next to her, and she felt lonely, sleeping by herself. Outside, she could hear Nat's boots on the prairie soil as he spread his bedroll. Then he was quiet and there was only the chirping of the frogs. At last she slept.

She woke up screaming.

She had not screamed when the Indians had searched the wagons. When the fighting started, she had squeezed into a corner of the wagonbed, behind the trunk filled with clothes and the box that held all of Ma's cooking pots. One corner of the quilt that covered the trunk hung down, hiding her head. She crouched in her hiding place, as quiet as the boxes that hid her.

She had not screamed, not even when she saw the dreadful

face of an Indian—bronze head shaved except for a crest of hair. She could see him clearly through a crack between the trunk and the box. He was laughing, a laugh that was almost a snarl, and he was saying something in a savage language to one of the others. She could see a knife in his hand, its bright blade flashing as he slashed open a bag of flour and sent up a cloud of fine white powder.

If she could see him, then surely he could see her just as clearly. In a moment, he would look her way, and she would scream as she had heard her sisters and her mother screaming a moment before. In a moment, he would find her.

She heard another Indian calling outside the wagon, a babble of guttural words that made no sense. The savage turned away from her hiding place; she felt the wagon sway as he jumped down from the wagonbed. And still she fought the scream that wanted to escape, wanted to rise like the howling of wolves.

In the dream, she could not stop the scream—it was too strong for her. And as she screamed, she knew that the Indian would return to take her scalp and leave her for dead. But she could not stop screaming.

"Jenny!" The voice was Elizabeth's, but Jenny felt the Indian's hands on her shoulders and fought him, lashing out with her fists. She struck someone, and the hands released her shoulders. "Jenny." Elizabeth's voice, more softly this time. "It's all right." A hand grabbed her fist so that she could not punch again. It was a soft hand, too small to belong to the Indian. Jenny opened her eyes. In the moonlight that filtered through the canvas, she could make out Elizabeth, sitting on the edge of the bed. Her hair was loose; the collar of her flannel nightdress rose around her neck.

"The Indians," Jenny said. "They were here." She sat up in bed and looked around the wagon, searching for the Indian with the knife.

A shadow fell across the opening to the wagon, and the wagon swayed as someone stepped up into it. Jenny started, staring wildly toward the figure that blocked the moonlight.

"No Indians here," Nat said. "No Indians for miles."

"It was just a dream," Elizabeth murmured. "Just a bad dream."

"How do you know?" Jenny said, clutching the quilt more

tightly around her and speaking to the shadowy figure of Nat. "How do you know there are no Indians for miles?"

Nat stepped into the wagon, filling the doorway. "They've taken their stolen horses and ridden away, afraid that more white men will come and kill them for the murder they've done."

"How do you know?" Jenny repeated. "They might be out there in the dark."

"I'd smell them if they were. But the wind is clean and sweet—nothing but the smell of prairie grass and buffalo." He crouched on the wagonbed beside her nest of blankets.

"You can smell Indians?" she asked. "What do they smell like?"

"Those ones left the smell of bear grease and whiskey and blood. And wild ponies and face paint and buffalo robes. And fear and hate—that, too."

In the light from the opening, she saw the glitter of his eyes—golden eyes, like no one else had. She reached out and took hold of his hand for reassurance. "If you can smell Indians, can you smell white men, too?"

Nat nodded. "White men reek of tobacco and black powder and oxen and wood smoke. Always wood smoke—they light so many fires to keep back the darkness."

"And there ain't any Indians near here?"

"No Indians. No white men. Just the prairie and the wolves."

Jenny lay back on her bed.

"Don't worry, little one," Nat said. "I'll keep you safe."

Jenny looked up at Nat. His face, illuminated by lantern light, was filled with concern. His voice was soft.

"Why?"

"Because my mama and papa are dead, too. So we have to take care of each other."

"You promise?"

"I promise."

"Will you go to sleep now?" Nat asked her.

"I don't want you to leave," she said, still clinging to his hand.

"I'll sing you to sleep," he said. "Listen now—I'll sing to you." He started to sing softly in a language she didn't recognize.

"What does it mean?" she asked. "I don't understand."

"It's a song my papa used to sing to me. It says 'Sleep, little one. The wolves will watch your bed and sing to you. All is well. Go to sleep and the wolves will keep guard.' Now hush." He kept holding her hand, and he sang again. She closed her eyes, thinking of the wolves that kept watch. The animals had Nat's golden eyes. When she fell asleep, she did not remember her dreams.

16

■

At dawn, Elizabeth woke to Nat's voice, speaking softly to the oxen. "Come on there, Oliver. Move along, Bill Sikes." The jangling of the harness was punctuated by the clanging of the bell that hung around Sweet Nancy's neck. The sounds faded slowly. Elizabeth guessed that Nat was taking the stock down to the river for water.

She dressed silently, leaving Jenny curled up in a tangle of quilts. The girl was sleeping peacefully now. When Elizabeth was fully dressed, she hesitated, looking at the gun belt that hung from the peg at the front of the wagon. It was Papa's belt, purchased in Independence and worn only a few times. Heavy leather, with a sturdy holster to hold the pistol. She strapped the belt over her dress and slipped the pistol into its holster.

The holster was standard Army issue: the leather pocket carried the pistol with the butt forward. To draw, she had to turn the back of her hand toward her body and pull the pistol out with a twisting motion. She tried it a few times, awkwardly at first, and then more easily.

The gun belt was tight around her hips; the gun was heavy in her hand. If her friends in Springfield could see her now, they would think she was mad. Elizabeth Metcalf, with a pistol in her hand, traveling across the prairie with a young man that she had met just two days before and a young girl whose parents had been killed by Indians. She slipped the pistol back in its holster, glanced in the mirror, and smoothed back a strand of hair that had escaped its braid.

She heard the snorting of the oxen returning from the river and she climbed down from the wagon. Nat glanced at the pistol. He made no comment, but he smiled when he saw it.

"Jenny is still sleeping," she said. "She's worn out. I'll wake her when breakfast is ready."

Nat nodded and began to turn away. Impulsively, Elizabeth reached out and touched his arm. "Wait, Nat."

He stopped, his eyes on her face. When he watched her so closely, she felt that she was being judged. The night before, when he was reassuring Jenny, he had seemed warm and kind. Now, she wasn't sure. She forced herself to go on.

"I just wanted to thank you for all you've done. For teaching me to shoot, for helping with Jenny. I don't know what would have become of us without you."

He nodded again. "Seemed like the only thing to do."

She looked down, avoiding his eyes. "Last night, when I was going to sleep, I listened to the wolves howling. And for the first time, I wasn't afraid of them." She looked up and met his eyes. "If you help me, I can learn."

He smiled then, and patted her arm gently. "You'll do fine," he said easily. "You and Jenny both." He turned away then, calling to the oxen. Elizabeth watched him, feeling that she had just passed a test of some kind.

At breakfast, Nat joked with Jenny and Elizabeth—friendly and easygoing. He was particularly solicitous of Jenny, insisting that she eat two helpings of corn bread. "You won't have the strength to lift that rifle if you don't eat," he joked.

As they traveled along the river, he stayed close by the wagon. After a time, he asked Jenny if she would like to ride on a horse, rather than on the seat of the wagon. When she said yes, he dismounted and hoisted her to the horse's back. At Elizabeth's insistence, Jenny rode as a lady should—sidesaddle with one foot hooked in the stirrup. She clung to the saddle horn with both hands at first. After a time, she relaxed and let one hand rest on the saddle horn, the other in her lap.

Nat led the horse and they walked at Elizabeth's side as she drove the oxen. The pistol was heavy on her leg; her arm was tired from wielding the whip, but she felt oddly comfortable, walking beside Nat.

As they walked, Nat began to sing the lively tune that he had been singing two days before, when he brought her oxen back to camp. Elizabeth could not identify the language, but she recognized the tune. She listened closely as Nat sang, and when he returned to the chorus, she joined in, mimicking his words as best she could. Nat rewarded her with a brilliant smile. On the third repetition of the chorus, Jenny sang as well, her voice as sweet as the chirping of the small birds that flew up from the prairie grasses at their approach.

"It's a pretty song," Elizabeth said when they were done. "So lighthearted."

"My father taught it to me," Nat said. "We sang it together when we were plowing the fields." His smile faded then.

Elizabeth hesitated, watching his face. "You miss your father," she said softly. "I understand. I miss my father, too."

"That's so," Nat said. He glanced at Jenny, who was barking at the prairie dogs in a prairie-dog village not far from the trail.

"You know," Elizabeth went on. "We're all three orphans here. So we aren't really alone. We each have the other two."

Nat nodded, but didn't reply. Elizabeth studied the set of his shoulders, and said no more.

When the sun was high in the sky, they stopped to rest the oxen and eat their midday meal. The trail ran close beside the river and the oxen grazed quietly, cropping the grass that grew on the riverbank. The river was wide here, with a low green island in the center. A few miles ahead, Elizabeth could see a sandstone outcropping rising from the flat land, a startling change in the monotonous landscape.

Elizabeth spread out a picnic—cold johnnycake, salted pork, lemonade—while Nat and Jenny went down the the river to fetch water. At Elizabeth's suggestion, Jenny took a bit of soap along. From her place by the wagon, Elizabeth heard the pair of them splashing. They came back with the bucket filled with water and both their faces washed clean of dust. Nat carried his hat in his hand. His hair was wet—he had washed it in the river and combed back with his fingers. One ragged lock was falling into his eyes.

Elizabeth shook her head and clicked her tongue when she

saw him. "Nat," she said softly. "I was just thinking—you would look nice with a proper haircut."

He ran his hand back over his head. "What's wrong with this one?"

She smoothed down her apron, wondering how honest to be. "Well, it looks a bit like you hacked it short with a hunting knife. I don't know what barber would treat a head of hair so cruelly."

Nat grinned. "Maybe so. But I don't see a barbershop anywhere nearby, so I guess it'll have to do."

"I could cut it with my sewing scissors," Elizabeth said. "I used to trim Papa's hair, now and again."

Nat ran a hand through his hair, then shrugged. "If you like."

After they ate, Elizabeth sat him on a boulder by the river and fetched a comb, her scissors, and a looking glass. "Now take a look at yourself," she said, holding the glass up to his face. "I want you to remember what you look like so that you'll know how much better you look when I'm done."

He made a face at himself in the mirror and then at Jenny. The girl watched him with wide eyes, but did not return his grin.

"Stop your larking and sit still," Elizabeth said, putting the glass aside. Sitting in front of her, he seemed much less formidable. He was, after all, very young. "We'll see what we can make of you, won't we, Jenny?"

She combed his hair back from his forehead and set to work. As she snipped at his hair, a prairie breeze caught the strands that she had cut free and carried them away.

"My hair is flying away," Nat said to Jenny. "Do you know where it will end up?"

Jenny shook her head, watching Nat intently.

"It'll fly away until it tangles in a clump of grass, somewhere far from here. And do you know what will happen then?"

"What?"

"Then a mouse will come out of her den to eat the grass seeds, and she'll find my hair tangled in the grass. She'll pick some up and take it into her burrow and use it to make her nest. And then when her little babies are born, they'll roll and squeak in a nest made of my hair."

Nat's hair was warm under Elizabeth's hands as she combed it out and snipped the ragged strands to make them even. Such thick dark hair, silky smooth beneath her hands. He smelled of soap and river water.

"What about the rest?" Jenny was saying. "What'll happen to the rest of your hair?"

"A meadowlark will find some, and she'll take it to build her nest, weaving my hair in with bits of grass and twigs to make a place to lay her eggs. And she'll sit on her eggs, keeping them warm until they hatch."

Elizabeth cut the hair around his ears so that it lay flat, rather than poking out awkwardly. There was something intimate about combing and cutting another person's hair, Elizabeth thought. She could never be a barber, for surely she would fall in love with every man whose hair she cut. She tried to dismiss that thought—she was being foolish and she knew it.

"And what about the rest?" Jenny persisted.

"Well, I reckon it'll tangle with another clump of grass and a buffalo will come along and stop to graze. She'll eat the grass and she'll eat the rest of my hair along with it, and go on her way, none the wiser. And there I'll be, all over the prairie, in the mouse's burrow and the meadowlark's nest and the buffalo's stomach."

Jenny laughed—a startling sound. Just the night before, Elizabeth would have said it would be a long time before Jenny was lighthearted enough to laugh.

"Here now," Elizabeth said, taking a stern motherly tone. She stood in front of Nat, taking a good look at him. Then she held up the glass. "In addition to spreading hair all over the prairie, we've improved the look of you, I think."

While Nat was looking in the mirror, she studied him. With his hair neatly trimmed and his face clean, he was a handsome young man. He glanced up and caught her looking. She blushed and took the mirror from his hand. "Enough of admiring yourself," she said. "We'd best be on our way."

That afternoon, the wagon ruts veered away from the river and climbed the low sandstone outcropping that Elizabeth had seen in the distance. Elizabeth called to the oxen, encouraging them to haul the wagon up the slope. She flicked the whip against the flank of Fagin, who was slacking off as usual.

When the trail reached the top of the bluff, she turned to look back. She could see for miles across the flat prairie. Far in the distance, she could see the green brush that surrounded the spring where they had camped the night before. Below, she could see the South Fork of the Platte, glittering in the late afternoon sun. It meandered across the prairie, bulging around the low islands and winding around the base of the bluff. Beside the river, she could make out the wagon ruts, a thin tracing of sandy brown. The trail was the only sign that humans had visited this vast landscape, and it was so faint that she could easily have missed it. She felt tiny and insignificant, an ant on a plate, following the trail of other ants.

"Come on, Elizabeth," Jenny called. She had walked ahead. "What are you waiting for?"

Elizabeth turned her back on the forbidding view and flicked the whip at Fagin. "I'm coming," she called. "I'm coming."

The trail followed the top of the bluff for a time, and then descended gradually into the valley down a slope that was bright with sunflowers. Here and there were strange mounds of earth—each one six to seven feet across and half a foot tall. Jenny and Nat, on foot now after a morning of riding, investigated and reported that the mounds were anthills, swarming with busy insects.

They reached the foot of the bluff late in the afternoon, and made camp where the trail passed close to the river. Nat watered the oxen and checked their hooves for any injury. The animals were doing well—working hard, but thriving on the grass of the river valley. Elizabeth took advantage of the late sun to air the bedding, spreading the quilts on the dry prairie grass.

While Jenny was gathering fuel for the fire, Elizabeth asked Nat for another shooting lesson. This time, he set a rock as the target, balancing it on the highest branch of a clump of scrubby bushes. Elizabeth loaded the musket under his supervision, and lifted it to shoot.

"Relax your shoulders," Nat said. "Make sure that your feet are set, like this." He planted his feet wide and lifted his own rifle to his shoulder. Feeling foolish, she imitated him. Her arms were tired from flicking the whip, but she did her best.

She shot at the rock and missed.

"You need to relax," he said. "Not so tense. Try again."

She reloaded and lifted the musket to her shoulder again. Nat moved to stand behind her and rested his hands gently on her shoulders. "Relax now," he said. She relaxed, but his hands remained where they were. "Line the end of the barrel up with the rock." She could feel his breath on her cheek. "Now, take the distance into account: aim high so that the bullet can drop as it flies." His hands left her shoulders. He reached around her and laid his hands on top of hers. His hands guided hers. "That's it. Keep your arms out straight. Now squeeze the trigger gently."

The gun jerked and flew upward. Elizabeth jumped at the sudden explosion. Her ears rang. She blinked at the target, but the rock was gone. Nat had released her. "I got it!" she said. "I hit it!"

She turned to face him, and found herself almost in his arms. For a moment, she did not move. She could feel the warmth of his body, smell the dust and sweat of the trail. It frightened her to stand so close to him—and yet she did not want to step away. She wanted to move closer—to kiss him or let him kiss her.

How strange to feel like this. She had never been one for flirting with men. Mama had died when she was only ten, and she had always known that she would take care of Papa. There had been no other man for her. Oh, once George Cramer, a young man who worked for Papa, had courted her. That was when Papa had been editing a newspaper, and George had written earnest essays about the importance of the Westward expansion. He had, once or twice, come to visit the house and sit with her in the parlor. At her cousin's wedding, he had danced with her, and then invited her out to take the air. In the shadows beside the house, he had taken her in his arms and kissed her. Reluctantly, she had pulled away from him and, standing a few paces away, had explained that she could never leave Papa. It was not long after that he had announced his intention to seek his fortune in the fur trade and write a book about the Far West. She had wondered, now and again, what might have happened if she had not avowed her intention to stay with Papa.

But Nat did not move to kiss her—though he must have known by the look in her eyes that he could. It would not have been proper to stand like this in Springfield, staring boldly into the eyes of a young man. But Springfield was far away. They were alone on the prairie and Nat was studying her face with his curious eyes.

"Thank you for teaching me," she said, and kissed his cheek in a sisterly fashion. A clap of thunder in the distance brought her back to her senses. "The quilts!" she cried, and ran to bring them in.

17

Nadya stood still, watching Elizabeth run to fold the quilts. For a moment, she could feel the lingering warmth of Elizabeth's body next to hers, the touch of Elizabeth's lips on her cheek. So soft, so gentle.

"Jenny!" Elizabeth cried. "Tie down the sides of the wagon."

Nadya helped Jenny tie down the wagon top's canvas sides, securing them against wind and rain. While they worked, Elizabeth ran back to the wagon, carrying the quilts. The thunder rumbled in the distance.

"Come on," Elizabeth called to them. "Come into the wagon."

Nadya and Jenny sat on trunks at the back of the wagon. Elizabeth was folding quilts, placing them on beds, rearranging boxes, filling the small space with activity.

"We'll have to have a cold supper," Elizabeth was saying as she rummaged among the boxes that held foodstuffs. "We don't want to get caught in the rain."

Elizabeth was nervous and excited, Nadya realized, and she was trying to hide it with talk and action. She would not look at Nadya; she was pulling smoked sausages from one box, a jar of pickles from another. The woman's scent was touched with fear and arousal.

Watching Elizabeth, Nadya remembered her friend Lottie, who had always been nervous about wolves and storms and Injuns and outlaws. Lottie's mother had filled her head with fears,

Nadya thought. Fear of danger, fear of bad men who would carry her away. It seemed likely that Elizabeth had the same fears.

Yet here she was, on the prairie with a strange man, a man who could do her harm. And she had stood close by this man, she had kissed him on the cheek. Nadya smiled, amused at the image of herself as a strange man, someone whom Elizabeth might find frightening—or perhaps attractive.

"Where you going to sleep tonight, Nat?" Jenny asked.

Blood rose quickly to Elizabeth's cheeks; she was blushing, probably at the thought of Nat in bed. She glanced up from her work and caught Nadya watching her. The fear in her scent intensified—and so did the excitement and arousal.

"Outside, where I usually sleep," Nadya said easily.

"But it's going to rain," Jenny said. "You can't sleep in the rain."

"You could sleep under the wagon," Elizabeth suggested in a sensible tone. "That would keep the rain off."

Nadya shook her head, imagining a night under the wagon. The axles reeked of bear grease and the underside of the wagonbed was thick with trail dust. "I'll do the same as I did when I was traveling alone," she said. "I'll rig a tent and that will keep me dry." She peered out the back flap of the wagon. No rain had come, though dark clouds had rolled in to cover the sky. She glanced at Jenny. "Come on, little one. You can help me set up my tent."

With rope and a gutta-percha tarp, she constructed a sort of lean-to: a clump of scrubby bushes served as the support on one side; the tarp angled down to the ground on the other. Under the tarp, she'd stay dry.

"Why don't you sleep in the wagon?" Jenny asked her, looking up at the dark clouds. "You could share my bed."

Nadya shook her head, imagining spending the night so near Elizabeth. The touch of arousal in Elizabeth's scent had left her feeling uncertain, confused.

She remembered the warmth of Elizabeth's hands on her head as she cut Nadya's hair. Nadya had talked and joked with Jenny to distract herself from that delicate touch. When Elizabeth had kissed her cheek, Nadya had felt the urge to put her arms around the woman and pull her close. Was this what it was like for a man, when a woman liked him?

"I'll be happier out here," Nadya said.

They dined in the wagon on smoked sausage and pickles and biscuits left over from the noon meal. Then Nadya retired to her tent. The moon hid behind the clouds and the night was dark, but she could see the white canvas of the wagon top not far away. She could hear Elizabeth's soft voice, singing Jenny to sleep.

The wind rattled the canvas that covered her, but still the rain did not come. At last, thinking of Elizabeth, Nadya drifted off to sleep.

She woke to the rumble of thunder. Lightning flashed behind a cloud, illuminating the sky for an instant, as if God had uncovered a lantern and then, thinking better, dropped the shutter again. The sky was black overhead. Thunder rumbled again, a deep drumming that made the ground shake as if a herd of buffalo were rushing past. A few drops of rain pattered against the gutta-percha cloth. She reached out of the blankets and made certain that her boots were tucked under the tarp, out of the rain. She relaxed then, confident that her boots would be dry for the coming day.

From her improvised tent, she could peer out at the prairie. She saw the wagon shake as the wind buffeted it, rattling the canvas cover. She breathed deep, enjoying the smells of the wet earth. With a painted canvas cloth beneath her and the gutta-percha tarp on top, she would stay dry while the rain fell around her.

Then the storm struck in earnest. Rain hammered on the gutta-percha and ran away in rivers. The thunder rolled overhead. Nadya watched as the lightning flashed again, a brilliant white light that illuminated the wagon and the empty prairie around it.

In that flash, Nadya caught sight of Jenny's face at the wagon flap, staring out into the storm. Darkness returned, and then another flash revealed Jenny, running toward Nadya, her white nightshirt caught by the wind.

"Nat!" Her voice was panicked. "Nat! Are you all right?"

Nadya peered out from her waterproof cocoon. "I'm fine. Go back to the wagon."

Jenny stood over Nadya. The next flash of lightning revealed that the child was already drenched and shivering. "You have to come into the wagon," she wailed over the thunder. "Come on!" She tugged at the tarp in the darkness and a blast of rain hit Nadya in the face.

"Go back," Nadya said again. "I'm fine here."

"Jenny!" Elizabeth's voice called from the wagon. "Jenny, come back." Nadya could see the flickering light of a lantern from the wagon.

Nadya gave up her attempt to stay dry and slipped from the tent, doing her best to leave the blankets beneath the cover of the tarp. She swept Jenny into her arms and ran for the wagon, the rain hammering down on her head. Her clothes were soaked by the time she was halfway there. At the wagon, she handed the wet child to Elizabeth and climbed in after her.

A single lantern hung from a hook in the hoop that supported the wagon's canvas cover. When the wind buffeted the wagon, the lantern swayed and flickered. The wagon's interior was filled with moving shadows.

Elizabeth stripped off Jenny's wet nightshirt and wrapped her in a blanket, scolding her all the while. "You haven't a bit of sense in your head—running out there in the rain."

The girl's eyes were still on Nadya, who stood awkwardly beside the canvas flap. Rain rattled on the canvas and thunder rumbled in the distance.

"Nat was in the thunder," Jenny said.

"Well, Nat's out of the thunder now," Elizabeth said. "And everyone's all wet. Maybe Nat's big enough to take care of himself, don't you think?"

Jenny shook her head, her eyes wide. "He might catch his death of the cold," she said, very softly. "Like your papa."

Elizabeth stopped toweling Jenny's hair and gave the little girl a hug. Nadya could not see her face. "Time for you to go back to bed." Elizabeth glanced back over her shoulder at Nadya, her eyes studying her frankly. Belatedly, realizing that the wet shirt clung to her body and revealed her breasts, Nadya plucked at the fabric, pulling it away from her. "There's a towel there on the peg," Elizabeth said after a moment. "You can dry yourself."

"Much obliged," Nadya said. She sat down on a wooden trunk and rubbed her hair with the rough towel, grateful for something to do.

"Now you go to sleep," Elizabeth told Jenny.

Jenny murmured an answer that Nadya couldn't hear.

"Nat will be fine," Elizabeth said.

"I'll be dry in a minute," Nadya reassured the girl. "Now you go to sleep."

Nadya dried her hair, untucked her wet shirt and spread it loosely, so that it no longer clung to her. Elizabeth gave her a comb, and she combed her wet hair. Jenny's breathing grew steady and even.

"She was worried for you," Elizabeth said at last. She was looking at Jenny, not at Nadya.

"Is she warm enough?" Nadya asked.

"I think so."

"I wish she hadn't run into the rain," Nadya said.

"I know." Elizabeth looked up. "I'd guess that your bed is soaked by now."

Nadya frowned, thinking of her boots and blankets. "You may be right."

"You'd best spend the night here. I can share Jenny's bed and you can have mine." She leaned over and opened a trunk. "Your shirt is wet. Here's a dry one—it was Papa's."

"I don't think. . . ." Nadya began.

"Don't be foolish," Elizabeth said. "You can't stay in those wet things."

Nadya turned her back and slipped out of her wet shirt and pants. The dry, clean linen felt warm against her skin and the shirt was large enough that it hung to her knees. Nadya sat on the edge of the bed. Elizabeth wrapped herself in a quilt and sat on the floor beside Jenny. Then she blew out the lantern.

"You know," Elizabeth said in the darkness, "one way or the other, you're a mystery. You come out of the prairie, like an angel from heaven, just when I need you the most. You call yourself Nat. . . ."—she let the name hang in the air for a moment—"and dress like a man. I suppose that's your business. I'll keep calling you Nat if you like."

Nadya could not see Elizabeth's face in the darkness. She hesitated. "My name is Nadya," she said softly. "I'm sorry I lied about that. It wasn't right."

"I suppose you had your reasons."

Nadya hesitated again. There was nothing she could say to make it right, but at least she could tell the truth. "There may be people looking for me. I . . ." She stopped, then reluctantly continued. "I killed a man."

"Why?" Elizabeth was just a voice in the darkness, nothing more.

"He killed my mother and father." Saying the words brought back her anger, her feeling of betrayal. "Hunted them down like animals and shot them. And he lied—he betrayed me. And when he came to our cabin, I took my rifle and I shot him."

She shook her head, remembering Rufus—the sweet touch of his hands on her body beside the river, his laughter when she reminded him of his promise not to hunt wolves, the smell of blood—her parent's blood—when he came to the cabin. "I'm not sorry, either. I'm glad I did it. But I had to run. So I took his horse and headed West."

She listened for a moment to the rain rattling on the canvas. She was glad that she could not see Elizabeth's face. "There may be people looking for a woman named Nadya. But no one is looking for a young man named Nat."

Thunder rumbled overhead and a flicker of lightning revealed Elizabeth's face, her eyes open in the darkness. "But the man you killed was a murderer," she said. "You were only protecting yourself."

There was no way to explain it all. Yes, Rufus was a liar and a murderer. But no one could see that. He had killed two wolves, and that was something any man would do. Killing Indians and wolves was acceptable; it was a good thing. Elizabeth would not understand that.

Nadya reached across the darkness that separated them and found Elizabeth's hand. Elizabeth clasped Nadya's hand in both of hers, and her touch gave Nadya the courage to continue.

"I had to run," Nadya said again. "People wouldn't understand. And I had to lie. I had to pretend to be a man. It wouldn't do for a woman to travel across the prairie alone. But a man could do it. I'm only sorry that I had to lie to you."

Elizabeth squeezed Nadya's hand gently. "I understand," she whispered. "It's all right."

Elizabeth accepted her. Even though Nadya knew that she didn't understand, she couldn't understand, it was wonderful to hear that Elizabeth accepted her, forgave her for her sins. For the first time since her parents' death, she felt safe with another person.

"It doesn't matter what you call yourself," Elizabeth continued. "I'll call you Nat, that doesn't matter. The only thing that worries me is that you'll vanish the same way you came. You'll just disappear one morning and never come back, leaving me and Jenny alone in the prairie."

"I won't," Nadya said fiercely, clinging to Elizabeth's hand. "I won't vanish. I promised Jenny that I'd keep her safe, and I will."

Elizabeth sighed. "That's all right, then."

Nadya lay down on the bed, still holding Elizabeth's hand. She fell asleep like that, holding Elizabeth's hand in the darkness.

The next morning, Nadya woke early and climbed quietly from the wagon. She pulled on her wet pants and hung her wet shirt over a bush to dry. The gutta-percha tarp had protected her blankets and boots from the worst of the storm. She shook out the tarp and the canvas ground sheet and spread them out beside her shirt.

She squatted on her heels, looking out over the river. The sky was clear and the rain had soaked into the sandy soil. The air smelled new and clean. Mingling with the smells of the camp, she could catch the scent of antelope and prairie dogs, and, somewhere far off, buffalo. It was a fine day.

Nadya heard footsteps and looked up to see Jenny running toward her across the wet grass. The girl stopped just a few feet away, studying Nadya intently. "Elizabeth says your name is Nadya," she announced.

"That's right," Nadya said, looking down at the solemn girl.

"That's a girl's name."

"That's right."

"You're a woman?"

"That's right."

Jenny frowned. "Elizabeth says we should keep calling you Nat. And she said that we'll pretend that you're her brother."

Nat nodded. "That sounds like a good idea."

Jenny studied her face and then apparently decided not to ask any more questions. "All right," she said. "I'll call you Nat." She started to head back to the wagon, then stopped. "If you wear trousers, then I can, too," she announced suddenly.

"You'll have to take that up with Elizabeth," Nadya said.

The girl ran toward the wagon, calling out to Elizabeth. Nadya watched her go, suddenly very happy.

There was a dreamy, timeless quality to their travel for the next week. Each morning, they woke at dawn, hitched up the team and drove until noon, then rested and continued until twilight.

Jenny convinced Elizabeth that she should be able to ride astraddle, like Nadya, and Elizabeth modified a pair of her papa's trousers into a set of baggy bloomers that gave the girl more freedom of motion. Nadya watched Elizabeth shake her head and smile when she saw the girl running harum-scarum across the prairie.

Some days, they made fifteen miles; others, only eight or ten. In the mornings, Nadya stayed with the wagon, walking at Elizabeth's side. Sometimes, Elizabeth told Nadya and Jenny about the stories she had read in her books. She talked about Oliver Twist, the boy after whom her papa had named the ox.

"He lived in a workhouse in England," Nadya said. "And everyone there was very cruel to him."

"What's a workhouse?" Nadya asked.

"It's a place where people have to live if they are very poor," Elizabeth said. "And they never gave Oliver enough to eat. But he was a sweet young boy and—"

"Why didn't he go hunt, if he was hungry?" Nadya interrupted. "If he brought home a turkey, then everyone could eat."

"They don't have any turkeys in England," Elizabeth said firmly.

Nadya shook her head. "Well, a squirrel or a coon or a deer then."

Elizabeth frowned, and Jenny chimed in. She had asked the same question when Elizabeth had read aloud to her from *Oliver Twist.* "You can't hunt in England," Jenny said. "Except for foxes." Elizabeth had shown her a picture in one book that showed a hunt.

"They hunt foxes?" Nadya imagined a roast fox and felt rather ill.

"That's right," Jenny said confidently. "They dress in red and hunt foxes. But Oliver couldn't go hunting because he didn't have any red clothes. So he was always hungry and he ran away."

"Well, that's not exactly—" Elizabeth began.

"And after he ran away, he met these thieves who stole handkerchiefs and watches and snuffboxes," Jenny continued excitedly. "They didn't hunt foxes and so they ate sausages and bread and butter, and that was better."

"The first thief who met Oliver was the Artful Dodger," Elizabeth said, attempting to regain control of the story. "That's what he called himself. His real name was Jack Dawkins. He and his friends were pickpockets and they stole from the ladies and gentlemen in the streets of London."

Nadya squinted, trying to imagine a boy who stole handkerchiefs in the city of London. Wolf Crossing was the biggest town she had ever seen, and she imagined something like that. She shook her head. If any boy in Wolf Crossing had stolen something, people would figure out who had done it pretty quick.

"Artful Dodger could slip a handkerchief out of a pocket without anyone feeling it," Jenny confided to Nadya. "But Oliver wasn't any good at stealing. He wasn't very clever, I don't think."

"Oliver didn't want to steal," Elizabeth corrected Jenny. "He was shocked when he learned that the boys were taking things that didn't belong to them."

"He had the brains of a grasshopper," Jenny whispered to Nadya. "It's too bad, but that's just how he was."

"He was smart," Elizabeth protested. "He was a sweet boy, too good for the evil world in which he found himself. He simply—Oliver!" she called suddenly, snapping her whip. The ox was slacking off and the team was slowing to match his pace. She snapped the whip against his flank and he moved more quickly. "Now, where was I? That's right—Oliver was a sweet boy. And he came into the clutches of Fagin."

She went on, talking about these strange people who ate foxes in a town where no one hunted for turkey. Nadya listened, and all in all she made more sense of Jenny's version than she did of Elizabeth's.

But she liked listening to Elizabeth talk, even when the things the woman said were nonsense. Since she had learned the truth about Nadya, Elizabeth had relaxed, or so it seemed to Nadya. The woman smiled more often, sang when she cooked dinner or milked the cow or combed out Jenny's hair each morning.

Nadya liked walking at Elizabeth's side. Sometimes, they sang as they walked. Nadya taught Elizabeth and Jenny Polish and French folk songs and Elizabeth taught them songs that she had learned in Springfield. One of Jenny's favorites was a cheerful tune called "There's a Good Time Coming."

Sometimes, when they stopped to rest the oxen at noon, Elizabeth gave Jenny lessons, teaching the girl to write. They used boulders as their chalkboards and pieces of soft rock as chalk. Nadya sat nearby, listening to Elizabeth's voice as she named each letter. Behind them, they left a strong of boulders marked with the ABC's in Elizabeth's neat hand and Jenny's scrawl.

In the evenings, Nadya gave Elizabeth and Jenny shooting lessons. That was, perhaps, Nadya's favorite part of the day. She could touch Elizabeth then, correcting her grip on the rifle, standing close behind her and adjusting her aim.

Nadya could not describe her feelings when she touched Elizabeth. This was something different, something new. When Rufus had taken her in his arms, she had felt an urgency touched with fear, a feeling that was sharp-edged and dangerous. When she touched Elizabeth, she felt a desire that was somehow softer, warmer, more giving. She wanted to be with Elizabeth, to touch her, to hold her near. But for now she was content to walk by her side, to listen to her voice, to sing with her as they traveled across the prairies.

It was strange that it should feel so reassuring to have Elizabeth nearby. Elizabeth was useless with a gun, easily frightened. But the touch of her hand offered comfort.

Every now and again, Elizabeth would raise the notion that they might find another wagon train, but from all indications, Nadya suspected that they were far behind the others in the westward migration. They camped where others had camped, but the camps were many days old; grass had grown up where the oxen had grazed; the hoofprints were worn smooth by the wind, not sharp-edged and fresh. But it didn't matter. They were happy traveling together.

They had been traveling along the river for three days without incident, when they reached the South Platte ford. The sandy bank was marked with wheel ruts and the hoofprints of cattle and horses. Just off to one side of the trail were five graves, marked with improvised crosses. Two looked fresh, left by the most recent emigration. Black tar on one cross identified the grave's occupant: ROBERT JONES, DROWND, 1847, RIP.

Nadya stood on the bank and studied the river. Over the last few days, they had crossed a few low creeks, deep enough to wet the wheels to the hub, but nothing like this. She guessed the river was more than half a mile wide. And according to Elizabeth's books, the Platte crossing was treacherous. The water hid quicksand, sand bars, holes in the bottom that could swallow a man or a wagon. The hazards changed position, and a path that had been safe one day would be disastrous the next.

"Look there," Elizabeth said, pointing to a pole standing above the water, evidently stuck in the river bottom. It wavered, but held steady in the rush of water. Halfway across the river, a short distance downstream, Nadya could see another pole, bent by the rush of water. At its tip waved a strip of red calico. "That must be the path that the last wagon train took," Elizabeth said. "They marked it with poles."

"Odd that they headed downstream," Nadya commented, squinting at the sloping bank on the far side.

"They angled downstream to the middle of the river," Elizabeth said earnestly. "Then turned the oxen to head upstream a bit. You don't want the current to hit the wagon broadside."

Nadya frowned at her. "How do you know that?"

"One of Papa's books says that's the best way to cross. First, you send a man across to mark the way. He uses a stick to test the bottom and places markers to show the path. Then the oxen and wagons follow along the marked path."

"Only one difficulty," Nadya said. "We haven't a man. But I suppose I'll have to make do. I'll cut a few sticks."

"We should water the oxen before we cross, so that they don't stop in mid-stream to drink," Elizabeth said. "You don't want to stop or you'll sink in the quicksand." She turned and examined the wagon with a critical eye. "Perhaps we had best raise the wagonbed as well, to keep it above the water. And I'll wrap Papa's books in tarpaulins for safety."

Nadya took to the cottonwood grove with a hatchet. Behind her, she could hear the ox chains jangling as Elizabeth and Jenny took the animals to the river to drink. Nadya chopped down a few slender saplings and stripped them of their leaves, using the hatchet to make a set of stakes, each one about six feet long. By the time she returned to the wagon, Elizabeth had a pot of boiling water for tea.

"We'd best eat before we cross," Elizabeth said. "To bolster our courage."

"Best not to eat too much," Nadya joked. "Shouldn't want to get a cramp if you fall in and have to swim."

Elizabeth did not look up from her cup of tea. "That won't be a problem. I don't know how to swim."

Nadya stared at her in amazement. Raised on the banks of the Missouri, she had been swimming since she was a child. "Well, then," she said, "I suppose we'll have to make sure you don't fall in."

Elizabeth nodded. "That would be the best, I imagine."

After tea, Nadya waded into the river, leaving Elizabeth and Jenny watching from the bank. The water was cool—refreshing in the heat of the day. Just a few steps into the water she could feel the current tugging at her trousers and sucking the sand out from under her boots. The water was laden with yellow-brown sediment, eroded from upstream banks, and she could not see the bottom.

She stepped forward cautiously, probing for the firmest ground with a long pole. In her other hand, she held the lead rope to Elizabeth's bay mare, a placid animal that would follow anywhere she led. Lashed to the saddle on the animal's back were her marker sticks.

She moved slowly, testing each spot before stepping. The water grew deeper—thigh deep, waist deep. The current pushed against her, a constant pressure forcing her downstream. Her stick sank into a patch of loose sand and she stayed where she was, searching for firmer ground. As she searched, she could feel her feet sinking. Even the firmest of sand was treacherous; the churning of the river water made it shift beneath her feet.

When Nadya found a firm patch, she had to tug her feet free, using the stick to help her along and dragging the reluctant mare after her. She planted a stick to mark the firm sand then dragged the mare forward again. The mare rolled her eyes and tossed her head. She was an even-tempered beast, but the river was more than even she could bear.

The water grew deeper still, reaching almost to chest height. Nadya had to use her pole to brace herself against the current. Just when she thought she might have to turn back, the water grew shallow again as she found one of the river's many sandbars. She risked a glance back at the wagon. So far away—and the other shore was just as far. Her legs were tired with the effort, shaking from the chill.

Keep moving, she reminded herself, then had to tug the mare forward again. Grateful for the sandbar, the animal had decided to stay in the shallow water. When Nadya pulled on the lead, the mare stayed put. "Giddap!" she shouted over the rush of the water and hauled on the lead. Abruptly, the animal leaped forward. Nadya stepped wrong and floundered. Suddenly, there was no ground beneath her feet. She lost the pole, but clung to the lead rope even as her head plunged beneath the water. She kicked, found her footing again, and emerged dripping beside the mare, who was once again standing with her feet firmly planted.

Nadya clung to the animal's neck for a moment, spitting out gritty water. She watched her pole float away downstream, spin in an eddy, then hang up momentarily on a snag, a fallen tree trunk that jutted up through the water, half buried in the river bottom. A current yanked the stick free of the snag and it whirled away, picking up speed. Nadya took another pole from the horse's back and continued.

She had to fight the current now, and the muddy water surged against her, making each step more difficult than the last. Finally, she struggled out on the far side, grateful for the dry land beneath her feet. She waved to Elizabeth and Jenny with more enthusiasm than she felt, tied the mare to a tree, and rested before starting back. The afternoon sunshine warmed her, and after a time her legs stopped trembling.

On the return journey, she followed the course that she had marked with her poles and did not have to constantly test the ground. But her legs were tired and she slipped twice, catching herself with her pole both times.

Jenny cheered when she staggered up the bank and Elizabeth wrapped her in a quilt and gave her hot tea and sweet biscuits. She sat in the sunshine, relaxing for a moment in the warmth. While she was crossing the river, Elizabeth and Jenny had used a jack to lift the wagonbed and wooden blocks to support it high above the running gear. The wagon looked as if it were standing on tiptoe—top-heavy and awkward.

The crossing had taken longer than Nadya expected. It was late afternoon by the time they hitched the oxen to the wagon. Nadya would ride her horse alongside the team and lead Nancy, the milk cow. Elizabeth and Jenny would ride on the wagon seat.

The wagon lumbered down the sloping bank into the river. It stuck for a moment with its tongue pointing at the foaming water. "Giddap!" Elizabeth shouted, snapping the whip over the oxen's backs. The lead animals leaned into the yokes, and the wagon lurched awkwardly into the water.

The sand-laden water roared through the spokes of the wagon wheels. The oxen snorted and protested. Once, Bill Sikes tried to turn back, but Elizabeth cracked the whip and he reluctantly returned to the proper course. The wagon moved slowly but steadily to the center of the river, following the path that Nadya had marked.

The milk cow was alarmed by the rushing water. Twice she planted her feet and Nadya had to tug on the lead to make her follow. Three times, she tried to turn back, lunging desperately for the bank that they had left behind.

They were more than halfway across and had just turned to head upstream when the cow planted her feet, stubbornly refusing to move. Nadya turned in the saddle to look back. In that moment her horse missed its footing. Nadya went down with the horse, losing her seat, underwater before she could react. She struggled to find the river bottom beneath her feet, but there was nothing but water. She surfaced, and caught a glimpse of the wagon a few yards distant. Her feet found the bottom, but she could not stand. The rushing water swept her away from the wagon, and she pushed desperately against the river bottom, struggling to reach it.

The strain of crossing the river twice had exhausted her, and the current was too strong. The wagonbed remained a few feet from her. She reached out as the river carried her past, but the wagon was too far away. Something tickled her extended hand and she grabbed it without thinking. A moment later, she found herself clinging to a coarse rope—Nancy's lead, no doubt, carelessly left dangling from the back of the wagon. The current buffeted her, but she kept hold of the rope and held her place, planting her feet on the bottom. The water was chest high, and she could not find the energy to fight it. Her legs were trembling in the cold water. She reached with one hand to pull herself closer to the wagon and almost lost her grip on the rope. Her hands were cramping in the cold.

"Nadya!" The wagon had stopped moving forward and Elizabeth's pale face peered from the back. She disappeared for a moment, and then returned. She had stripped to her white chemise and she was clutching a second rope. The current shifted and Nadya was splashed with yellow-brown water. When her view was clear, she saw Elizabeth lowering herself into the water.

"Don't!" Nadya called. "Stay on the wagon!" But the roar of the river drowned out her words.

The water caught at Elizabeth's chemise, lifting the light fabric. The woman found her footing on the river bottom. Clinging to her rope and pushed by the current, she reached Nadya quickly, coming up beside her and putting an arm around her shoulders. "Here now," she shouted over the rush of water. "Put your arms around my waist and hold tight." Nadya released her grip on the rope and, supported by Elizabeth's arm, embraced the woman. "All right—we're heading back."

Nadya clung to Elizabeth as she pulled them in, hand over hand, on the rope. She did her best to help by pushing against the river bottom, but most of her attention was focused on keeping hold of Elizabeth. When they reached the wagon, Elizabeth awkwardly hoisted Nadya into the back, then tumbled after her.

"I have her," Elizabeth called to Jenny. Then she scrambled forward again. Nadya heard her shout "Giddap!" The shout was followed by the crack of the whip and the bellowing of an ox. The wagon lurched once, then jerked again, and then moved steadily.

"You lazy good-for-nothing beasts," Elizabeth was shouting. "Move, you chicken-hearted sons of Satan, you fools of oxen." Nadya lay shivering in the back of the wagon and listened to sweet Elizabeth curse the oxen.

Nadya's horse was waiting by Elizabeth's mare on the far side of the river, idly cropping the grass. The milk cow had followed after the oxen, ending up a bit downstream, but finding her way to camp soon enough.

When Jenny had a small fire going, Elizabeth helped Nadya from the wagon. When Nadya was settled, she went back to the wagon and returned, wearing her dress once again and carrying her wet chemise and a bottle. Her hair was wild—damp tendrils had escaped the braids and curled around her face. "As a rule, I don't hold with drinking spirits," she told Nadya. "But I think we need something to warm us. And a spot of brandy in a cup of tea won't do any harm."

Nadya accepted the brandy-laced tea and sipped it, watching Elizabeth's face. "You did a fine job of cursing the oxen," Nadya said at last. "I couldn't have done better myself."

Elizabeth colored slightly. "It seemed to me that they needed encouragement."

"I'm grateful that you found the proper words to do it."

"We had a hired hand who used very colorful language." Elizabeth sipped her tea. She was, Nadya thought, suppressing a smile. "I probably shouldn't have listened."

"If you hadn't listened, we'd still be in the middle of the river," Nadya said. "I think a few cuss words were just what the oxen needed. Gentle words wouldn't have moved them."

Elizabeth smiled then. "I suppose you're right."

When they had finished the first cup of brandy-laced tea, they had another at Nadya's suggestion. Elizabeth put a pot of stew on the fire, and then they had a third cup of tea with brandy. It seemed only right to have another—the medicinal value could not be argued.

Nadya found herself watching Elizabeth—pouring tea, ladling stew into bowls, adding another buffalo chip to the fire. She had combed out the tangles in her hair and it hung loose around her shoulders.

"Tell me again about how Elizabeth pulled you out of the river," Jenny asked, snuggling up to Nadya's side. Left in charge of the oxen, she had missed seeing the actual rescue. Nadya had recounted the story twice and Elizabeth had told it once, but Jenny wanted to hear it again.

"Maybe tomorrow," Nadya said. She was warm and comfortable, at ease with her companions and the world. The sun had long since set. In the twilight, a distant wolf pack howled.

"Can you hear what they're saying?" she asked Jenny.

"They're not saying anything," Jenny said. "They're just howling."

"Now, that's not so. They're talking to each other, just as sure as I'm talking to you. Listen here." She barked once, then howled. The distant pack answered with a chorus of howls.

"What did you tell them?"

"I told them we were here. I wished them good hunting. They're off to chase the buffalo."

"Can you teach me to howl like a wolf?" Jenny asked. "Like you do?"

"Sure I could," Nadya said, putting her arm around the girl's shoulders.

"Some other night," Elizabeth interrupted. "It's late now. And we've had a long day. Time for bed."

Nadya nodded, soothed by the brandy and ready for bed. Jenny protested a bit, but she was tired too, and finally she went with Elizabeth into the wagon and to bed. Nadya was laying her bedroll on the ground beside the fire when Elizabeth returned.

"I wanted to say good night," she said. She swayed a little, standing by the fire. The brandy had softened her voice and her eyes were half-closed.

"Good night," Nadya said.

In the distance, the wolves howled again. Nadya smiled, listening to their singing.

"I've never heard anyone talk about wolves as you do," Elizabeth said, watching Nadya closely. "I don't know what to make of you. You aren't like anyone else I have ever known." She studied Nadya's face intently. "You frighten me sometimes. And sometimes, sometimes I. . . ." She shook her head and looked down at her hands.

"There's nothing to be frightened of," Nadya said. She wanted to reach out and brush the hair back away from Elizabeth's face, to feel her warm skin beneath her fingers.

"I know I'm just being foolish." Elizabeth looked up from her hands, her face composed again. "Time for bed, I suppose."

Later, lying by the wagon and looking up at the stars, Nadya thought about Elizabeth, about the look in her eyes when she said that Nadya frightened her. At that moment, Nadya thought she had caught the musky scent of desire. But she might have imagined that. Nadya fell asleep wondering.

18

Elizabeth walked beside the oxen, whip in hand. When any of the animals slacked or slowed its pace, she called to them. "Giddap there, Oliver. Move along, Dodger."

She had grown used to driving the oxen. She could snap the whip sharply. When an ox failed to pull, she did not hesitate to twist the offending animal's tail. She remembered her concern when she had watched Edward do the same, but that seemed long ago.

The weather was hot; the air, thick with humidity. They were making their way north across the high lands that divided the South Fork of the Platte from the North Fork. Leaving the softly rolling hills of the South Fork behind, they traveled through a barren landscape of abrupt canyons and ridges that ended in sheer cliffs. The wind was constant—it swept over the bluffs and whistled through the spokes of the wagon wheels, tugged at the bonnet that Elizabeth had tied firmly under her chin and whipped her skirts around her legs.

The trail followed a ridge, sometimes dipping into a small gully and sometimes climbing a rise. All around her, Elizabeth could see more of the same: windswept ridges to which sagebrush and grasses clung. Such a lonely place. Worse, she thought, than the flat prairie land, for here there were terrifying canyons into which the wagon could tumble.

"Stay back from the edge," she called out to Jenny for what seemed like the hundredth time. The wind caught her voice and carried it away. The girl wandered ahead of the wagon, peering over the edges of the bluffs or climbing to a higher vantage point to look out over the landscape. Allegedly, she was keeping watch for Indians. Jenny waved a hand in response to Elizabeth's plea, but did not reply or move away from the edge.

Elizabeth noticed with a sigh that the girl had taken off her bonnet once again. At least three times each day, Elizabeth tied the bonnet back on the girl's head. Jenny's face was growing a very unladylike brown. Some of that was dirt, Elizabeth was confident, but some was tanning from the sun.

"Jenny, where's your bonnet?" Elizabeth called. "You'll be as brown as an Indian if you don't wear it."

"There's Nadya!" the girl cried, waving her hand frantically. "She's coming this way."

Elizabeth clucked her tongue to the oxen. They picked up their pace—shifting from a slow shamble to a slightly faster stroll. The trail angled upward and they leaned into their yokes as they pulled the wagon up the slight incline. Elizabeth could see the North Platte far below. The ridge top on which she stood broke into ragged bluffs on two sides, but the trail wound up and over another hill, this one sloping smoothly down into a hollow.

Nadya appeared at the top of the hill and trotted down to meet Elizabeth. "Good camp ahead," Nadya called. "And we'll have a fine dinner—fresh antelope meat."

Elizabeth looked at the steep trail that led up the hill and the equally steep slope on the other side. Going over the top was preferable to following the side slope. The high wagonbed was ideal for fording rivers or traversing boulder-strewn trails, but on a side slope it was in constant danger of tipping over and tumbling.

"Giddap there, Bill Sikes," Elizabeth called. "Giddap, Dodger."

They pulled easily along the ridge top, but balked at the steep incline. When Elizabeth cracked the whip and shouted, the oxen leaned into their yokes. But their hooves slipped on the loose soil, worn bare by passing wagons. "Giddap there, Oliver. Giddap, Mr. Bumble." The wagon barely moved, even with the team pulling in unison. One iron-clad wheel clattered over a stone and the wagon rocked slowly forward and inched up the hill.

Fagin tossed his head and eased up on the yoke, letting Bill Sikes take the full weight of the wagon. Elizabeth snapped her whip against Fagin's flank, and the beast leaped forward. Elizabeth heard a sudden crack as one of the chains that linked the yokes snapped. A sudden confusion—some oxen pulling forward against the wagon's weight, others bellowing in protest as the wagon pulled them back. "Whoa," Elizabeth shouted. "Whoa there."

The wagon slid to the bottom of the hill, losing the few feet they had gained. Still protesting, Fagin tossed his head and the loose chain, broken at a weak link, jingled. The other oxen bellowed and shuffled in their traces. It took both Nadya and Elizabeth to calm them.

Elizabeth examined the broken chain. "We can fix it easily enough," she said. "Papa packed extra links in the tool kit."

Nadya nodded. "Even so, we need to lighten the load."

Elizabeth nodded. She had known it would come to this sooner or later. She looked at the oxen. The animals were lathered with sweat from the brief effort. They were thinner than they had been in Independence, worn from the days of hard hauling. If she kept working them this hard, they wouldn't make it over the Rockies, let alone to California.

Nadya helped her carry things from the wagon: two big pots, larger than they needed for cooking on the trail. A cast-iron stove that Papa had carefully taken to pieces and packed, so that they would have something fine to cook on when they reached California. Elizabeth's china tea set. A trunk filled with Papa's clothing. And finally, to Elizabeth's sorrow, Papa's cast-iron hand press, the one he had hoped to use to establish a publishing house. It was so heavy that Nadya and Elizabeth working together could barely lift it and tip it out the back of the wagon. It tumbled into the dust in the middle of the trail, and unable to move it farther, they left it there. The next wagon train would have to move it or make a new trail around it.

Elizabeth shouted to the oxen and cracked the whip. When they pulled, the newly repaired chain jingled and pulled taut. The wagon moved forward, creaking in a new rhythm: lighter and easier.

That night, they reached Ash Springs and the North Fork of the Platte. There, the trail turned westward again, running along the gently sloping land that bordered on the marshy meadows of the river's bottomlands. The next day, Elizabeth caught sight of Courthouse Rock, a landmark that all of the books had mentioned. According to her books, the massive outcropping of red sandstone was some ten miles off the trail. In the clear air, it looked to be much closer. A few days farther on, they made camp in sight of the Chimney, another landmark. The limestone column rose to a height of some two hundred feet above a rounded mound of limestone and clay.

The days had a natural rhythm. Nadya hunted for fresh meat, and they dined on prairie chickens, antelope, and buffalo. The meadows beside the trail bloomed with black-eyed Susans and buzzed with mosquitoes. In the distance, sandstone cliffs rose like the ruins of some long-abandoned city.

As she walked alongside the wagon, Elizabeth studied the cliffs, letting her imagination shape them into the walls of a castle—now broken and worn. Sometimes, she thought about what California might be like: a golden state where the climate was perfect and the snow never came. More castles in the air. But it was better to think of the future than the past. She was abandoning her old life, one piece at a time, leaving it all behind. All her life, she had maintained a placid exterior—a perfect daughter to her father, an intelligent and gentle woman with her friends. But that exterior no longer served. She was a different woman now—she could wade into a rushing river, shoot a rifle, drink brandy by the fire, and listen to howling wolves without a shiver. A gentle woman would not curse an ox or twist its tail, but she had done these things and would do them again.

And then, there was Nadya. Elizabeth did not know how to deal with this strange young woman. By day, Elizabeth could forget her—Nadya rode away from the wagon in search of game, leaving Elizabeth and Jenny to follow on the trail. But in the evening, when they sat together by the fire, Elizabeth found herself confused by feelings that did not fit into any category she could name.

When she had thought that Nadya was a man, she had had a name for the feelings. She was falling in love—inappropriately, to be sure, but in love, nevertheless. Now she tried to interpret those same feelings as sisterly affection—with more limited success.

It made no sense, this longing that possessed her. The desire to touch Nadya, to smooth her hair back on a hot afternoon and kiss her forehead, to take her hand as they sat together in the evening. It was all very foolish and she did her best to put these thoughts from her mind. She read her books, she wrote long notes in her journal, describing the scenery, the trail. She worked very hard, confident that the labor would help her sleep soundly. But somehow, despite all her efforts, she lay awake at night, thinking of Nadya lying just outside the wagon.

The heat was an oppressive weight, slowing Nadya down, making each movement an effort. The air was still, as if a storm were coming, but no storm came. Nadya found it difficult to sleep. She lay awake and watched the stars wheel overhead.

When she slept, she dreamed of Rufus. Or perhaps it wasn't Rufus at all. She dreamed of kissing someone, of someone kissing her. Someone's hands touched her breasts—a tentative touch, far more gentle than Rufus's eager groping. Someone stroked the tender skin of her inner thigh—tickling her, teasing her. She dreamed and woke in the moonlight. The frogs in the meadow called out to each other, each one seeking a mate.

From her experience with Rufus, she knew about falling in love. Falling—one wrong step and you were out of control, limbs flailing, body tumbling, no way back. In love—but love didn't seem like the right word for it. Love was sweet with roses and valentines. Not the right word for a feeling that comes so urgently. Obsession, desire, a yearning to touch and be touched.

When the sun rose, she watered the oxen and they began another day's journey. Sometimes, she and Jenny tramped in the meadow beside the trail. Their noise startled the frogs that lived in the boggy places, sending them leaping into puddles and burrowing in the mud for safety. Jenny startled a grass snake, as green as the grass itself—and it slithered away to vanish among the leaves.

"Elizabeth likes flowers," Jenny said.

Nadya grinned conspiratorially. "Let's pick her some."

Together, they gathered armfuls of black-eyed Susans and marsh daisies, laughing as they splashed through the mud to get the finest blossoms. Triumphantly, they brought them to Elizabeth and spilled them in a bright tumble on the seat of the wagon. Elizabeth smiled and tucked one behind her ear. Jenny made the rest into a daisy chain, which she draped over the oxen, giving the beasts a festive air.

The days passed and the moon faded to nothing then returned, growing fat once more. Nadya grew restless with the waxing of the moon. She could feel its pull in her belly and her groin and she could not sleep at night.

She lay awake, watching the moon. Sometimes she read her mother's cards, wanting to learn what the future held for her. Sometimes, she drank brandy from the bottle that Elizabeth kept for medicinal purposes. She was drinking it to help her sleep, and surely that was medicinal.

More often than not, the brandy didn't help her sleep. Instead it muddled her thoughts and left her lying alone on her bedroll, thinking about Elizabeth, about how the sunlight looked on her hair in the morning, about her smile and her happy laughter when Jenny and Nadya brought her flowers. About her warm, inviting scent.

Sometimes, she thought that Elizabeth returned her affection. But then she felt the pull of the moon and she knew that Elizabeth could not love her; Elizabeth did not know her. Elizabeth would fear her when the full moon came. At times like that, she wondered if she should leave them, if she should travel alone, so that there would be no one to fear her, no one to care for her. At times like that, she lay awake and watched the moon.

At night, Elizabeth heard Nadya's footsteps, prowling the camp—restless and unhappy. When the moon was three days from full, Elizabeth caught the sound of liquid splashing into a tin cup. She looked out the back of the wagon and saw Nadya sitting on her blankets beside the ashes of the campfire. By the light of the moon, Nadya was studying something that lay on the blankets before her.

Elizabeth pulled a shawl around her shoulders and went to Nadya's side. She could smell brandy on the night air; a cup rested on the ground beside Nadya. A pattern of cards lay on the blanket in front of her. Nadya's head was down; her shoulders bowed.

"I can't sleep, either," Elizabeth said. "It's the moonlight, I think. It's too bright to sleep."

"Yes," Nadya said. "It's the moon." She spoke slowly and carefully, like someone who has been drinking but does not want to sound drunk.

"You're drinking brandy," Elizabeth said.

"That's so," Nadya agreed gravely. She did not seem inclined to apologize or to listen to a temperance lecture.

"What cards are these?" Elizabeth asked. Uninvited, she sat on the blanket beside Nadya. "I've never seen anything like them before."

"They belonged to my mother," Nadya said, her voice barely a whisper. "She used them to tell the future."

Elizabeth studied the cards. In the moonlight, the pictures had no color—the bold lines and shapes were in black and white.

"Heartbreak," Nadya murmured, tapping her finger on a card that showed a heart, thrust through with swords. "Betrayal." She pointed to another card. It pictured a man lying facedown with swords thrust in his back. "Imprisonment and confusion." A woman, blindfolded and bound to a stake. "The future doesn't look good. Maybe it's a bad time to read the cards." Nadya swept the cards together, wrapped the deck in a scarf, and tucked the package into her saddlebags. She picked up the cup and sipped her brandy.

Elizabeth reached out and put her hand on Nadya's shoulder. Nadya did not speak or look at her. "What's wrong?" Elizabeth asked. Nadya seemed like a stranger, so silent and unsmiling. "What can I do?"

"The moon is almost full," Nadya said.

"Why does that make you sad?"

"When the moon is full, I'll go hunting." There was an urgency in Nadya's voice that Elizabeth did not understand. "While you and Jenny sleep, I'll hunt. Don't come looking for me."

"You'll hunt at night? Why?"

Nadya looked up at Elizabeth. "I have to." The moonlight reflected from her eyes: bright and unreadable, the eyes of a wild animal. "Sometimes I think you might be better off traveling alone."

"Why?" Elizabeth asked. "Why do you think that? I . . . we . . . Jenny and I need you."

"I don't belong here," Nadya continued, as if she hadn't heard. "I don't belong with you."

"Yes you do," Elizabeth said. "Of course you do."

"I killed a man," Nadya said, her eyes on the cup in her hand. "I dream of him sometimes."

"You told me that," Elizabeth said. "I understand. It was self-defense."

"No, you don't understand," Nadya said. She looked up at Elizabeth and her eyes were wet with tears. "Heartbreak and betrayal," she said. "It would be better if I went away. I should be alone. But I don't want to be alone."

Elizabeth slipped her arm around Nadya's shoulders, as if she were comforting a child. "You're not alone," she said. "I'm here. Jenny's here. We won't let you go."

"When the moon is full, I'll go hunting," Nadya murmured.

"Sleep now," Elizabeth said. "I'll lie down with you. Try to sleep." Elizabeth lay on the blanket and gave Nadya her shoulder as a pillow. She cradled Nadya in her arms and sang the lullaby that Nadya had taught her. At last, when Nadya's breathing grew steady and even, Elizabeth fell asleep.

* * *

Jenny watched Nadya, watched Elizabeth, knowing that something was going on, though she did not know what. They were polite enough, and on the surface they seemed happy, but there was a tension in the air, unspoken words hanging between them.

One night, just after they made camp, Nadya went off with her rifle, saying she'd get fresh meat for dinner. Jenny was on her way to the river to fill a bucket with water when she heard a shot. She headed toward the sound. Not far away, she found Nadya, disemboweling an antelope. The entrails steamed in the evening air.

Nadya's attention was on the work at hand. She did not hear Jenny coming up behind her. She flipped the body to one side to let the blood drain from the body cavity. As Jenny watched, she got to her feet, holding her knife in one hand and a bloody piece of meat in the other. With an air of relish, like a child with an unexpected treat, she sliced off a bit of meat, still warm and bloody, and popped it in her mouth.

"Nadya," Jenny called, startled.

She turned to face Jenny, licking a drop of blood off her lips. She studied Jenny for a moment, her face expressionless. "Fresh meat for dinner," she said.

Jenny took a step back, momentarily frightened, but Nadya remained motionless.

"Come and help me carry it to camp," she said.

Jenny hesitated for a moment, and then went to her. That night, Jenny helped Elizabeth chop the antelope meat for stew. When Elizabeth wasn't looking, she tasted a bit of the raw meat. Salty and harder to chew than cooked meat, but not so bad.

Just before sunset, on the night of the full moon, Nadya walked away from camp, following the river west. She had told Elizabeth and Jenny that she was going hunting, and she carried her rifle tucked under her arm. Behind her, she heard Jenny asking Elizabeth, "Why is Nat going hunting now? It's going to be dark soon." She could not hear Elizabeth's murmured response.

So strange, to be alone again, after spending a month in their company. She walked along the trail, sniffing the breeze that blew over the prairie. Somewhere, not too far, there was a herd of buffalo. Many animals, with a scent as warm and inviting as newly baked bread. She had seen buffalo herds while hunting away from the trail, but she had not pursued the beasts. Such massive creatures—more meat than she and her companions could eat in a week. It seemed better to shoot the smaller game that was so abundant on the prairies: jackrabbits, prairie chickens, ducks on the river, and pronghorn antelope. Instead of giving chase, she had simply watched the herds from a distance. They moved as if they were part of the land, the hills come alive.

Beside the river, about a mile from camp, she undressed. She wrapped her rifle in her clothing to protect it from the dew. Standing beside it, she stretched, reaching up toward the darkening sky. It was a warm, clear evening, promising a beautiful night to come, and she felt exhilarated. She had been anticipating the Change with apprehension, knowing that Elizabeth would fear her in her altered form. But now, alone under the prairie sky, she did not care about Elizabeth's reaction. A great horned owl flew overhead, its wings silent. The breeze carried the scent of buffalo. She felt young and strong and filled with joy. She felt the pull of the moon and smiled.

The moon rose and she Changed. A gray wolf stood beside the river, lifting her head to sniff the breeze. She followed the scent of buffalo away from the river, trotting through the prairie grass.

She was in no hurry—Elizabeth had cooked supper before she left and she wasn't hungry. She stopped to investigate the intriguing scents of a prairie-dog town, digging into one burrow and sniffing the dirt. She could hear the tiny squeaking of the rodents underground. She passed a skunk that was hunting mice in the tall grass. The skunk returned Nadya's stare and Nadya kept moving. When she was younger, she had been sprayed once by a skunk and she did not care to repeat the experience.

She found the trail left by the buffalo herd, a broad area where the animals had grazed. She followed the animals eastward, content to be alone on the prairie, exploring the world.

* * *

That night, Elizabeth had to sing Jenny to sleep, sitting beside the girl as she dozed off. Jenny kept asking why Nadya had gone hunting at night, why she hadn't waited until the next day. Elizabeth had no answers. "I don't know," she told Jenny. "You'll just have to ask Nadya when she comes back."

After Jenny fell asleep, Elizabeth found herself unable to settle down. Nadya's gear was just under the wagon, the place she always left it when they made camp, but the camp felt empty without Nadya there.

Elizabeth left the wagon and walked to the river bluff. The full moon cast a silver light so bright that she could see her shadow on the prairie grass. The night breeze raised ripples on the smooth surface of the river.

She listened to the sounds of the prairie—the murmur of the flowing water, the creaking of frogs. No human sound disturbed the silence. She sat atop the bluff, where the grass grew thick and she could see the wagon and the river. She could not sleep, with Nadya gone. Suppose Indians came to the camp. Who would protect her and Jenny?

The light of the full moon had washed away the Milky Way. She lay on her back and looked at the stars. Long, long ago, when she was just a child, Papa had told her about the stars. He had said that the stars were big balls of fire that were very, very far away. He had shown her how to find the Big Dipper and how to follow the pointer stars to the North Star, so that she would always know her way. She listened to Papa and learned what he had to teach.

But she remembered another story about the stars, a story her mother had told her before she died. Her mother had said that the stars were angels watching over everyone on earth. At night, when evil was strong, the angels kept guard and protected God's children.

A falling star traced a bright path across the sky. Her mother had told her that each falling star was an angel, coming to earth to help someone in need. Elizabeth hoped that this angel would watch out for her and Jenny and Nadya, wherever she was.

The wind blew in the grass, whispering secrets that Elizabeth could not understand. There were so many things she did not understand. She did not understand why Papa had died. She did not understand why Nadya had come to save them. She did not understand the feelings that she had when she lay down with Nadya in her arms.

Under a sky filled with stars, she sang her favorite hymn. Nadya didn't like the song, but Nadya was somewhere far away, on some mysterious business, and Elizabeth sang softly, just for herself and the stars: "Jesus, watch your wandering sheep; keep us safe from harm."

She lay back and looked up at the stars. She could turn her head in one direction and see the wagon; in the other direction, she could see the river. The air was warm and the wind teased her with secrets. If she listened just right, perhaps she could understand what it was whispering. Perhaps it would tell her where Nadya had gone.

The line between wakefulness and sleep is ill-defined, as vague as the line between sisterly affection and love. Elizabeth may have slept. If she did, her dreams were filled with wind and stars and secrets that she could not grasp. The stars wheeled overhead, circling the North Star in their nightly dance.

Perhaps it was in a dream that she saw the gray wolf trot along beside the river and lift its head to catch a scent on the wind. The moon was setting and the first light of day touched the eastern sky.

In the dream, if it was a dream, her hand groped for the handle of the pistol that was holstered at her side. She realized as she reached for the gun that it was back at the wagon. She was not wearing her holster. Besides, she had promised Nadya that she would not shoot wolves. And so she just watched the wolf. It stopped for a drink, standing with its great paws planted on the muddy bank. It lifted its head from the water and turned, as if it had caught her scent on the breeze. It watched her—its head high, its ears cocked forward, as if waiting for her to speak.

She did not speak. She watched the wolf come toward her, following a game trail that climbed up from the riverbank. In the predawn light, its fur was silver, shading to black where the water had wet its paws.

The trail wound around a rock outcropping, and she lost

sight of the wolf for a moment. In the dream, if it was a dream, she sat up, anxious that the wolf would not come upon her unawares. She could not shoot the wolf—she had promised that. But it seemed to her that if she looked the animal in the eye, it could not harm her. In the dream, she knew that was true.

But no wolf appeared around the outcropping. Instead, she saw a dark-haired woman, silhouetted against the dawn glow. She was naked. Her body was sturdy and square-shouldered.

Elizabeth called out to Nadya. Unconcerned with her nakedness, Nadya walked through the grass toward Elizabeth, smiling joyfully. Elizabeth could see her muscles moving beneath her skin as she strode through the grass.

"Where is the wolf?" Elizabeth asked.

Nadya laughed and stretched her arms wide, as if embracing the sunrise and the day to come. "Right here," she said.

In the dream—was it really a dream?—Elizabeth stood and opened her own arms to embrace the naked woman. Such a beautiful woman: her hair wet with river water, her body touched with the red light of the dawn. "You're so beautiful," she told Nadya.

Nadya laughed again and came into Elizabeth's open arms, her skin wet against Elizabeth's nightgown. "You mustn't get your nightgown wet," Nadya said. She unbuttoned the nightgown and slipped it off Elizabeth's shoulders. Elizabeth could feel the breeze against her skin, touching her breasts and making her nipples crinkle.

In the dream—surely it was a dream, Elizabeth knew it was a dream—they lay in the grass together, naked as Adam and Eve. Nadya's hands stroked Elizabeth's naked breasts. She felt Nadya's kisses—fierce kisses—on her belly, her thighs. She felt Nadya's hands—eager, insistent hands—on her breasts, between her legs. Was it the sunlight that warmed her, or did the warmth come from within her, blossoming outward to fill the day? It's difficult to say. Perhaps it was a dream—a sweet dream of fingers and tongues and kisses and caresses. At the time, all that mattered was the warmth and the sweetness and the beauty of the day.

19

On the night of the full moon, Jenny had fallen asleep, listening to Elizabeth's singing. She woke to sunlight shining through the canvas wagon top and the sound of voices. Elizabeth and Nadya were outside the wagon, talking softly. She could not make out the words. Nadya laughed, and Jenny sat up in bed.

Jenny pulled on her dress and shoes and scrambled out of the wagon. "Good morning, sleepyhead," Elizabeth said. She and Nadya were sitting by the fire circle, drinking tea. "Come here and I'll comb those rats' nests out of your hair."

Jenny ran a hand through her hair, pushing it back out of her eyes. "Ain't we moving today?"

Elizabeth shook her head. "Not today. The oxen need a rest, and I need to do laundry."

Jenny made a face. Laundry was an awful chore. She didn't want to spend the morning pounding clothes on the rocks by the river.

Nadya grinned at her. "Help with the laundry, and we can go for a swim in the river later."

Elizabeth and Nadya had already had breakfast and Jenny ate cold johnnycake and honey for hers. Then she and Nadya went down to the river, leaving Elizabeth behind to spread the quilts to air. Nadya carried Elizabeth's biggest kettle, stuffed full of dirty clothes, and Jenny carried a bucket.

They followed a small trail, worn by wild animals and widened by the oxen of emigrants, until they reached the broad, muddy beach by the river. There, they walked side by side. Jenny glanced up at Nadya's face more than once. Nadya was smiling and Jenny was glad. For the past week, Nadya had been sorrowful and distant. Now something had changed and Nadya was happy again.

The river was wide and slow-moving. On both sides, the water lapped at broad, muddy beaches. By the far shore, a great blue heron stood motionless in the shallows. The bird had frozen in mid-step, one leg lifted. Its gaze was fixed on something under the water. As Jenny watched, the bird struck, plunging its bill into the water and coming up with a struggling fish. The heron tipped back its head, swallowed the fish, then set its foot down in a slow deliberate step, taking no notice of the two humans on the other side of the river.

Nadya walked across the muddy ground to the river. At her approach, a young snapping turtle slid into the water. Jenny followed, peering at the mud at her feet. Marks showed where the turtle had rested. She could see the flat spot where its shell had flattened the mud, the scrapes where its feet had pushed off the bank. The turtle's resting place was surrounded by footprints left by other animals.

Jenny set her bucket on the beach and stooped to examine the mud. "Look," she said, pointing to tiny handprints in the mud. It looked for all the world as if babies had been playing at the water's edge.

"Raccoons," Nadya said.

Wading birds had left delicate prints that ran one over the other. The overlapping lines formed intricate patterns that reminded Jenny of the type in Elizabeth's books. Cutting across the patterns of bird prints were footprints that looked like those of a large dog.

"What are these?" Jenny asked, pointing to the prints.

"Wolf," Nadya said, smiling down at her.

"Just one," Jenny said. "I wonder where the others are."

"Just one. Sometimes wolves travel alone."

"He must be lonely," Jenny said, studying the tracks. "One wolf, all alone."

Nadya set the big kettle on the beach beside Jenny's bucket, then stooped down and made her hand into a fist. The fist just fit into a single wolf print. "Maybe she has friends somewhere else," she said easily. "Maybe she just likes to hunt alone."

"Why did you go hunting by yourself last night?" Jenny asked.

Nadya shrugged, but did not look up from the footprints. "When the moon's full, I go hunting." Her voice was soft and steady.

"Maybe next full moon, I could come with you," Jenny suggested.

Nadya shook her head. Still squatting, she looked up at Jenny, then put her arm around Jenny's shoulders. "I'm sorry, little one. I know you were worried about me. But when the moon's full, I hunt alone."

"Why? Why can't I come?"

"You can't."

"Why not?"

Nadya's expression was solemn. She studied Jenny's face. "When the moon is full, I change."

"How do you change?"

Nadya glanced down at the beach. "These are my footprints," she said slowly. "When the moon is full, I hunt like a wolf and no one can come with me."

"You turn into a wolf?" It seemed to Jenny that she should be scared that Nadya was saying something so crazy, but she wasn't. Nadya's arm was warm around her shoulders. It was a regular human arm, just like always. Jenny had heard ghost stories about men who turned into wolves, but those wolves were always wicked; they came and tore people apart. Nadya wasn't wicked. Jenny was sure of that.

"Yes, I change," Nadya said. "And then I hunt."

Jenny thought about this. It was an amazing thing, but she had seen many amazing things in her lifetime. Once, in a carnival wagon, she had seen a mermaid—half fish, half human. That had been all dried up and dusty, with staring glass eyes, but it was remarkable nonetheless. Nadya's claim that she turned into a wolf seemed plausible. After all, she had seemed like a man when they met, then she turned into a woman. She had two names—Nat and Nadya—and she answered to either one. She was mysterious and wonderful, and turning into a wolf seemed like something she might do.

"When you're a wolf, do you remember me?" Jenny asked.

Nadya hugged Jenny. "I never forget you altogether. Sometimes, the memories aren't clear. But when the moon sets, I remember."

"So you won't forget to come back to the wagon?"

"I won't forget."

"What do you do when you're a wolf?" Jenny asked.

"Last night, I hunted buffalo," Nadya said. "It was wonderful."

"Tell me what it was like, hunting buffalo," Jenny said, leaning into Nadya's arm.

"What's the best smell you can think of?" Nadya asked Jenny.

"Apple pie baking."

"That's what the buffalo smell like to a wolf. A wonderful warm smell. In a big herd, there are so many buffalo that you can't see the grass beneath their feet. Their shaggy fur is dusty and they move as if they were part of the land, the hills come alive."

Nadya was happy to sit on the riverbank, with the sunshine warm on her face, and tell Jenny about the buffalo. She had found the herd. Though she had not pursued the beasts—one wolf alone cannot bring down a buffalo—she had stayed with the herd for a time, savoring their rich scent.

"Do you like being a wolf?" Jenny asked her.

Nadya frowned for a moment, thinking about the night before, remembering the previous full moon when the pack had chased her over the prairie. "Sometimes it's wonderful," she said slowly. "And sometimes, it's frightening. But it's who I am. I don't reckon I have much of a choice in the matter."

"I'd like to be a wolf," Jenny said confidently. "I'd be very fierce and strong. And no Indians would scare me then."

Nadya put her arm around Jenny's shoulders, feeling the tension in the girl. "I'll keep you safe, Jenny," she said. "Don't worry."

"Hello!" Elizabeth called in the distance. "Where are you?"

Nadya and Jenny ran up the trail to help her carry laundry down to the river.

For the next two hours, they did laundry: filling the kettle with clothes and water and lye soap, pounding the clothes on the rocks by the river, emptying the kettle and filling it again to rinse the clothes. Nadya had her doubts about the utility of all this effort. The clothing emerged from the water no cleaner than it went in. The dirt was more evenly distributed and the grime of the trail had been replaced by the yellow silt of the Platte. But the process seemed to make Elizabeth happy, and that was enough for Nadya.

Watching Elizabeth step carefully into the shallows and dip up a bucket of river water, Nadya was filled with joy. Elizabeth smiled at her, and she felt warm and cared for. She remembered the moment when she came up from the river and saw Elizabeth in the grass, waiting for her.

Nadya's memories of making love to Elizabeth blended with her memories of the Change. It seemed to her that Elizabeth must have Changed in the night as well, Changed in some way that Nadya could not quite fathom.

After the laundry was washed and rinsed, Nadya helped Elizabeth spread it to dry on the bushes by the river. Then she and Jenny went swimming. The sun was hot, and Nadya stripped off her clothes without hesitation, wading until the water was waist deep, then plunging beneath the surface. The water was cool and the current stroked her skin like a lover's hand. She kicked a few times, swimming parallel to the bank, then dove beneath the surface. She burst back into the sunlight, her hair streaming with river water. "Come on," she called to Jenny and Elizabeth. "The water's fine."

Jenny followed, wading carefully into the river, her body pale in the sun. "I'll stay here," Elizabeth called back. "I want to wash my hair." She had pulled off her dress, but she still wore her white chemise. "I have soap here. You and Jenny could wash while you swim."

They washed and swam while Elizabeth stayed in the shallows. Then they gathered the clothes and returned to camp. That afternoon, Elizabeth taught Jenny her alphabet. Nadya lay down in tall grass nearby. She could hear Elizabeth's soft voice, correcting Jenny as she read. Insects hummed in the grass and Sweet Nancy's bell rang softly as the cow cropped grass. She slept, at ease for the first time in months.

She woke late that afternoon, feeling rested and content. Nadya sat up and saw Jenny sitting nearby. She was peering at a book and looking a little bored. "Hello," she said.

Nadya stretched, feeling relaxed and well rested. "Where's Elizabeth?" she asked.

"Down by the river, folding clothes."

Nadya nodded. "Maybe I'll see if I can find us some dinner," she said.

Jenny set down her book. "Can I come with you?" she asked eagerly.

Nadya smiled at the girl. "If you like."

They walked away from camp. Walking through the sage grassland with Jenny at her side, Nadya remembered the first time her father had taken her hunting. So long ago. They had followed a path along the river and Nadya had shot a turkey. They brought it home and Nadya's mother had made a fine dinner. It was a good memory. For the first time since Nadya had left Missouri, remembering her father made her happy, rather than sad.

They strolled along the river and there Jenny shot a jackrabbit, her first successful use of her new skill with a rifle. On the way back to camp, they gathered buffalo chips for the fire, and when they returned to camp, Elizabeth cooked the rabbit. They had a fine dinner.

After dinner, when the moon was rising, Nadya tipped back her head and howled. Elizabeth looked up from the pot that she was washing, and Nadya grinned. "Just saying hello to the moon," she said.

She tipped her head back again, barked once, and let loose another howl that echoed across the empty land.

"Could I howl?" Jenny asked.

Nadya nodded. "You could try."

Cautiously, Jenny barked once, a small sound that was barely louder than the croaking of the frogs in the river.

"You bark like a puppy," Nadya said, laughing. "You can do better."

Jenny barked again, louder and deeper this time.

"Better," she said. "Now howl. Let the moon hear you."

Jenny fixed her gaze on the moon's pale face and howled. The sound began small and then swelled, as if it had been waiting, deep inside her, for this moment. Nadya joined her with a deep wail that made the air ring.

The moon shadows shifted in the moving grass. Jenny barked

again then wailed, her howl rising on the wind.

"That's enough there," Elizabeth said easily, carrying the clean pot back to the wagon. "It's time for you to be in bed." Elizabeth took Jenny to the wagon.

Nadya spread her bedroll by the ashes of the fire and listened as Elizabeth sang Jenny to sleep. Her voice blended with the peeping of frogs by the river, with the hooting of an owl, down by the river.

It was a warm night and the sky was clear. Nadya watched the moon, one day past full, rise in the east, and its pale light warmed her, reminding her of the heat of the Change. She could feel the moon's power, muted now, but still present.

After a time, Elizabeth's voice fell silent. Then Nadya heard the wagon creak as Elizabeth climbed down. "Nadya," she said softly. Nadya sat up on her blanket. Elizabeth sat on the blanket beside her. "Jenny's asleep," she said softly.

Nadya turned to look at her. "I'm glad you've come back," she said. "I wasn't sure you would." She studied Elizabeth's face in the moonlight. "There are things I should tell you. About where I go when I hunt at night. About—"

"Hush," Elizabeth said, reaching out and taking Nadya's hand. "Don't talk." Her blue eyes were dark in the moonlight. She put her arms around Nadya and kissed her.

Her lips were soft and her body was warm against Nadya's. All that Nadya wanted to say left her in that moment. Words didn't matter. What mattered was Elizabeth's body against hers.

When Nadya woke in the morning, Elizabeth was gone, having returned to the wagon in the night. When she emerged from the wagon, she greeted Nadya cheerfully. They traveled by the river that day, and the next, and the day after that.

As they traveled, Nadya came to think of Elizabeth as two people. The daylight Elizabeth was all words—her thoughts were carefully expressed, bounded, controlled by words. At night, Elizabeth fell silent. When she came to Nadya's bed, she did not speak. Nadya learned to interpret a kiss, a touch, a sudden breath, a sigh.

The nights were warm and they lay on top of the blankets that served as Nadya's bed. Nadya undid the buttons of Elizabeth's nightgown and pulled the flannel garment off to reveal her naked body, unwrapping her like a Christmas gift. She came to know Elizabeth's body by starlight—a study of silver and shadow.

Elizabeth closed her eyes when they made love. Nadya wondered at that. She kept her own eyes open, wanting to see each curve of Elizabeth's body, each shadow and fold of the flesh, each passing expression of wonder and surprise. Nadya loved to see Elizabeth's expression change as they made love—at first, she always looked startled, as if Nadya's hand on her breast were surprising, unlooked for, as if all this were unexpected no matter how often it had happened before. The surprise deepened to a look of wonder—what were these mysterious feelings? And after, her face relaxed, as peaceful as one of the angels pictured in her Bible.

Sometimes, Nadya stayed awake until Elizabeth slipped back into her nightgown and returned to the wagon. Sometimes, she fell asleep with her head pillowed on Elizabeth's arm. But always, she woke alone.

She did not question this. She liked waking up alone, hearing the first morning calls of the birds in the bushes, watching the morning sky lighten with sunlight. Elizabeth never told her why she always slipped away in the night. Nadya supposed that it had something to do with propriety, with the right way to do things. But she never asked. She knew, somehow, that Elizabeth would not welcome the question.

Each day, they traveled. The grass was good and the oxen were healthy and they made good time, traveling maybe twelve miles in a day. Nadya could see Laramie Peak in the distance, rising above the prairie, its crest capped with snow even this late in the season. According to Elizabeth, they were approaching Fort Laramie, a fur traders' outpost built in 1834.

Nadya began to notice the scents and signs of other people along the trail. In the grass of the prairie, she found the bones of dozens of buffalo—bleached by the sun and scattered by wolves. A white man's kill, she guessed—trappers and soldiers often shot far more than they could eat, taking the most delicate parts of each animal and leaving the rest.

Nadya smelled the smoke and the scent of white men before

she caught sight of the fort itself. It was early in the morning, and the smoke of cooking fires hung in the air. The trail climbed a small rise. From the top, Nadya looked down on a broad valley. In the distance, she saw several tepees in front of a wall of adobe bricks. Nadya could see men atop the wall, looking in their direction.

Dogs barked as they passed the tepees, and Nadya barked back, growling so ferociously that the Indian dogs bristled and backed away from the wagon. Naked children ran from the Indian encampment to watch the wagon pass.

The wooden gate in the thick adobe stockade wall stood open. Elizabeth drove the oxen through the opening, halting them in the large central courtyard. Nadya rode in beside her.

After a month on the prairies with only Elizabeth and Jenny for company, the stench of the fort was almost more than Nadya could bear. The air was thick with the smells of unwashed bodies, dirty buckskin clothing, tobacco, whiskey, smoked meat, the rancid reek of bear grease used as hair pomade, horse manure and human waste, and furs of many dead animals.

Indians and traders, reclining at ease on the low roofs of the adobe buildings within the stockade walls, stared down at the wagon. By the open doors, squaws sat in the shade. They were busy with needlework—stitching moccasins, decorating buckskin with elaborate patterns of beads. Everywhere there were children: dark-faced and curious, most of them half-naked.

A small dark-haired man burst from one of the buildings, scattering children before him like pigeons before a fox. He was shouting in French—about no wagons in the stockade, about the ancestry of emigrants and how they were likely related to the oxen they drove, about how oxen were more intelligent than emigrants, for oxen knew better than to come into the stockade.

In French, Nadya shouted over his rant, advising him to watch his tongue: there were ladies present. She waved a hand at Elizabeth, who stood by the oxen with her whip in hand, and Jenny, who perched on the wagon seat.

The man stopped abruptly, staring at Nadya with an air of amazement, like a man witnessing a conjurer's trick. He studied Elizabeth and smiled, displaying crooked teeth stained yellow with tobacco. "Ah, mademoiselle, my apologies," he muttered.

He held out a dirty hand. Elizabeth hesitated, then transferred her whip to her left hand to shake hands. Nadya could smell her fear. She did not like this place; she did not like this man. "Don't worry," Nadya said to her softly. "We'll soon be on our way."

The Frenchman's grin widened. The children crowded around, and the man waved his hands to shoo them away. "They are curious," the man told Elizabeth in French. "Every visitor is a novelty."

Nadya swung down from her horse. "My friend doesn't speak French," she said.

"I see." The man studied her. "But you do."

"My mother was French," she said. She looked down at the children, who were coming back again, reaching out to touch Elizabeth's skirts. "But surely we are not such a novelty. You must have many emigrant groups come to trade."

"But not so late in the season. And such an unusual party. A woman, a young man, and a child." He studied Nadya through half-closed eyes. "But if you wish to trade, I am pleased to help you." He spread his hands as if offering her everything in the fort. "I am always pleased to assist travelers whenever I can."

"We want to buy coffee and tea and black powder."

The man smiled. "Of course. I can offer you fine flour, buffalo meat, coffee, tobacco, black powder, whiskey—whatever you need."

Nadya studied his face, knowing that the flour was probably full of weevils, the meat was rancid, the whiskey was watered, and he would charge her top dollar for the rest. Still, they had to have a few things. She settled down to bargain.

Elizabeth found Fort Laramie strange and frightening. After weeks alone on the prairie, it was strange to see so many people. There were Indians: tall, dark-skinned men who stared at her with enigmatic expressions, young women who called to their children in a language that sounded more like the singing of birds or the sounds of animals than it did like human speech. The white men looked as barbaric as the Indians: unwashed, uncombed, their clothing tattered and patched, their faces burnt brown from the sun.

She pushed her bonnet back on her head and sat on the wagon's running board, where she could keep an eye on Jenny, who was having a discussion of sorts with a little girl who lived in the fort. The other girl spoke a mixture of French and an Indian language, with a few English words thrown in. The two girls were doing their best with the limited vocabulary that they had in common.

Elizabeth was glad when Nadya returned to the wagon carrying burlap sacks filled with supplies, glad when Nadya suggested they move on that day. Before reaching the fort, she had thought it might be nice to sleep with a roof over her head. Now, seeing the fort, she wished only to be alone with Nadya and Jenny, away from these savage-looking people. Nadya seemed to understand; she was not eager to stay in the fort, either. Elizabeth was grateful for that.

Past Fort Laramie, the trail climbed into the Black Hills, still following the North Fork of the Platte. That night, they camped on Bitter Cottonwood Creek, which flowed down from the direction of Laramie Peak. The water was clear, a welcome change from the warm, silt-laden waters of the Platte. The air was cooler, a relief after the heat of the prairie.

They traveled as they had before. Each night, Elizabeth wondered if she would go to Nadya again. Each night, she waited until Jenny slept, then slipped from the wagon to join Nadya.

Her body had always been something that obeyed her, something she controlled. Her body was her servant. But now the will of the body was her will. At night, her body kept her awake, tormenting her. It was her body that lusted, her body that took her to Nadya's bed.

Sometimes, she prayed for guidance. But even then, she did not know how to phrase her prayers. Should she ask the Lord to guide her away from temptation? What did she mean by temptation? Was Nadya's body a temptation? It was. But making love was so sweet, surely it couldn't be wrong?

Was it love, this feeling she had? She needed Nadya; she wanted Nadya. But did she love Nadya? She could not answer that question.

Sometimes she feared Nadya. Such a strange young woman. At the fort, when Nadya had traded with the Frenchman, she had seemed so hard, so grim. And on the night of the full moon, when she went hunting . . . Elizabeth shied away from that thought. It had been a dream, the wolf that had come up from the river, coming toward her. Just a dream.

She did not think about that except at night, sometimes, when she lay in Nadya's arms after making love. And when she thought of the wolf, she left Nadya and returned to the wagon, retreating to the safety of her own bed.

20

The trail made its way through the hills, crossing mountain streams every few miles. The land was beautiful: Jenny picked wild currants by the trail; blue flax, larkspur, and wild roses bloomed in sheltered places. Pine trees and cedar clung to the bluff tops. The air was clean and sweet after the dust of the prairie. Once, they camped at a warm spring, where Elizabeth bathed and washed all their clothing, spreading it on the grass to dry.

But the sandstone that made up the trail was hard on the oxen. The rock was abrasive—as hard and rough as the whetstone Nadya used to sharpen her knife. On the fourth day after they left Fort Laramie, Nadya noticed that Mr. Bumble and Oliver were limping. She checked their hooves and found cuts where the stones had injured them.

Jenny helped her wrap the injured hooves in scraps cut from a buffalo robe. She covered each hoof, tying the covering in place with a leather thong. The other four oxen pulled the wagon, while Mr. Bumble and Oliver followed behind.

Nadya worried about the animals. The grazing was scant. Sometimes, she cut branches from the poplar trees that grew beside mountain streams and tossed those to the livestock to supplement the meager grass. Even so, the animals lost weight.

At several points, the trail returned to the Platte River and divided—one branch crossing the river to the north bank, the other continuing along the southern shore. Reluctant to cross the Platte again, Nadya stuck to the southern trail until they reached a place where the only trail was the one crossing the river. There, the river was shallow—a couple of feet at its deepest—and much narrower than it had been in the prairie. They crossed without incident—Elizabeth driving the wagon and Nadya riding beside—then they celebrated the crossing with a glass of brandy and camped that night on the north shore.

Not far from the Platte River ford, the trail left the river, heading for a low pass through the hills. They camped at a trickle of water. Consulting her books, Elizabeth guessed that they were at the place called Poison Spider Creek. "It's two days' travel before we reach the Sweetwater River," she said. "There's no good water along the way."

Nadya nodded. Mr. Bumble and Oliver were still limping, despite her efforts to treat their injuries. What the animals needed was a long rest, in a place where the grazing was good. Perhaps at the Sweetwater they would find such a place.

They set out before the sun came up, having watered the oxen and filled three kegs with water from the creek. By mid-morning, they were following a blasted-looking trail that wound among the rocks. As far as the eye could see, the land was barren and broken—gray-green sage clinging to dusty rocks. Patches of clear ground were dusted with white alkali, a biting poison that burned if you touched it. The air stank of rotten eggs. In a few places, mineral springs bubbled from cracks in the rock. The water was unhealthy-looking, tinted yellow or red with minerals and laced with poisonous alkali.

Nadya wore her kerchief over her nose and mouth, but the cloth could not keep out the alkali dust. It seeped through the cotton, worked its way around the edges. She drove the oxen for a time, letting Elizabeth rest her voice and her whip hand. The rest of the time, she tended to Mr. Bumble and Oliver, keeping the thirsty animals from sampling the poisonous pools.

They stopped at noon and rested in the shade of a dry canyon, then continued on until past sunset. Finally, exhausted and thirsty, they camped in a dry canyon and rationed the water they had carried. Jenny, Elizabeth, and Nadya each drank of cup of water. Warm from the sun, the water tasted slightly of sulphur. Each animal got a drink from a bucket.

Nadya and Elizabeth sat up after Jenny had collapsed in her bed. The oxen were thirsty and restless, and Nadya could not sleep, listening to them bellow. Elizabeth sat close beside her.

"I'm glad you're here with me," Elizabeth said softly, taking Nadya's hand. "This is a dreadful place, and I'd be very frightened if you weren't here."

Nadya squeezed Elizabeth's hand gently. "We'll reach water tomorrow," she said. Her throat was dry.

"We'll reach the Sweetwater River and then we'll travel up the river to South Pass. We'll cross the Rockies and come down on the other side." Elizabeth's voice had a dreamy tone as she recited the trail that they would be traveling. "And then. . . ." She paused, then continued, her voice strained. "And then the trails divide. The way to Oregon and the way to California are not the same."

Nadya glanced at her, startled. She had not given any thought to the division of the trails. For her, traveling was enough.

"What are you looking for, up there in Oregon?" Elizabeth asked, her voice trembling a little.

Nadya frowned. "It was where my papa wanted to go. He thought there'd be a place there where we could live, where people wouldn't bother us. A place of our own."

"A home," Elizabeth said. She was looking down at their hands and her grip on Nadya was strong. "But you have a home now. You have a home with me and with Jenny. I wish. . . ." She looked up and a tear had traced a path through the dust on her cheek. "I wish you would stay with us. Come to California with me."

Nadya reached up and brushed the tear away, then pulled Elizabeth into her arms. Elizabeth needed her. Elizabeth wanted her. Her thirst and weariness no longer mattered. "If you want me to come to California and stay with you always, I will."

That night, they slept in each other's arms.

The next morning, they got started before the sun came up. Nadya gave each oxen half a bucket of water. Jenny had a cup of water; Nadya and Elizabeth split a cup, barely enough to wash the dust from their throats. But the kegs were empty and they had no choice but to continue.

The trail led downward, past sulphurous pools and a marsh that stank indescribably. Nadya was driving the team, while Elizabeth and Jenny tended to Mr. Bumble and Oliver, who followed on behind.

They were halfway up a small rise when Elizabeth hurried up beside Nadya. "There, look!" Elizabeth cried. "There's water."

Nadya looked. Behind them, some distance away from the trail, she could see a lake, shimmering in the heat. She blinked at it. The still water reflected the green trees that grew beside it, lush and welcoming. She sniffed the breeze. No smell of water. Just dust and sulphur.

"A mirage," she said.

"No, it must be real," Elizabeth insisted. "Can't you see the trees around it?" She took a few steps off the trail. "Let's go."

"We didn't see it when we passed."

"It was hidden by that hill." Elizabeth was impatient. "But you can see it now, plain as day."

"Look at the oxen," Nadya said. The animals stood with their heads down, showing no interest in the distant lake. "They don't smell water."

Elizabeth shook her head, still staring in the direction of the mirage. "It seems so close," she murmured.

"Nat!" Jenny cried from behind them. "Nat!"

Nadya and Elizabeth left the oxen where they stood and hurried back along the trail. Jenny stood beside a still pool of brandy-colored water. Mr. Bumble was struggling to get to his feet. The ox was breathing heavily, and his tongue lolled from his half-open mouth. His hind legs had collapsed beneath him. Oliver stood a few feet away, his head hanging low.

"He drank from the pool," Jenny said. "I chased Oliver away, but I couldn't stop him. He wouldn't stop."

The ox gave up the struggle as his front legs gave way beneath him. He snorted, as if trying to clear dust from his nose, then his head fell back and he lay still.

Jenny stood beside the ox, her hand resting on the animal's head. "He didn't drink so much," she said. She was crying, and the tears traced clean paths through the dust on her face.

Nadya put her arm around the girl's shoulders. "Come on, now. We've got to go. We'd best get Oliver away from here, so he won't be foolish and drink as well. Come along."

Nadya tied Oliver behind the wagon with Sweet Nancy. Elizabeth drove the oxen, and Nadya walked with Jenny. "We'll camp at Willow Springs tonight," Nadya said, trying to cheer the girl. "We'll have all the water we want to drink."

Jenny nodded but did not look up.

That night, they reached Willow Springs, an oasis of green grass and fresh water. Jenny helped water the oxen and then she sat by Nadya and watched as Nadya checked the animals' hooves. Worn down by the rocks and burned by the alkali, the oxen's hooves were cracked and splitting. Nadya smeared each hoof with ointment and adjusted the boot that protected Oliver's injured foot.

When Nadya finished and tethered the oxen where they could graze, Jenny sat with her beside the pool of water. A willow tree shaded them from the setting sun. Nadya could hear Elizabeth setting up camp.

Nadya took off her shoes and dangled her feet in the cool water. "Tomorrow, we've got another long pull through dry country," she said. "Then we get to Independence Rock and the Sweetwater River."

Jenny glanced up at where the oxen were grazing. "I'm sorry I didn't watch Mr. Bumble better today," she said.

"Nothing you can do about it," Nadya said. "I'm surprised we didn't lose an ox before now. We've been lucky."

Jenny didn't reply. She was looking down at her feet.

Nadya reached over and put her arm around Jenny's shoulders. "Don't worry about it, Jenny. We'll be fine."

"My pa would have whupped me for doing something stupid like that," Jenny said quietly.

"Well, Elizabeth and I ain't going to whup you. So you just have to forget it and forgive yourself."

Jenny bit her lip, still watching her feet. "Did you ever do something so silly?"

"Oh, I've done things that were much sillier than that," Nadya said.

"Did you forget it and forgive yourself?"

Nadya glanced down at her, thinking about Rufus and remembering her mother and father. "No, not yet."

Impulsively, Jenny put her arms around Nadya and hugged her quickly. "I'll try to forgive myself if you do the same."

"I don't know if I'm ready to do that. I don't. . . ."

"If you do, then I will," Jenny said. "If it's good for me to do, then you should do it, too."

Nadya smiled then. "I'll try."

"So will I."

21

Independence Rock was a lump of granite some seventy feet high and about a mile around. It stood alone on a plain of sagebrush. The Sweetwater River curled around its base, not ten yards from the rock itself. To the north, the Rattlesnake Range rose above the plain. Five miles to the west, the Sweetwater Mountains began.

The monolith was named in 1830, by trappers of the American Fur Company who spent Fourth of July camped by the rock. Those men painted their names on the rock, adding to the Indian petroglyphs that had decorated the granite before they came. By the time the explorer John C. Frémont reached the rock in 1842, many travelers had added their names to the earlier ones, painting on the rock with wagon paint or axle grease mixed with black powder.

At Willow Springs, Elizabeth read Frémont's description of the rock aloud to Nadya and Elizabeth. "'Everywhere within six or eight feet of the ground, where the surface is sufficiently smooth, and in some places sixty or eighty feet above, the rock is inscribed with the names of travelers. Many a name famous in the history of this country, and some well-known to science, are to be found mixed among those of the traders and of travelers for pleasure and curiosity, and of missionaries among the savages. Some of these have been washed away by the rain, but the greater number are still very legible.'"

Nadya, Elizabeth, and Jenny, traveling southwest from Willow Springs, came to the great rock late in the afternoon. The sky was a cloudless blue and the Sweetwater River was a ribbon of silver on the gray sagebrush plain.

The oxen lifted their heads and sniffed the scent of water in the air and pulled with greater enthusiasm. The animals were gaunt and weary, and Nadya was worried about Oliver, whose injured hoof had still not healed. They needed to find a pasture where the grass was thick and the oxen could rest and recuperate.

They reached the rock well before sunset, and made camp close by, where the rock's bulk would block the winds that swept across the plains. The land was sandy and the grass was scant—they would have to look farther for a good pasture, but the oxen needed water and they could travel no farther that day.

That night, Nadya went to sleep alone. Elizabeth was sleeping in the wagon; she had said that she couldn't bear another night on the ground. But Nadya had wanted to watch the stars wheel overhead, smell the sage on the breeze. The moon would be full on the following night, and she was restless.

She was just beginning to doze when a coyote yapped, not far from camp. She sat up. Something was not quite right about the sound. An answering howl came from the other side of camp and she listened carefully. Not coyotes. People, using coyote howls as signals to communicate.

She slipped from her blankets and went to the back of the wagon. "Wake up," she whispered to Elizabeth and Jenny. "I think there are Indians outside of camp. You get your guns and keep watch. I'll scout."

Indians rarely attacked a wagon train directly. More often, they stampeded the stock—first cutting the animals loose from their tethers, then rushing in on horseback with whoops and hollers to panic the animals. With their horses and cattle run off, the emigrants could not give chase.

Nadya went to her horse, untied his tether, then tied the rope securely to the wagon wheel. If the other animals stampeded, he would likely remain, and she could follow. Then she slipped away from camp, carrying her rifle under her arm. When she heard the next coyote howl, she was near Oliver, the ox tethered farthest from the wagon. She squatted beside the animal, blending into the darkness. She stared in the direction from which the howl had come.

A shadow moved. At the same time, she caught the scent of whiskey and human sweat. Something glittered in the Indian's hand—a knife, ready to cut the tether.

Nadya waited as the Indian moved past Oliver. Silently, she set her rifle down beside the ox. A shot would give her away and spook the animals. Moving quickly, she caught the man from behind with a low tackle, taking out his knees and bringing him down heavily on his face. Surprise worked in her favor—he fell heavily with a grunt. She was on his back before he could recover. He started to roll over in an effort to free himself, but she rammed her knee between his thighs from behind, striking up sharply into the groin. The man twisted beneath her, and she slammed an elbow into the side of his head, a stunning blow. He was dazed, but he clung to the knife until she took hold of his wrist with both hands and twisted the joint sharply until the man cried out and dropped the knife.

Still holding his injured wrist in her right hand, she pulled the kerchief from her neck and stuffed it in his mouth to keep him from crying out again. The smell of whiskey was very strong. He tried to bite, but she yanked her hand away. She took the knife in her left hand, cut the leather thong that hung around his neck, and used it to lash his hands together. She used her belt to tie his feet together.

She looked down at him for a moment. A young man, not much older than she was. He smelled of fear, but the dark eyes that watched her were impassive.

She felt fine. The air was cool and clear and the stars were bright. Excitement sang in her blood. Nadya moved to stand beside Oliver and laid a reassuring hand over the beast's neck. He was a placid animal. Though he had shied away from the wrestling match at his feet, he had not panicked. "Easy there," she murmured.

From somewhere nearby, another Indian yapped, a questioning sound. Nadya grinned. She moved silently among the oxen, using the animals for cover. The beasts shifted uneasily, disturbed by the movement around them. Bill Sikes and Artful

Dodger had been cut loose, but they remained with the others. Nothing had happened to panic them.

Nadya circled until she was downwind of the second Indian. He was not far from the wagon, crouching as he slipped close to cut loose Elizabeth's mare. Nadya could see Elizabeth standing by the wagon, some hundred yards off. She was staring out into the darkness, the rifle clutched under her arm, but she was looking in the wrong direction.

Nadya slipped up silently behind the Indian, her rifle ready. Standing a few yards distant, she spoke. "Hold it there, or I'll shoot." The Indian turned and froze, staring at her. "Jenny," Nadya called. "Bring me some rope. Elizabeth, you stay there."

She smiled at the Indian, showing her teeth. "That mare belongs to my friend," she said conversationally.

"Friend," the Indian said eagerly. "Yes. We friends."

Nadya regarded him steadily but didn't reply. Jenny ran toward her, awkwardly clutching a length of rope and her pistol. The girl was pale and she was gripping the pistol so hard that her knuckles were white. She stared at the Indian, pointing the pistol at him with a shaking hand. "Why didn't you shoot him?" Jenny asked.

Nadya frowned. "We don't need to shoot anyone," she said. "You just tie his hands together—real tight, like you were trussing a hog."

Jenny stared at Nadya. "We have to kill them, or they'll kill us," she said.

"Tie him up," Nadya repeated. "Hands and feet."

When the Indian was tied, Nadya told Jenny to run back to the wagon. She left the Indian where he lay and headed upwind. Earlier, she had caught the scent of unfamiliar horses. Now she cautiously headed in the direction of the scent, using boulders and clumps of greasewood for cover. The scent grew stronger. Four ponies and one man, by the smell of it. She spotted the ponies and circled wide, so that she would come up on the guard from the west, away from the camp.

She could see him, peering in the direction of the camp. A big man, older than the other two. He held a whiskey bottle in his hand. By now, his friends should have returned, ready to ride into the camp and stampede the stock. Something had gone wrong, he knew that. But he hadn't decided what to do about it.

She tried the same approach she had used on the first Indian, a low tackle and a knee to the groin. The whiskey bottle flew from his hand. This man was bigger and perhaps less drunk than the other. He turned before she could knee him. But as he turned, she locked her arm around his throat, squeezing to put pressure on the carotid artery. Against the inner surface of her bare arm, she could feel the beat of his pulse, slowing as the pressure continued. Just before he lost consciousness, he reached back, striking at her face. She growled and clamped her teeth on his hand, an instinctive response. The taste of dirt and blood filled her mouth. For a moment, he struggled, then his pulse slowed at last and he slumped in her arms.

Nadya dragged the Indian into camp by the feet, pulling him across the sand and sage. Elizabeth was waiting by the wagon, looking wild-eyed. Her hair was loose, falling in tangles around her face.

"What are you doing?" she asked Nadya in a low whisper. "Why are you bringing him here?"

"Just watch him," Nadya said. Her arm ached where she had scraped it against the ground in the struggle, but that didn't matter. She could smell the Indian's sweat, touched with fear. When she licked her lips, she tasted blood. The joy of the fight sang in her veins. "If he wakes up, show him your rifle," she told Elizabeth. Then she went back for the other two.

In the moonlight, Elizabeth watched as Nadya urged the other two Indians forward with the barrel of her rifle. Nadya's shirt was torn. In the moonlight, her arm looked black—blood, Elizabeth realized. There was blood on her face as well, at the corners of her mouth. One of the Indian's hands was mangled, as if by an animal, and Elizabeth didn't care to think about how that had happened. What frightened her the most was the look on Nadya's face: she was grinning from ear to ear.

She pushed the Indians down by the firepit. Then she went back for the ponies. Elizabeth stood over the Indians. All three were awake and watching her with dark unreadable eyes. Two of them were young—surely no older than Nadya. The other was just a few years older.

"What's Nadya going to do?" Jenny asked her. Jenny stayed in the shadow of the wagon, looking out at the Indians with terrified eyes.

"I don't know," Elizabeth said.

Nadya returned with four Indian ponies. She tied them to the wheel of the wagon and returned to stand beside Elizabeth.

"What are you going to do?" Elizabeth asked.

"Make sure that these fellows don't try stealing our horses again," she said.

"Shall I light the lantern?"

Nadya shook her head. "Moonlight is better for this work."

She stepped away from Elizabeth, her eyes on the oldest of the three Indians. She squatted on her heels in front of him. "You," she said. "You tried to steal my horse. I don't much care for that. You reckon I ought to kill you?"

He watched her impassively.

"Nadya," Elizabeth said. "Maybe he doesn't understand." Her voice was tight and fearful. She was afraid of the Indians. But in that moment, she was afraid of Nadya as well. Surely Nadya wouldn't kill the men in cold blood. She had set her rifle down, but she held a knife—one of the Indian's knives, Elizabeth thought—ready in her hand.

"You speak English?" Nadya asked. "You understand when I say that maybe I should kill you?"

The youngest of the Indians, the first Nadya had tackled, moved his head and grunted through the kerchief that Nadya had stuffed in his mouth. She moved to him and removed the kerchief that gagged him.

"I understand," he said. "I talk this talk."

Nadya remained where she was, staring at the Indian, still smiling. "Three of you came to steal my horses." She pointed at them, one by one. "One, two, three." She held up three fingers. "There's only one of me." She tapped on her chest with her hand. "One." She held up a single finger. "And I knocked all three of you down and brought you here."

She stood looking down at the Indians. "When I walk at

night, you can't hear me. You can't see me. I pass among you like the night wind. But I can see you, I can smell you. I can smell fear; I can smell a lie. I have very strong medicine, stronger than yours." She grinned, and her teeth gleamed in the moonlight.

"I can smell you when you come prowling around here. If you come to steal my horses again, I will tear out your throat. You understand?" She squatted again and laid her hand on the oldest Indian's neck. "I'll tear your throat and I'll bury your body so that your tribe can never find you. Your body will rot beneath the earth. You understand?" Her hand tightened on the Indian's neck, but the man did not move.

Elizabeth shifted uneasily. The moon shadows shifted on Nadya's face: sometimes, when the moonlight caught in her eyes, she did not look entirely human. There was a restlessness in her: she moved like an animal caught in a cage, pacing, glaring. She did not care about the blood on her arm, the tear in her shirt. Watching Nadya now, Elizabeth thought she seemed as barbaric as the Indians.

"Tell them that," Nadya told the youngest Indian.

The young Indian babbled in a language that Nadya couldn't understand. The other Indians grunted.

"They understand," the young Indian said.

Nadya released the Indian's throat and tipped back her head. She howled, a long low cry that made the hairs on the back of Elizabeth's neck stand up. Somewhere far away, a wolf answered. "I have friends," Nadya said, her voice low, almost a growl. "Many friends. You understand?"

"I understand," the youngest Indian repeated.

"If you are my enemies, I will kill you now. If you are my friends, I will let you live. I will take one of your ponies and let you keep the rest. We will smoke together and we will have peace." Nadya watched the Indian closely, still squatting in front of him. "Tell the others what I have told you."

The Indian spoke to the others in a language that Elizabeth could not understand—quick and guttural, a collection of noises that did not seem like words at all. The other Indians responded with grunts, glancing now and then at Nadya.

"What do you say?" she asked then. "And remember: I can smell a lie."

"I talk only truth," the youngest Indian said with dignity. "Only truth." He glanced at his companions. "We give you pony. You don't kill us. We smoke pipe."

"Elizabeth, get the tobacco and your papa's pipe from the wagon," Nadya said. "And we'll need some things to give away—some gifts in exchange for the pony."

Elizabeth fetched Papa's tobacco pouch from a peg inside the wagon. She brought Papa's match case and his well-used briar pipe. She did not know what Nadya wanted in the way of gifts, but she opened a trunk in the back of the wagon. It was Papa's trunk—where he had put some of his fancy things. In the darkness, she operated by feel, snatching up the first few items that she could identify as things they could do without: a top hat, a fancy satin vest with mother-of-pearl buttons, and a Chinese paper parasol that Papa had planned to give his sister-in-law when they reached California.

When she returned, Nadya had untied the Indians' hands and feet. They sat cross-legged on the ground in a circle.

"Sit here by me," Nadya said. Elizabeth sat down, putting the gifts on the ground beside her. "Give me the pipe."

Nadya took a plug of tobacco from the pouch and used her knife to cut a small piece. The tobacco was stale, but still fragrant. The smell reminded Elizabeth of Papa, and she thought of how far she had come since his death. What would he think of this strange primitive ceremony? He would be curious, she thought, intrigued by the Indians and their ways. The thought gave her comfort. She watched the Indians and tried to see them as Papa would have seen them.

Nadya handed Elizabeth the pipe, and she held it while Nadya opened the match case and struck a phosphorous match. Nadya lit the pipe from the match, drawing so that the flame dipped down into the bowl and the tobacco caught. She blew out a cloud of smoke.

"There will be peace among us," Nadya said. "You will not steal our horses, you will not stampede our cattle." She looked at the Indian who spoke English. "Tell the others."

The Indians all nodded. Nadya drew deeply on the pipe. She blew the smoke toward the sky, then passed the pipe. Each man smoked, solemnly puffing on the pipe. It seemed to Elizabeth that it all took a very long time. She was very aware of the rifle that rested across her lap. Suppose the Indians decided to kill them all, rather than smoke the pipe. She would need the rifle then. But the Indians made no move to kill them.

When the pipe was done, Nadya picked up the satin vest, shaking it out so that the mother-of-pearl buttons caught the moonlight. The satin backing was red, but in the moonlight it looked black. Nadya looked at the three Indians.

"These gifts will seal the bargain between us," she said. She jerked her head at the oldest Indian. "What's his name?" she asked.

The youngest Indian said something in his guttural language and Nadya frowned. "At fort, they say 'Angry Dog,'" he said.

"Angry Dog," she said, and held out the vest. Angry Dog accepted it eagerly. He fingered the fabric and examined the mother-of-pearl buttons, exchanging comments with the other two Indians.

"He wants to know how you put it on," the youngest Indian told Nadya.

"Show him how," Nadya asked Elizabeth.

She went to the Indian's side and sat on the ground beside him. It was frightening to be so close—she could smell the rancid bear grease in the man's hair. But he held out the vest, and she showed him how to undo the buttons and button them again. She watched as his fingers clumsily fastened the buttons, then unfastened them. He was like a child, fascinated with the simplest thing.

"Your arms go here," she said, putting her hand through the armhole. The youngest Indian translated, and Angry Dog nodded enthusiastically and slipped his arms through the holes, putting the vest on front to back. "The other way," Elizabeth said, but he frowned when she mimed taking the vest off and putting it on the other way. "Well, I suppose it would work just as well this way," she said, and fastened the buttons running up the Indian's back. Angry Dog grinned at Nadya and nodded, running his hand up and down the smooth fabric.

"And here," Nadya said, "here is a wonderful thing." She held up the parasol, then suddenly opened it. The Indians jerked in surprise at the sudden movement. She twirled it in her hands, giving them a chance to admire the delicate paintings of flowers and birds. She indicated the second-oldest Indian. "What do the traders call him?"

"Fat Bear," the youngest Indian said.

"Fat Bear," she said. "This is for you." She closed the parasol and held it out. The man took it carefully. When Elizabeth offered to take it and show him how to open it, he wouldn't let go. Finally, he let her push it open while he held it, and watched carefully how she made it open and close. Then he tried it himself, and smiled broadly when he succeeded.

"Good," Elizabeth said. They were like children, willful children.

"And what do the traders call you?" Nadya asked the youngest Indian.

"I am Spotted Crow."

"Spotted Crow," Nadya repeated. She held up the top hat. "This is for you. This is the kind of hat that very rich men wear in the white man's cities. Very powerful men." She looked at him thoughtfully. "Do you understand?"

He nodded solemnly. Nadya reached out and placed the hat on his head. Then she looked at the three of them. "I give you these gifts to seal the bargain between us." She stood and went to the ponies. Choosing one of the four, she untied the other three. "I will keep this pony, but the others are yours. Take them and go. Tell your people that there is peace between us."

The Indians took their ponies and went, riding away as quickly as they could.

The next day, the day of the full moon, Nadya, Elizabeth, and Jenny traveled up the river. Earlier, they had talked about climbing Independence Rock to paint their names on the granite, but after the encounter with the Indians, Elizabeth wanted to hurry along.

Jenny rode on the Indian pony. About five miles from Independence Rock, the trail left the river and made its way into the Sweetwater Mountains. In the distance, Elizabeth could see a slim ribbon of silver where the river plunged through a gap in the low mountains. The narrow gorge was called Devil's Gate in Elizabeth's books. Though the waterfall was far away, Elizabeth could hear the rumbling of the torrent as it tumbled through the opening.

They camped early that afternoon, stopping near the river where bunch grass provided some grazing for the oxen and rock outcroppings offered shelter from Indian attack. Elizabeth gathered bits of wood for their evening fire, searching among the boulders for scraps to burn.

She was reaching for a branch of dried greasewood when she heard a strange hissing sound. Something thumped against her right leg, and she felt a searing pain. She cried out as she fell, and a rattlesnake slithered away from her, sliding into a crack between the rocks. Nadya ran to her side.

The snake had struck at her ankle. Nadya unlaced Elizabeth's boot to examine the bite. One fang had struck the leather of her boot; the other had grazed her skin, sinking partway into the flesh. Already, her ankle was swelling from the poison and her leg burned with pain.

Elizabeth's breathing was ragged. She could feel her heart pounding, carrying the poison through her body. She took a deep breath, tried to calm herself. "You have to cut the bite with a knife," she managed to tell Nadya. "I've read about it. Cut the bite with a knife so that the blood flows and suck out the poison and spit it out. Hurry."

Nadya pulled her knife from her belt. Elizabeth turned her head away. Nadya's knife was cold against her skin: she felt it in the center of the great hot pain of the bite. Her blood flowed down her leg to drip into the desert sand.

Elizabeth looked up to see Jenny standing nearby, her face pale. "Here now," she said, forcing her voice to remain even. "Get the bed in the wagon ready. Nadya will help me get there."

She leaned on Nadya and hopped on her other foot and made her way to the wagon. By the time she got there, she was weak and dizzy.

"I'll need water to drink," she muttered to Nadya. "And you'd best wash the wound and bandage it." She lay back on the bed and closed her eyes against the sudden dizziness.

"Will she be all right?" she heard Jenny ask Nadya fearfully.

"It only got one fang in her, and that one not too deep. She's got a chance. You've just got to keep her still and quiet. You have to keep watch over her. Tonight, I go hunting."

Then the voices faded as she slipped into unconsciousness.

Nadya made Jenny and Elizabeth a meal of sorts from leftover johnnycake and salted pork. Not long before the sun set, she walked away from the camp, leaving Jenny in the wagon with Elizabeth. Just out of sight of the camp, a little ways up the river, she found a patch of level ground where the view to the east was clear. She took off her clothes, folding them and placing them on a boulder by the river.

The sun was going down. The western sky was pale pink, fading to deep blue overhead, and she could feel the full moon, just below the horizon, tugging at her blood. She did not want to leave Elizabeth alone; she did not want to Change. But the moon was rising and the Change was inevitable.

She stood naked in the fading sunlight. She closed her eyes for a moment, sniffing the wind from the west and listening to the sounds of the open land. Then she cocked her head and listened closely. Drums—a faint rhythm pounding in the distance, so faint that she could almost believe that she imagined the sound. As she Changed, she heard the drumming continue, as steady as the pulsing of her own blood, constantly pounding.

22

Painted Wolf pounded on the medicine drum and called out in the language of the People. "Come closer, curious one. Come closer now."

He had been dancing since the full moon rose. Now the moon was sinking toward the western horizon. His legs ached from dancing; the fingers of his right hand were nearly numb from pounding the drum. He ignored the weariness and pain. When he was young, he had danced for four days and four nights in the Sun Dance Ceremony. He was not a young man now—he had seen fifty summers come and go. But he was still stubborn and he would dance all night to draw this spirit close.

The braves who returned to the village the night before had told a strange tale of a spirit that dressed like a white man but slipped through the darkness like a wolf. Painted Wolf had set out to find the truth of the matter.

Painted Wolf was of the Tsistsistas. The white men called his people the Cheyenne, after the Sioux word "Shahiela," or "people who speak a strange language." But their proper name was Tsistsistas, the People.

Painted Wolf was, in the language of the People, *hemaneh*—half man, half woman, a position of power between the masculine and feminine principles. *Hemaneh* called each other sister. They dressed in women's clothing and were skilled in women's work. They were also valued members of any war party and capable hunters. A member of the Bare Legs family, Painted Wolf was a doctor with strong powers. He possessed the strongest love potions; he had been the keeper of scalps in the victorious Scalp Dance. He was counted as a clever person, knowledgeable in the lore of men and the lore of women and borrowing from both sides.

Painted Wolf drummed and danced, knowing that the spirit's curiosity would draw it near. Spirits were always curious—like the prairie antelope that could be lured in by a waving flag, a spirit would come to investigate anything out of the ordinary. Such as a *hemaneh* singing and dancing alone. The braves had said that this spirit might be Coyote—appearing as a white man to fool them. Coyote was always curious.

This spirit, the braves had told him, did not speak the language of the People, but rather the white man's talk. Painted Wolf spoke the white man's tongue—as a young person, he had traveled with a group of trappers, showing them the best trails, guiding them through the Cheyenne's country, and learning their ways. He found the white men to be strange people—they smelled odd; they ate peculiar foods.

While among the trappers, Painted Wolf had sampled the white man's whiskey—a powerful drink that brought visions and took a man to other worlds. But the white men ignored the visions and brought no wisdom back from the worlds they visited. It would be interesting to talk to one of the white man's spirits, to learn more about the strange people who traveled through the land of the Tsistsistas.

Though he pretended to be absorbed in his drumming and singing, Painted Wolf kept watch as he danced. He swung his head so that his hair covered his eyes, but he peered through his hair and caught a glimpse of movement among the rocks.

He danced more furiously and beat the drum harder. Again, he saw movement in the rocks—closer now. When his hair flew back, he caught a glimpse of the spirit: a gray wolf, watching him from beside a boulder. Its eyes gleamed in the moonlight.

The spirit circled the fire, circled again. It would not come nearer, but the beat of Painted Wolf's drum would not let it go. Painted Wolf chanted, calling the spirit to him; he whirled and leaped about the fire, but the spirit remained just outside the circle of firelight.

The eastern sky was growing light; the night was almost over. With the coming of day, the spirit might flee, and he would lose his chance to gain power from this strange creature. With a great cry, he leaped as high as he could, then collapsed on the ground and lay motionless.

Beside him, the fire crackled and spat, filling the air with the scent of burning sage. He could feel his heart pounding from the exertion of the dance. He waited, relaxing on the cold ground. He could feel the heat of the fire beside him: his left side, the side near the fire, was warm; his right side was chilled by the morning breeze. His heartbeat slowed to a steady rhythm; the heat of the fire faded as the fire died to embers.

He did not think about the spirit that watched him from behind a boulder. He relaxed on the ground, against the breast of Grandmother Earth. He listened and caught a whisper of sound—the breath of the spirit that watched.

From behind the curtain of his hair, he saw that the light was changing: the rising sun touched the sand with red; the moon was setting and its pale light left the world. At that moment, he lifted his head and smiled. Despite his sore muscles, he stood quickly. "Hello, elder brother," he said in the language of the People, speaking with familiarity and respect.

A pale-skinned young woman with black hair studied Painted Wolf without fear. She was naked. Her hair was cropped short.

Her eyes were golden and they caught the morning sunlight and reflected it back. She took a step back when Painted Wolf stood, then remained still.

"I don't understand you," the young woman said in the white man's language.

Painted Wolf laughed. How odd that a spirit woman with the eyes of a wolf should speak only the language of the whites. "Hallo," Painted Wolf said, as the white men did. "Hallo, friend." The young woman studied Painted Wolf's face. "Friend," she repeated softly.

She looked around at the drum that lay at Painted Wolf's feet, at his medicine bag. "Why were you drumming?"

Painted Wolf smiled at the woman. "Drums call you. You listen. I bring you here."

"Who are you?"

Painted Wolf told her his name in the Cheyenne language. She frowned and he repeated the name that the trappers had called him. "Painted Wolf," he said. "Man and woman, all together. You understand?"

She nodded.

"Very strong medicine," he said. "Very powerful."

The spirit cocked her head to one side, studying Painted Wolf with her strange eyes. "You have strong medicine," she said.

"Very strong."

"My friend—she was bitten. By a rattlesnake." She moved her arm back and forth in a sinuous movement. "Bite," she said, and her hand darted forward like a striking snake.

Painted Wolf nodded.

"She is very sick. Do you have medicine for a rattlesnake bite?"

Painted Wolf smiled. It was always wise to befriend a spirit. "Yes," he said. "Strong medicine."

Jenny stared at the Indian—a tall figure wrapped in a black blanket. Looking at him, she could not tell if this Indian was a man or a woman. The Indian's face had delicate features, like a woman. But the Indian's voice, when Jenny heard it, was a man's voice. Where the black blanket fell open, the Indian wore a buckskin tunic, elaborately decorated with beads, quills, and feathers, like the ones she had seen Indian women wearing.

"He has medicine that will help Elizabeth," Nadya said.

Nadya had awakened Jenny just after dawn. Jenny had curled up in a buffalo robe beside Elizabeth. She had planned to keep watch; she hadn't thought she would fall asleep at all, and she was disoriented when she woke. And there was this Indian, crouching in the door to the wagon.

Jenny moved to the far end of the wagon, as far from the Indian as she could get. She watched as Nadya laid a hand on Elizabeth's head. Elizabeth murmured in her sleep, but did not awaken. Nadya pulled back the covers and undid the bandages to reveal Elizabeth's leg. The flesh around the bite was black. The slashes from Nadya's knife were dark with clotted blood. The leg had puffed up and turned an awful shade of red.

The Indian grunted and bent to examine the wound.

"Don't let him touch her," Jenny cried without thinking. "Don't let him hurt her."

"Hush," Nadya said. "He's here to help her."

"No," Jenny cried. "He'll kill her. I know it."

The Indian looked up at her, watching her with dark curious eyes. He grunted something to Nadya, and she said, "Indians killed her family. Pawnee."

The Indian frowned. "Pawnee—they are bad, very bad." He studied Jenny for a minute. "I am Tsistsistas. Not Pawnee."

Jenny bit her lip and watched as the Indian laid his hands on the tender flesh of Elizabeth's leg. Elizabeth moved in her sleep, muttering something that Jenny couldn't understand. Jenny crept toward the head of the bed, hoping to escape the Indian's notice. He was taking bits of leaves and bark from the pouch at his belt, spilling them onto the quilt at the foot of the bed.

Jenny stroked the hair back from Elizabeth's face. Her forehead was hot and her eyelids flickered as if she were waking.

She glanced at the Indian. Using a piece of bandage, he was gently wiping the clotted blood away from the wound.

Elizabeth cried out at his touch and shifted in the bed. "There now," Jenny said soothingly, stroking her forehead. "Easy now."

She lifted her head and saw the Indian nod.

"Good," he said, nodding, and continued his work. He took a handful of the dried leaves and chewed them. As she watched, he spat a lump of chewed leaves onto the bandage. With his fingers, he spread the leaf pulp over the wound, pressing it into the slashes.

"I'll get clean bandages," Nadya said, and brought him strips of cloth torn from a shirt.

When the wound was bandaged, the Indian sat back.

"Will she be all right?" Jenny asked.

He looked at her. "Strong poison," he said, and then he looked at Elizabeth's face. "Strong woman." He shrugged.

Nadya and the Indian left the wagon and Jenny tucked the covers around Elizabeth once again. With a damp cloth, she wiped the sweat away from her forehead. She heard them talking outside. After a few minutes, Nadya came back into the wagon and gave Jenny a hug.

"I've never been so scared," Jenny said.

"You did good," Nadya said. "You just keep taking care of Elizabeth." She looked down at Elizabeth's face. She was sleeping peacefully now. "We're going to move today. Just a few miles to a good pasture." She hesitated. "It's where his tribe is camped. But the oxen can rest there. And we can stay there until Elizabeth gets better."

Or dies, Jenny thought. But she did not say that out loud.

Nadya drove the oxen and Jenny rode in the wagon, keeping watch over Elizabeth. Painted Wolf walked beside Nadya.

Nadya smelled the Indian camp before she could see it. Burning sage and greasewood, horses and mules, buffalo robes and human sweat. They came over a low hill and looked down on the Indian encampment.

So many tepees—Nadya guessed there were hundreds of them. The smoke from cooking fires rose to darken the sky. Behind the tepees, a patch of willows provided shade. She could see people moving nearby, coming out to look at the approaching wagon. Horses and mules grazed in the surrounding grassland.

"So many people," Nadya said.

"All the people come for *Massaum,*" he said. "Come from everywhere." He waved a hand in a great circle, indicating all points of the compass. "Hunt for buffalo, dance." He nodded in satisfaction.

As she watched, young men ran from the camp to catch horses. Mounted, the Indians raced toward the wagon. She could hear them whooping in the distance. She glanced at Painted Wolf, who continued to walk beside her.

As they approached the camp, she saw the three men who led the group: one wore a top hat, the second wore a vest, and the third carried a brightly colored parasol, closed now and held like a battle lance.

Spotted Crow rode up beside the wagon. "Hallo," he called to Nadya. His hat had been decorated with feathers, and he wore it with obvious pride. "You will meet my father now."

"I suppose I will," she said.

He grinned.

They made their way to the Indian camp, with the mounted braves escorting them. The dogs barked at their approach; women came from the shade of the trees, naked children hiding behind them.

"Ho!" Nadya called to the oxen. They came to a stop at the edge of camp.

A tall man walked from the crowd, obviously the chief. He stood two heads taller than Nadya. His upper body was naked, and his chest glistened in the sun. He wore leggings of fringed buckskin and a breechcloth. His ears were slit and a polished brass ring hung from each earlobe. On his right arm, he had two silver armlets and on his left was a ring of polished copper. Around his neck hung a string of red beads with a silver medal at the center. His dark braided hair was decorated with feathers and bright discs of silver.

Nadya looked up at him. His face was impassive. She wondered what she could say that he might understand.

The savage chief held out his hand. "Hello. I am pleased to meet you," he said in excellent English. "It is very kind of you to come."

23

Vipponah, the Cheyenne chief whose name white traders translated as Chief Slim Face, was a respected man in his tribe. In his youth, he had been a brave warrior, counting coup in battles against the Crow and stealing many horses. His lance was decorated with scalps and he was head of the Coyote society, one of the tribe's six military societies.

With age, Slim Face had settled down as a good Cheyenne should. He was known to be a good-natured man, generous, slow to anger, and noted for his fairness—all traits valued by the Cheyenne people. He became a peace chief, one of the council of forty-four men responsible for maintaining peace within and outside the tribe.

In 1844, Chief Slim Face had accompanied a group of traders to Saint Louis, Missouri. He went to Saint Louis to ask the American government to stop the traders from selling whiskey to his people. He had seen that the liquor poisoned the young men, leaving them weak against the Crow and their other enemies.

One afternoon in Saint Louis, determined to know how many white people lived in this strange place, he sat on a street corner with a stick and made a notch each time a person passed. By sunset, there was no room on the stick to make another notch, but still the people came, too many pale faces for anyone to count.

Another day, one of the traders took him to see a circus where he saw a camel, an elephant, a flock of trapeze artists, a tightrope walker, a contortionist, and three trick riders. He shook his head at the camel and the elephant, such strange and misshapen beasts, marveled at the trapeze artists and rope walker, and speculated on the sexual abilities of the contortionist. But the trick riders had been the only act that truly impressed him.

The horses wore plumes and glittering saddles, and the men rode better than Indians. There was a man who somersaulted over the horse's tail, ran across the ring, then leaped onto the animal's back. Another man did a handstand on a galloping horse. Another balanced an apple on his head while standing upright on the back of a horse.

This display of horsemanship was, Slim Face thought, the only evidence of anything positive in what the white men regarded as civilization. The rest, in his opinion, they could keep. He saw no value in their wooden houses and crowded streets. Why would so many people crowd together, so far from any hunting ground?

An intelligent man, he learned to speak as the white man spoke, and his vocabulary included the curses of the bullwhackers on the Santa Fe Trail and the rough language of traders. In Saint Louis, he had stayed with the family of a trader. The trader's wife, Mrs. Marson, a genteel woman who had been raised in the best society, had educated him further. He had returned to his people with stories that would have been deemed unbelievable, had he not been such a respected man.

Slim Face greeted the travelers that Painted Wolf brought to his camp just as Mrs. Marson had always greeted her visitors.

"This is a very powerful spirit," Painted Wolf said in Cheyenne. "She is my sister: she looks like a man, but she is a woman."

Slim Face nodded, studying the spirit. Not such a large person. It seemed strange that she could have overpowered three warriors in open combat. Fat Bear had described the battle when they returned to camp. This stranger had slipped through the night like a wolf stalking buffalo—though the men were alert and ready, she had caught them unawares. She had dodged Angry Dog's arrows—the man was the best marksman in the tribe. When Fat Bear charged at her, she had caught the brave around the waist, hoisted him over her head, and hurled him across the camp. She had grabbed Angry Dog by the throat and caught the brave's hand in her teeth, then whirled him around three times before she let him spin away to fall upon the ground. The bruises around Angry Dog's throat and the bite on his hand supported the story. And then the spirit had smoked with the warriors and given them gifts.

Of course, Spotted Crow, Slim Face's son, had said little about the battle. Slim Face did not believe the entire story—

though the braves had returned with one fewer pony and with splendid gifts. He suspected that he was not hearing a full account. But he did believe that this young woman had bested the three in a fight, and that was impressive.

"She does not understand proper language," Painted Wolf told Slim Face in Cheyenne. "She only speaks the white man's tongue."

Slim Face nodded. "Is she a friendly spirit or a dangerous one?" he asked in Cheyenne.

"Friendly," Painted Wolf said with confidence. "Her wife was bitten by a snake, and I have helped her, so she is friendly. Her name is Nadya."

"Nadya," Slim Face said, pronouncing the name carefully. It had a strange and awkward sound. He was always puzzled by the names of whites, names that meant nothing but a sound. "Why do you come to my land?" he asked in English.

"We're going to California," Nadya said, waving a hand westward. "Over the mountains. Far from here."

Slim Face nodded. So many white men went to the places they called California and Oregon. Obviously, their spirits had to follow. When the Tsistsistas traveled, their spirits led the way. But white men were different.

"My friend is sick," Nadya said. "My oxen are hungry. I ask your help."

Slim Face nodded. This spirit was better mannered than most of the white men he had met. "Your oxen may eat the grass and grow fat," he said. "Now will you come into my lodge and smoke with me?" Mrs. Marson had always asked her visitors if they would like a cup of tea, but Slim Face had never developed a taste for that beverage. "Come now."

The chief led the spirit into his lodge. His was a large tepee, sewn from the hides of twenty buffalo. Before erecting the tepee, his wife, Calf Woman, had dug down into the sod, creating a bare dirt floor and a sod sleeping bench that extended all around the perimeter. A lining sewn of buffalo hide was tied halfway up the supporting poles and extended over the bench, so that no wind could blow between the tepee cover and the ground. The sod bench was well padded with grasses. While the men had been hunting, Calf Woman had woven new mats of willow branches. These were attached to tripods and covered with buffalo robes to form backrests, so that people could sit comfortably.

Slim Face was proud of his lodge. It was spacious and comfortable. On the hides that lined the lodge, his wife had painted scenes from his adventures as a young man—when he fought the Crow and counted coup five times in a single afternoon, when he stole sixteen horses by slipping into a Pawnee camp and stampeding them out into the prairie, when he traveled to visit the white man's city. The white man's city was painted as many tepees, packed close together, with white-faced people looking out. He had tried to describe the square buildings of Saint Louis to Calf Woman, and she had painted a few boxy structures among the tepees. But she had argued against painting a city full of boxes. If she did that, she had said, how would anyone know that this was a place where people lived?

Slim Face showed his strange visitor to the place of honor at the back of the lodge. She sat beside Painted Wolf on the buffalo robe.

"I danced all night," Painted Wolf was telling the warriors who had followed them into the lodge. Painted Wolf was noted for his ability as a storyteller, particularly when he was telling a story about himself. He had a smooth voice—higher than a man's, but not so high as a woman's, and his stories were always exciting. "All night long, as the moon passed overhead, I danced. She came near when I danced, drawn by the power of my drumming. She came to me in the shape of a wolf, eyes gleaming like stars in the night."

The stranger's eyes were half-closed. She looked very tired.

"Are you hungry?" Slim Face asked, leaning close to her. When she nodded, he waved to Calf Woman and told her to bring food for the visitor. She brought a pottery bowl filled with the stew that simmered on the fire and a horn spoon. The visitor sampled the stew carefully, then ate eagerly.

"A gray wolf," Painted Wolf was saying to the warriors. "She came to watch me dance. And when I faltered in the dance, she leaped on me, thinking to throw me across the camp, as she had done to Angry Dog. But I have power too, and I danced away from her, so that she could not catch hold."

"This is very good," Nadya told Slim Face quietly. "Thank you."

"You are welcome," he said.

"You speak English very well," she said.

He nodded. "I traveled to Saint Louis when I was younger," he said carefully. "We must talk about it sometime."

She nodded. He watched her finish the stew and gestured to Calf Woman to come forward and take the bowl. Painted Wolf was still telling his story.

"We danced and we fought until we both were weary," Painted Wolf continued. "Then she lay down on the ground, captured by my power. We talked then. We spoke of great things. I asked her about the buffalo, asked her why the white men killed not only the buffalo, but also the buffalo calves, leaving none to grow big for summers to come. I asked her if she would come to *Massaum,* and she said that she would."

The strange woman was listening to Painted Wolf now. Clearly, she did not understand what he was saying. "What's that word?" she asked Slim Face. "*Massaum.* What does it mean?"

"All the people have gathered here for *Massaum,*" Slim Face told her. "Painted Wolf has called all the tribe together. We have come here for *Massaum.*" He thought for a moment, trying to come up with the right words for the ritual dance. Mrs. Marson had taken him to church and told him about the white man's rituals, but that was a very different thing. "The buffalo," he said. "There are not so many of them as before. The hunt is not good. *Massaum* will bring back the buffalo."

She nodded, still frowning.

Spotted Crow leaned forward. He was sitting beside his father. "It's the Crazy Dance," he said. "Good fun."

Slim Face nodded tolerantly. Yes, the dance would be fun, but it was also a powerful thing, not just a time to show off one's dancing skills. "It calls the buffalo," he told Nadya.

"I am *hemaneh,*" Painted Wolf was saying to the cluster of braves. "She is the white man's *hemaneh*—half woman, half man. And she has the power of the wolf in her blood, in her eyes. The spirits whispered to me of this one, and I went to find her. Together, she and I will bring back the buffalo, so that the tribe will be strong. The buffalo will return, and the world will be right again."

Slim Face glanced at Nadya. She was leaning back and her eyes were closed. He listened, and her breathing was steady and even. The white-woman spirit was asleep.

"She is a powerful spirit," Painted Wolf was saying. "Very powerful. She will bring buffalo for us to hunt; she will help the people grow strong."

Jenny sat in the wagon, with the pistol on her lap. Nadya had told her to watch over Elizabeth, and that was what she would do. Once, the Indian that Nadya called Painted Wolf had poked his head in the back of the wagon, but Jenny had told him to go away and had pointed her pistol in his direction. He had left quickly.

She had heard the Indians talking outside the wagon, heard chains rattling as the Indians unfastened the oxen. She worried about that, but she stayed inside with Elizabeth. Let them take the oxen. Nadya would get them back. Jenny did not want to leave Elizabeth alone.

She was afraid, but she had her pistol and she knew Nadya would come back. Nadya had said that she would come back, and Jenny believed her.

Every now and then, she wiped Elizabeth's forehead with a wet cloth. Jenny thought that maybe Elizabeth was sleeping easier now: she did not moan and toss and turn as she had the night before.

She heard a rustling sound at the back opening and glared in that direction, expecting to see Painted Wolf again. Instead, a little girl looked in through the back of the wagon. Jenny had seen her in the crowd of Indians just before Nadya left with the chief.

The little girl made a bunch of sounds—words, Jenny guessed, but not ones that made any sense to Jenny.

"Can't understand a word you're saying," Jenny said crossly.

The little girl repeated the same unintelligible sounds, more slowly this time, and held out the pottery bowl that she carried. The warm aroma of stew rose from the bowl. Jenny realized that she was very hungry.

"You don't make any sense," Jenny complained.

Looking back over her shoulder, the girl climbed up into the wagon, holding the bowl carefully level. She stood in the wagon, looked solemnly at Elizabeth, and said something in a sympathetic tone.

Jenny fought back tears. "She's sick," she said. "Real sick. I hope she doesn't die."

The girl held the bowl of stew out to Jenny. Jenny hesitated, then put her pistol aside and took the bowl. "Thanks," she said.

The girl sat down beside Jenny and gave her a comforting hug. The Indian girl smelled of wood smoke and sage, but she patted Jenny on the back and murmured things that sounded vaguely reassuring.

Nadya woke to the smell of human sweat and smoke and buffalo robes and eagle feathers and wolf fur, a warm, pungent mixture of aromas. She blinked in the dim light. Somewhere in the distance, she heard whooping and calling.

Two women sat to one side, talking quietly to each other as they sewed; two naked children were playing nearby, wrestling like puppies on a buffalo robe.

She sat up, and the women looked up from their work. "Good morning," one of the women said carefully. "Good morning."

"Good morning," Nadya replied. "How long have I been asleep?"

"Good morning," said the second woman, smiling broadly. "Good morning."

Nadya stretched and stood up. "Good morning," she repeated, guessing that the greeting had exhausted the women's English. "Thank you."

She went to the opening in the wall of the tepee and looked out. Early afternoon by the look of the light—she must have slept for a few hours. She left the tepee, and the naked children followed her, calling out, "Good morning! Good morning!"

She could still hear men shouting and dogs barking on the far side of camp. She ignored the noise and headed for the wagon. Jenny might be worried about her; Elizabeth might have taken a turn for the worse.

She heard voices as she approached: Jenny speaking in English and another girl speaking in Cheyenne. Nadya climbed into the back of the wagon. Elizabeth was sleeping peacefully. A Cheyenne girl about Jenny's age sat on the trunk beside Jenny.

"Nadya," Jenny cried and went to hug her.

"How are you doing?" Nadya asked. "How is Elizabeth?"

"I was scared for a while," Jenny said. "But she came along and I figured you'd be back sometime." Jenny glanced at the girl. "Her name is Wokaiwo. . . ." Jenny faltered, making a valiant effort to pronounce the unfamiliar sounds of Cheyenne.

The girl giggled. "Wokaihwokomais," she said, pointing to herself. Then, in awkward English, she managed, "White Antelope." Then she pointed to Jenny. "Jenn-eee. Jenn-eee."

Nadya smoothed the hair back from Elizabeth's forehead. Her face was no longer quite so hot, and her color looked better. Her eyelids fluttered. "Nadya?" she murmured.

"I'm here," Nadya said. "How are you feeling?"

"My leg. It hurts." A dog barked nearby and Nadya could hear two Indian women, talking in their incomprehensible language. Elizabeth frowned. "Where are we?"

"In an Indian camp," Nadya said. "Painted Wolf, their medicine man, brought us here."

"In an Indian camp," Elizabeth said quietly, as if the information were more than she could absorb. The look she gave Nadya was disbelieving.

"Hello!" Nadya heard Painted Wolf call from outside the wagon. White Antelope responded with a rush of words and he climbed in the back of the wagon.

"This is Painted Wolf," Nadya said. "He's been treating your snakebite."

Elizabeth watched Painted Wolf as she might have watched a snake that was coiled and ready to strike. "I've had such dreams," she murmured. "Awful, frightening dreams. I dreamed I was surrounded by savages, painted savages all around me. I couldn't run; my leg was hurt and I couldn't run."

"Bad dreams," Painted Wolf grunted. "From the snake's poison." He nodded sagely.

"You've been very sick," Nadya said. She stroked Elizabeth's hair. "That snake almost killed you."

"I need to look," Painted Wolf said, gesturing at Elizabeth's leg. "See how bite is healing."

"I don't want him touching me." Elizabeth's voice was softer now, the voice of a peevish child.

"Painted Wolf is our friend," Nadya repeated. "He'll help you." She put her arm around Elizabeth's shoulders, holding the woman close to her body. "You just rest now. Just rest." She held Elizabeth and sang the lullaby that she had used to soothe Jenny on the night of the storm. "Sleep, little one. The wolves will watch your bed and sing to you. All is well. Go to sleep and the wolves will keep guard."

Elizabeth's breathing grew steady. When she was asleep, Nadya nodded to Painted Wolf. He crouched by the bed and examined the wound. Nadya watched as he placed wet leaves on the wound, chanting softly under his breath as he did so. When he was done, he touched Nadya's shoulder gently, a reassuring touch, and then left quietly.

Elizabeth slept for the rest of the afternoon, and Nadya dozed with her, tired after her sleepless night. She woke to find Elizabeth awake. She had slipped from the bed and she sat at the back of the wagon where she could look out through the opening. Her head was turned away from Nadya: she was listening to the sounds outside the wagon. Children at play—calling out in Cheyenne. Then Jenny's voice: "My turn! Let me try."

"How do you feel?" Nadya said softly. "How's your leg?"

Elizabeth turned to look at Nadya. Her face was pale and her eyes were weary. "Better. Still hot and stiff, but not so much pain. My head aches."

"It'll take a few days to wash the poison out of your body. That's what Painted Wolf says."

Elizabeth was silent for a moment. "It's hard to believe that savage speaks English," she said at last.

Nadya frowned. "A little English; a little French. Chief Slim Face speaks English very well. He's been to Saint Louis."

Elizabeth stared at her with disbelief.

"He has," Nadya insisted.

Elizabeth looked down at her hands, then looked out at the camp again. "How long will we stay here?"

"Until your leg is better and the oxen are well fed. They need the rest," Nadya said. "I think that's best."

"All right," Elizabeth agreed. "For a little while, then."

The next day, Nadya sat by the bed while Elizabeth slept, keeping watch so that she would not be frightened when she woke. Often, Painted Wolf came and tended Elizabeth's wounds, then sat with Nadya. He talked with her in his limited English and taught her a few words of Cheyenne.

She liked having him there. When he sat still, he was very quiet—as placid as a pool of water. Elizabeth, when she was awake, was moving even when she sat still. Her thoughts and words darted here and there—ahead to California then backward to Illinois—as if she could not bear to be still, to think about where she was.

Nadya talked with Painted Wolf about the white men who passed through the Cheyenne's land. "The white man's world—it is very small," Painted Wolf said.

"Oh, no," Nadya said. "It's big, very big. Big cities, many, many people."

Painted Wolf shook his head. "Many people, but very small. Like the canyon." He held out his hands with the palms facing each other. "Very small."

"Narrow," Nadya said.

"Narrow," Painted Wolf repeated carefully. "No room for the Indian. No room for the wolf. No room for buffalo." He pushed his hands together as if crushing something between them. "Small. Narrow."

Nadya nodded. "That's so."

He studied her face. His scrutiny did not bother her. She had the impression that she was a puzzle that he wanted to figure out, a mystery to solve. "You are wolf," he said softly. "No room for you in white man's world."

She shrugged. "Sometimes, I am a wolf."

"Always you are wolf."

She shrugged again. "Maybe so. But mostly I don't look like a wolf."

He shook his head and tapped a finger beside his eye. "Always you look like wolf. Your eyes—they show it. Wolf."

"To you, maybe. To most folks, I don't look like a wolf."

"Very strong," he said, taking hold of her hand. "Very strong wolf medicine. You don't know."

"What don't I know?"

"That wolf medicine is very strong." He squinted at her face. "You stay here for dance. For *Massaum.*"

"What happens in *Massaum?*"

"We call on the animals. The spirits come to us, and if the dance is good, the animals will come. The buffalo, the antelope. We dance, and then we hunt. You must dance, and the dance will be very strong."

"When is the dance?"

"Soon. Few days. Very soon." He nodded, looking into her eyes. "Dance make you strong, make Tsistsistas strong. Very good medicine. Then we hunt for buffalo."

"All right," Nadya said. Elizabeth needed to rest; the oxen needed to graze. And it seemed important to Painted Wolf that she stay for this dance. "We'll stay. A few days."

Elizabeth grew stronger under Painted Wolf's care. Nadya was careful to sit at Elizabeth's side whenever the medicine man attended to her wound, because she knew that Elizabeth still feared the Indian. But fearful or not, Elizabeth grew stronger. Jenny played with White Antelope and forgot her fear of Indians. The oxen grazed and grew fatter, and that was good.

24

Painted Wolf sat in Chief Slim Face's tepee, talking with the chief. The tepee was filled with the chief's sleeping family, but the chief did not want to sleep. He was in a sad and bitter mood. A group of warriors had arrived at the encampment that day, bringing the news that his cousin, a chief the whites called Old Tobacco, had been shot and killed by a group of soldiers. Old

Tobacco had been going to warn the soldiers of a Comanche war party that was camped nearby. But when the soldiers saw an Indian riding toward them, they shot without waiting to find out what his mission might be.

"The whites are mad," the chief said to Painted Wolf. "Like rabid dogs, biting anything and everything in their path."

Painted Wolf nodded. "They make even less sense than the Pawnees," he agreed. "And everyone knows that the Pawnees are crazy. But it doesn't matter. They may come here for a time, but it will not last. The land does not want them here. It is filled with our spirits, and they cannot stay here long."

The chief shook his head. "There are so many of them," he murmured. "In the place they call Saint Louis, I could not count all the white faces. More than all the buffalo on the plains."

"Do not worry about the whites," Painted Wolf told him. "We have made agreements with them."

The chief shook his head again. "They have broken their agreements before."

"If they break their agreements, we will fight them. We are equally numerous. I have never seen such a large encampment, so many strong braves, so many women and children. The dance will go well. It will make us strong."

The chief would not be comforted. He shook his head again, sorrowful and filled with uncertainty. "What about the white spirit, this Nadya? How will she affect the dance?"

Painted Wolf frowned. He had spent many hours talking with Nadya, but he still did not understand her. She was a powerful spirit—he could feel that power in her—but she did not seem to know her own power. "I have talked with her. She will join the dance and make us stronger," he said.

It was late when Painted Wolf stepped outside the chief's tepee into the moonlight. Even so he could hear the steady beat of the drum from the lodge where the Wolf Warriors, one of the tribe's military societies, held their secret rituals. They were preparing for the dance—smoking and drumming together.

It made him glad to see how large the encampment was. This dance was his doing. When the first grass was sprouting, he had traveled across the prairie, seeking out every scattered band of the People. He had brought gifts and tobacco and told them all to come to this place on the river for *Massaum*. Over the last week, all the bands gathered. There had been parties and feasting—it was rare for so many to gather in one place, and this was a time for courting, for making new friendships and renewing old ones.

Now they were making preparations for the dance itself. The lodge that housed the sacred medicine bundles had been built and sanctified. Corn Woman had undergone purification rituals: she slept alone now, and each day she painted symbols of strength on the sacred wolfskin. That morning, the women had finished building two great barriers of brush, positioned in a vee, while the men constructed a corral at the point of the vee. The structure was identical to that built for an antelope hunt: in a hunt, the hunters drove the antelope into the wide part of the vee and captured them in the corral, where they could be slaughtered. In *Massaum*, the dancers would be chased into the vee and captured in the corral.

He walked by the wagon where Nadya and her companions stayed. Nadya was sitting on a blanket beside the wagon, studying cards painted with pictures.

"Hello, sister," he said in English. "You don't sleep?"

Nadya looked up from the cards. "Not just now. The drumming kept me awake."

Painted Wolf nodded. "It is a good sound," he said. He squatted on the blanket beside her, peering at the cards. "What are you doing, sister?"

"Reading the cards," she said. "Reading the future." She shook her head and gathered the cards that lay on the blanket, shuffling them together.

He had been waiting for her to show him some of her magic, some of the power that he sensed in her. "Will you show me?"

Nadya shuffled the cards, studying Painted Wolf's face. "Sometimes, the future is not good," she said softly. "Are you sure you want to know what is to come?"

"If we know what comes, we can be ready to meet it," Painted Wolf said.

Nadya nodded slowly. "As you will," she said. "I will read your future."

"Not my future," he said. "The future of the People. Tell me when the buffalo will come, whether we will fight the Crow and win, whether the dance will go well. Tell me how it will go for my People."

She shuffled the cards and laid them on the blanket, one by one. One picture showed a man who had been stabbed in the back with swords, lying facedown in the sand. In another, a woman in a black cape stood beside three cups that had been overturned, spilling their contents on the ground. On a third, a group of men fought one another with long staffs. On the next card, a woman stood bound and blindfolded, fenced in by swords that stood point down in the ground. Another showed a smiling child, standing beneath a bright sun.

"This is behind you," Nadya said, pointing to the child. "*Le Soleil*, The Sun. Joy and contentment in the world." She frowned at the other cards. "There will be much fighting."

"Who will we fight?"

She shook her head. "Who do you think you will fight?"

"The Crows, the Pawnees." He hesitated. "The white soldiers?"

She nodded. "I don't need the cards to tell you this," she said. "Don't trust the whites. They do not love you." She looked down at the pictures again. "There will be betrayal," she said. "There will be loss." She gathered the cards from the blanket. "It is not a good time to read."

"After the dance," Painted Wolf suggested. "After the dance, you can read the future for me."

Painted Wolf left her there, shuffling the pictures that could tell the future.

Nadya followed White Antelope through the camp. Every now and then, the girl looked over her shoulder and said something encouraging in Cheyenne. She had come to the wagon to tell Nadya that Painted Wolf wanted her.

The air around Nadya throbbed with the pounding of drums. The drumming had started two nights before, and had continued all day and all night since that time. The rhythmic pounding was occasionally punctuated with the shrill piping of eagle-bone whistles and the barking of dogs.

The morning air was hot and still, and her pulse seemed to beat in time with the drums. It was, according to White Antelope, almost time for the dance to begin.

White Antelope stopped in front of Painted Wolf's tepee. "You go here," she said, waving at the door flap. Then she smiled and turned away, running through the encampment.

"Painted Wolf," Nadya called. She ducked through the door flap. In the dim light of the tepee's interior, she saw Painted Wolf rising to his feet. He wore only a breechcloth, a flap of soft leather hanging from a leather thong that was tied around his waist. His body was painted with the geometric designs; his face was a mask of color.

"Good," he said. "You come and dance." He held a breechcloth out to her. "You wear this."

She took it and eyed it doubtfully. The leather was soft and supple.

"Sit," Painted Wolf said abruptly. "Sit now." He gestured to a buffalo robe, then, when she hesitated, half pushed her onto it. He poured two cups of tea into pottery cups. "We drink."

Nadya could hear the drumming, the whooping of the men, but the sounds were muted by the walls of the tepee. She sipped the warm tea. It had a nasty, bitter taste.

"Drink," Painted Wolf said. "It is almost time for the dance."

"Painted Wolf," Nadya said. "Perhaps I shouldn't dance with you. I don't know how. I think—"

"You think too much," he said. "Talk too much." He gestured at the tea. "Drink."

She flushed, momentarily angry. Then she took a deep breath. She owed Painted Wolf for Elizabeth's life. Joining in their dance was little enough to ask in return. "All right," she said, and drank the tea. He refilled the cup. "Too much," she protested, but he ignored her.

"You must drink," he said. "Very strong."

Nadya wasn't sure whether the tea was very strong or it would make her very strong, but she drank. Painted Wolf sat beside her on the buffalo robe. She could smell his excitement—not a sexual arousal, but a mixture of sweat and fear and anger. "Drink all."

She drank the second cup. The taste was not so bad, she decided. Not so bad at all. The tea's warmth filled her and seemed to spread from her belly out to her hands and feet, making her skin tingle. She was aware of the texture and weight of the cup in her hand. The designs painted on the rim seemed to draw her in. Triangles and spirals, repeated in an endless border. She studied them, fascinated by the sharp points of each triangle, the flowing line of each spiral.

"Here," Painted Wolf said, and she looked up from the cup. The lines painted on his face shifted and changed. First, she saw his face, painted with strange designs. Then the lines shifted and the paint became part of his skin: not his face at all, but the face of an animal, the muzzle of a wolf. She laughed aloud, then blinked in the dim light, trying to focus.

Painted Wolf took the cup from her hand and set it on the dirt floor. "No clothes," he said again, and began unbuttoning her shirt. He seemed intent on removing her shirt, so she helped willingly enough, delighting in the sensation of the buttons against her fingers. So smooth and cool and hard—and the linen was soft and warm when it brushed her skin.

Painted Wolf removed her boots, then made her stand. She felt unnaturally tall—dizzy she was so tall—but he supported her as he untied her trousers and tugged them down to her ankles. The air in the tepee was warm against her skin; she was naked, just as she was when the Change was coming. He reached around her waist and tied the leather thong around her. Where his fingers touched her skin they left warm trails behind. The breechcloth hung around her, covering her pubic hair.

With a brush made of hair cut from a pony's mane, he painted her. The brush tickled; the drying paint was cold on her skin. She closed her eyes as he painted her face. She wondered if her face would change beneath the paint as his had, changing from a human face to an animal mask.

As he worked, Painted Wolf chanted softly in Cheyenne. Nadya did not understand what he was saying, but the words were a soothing murmur, blending with the drums and the shouting from outside. Words were not important anymore. She could feel her heart beating, could feel the rush of blood through her body, could feel the heat rising from her skin.

"Good," Painted Wolf said at last. "Now we dance."

She blinked at him, startled to hear English words again. She struggled to reply, bringing the words from an enormous distance. "How . . . how will we dance?"

"Like wolves," Painted Wolf said. "We dance like wolves."

Nadya tried to speak again, but words had left her. Painted Wolf was stooping and picking up a drum and stepping away from her. She followed him—she had to follow, drawn by the sound of the drum, by the painted symbols on his skin.

He threw back the tepee flap and stepped out, howling and pounding on the drum. The sun was brilliant after the darkness of the tepee, and Nadya closed her eyes against the light. Even so, the sunlight was warm on her bare skin—on her breasts, her back, her legs, all the skin that had been clothed so long. The ground was hot beneath her bare feet. She tipped back her head and howled with Painted Wolf, a long wailing cry that cut through the drumming and shouting.

Painted Wolf shouted in Cheyenne and pounded on his drum. She opened her eyes and saw him leap in the air and land in a crouch. He left the drum there on the ground and leaped again, like a wolf pouncing on mice in the grass. Nadya tried to laugh, but the sound that came from her mouth was more like a bark. He looked back at her, and she saw him as a brother and a sister: half wolf, half human, half man, half woman. He whined in his throat, an entreating sound, and she followed him, stepping carefully forward, head high, testing the scents on the breeze.

She ran when he ran, dodging among the warriors and women. The people were painted and the air was thick with the earthy scent of paint and the animal smells of the feathers and skins that they wore. A camp dog was barking, and she snarled, angered by the sound. She would hunt the dog down and tear out its throat. But the drumming distracted her, and she kept running.

Somewhere, somehow, Painted Wolf fell behind her, and she found herself leading the way. She ran through the encampment, circling the chief's tepee, running past the wagon. She was only dimly aware of Painted Wolf, running behind her. She felt dizzy and the world was blurred around her: the colors were fading to black and white. Her skin was hot and she felt the Change coming to her.

Other people were following her, dancing just behind her

and howling like wolves. She growled and snapped at the ones that came too close. She was mad with the heat, with the coming Change. She ran from the people and met a barrier, a great wall of brush that forced her back. She ran to the side and found another barrier. Only one way was open to her: she ran between the barriers toward the shaded pen. Painted Wolf was with her, running at her side and growling.

There was a power in her, a wild mad strength. She could share that power with these people; they would grow strong through her. Dancing warriors followed her into the pen: young men with the faces of wolves, leaping and running just as she did; snarling as she snarled. They were her pack. She was the leader. Since her parents died, she had had no pack, no other wolves to run with. When she howled, they howled. She was one of them. She felt wild and savage—and a little empty. She was leaving something behind, but she could not remember what.

A woman's voice cut through the drumming—a high, desperate shout above the noise. "Nadya! Nadya!" The name meant nothing to her. An awkward sound. But the voice called to her, just as the drums called. She turned toward the voice.

A woman pushed through the dancing warriors. Her dress was torn; one cheek was scratched where she had been pushed into the brush barrier. Nadya could smell the blood that smeared her cheek, smell her sweat and the musky scent of her sex. Familiar smells.

A wolf warrior grabbed the woman's arm. Nadya growled, low in her throat, warning him away. He ignored the warning and started to drag the woman out of the enclosure. She struggled, trying to pull her arm free, and fell, her leg giving way beneath her. The warrior tugged her to her feet. He was speaking words, but words meant nothing.

Nadya growled and leaped for the man. He turned to see her, and she caught a glimpse of his face: eyes wide and frightened, arm up to shield his throat. He was on the ground beneath her and she tasted sweat and paint and blood. She felt arms reaching around her and she turned to fight another enemy, but it was the woman, who held her close and murmured, "Nadya, Nadya. Come away from here. Come with me."

Nadya closed her eyes, lost in the familiar smells, the touch of Elizabeth's hand on her bare back, the sound of her voice. The drums faded.

When Nadya woke, she was wrapped in a quilt in Elizabeth's bed in the back of the wagon. Elizabeth was slumped in the chair beside the bed, sleeping. It was strange to see her sitting there, in the place where Nadya had waited to see if Elizabeth would recover from the snakebite. She could see Jenny's sleeping form, curled up like a cat in her corner bed.

It was dark, except for the dim light of the moon, shining through the canvas. Nadya sat up slowly. Her muscles ached and her body was sore all over. She looked down at her naked body: Elizabeth had washed away the paint and blood and dirt. Her breasts and back were scratched where she had run against the brush barrier; the scabs pulled painfully when she reached out to Elizabeth.

"Elizabeth?" she whispered. She took Elizabeth's hand. "Elizabeth?"

Elizabeth's eyes fluttered open. Then her hand tightened on Nadya's and she leaned closer. "Nadya—you know me. You're back."

Nadya nodded. She was back. The dance was over. She had felt the Change coming. In the middle of the day, when the moon was not full, she had felt the Change. And then Elizabeth had come to her and the Change had not come. "It was so strange," she murmured. "Something was happening, Elizabeth. Something I didn't understand. I was Changing. But the moon wasn't full. I don't know what would have happened."

"Don't try to talk," Elizabeth whispered. "You're tired; you need to rest." She left her chair and sat on the edge of the bed, still holding Nadya's hand. "I was so frightened. So frightened. You didn't know me. But when that Indian grabbed my arm, you came to save me, howling like a madman." She shook her head. "Covered with blood and paint." Softly, she traced the line of a long scratch that ran from Nadya's shoulder, across her breast, across her belly. Her fingers were cool against Nadya's skin.

Pain and pleasure—a thin line of fire along the scratch. Nadya took Elizabeth's hand and brought it to her mouth. She kissed

Elizabeth's fingers, soft and smelling of salve.

"We can't," Elizabeth said. "You're hurt."

The pain didn't matter—small aches, twinges of pain. She pulled Elizabeth into the bed with her, silencing her protests by kissing her, by reaching under her nightgown and stroking the soft skin of her thighs, by unbuttoning her dress. The pain didn't matter.

Afterward, Nadya lay on the bed, with Elizabeth's head pillowed on her shoulder. "Tomorrow," Elizabeth said, "we'll leave for California."

Nadya nodded. She thought about saying goodbye to Painted Wolf, to Slim Face, then realized that it didn't matter. She had made her choice; she had said goodbye. She was already far away.

Early in the morning, when the air was still cold, Nadya went to Painted Wolf's tepee. Her muscles were stiff, and she moved like an old woman. As she made her way through the village, she saw Calf Woman carrying a pottery jug filled with water from the river.

"Good morning," Nadya said, but the woman turned away without speaking.

Painted Wolf was not in his tepee. The flap was tied open so that she could look inside. The paints that he had used the day before were still laid out on a buffalo robe. She picked up the clothes that she had left there the day before, and went to Chief Slim Face's lodge. Calf Woman was bathing a small naked boy, one of the chief's sons, in water from the river. The boy submitted to the cold bath with good nature, smiling as he shivered. The chief sat by the fire, his head bowed.

"Good morning," she said to him.

He looked up from the fire, as if surprised to see her there. He studied her face with dark, unreadable eyes.

"I was looking for Painted Wolf," she said.

"He has gone," the chief said.

"Gone where?"

"Gone to fast. To pray. To ask the spirits what he must do." His voice was quiet. "You are leaving?"

She nodded. "I must go to California with Elizabeth and Jenny."

"I am sad that you are going," he said. "Painted Wolf thought you could teach us the ways of the white man's spirits. He thought you could make us strong."

She shook her head. "I'm not a spirit," she said slowly. "I can't save you. And I belong with Elizabeth and Jenny. They're going to California, and I must go, too."

"I think maybe you don't know where you belong." His voice was quiet.

"I wish I could stay. I wish things could be different."

"I think the world is changing," Chief Slim Face said. "The buffalo are going, the white men are coming. I think maybe I will not like this new world." He shook his head slowly, frowning. "Goodbye," he said. "Good luck."

25

They left the Indian camp and traveled up the Sweetwater River, over mile after mile of rolling land. Elizabeth rode on the mare. Her injured leg made riding sidesaddle difficult, so she hiked her skirts up to sit astraddle. Her leg ached, especially toward the end of the day's travel, but she didn't care. She was happy to be moving again.

That night, they camped beside the river and Elizabeth built a fire of cottonwood and made a dinner of pork and johnnycake. Jenny went to bed early, but Elizabeth sat by the fire, happy for the first time in weeks.

"I'll sleep well tonight," she told Nadya. She had never slept easily in the Indian camp. Always, there were sounds that disturbed her rest: voices calling to one another in an alien language, savages laughing, dogs barking and growling, and drums pounding, a rhythm that lay beneath all the other sounds, as constant as the beating of her heart. She had been afraid there, always a little afraid.

Nadya sat by the fire, watching the flames. Watching her face, painted red by the fire's glow, Elizabeth remembered the dance at the Indian camp.

It had been mid-afternoon when she heard Nadya's voice, howling like a madwoman. Elizabeth had left Jenny in the wagon, telling her to stay there, whatever happened, and she followed the sound of Nadya's voice, pushing her way through the dancing Indians.

She could walk, but her leg was still weak. Her ears rang with the rumble of the drums, the hideous whooping, the high piping of bone whistles, the mad barking of dogs. Sweating bodies crowded close around her. The air was thick with dust raised by dancing feet, with the smells of sweat and blood and burning herbs. The sun beat down on her head, and her own clothes stank of sweat.

A man was bleeding from a wound in his chest, a great slash just above his nipples, a ritual sacrifice of some barbaric sort. His eyes were closed, his vision turned inward. Another had a wooden skewer threaded through the skin of his back. A rawhide rope was wrapped around the skewer and a buffalo skull hung from the rope. The weight of the buffalo skull pulled at the skewer, tearing the skin so that blood ran down the man's back, mixing with the patterns painted on his bare skin. He was chanting as he danced, a high-pitched wailing.

She drew close to the lodge and the drums pounded in her head and her head ached from the piping of whistles. A dancing Indian jostled her and she almost fell, her injured leg giving way beneath her.

She saw Nadya then: naked except for a scrap of leather, her bare breasts painted with heathen designs, her body glistening with sweat. Elizabeth called to her and Nadya turned toward her. But there was no recognition in Nadya's eyes—wide and yellow, the eyes of an animal. "Nadya!" Elizabeth called. But Nadya turned away again, following the Indians.

Elizabeth hobbled forward to stop her. An Indian had grabbed her arm to pull her away and Nadya had come to save her: fierce and savage, leaping on the Indian with a low sound in her throat, a growl, a warning. There was blood and Elizabeth was pulling Nadya away, calling to her, calling her back.

It had been terrible and frightening, seeing Nadya bloody and howling. That was a moment of madness, of a passion beyond words. But remembering that moment now, Elizabeth felt a strange excitement. Mixed with the memory of terror and confusion was a powerful attraction. Nadya was not like anyone she had ever known. She remembered making love in the wagon, after the dance. When she lay with Nadya in the wagon, her dress undone, her skirts pushed up around her waist, her legs spread to Nadya's touch, the excitement came back to her. She remembered the beat of the drum, the wailing from the lodge, Nadya's naked body shining in the sun. And the power of it all swept over her and took her away.

Now, sitting at Nadya's side by the fire, she put her arm around Nadya's shoulders. Nadya's body was warm against hers. "I'm glad we're away from there."

Nadya continued staring into the fire, looking troubled. "I don't understand why you were afraid of the Indians. They helped us when we needed it. And they're just people, like you."

"Not like me," Elizabeth said sharply.

"How are they so different?" Nadya asked quietly.

"They are savages, heathens. That dance, the blood, the howling." She stopped, unable to put her feelings into words. "They aren't like me."

"But perhaps," Nadya said softly, "perhaps they're a little like me. Or I'm like them. Maybe I should have stayed with them, finished the dance. During the dance, I felt I could belong there. When the moon is full—"

"Oh, Nadya," Elizabeth interrupted her quickly. "Don't be foolish. You belong with me." She pulled Nadya close.

They made love under the stars and there was no more talk that night of where Nadya belonged or what happened when the moon was full.

They traveled as they had before: up each day before the sun had warmed the morning air; milk the cow, eat a light meal, hitch the oxen; travel until the sun was high, then rest for a few hours and travel again until late in the afternoon. Elizabeth resumed Jenny's lessons, and each day at noon she read to Nadya and Jenny from her books: poetry, essays, stories. Each night, Elizabeth came to Nadya's bed, and each morning, when Nadya woke, she was gone.

The trail westward crossed the Rockies at South Pass, a smooth gap in the mountains with a gentle grade leading to the summit and an easy descent. As they climbed, the nights grew colder. At the higher elevations, there were patches of snow beside the trail: crusted over and dusty, but still frozen even at midday. Nadya had never seen such a thing before—snow that persisted even in summer—and she marveled at it as they passed. Each morning, the water that was left in the bucket had a thin scum of ice.

The weather grew warmer as they descended from South Pass. The trail followed a creek to a river bed—the Dry Sandy, according to Elizabeth's guidebooks, a river that flowed only in the wettest of years. Following a faint set of wagon ruts, they took a cutoff that led directly west, rather than dipping south with the main trail. It led to the Big Sandy, a cheerful stream where Nadya shot two sage hens for supper.

They made their way across a stretch of dry land to the Green River, where a ferryboat run by two Mormon brothers took them across. The brothers were surprised to see any travelers so late in the year. It was three dollars for the ferry, but they spent the money rather than brave the river.

The trail led to the Bear River, then headed north, up to Soda Springs, a place where dozens of springs gushed from a mound in the earth. The waters bubbled even though they weren't hot. Nadya sampled the water carefully, at Elizabeth's suggestion. It tasted of the saleratus powder that Elizabeth used in cooking, and Nadya didn't care for it. But Elizabeth, quoting her books, claimed that the fizzing water had healthful qualities, and drank cup after cup of it. A short distance farther on, they found Beer Springs, a pool of golden water that tasted a bit like flat lager. They stopped for a time at Steamboat Spring, where the water boiled from a gap in a rock. Every now and then, a cloud of steam shot from an opening in the rock, and the spring made a low hooting noise, like the whistle of a steamboat.

The weather was good and Nadya was content. The oxen had gained weight grazing on the lush grass that grew beside the river, and the trail was level, making for easy traveling.

Past Soda Springs, the river turned south and the trail headed up between two low mountain ranges, past Mount Putnam, over rough land, to the Snake River, where the three great mountains known as Three Buttes stood over the adobe walls of Fort Hall.

They stopped for two days at Fort Hall, lingering to have the horses reshod. The fort, an outpost of the Hudson's Bay Company, was quiet. Most of the men were gone on an expedition to trade with the Snake Indians. Only two white men and half a dozen Indians remained. One of them, the clerk at the trading post, was drunk, as near as Nadya could tell, the entire length of their stay at the fort.

The other, the blacksmith, was a burly man with only one ear, the left one having been sloppily removed in a long-ago knife fight. Nadya guessed that he had been a handsome man before the injury. He had fine dark eyes, dark hair. The right half of his face was well proportioned. But scar tissue pulled the left half of his face to one side, giving it a demonic twist, so that half of his mouth was always smiling.

After shoeing the mare, the blacksmith offered to check the wagon's harnesses and running gear for weakness and wear. He did a thorough job, inspecting each axle and wheel, tightening the iron tire that encircled one wheel. As he worked, he chatted with Nadya about the trail ahead, glancing frequently at Elizabeth who sat nearby, neatly patching a skirt that she had torn.

"The trail to California's a hard way to travel," he said. Half his scarred face still grinned, but the other half was grim and serious. "It ain't fit for wagons. That first grade down into Big Goose Creek is worse than anything you've seen yet. And the Injuns are bad. You got two kinds of Diggers out that way: hungry dirty ones that will come around begging for food and steal what they can and mean dirty ones that will shoot your cattle from the hills, run off your horses and steal what they can. Odds are, you won't have anything to pull a wagon afore long. And even if you do manage to keep your stock alive all the way to the Great Meadows at Mary's River, you still have to cross the desert." He shook his head and continued gloomily. "The desert kills even more oxen than the Indians, I'd guess. And if you get across the desert, you still have to make it over the mountains."

Nadya glanced at Elizabeth, who had lifted her head to listen. "Others have managed it," Elizabeth said in a calm voice. "It isn't an easy road, but it can be done."

"Some," he said. "But those trains had a dozen men to clear trail and drive oxen and fight off the Diggers. I don't reckon that you can do all that on your own. Besides, it's mighty late in the season to be risking that trail. A few delays, and you'll be caught in the winter snows."

"That can't be so bad," Nadya said uneasily. It snowed sometimes in Missouri—a light powdering that lingered a few days, then melted. At worst, they would be delayed. It wouldn't be good, but they could do it.

The blacksmith was shaking his head. "It's bad—worse than bad. There was a wagon train snowbound in the California mountains last year. Headed up by a man named George Donner. They were coming up from the desert early in October, but the snow shut down the pass at Truckee Lake before they could make it over."

"Donner?" Elizabeth said. Her voice was strained. "George Donner? Was his wife's name Tamsen?"

"I don't know his wife's name, but his name was George. They didn't pass this way. They went by way of Fort Bridger, following a trail blazed by some fellow who had written a guidebook." The man shook his head. "Eighty souls, trapped in the snow for most of the winter. They ate all their supplies. They ate their oxen and boiled the hide and the bones for soup. They ate the pet dog that one family had brung along from Illinois." He dropped his voice still further. "And then they say they ate their dead. Mad with hunger, they ate human flesh, roasting heart and liver over the fire." He stared at Nadya, the right half of his face set in grim lines, the left still wearing its demon grin. "Half of them died in the snow. The other half escaped with their lives, leaving all their belongings to the snow and the Indians." He shook his head. "I wouldn't take that trail with a wagon. It ain't worth my life."

"They were from Springfield." Elizabeth's voice was soft but steady. "I met them before they left."

"Tell me," Nadya said to the blacksmith. "What would you recommend we do? We can't very well turn back."

"Head for Oregon," he said. "The trail's bad, but not so bad as the California trail."

Nadya glanced at Elizabeth. She was shaking her head, her expression grim but determined. "My uncle lives in California," Elizabeth said. "We have to go there."

"Then hurry along," the blacksmith advised. "Stop for nothing. You must get over the mountains before the snows."

"We'll make it." Elizabeth's voice was determined. "We'll be fine."

The blacksmith shook his head, looking at Nadya. "Your sister is a strong-willed lady. But I wouldn't take a wagon on that trail. It ain't worth my life."

They left Fort Hall early in the morning, traveling down the winding Snake River. At Raft River, they turned south and the trail grew rougher. The hill leading down to Big Goose Creek was as bad as the blacksmith had said. Nadya had to chain the wagon wheels together to act as a brake, so that the wagon wouldn't overrun the oxen. It was a long and dangerous road, finally fetching up at a sage-filled gully where a trickle of water flowed. The trail continued through a valley, where the wind had etched rocks into strange and fantastic shapes.

In the valley of Big Goose Creek, they met a band of Indians—dirty, hungry Diggers, according to the blacksmith's categories. Small, bowlegged, misshapen people, they begged for food and Elizabeth gave them johnnycake so that they would go away. She felt sorry for them, but she shrank back when they tried to finger her dress, touch her skin. They were naked and dirty and thin, very thin. They ate all the johnnycake she made, and begged for more. When she shooed them away, they complained bitterly in their own language, which sounded to Elizabeth like the growling and barking of puppies. That night, when Elizabeth came to Nadya's bed, she found Nadya sitting up.

"What are you doing?"

"Keeping watch," Nadya said. "I smell hungry Indians on the breeze, and I thought I'd best keep an eye out."

When Elizabeth woke, Nadya was still keeping watch, and the

next day she fell asleep at the noon break. That night, Elizabeth insisted that she take the first watch. Nadya argued, but in the end her need for sleep won. From that point on, they split the night in two, with Elizabeth taking the early watch and waking Nadya late in the night. Jenny slept in the wagon, and Nadya and Elizabeth slept out by the oxen, one sitting up and keeping watch while the other slept.

During her turn, Elizabeth would sit wrapped in a quilt, with Papa's rifle across her lap. She watched the stars wheel overhead, cool and distant, and watched Nadya sleep. It was strange, sitting alone in the darkness, watching over the grazing oxen.

The place where the snake had bitten her ached constantly. Her whole body ached: arm muscles sore from raising the whip; lips chapped; face burned by the sun.

She distracted herself from the pain with thoughts of California. In her thoughts, the town of Yerba Buena where her uncle lived was like Springfield, but warmer and filled with flowers. Her uncle and his family would welcome Nadya and Jenny like sisters. And they would all rest and eat and be happy. She would open a library with Papa's books, and a school for young ladies. Jenny would be her first pupil. They'd live together in a lovely little house surrounded with flowers.

When she woke Nadya, she would lie down and continue her dream. In the morning, they moved on. The land was gray and flat with distant mountains indistinct against the sky. She was tired, always tired. Dust rose from the trail, blurring the landscape around her.

On one chalky cliff, they found the names of others who had passed that way, carved deep in the soft stone. Elizabeth understood the urge to leave a mark behind; in this monotonous land, she felt that she herself was fading away, blurring at the edges, becoming one with the gray soil, the rocks, the graves alongside the trail. A valley of ghosts, always willing to welcome another spirit.

There were graves along the trail, weathered mounds of gray soil, sometimes ringed with stones, sometimes headed with wagon boards. On the boards, people had painted names, ages, causes of death. A child run over by a wagon. A woman, dead of the fever. A man killed by Indians. So many ways to die on the trail.

Beside the graves there were the bones of oxen—picked clean by scavengers and bleached white in the sun. Their own animals were gaunt, having lost the little weight they had gained during their time among the Cheyenne. Sweet Nancy's milk had dried up; Elizabeth could see the cow's ribs beneath her skin.

They went down Big Goose Creek into Little Goose Canyon, a fearsome place where the trail ran through the water as much as beside it. There they lost Bill Sikes to Indian arrows. Elizabeth was on watch and she never saw the attackers. She was dreaming of California when she heard an ox bellow in pain. Nadya was awake instantly, and she stood quickly, her rifle in hand, moving to Bill Sikes's side, keeping the ox's body between herself and the canyon walls. Elizabeth pointed her rifle up at the dark canyon walls, but she could see nothing to shoot. Nadya took sight on something that Elizabeth couldn't see, and fired her rifle. The echo of the shot rolled up and down the valley.

"Missed," Nadya grunted. "But close enough that he won't be back tonight."

Bill Sikes had been wounded by two arrows: one in the shoulder and one in the neck. Elizabeth tended the wounds as best she could, anointing them with the patent medicines that she had brought along and bandaging them to keep out the flies. Even so he died on the second night after the attack. They left him by the trail and moved on.

Down Little Goose Canyon, past Rock Springs, resting for a day at Thousand Springs Valley, where the grass was thick and the oxen could graze. There, the moon was full and Nadya went hunting.

On the evening of the Change, she walked away from camp, wandering across the valley to find a place where she could be alone when the Change came to her. She was not far from the camp when she heard rustling in the grass behind her. She stopped and waited, and Jenny came up behind her.

"Why are you following me?" Nadya asked.

"I thought . . . I wondered. . . ." Jenny looked at her feet, then raised her eyes to meet Nadya's. "I want to come hunting with you."

Nadya squatted down so that she could look into Jenny's face. "I know that, little one," she said gently. "But I told you: I change when I hunt. You can't follow me then."

"But I thought . . . maybe you could change me, too. You could make me into a wolf, like you." Jenny's face was solemn. "Then, you wouldn't have to go hunting by yourself. I could help."

Nadya shook her head. "I'd like that. But I can't change you, any more than I can stop myself from changing. The moon rises, and the wolf comes to me. I have nothing to say about it, no way to stop it." She stood up and looked down at the girl. "But if I could, I'd be glad to do it. You'd make a fine wolf, and I'd be glad to have you hunt with me."

Jenny nodded, biting her lip. "I don't like it when you leave," she said at last. "I'm afraid."

"What are you afraid of?" Nadya asked her. "You can take care of anything that comes along."

"I'm afraid you won't come back."

"I'll come back," Nadya said, smoothing the girl's hair back from her eyes. "I'll always come back for you. Now you have to go and take care of Elizabeth. I would worry, leaving her alone. But I know that you'll protect her."

Jenny nodded. "I will."

"So you go back to camp." Nadya watched the girl until the trees hid her from view.

Nadya found a grove of trees on the far side of the valley, and there she stripped naked, relishing the evening breezes on her bare skin. The moon was just below the horizon and she could feel its pull. Through the trees and across the meadow, she could see the flickering light of the campfire that Elizabeth had built. Looking at the distant flame, Nadya felt divided. A part of her longed for the warmth of the fire, Jenny's easy companionship, Elizabeth's daytime chatter and nighttime passion. But another part, deep and wild, feared the fire and yearned for the less certain light of the moon.

Nadya felt the touch of moonlight on her skin, a warmth that came from within her, like the first flush of sexual arousal. She Changed, shedding her human form and coming into her animal self. The gray wolf that was Nadya gazed up at the moon and voiced Nadya's longing and uncertainty by tipping back her head and howling, a long low cry that echoed across the valley. From the camp came an answering howl, Jenny's voice, not so deep but also touched with yearning.

Elizabeth was in the wagon, preparing for bed, when she heard Jenny howl. She climbed down from the wagon and went to sit by the dying fire. "That noise sends chills up my spine," she said softly.

"I just wanted to let Nat know we were here," Jenny said.

Elizabeth poked the fire, frowning. She did not want to think about Nadya being out there in the darkness. From the hillside came a long howl, answering Jenny's. Jenny joined in, adding her voice to the howling of the wolf. Two thin lonely voices echoing across the valley.

Elizabeth shivered and pulled her shawl tighter around her shoulders. "I wish Nadya were here with us," she murmured. She sat by the fire, her shawl pulled around her shoulders. The distant wolf howled again.

Jenny remained silent. She was leaning back on her elbows in the grass, looking up at the stars. "That's the Big Road," she said, pointing up at the Milky Way. "Coyote made it when he was putting up the stars."

Elizabeth felt a sudden chill. "What are you talking about?"

"White Antelope says that Coyote put all the stars up in the sky," Jenny said. "And she told me about the animals that live there. There's a wolf over there, and a bear—"

"Jenny," Elizabeth interrupted. "You know better than that. God and his angels put the stars in the heavens. I don't know who this Coyote is, but—"

"Coyote is someone who plays tricks," Jenny said. "Someone very clever, very sly. White Antelope said that maybe Nadya was really Coyote. She said it would be just like Coyote to show up looking like a white woman to fool everyone."

Elizabeth shook her head. They had left the Indian camp none too soon. The child had been exposed to all manner of nonsense. "Listen to me," she said sternly. "God put the stars in the sky, not some Indian spirit named Coyote. And Nadya is no more an Indian spirit than I am."

"Then why does she go hunting?" Jenny asked. "If she was Coyote—"

"Hush! I don't want to talk about this anymore. Tomorrow, I'll read to you from the Bible and you'll hear how God created the heavens and the earth. No more of this nonsense."

"But Elizabeth—"

"No more," she said quickly. "I won't have it."

Jenny fell silent. Elizabeth did not want to talk about Nadya and hunting. It was enough to accept that it happened, to wait quietly for Nadya to return. Talking made it real. She did not want to acknowledge the strange change that came when the moon was full.

"Here now," Elizabeth said. "It's time for both of us to get to bed anyway. Come along."

In the wagon, Jenny crawled into her small bed. The girl was very quiet and Elizabeth thought she might have been too stern. She was on edge, listening to that dreadful howling and trying not to think of Nadya. "You go to sleep now," she murmured to Jenny. "That's what you need. I think we've been out here too long. When I started traveling, I didn't know California was so far away. If I'd known that, I might have stayed in Springfield.

"Things will be better when we get to California," Elizabeth said, reassuring herself as well as Jenny. "We'll sleep in clean sheets—no fleas in the beds. And we'll have clean dresses to wear. We'll sit in regular chairs, not on rocks by the fire."

The girl's eyes were closing now. "When I was your age, I learned to play the pianoforte and sing. When we get to California, I'll teach you to play. You'll like that."

"Would you sing to me?" Jenny said. "Sing the song that Nadya sings."

Elizabeth stroked the girl's hair and sang the lullaby that Nadya had taught them. Jenny did not say anything. Her breathing was regular. Elizabeth smiled down at her. They would get to California and find her uncle, and they could leave all this behind them. She pictured the three of them in her uncle's drawing room, gathered around the pianoforte. She and Jenny were wearing new dresses. She could not quite imagine Nadya in a dress, but she was wearing clean trousers and a new linen shirt.

Things would be better when they reached California. Surely they were almost there.

The next day, they moved on, down along a small creek and across a dry stretch, always heading west, until they reached the headwaters of Mary's River. There they lingered again, resting in the meadow and preparing for the next leg of the journey.

For three hundred miles, this muddy stream named for the sacred Virgin followed a meandering course toward California, a trickle of water laced with alkali. In dry years, the water almost disappeared and the grass did not grow. In wet years, the mud washed over the grass, leaving the banks barren.

For the first few days of their journey downriver, the grass was good. Then the valley narrowed, closing in like a trap, and grass grew scarce. The river water had a poisonous milky color. Elizabeth boiled all the water they drank to kill the small wiggling creatures that swam in every bucketful. But even the strongest tea could not cover the taste of sulphur and salt. Drinkable, yes, but not palatable. Elizabeth dreamed of the well water back home: cool and sweet and tasting of greenery.

Day after day, the mountains looked the same, as if the oxen and wagon remained stationary despite their efforts to move forward. Not even a tree to break the monotony—three hundred miles of barren land.

Elizabeth was always tired now, always sore. Cracked lips, throat burned by the alkali dust, always a little thirsty but unwilling to drink too much of the foul water from the river, leg aching. By day, the sun beat down, broiling any exposed skin. At dusk, when the heat of the day eased, mosquitoes swarmed about her, attacking through her dress and raising welts that itched for days.

Traveling was like sleepwalking, like moving through an unpleasant dream. Sometimes, as she walked beside the oxen, she dreamed of California—waking visions of a better life. And sometimes, as she lay sleeping beside Nadya, she dreamed that she was walking beside the oxen, driving them even in her sleep. The animals were thin, and the four remaining oxen all worked hard.

By the river, the mud was bad, miring the wheels and tiring the oxen. When the road left the river and ran through the hills, the dust was worse. There was no water fit to wash in, and she and the others had weathered to a uniform gray color. Each day, the river grew fouler and smaller—a series of nasty pools connected by a bare trickle of water. White alkali glistened on the banks of the river like frost on a winter morning.

Indians haunted them, hungry ghosts in a gray land. At night, Elizabeth saw their fires burning brightly in the hills. Nadya would not allow her to build a fire, saying that the blaze would attract the unwelcome attention of the Indians. As Elizabeth sat in the fireless chill, she came to hate the Indians. If there had been no Indians, she could light a fire for warmth, she could sleep at night. One night, they lost Charlie Bates to Indian arrows. The next morning, they had to harness Sweet Nancy to the wagon and she pulled with the others.

Elizabeth kept watch at night, but her head drooped as she sat by the wagon. She slept sitting up—or maybe she dreamed that she was sleeping, for the two were so similar that she could barely tell the difference. In her sleep or her dream of sleep, she saw movement: Indians drifting down the hills toward her. It was nearly dawn: the sun was coming up and touching the sky with red, but she was still cold, just as she had been all night long. Nadya was asleep beside her, breathing steady, face relaxed.

Elizabeth stood up, letting the quilt fall, and the cold air made her shiver. She saw a quick movement near the wagon, someone running, and she leveled her rifle and fired without thinking. The rifle slammed into her shoulder and her ears rang with the sudden shot. In the distance, the running man fell. There were other men, running toward her now, and Nadya was sitting up in her blankets, snatching up her rifle.

Elizabeth was awake now, and the cold didn't seem to matter. "I saw an Indian near the oxen, and I shot him."

Nadya was standing now, holding her rifle where the Indians could see it, and Elizabeth snatched up the pistol and stood beside her.

"Reload," Nadya said, and ran toward the fallen man. Elizabeth's hands were shaking as she reloaded, spilling powder on the robe in her haste. There was a taste of blood in her mouth—

she had bitten her lip when the rifle fired. Her ears were ringing with the explosion from the rifle, an endless echo. Her hands would not stop shaking.

Nadya stood by the body. The Indians had fled. Elizabeth went to Nadya and looked down at the Indian she had killed. In one hand, he clutched a knife—he had cut two of the oxen loose. He would have left them with only a milk cow and a single ox.

He was a very small Indian, Elizabeth thought. Not much older than Jenny. "He's just a boy," she said. "Just a boy."

"Come on," Nadya said, tugging on her arm. "They may be back."

Elizabeth resisted. She could not stop staring at the dead boy. The bullet hole in his chest did not seem like it would be enough to kill him. She remembered the morning, so long ago, when she had strapped on Papa's holster. Back then, it had seemed like an adventure.

"I didn't mean to kill him," she murmured, but even as she said it, she knew it was a lie. She had meant to kill him, to kill all the Indians who tried to steal their oxen. "We should bury him."

"His people will come back for the body," Nadya said. "Come on."

"I want to say a prayer for him."

"All right, then. As you like."

Nadya waited beside her as she bowed her head. Elizabeth tried to pray, but no words came to her. Where words had once been there was a blankness, a void. She could not think, she could not speak.

After a time, Nadya put her arm around Elizabeth's shoulders. "It's all right," Nadya murmured. "We'd best be going." Elizabeth let herself be led away.

26

■

"Giddap!" Nadya cried, snapping the whip over Oliver's flank. "Giddap there!" Her throat was sore from shouting. She was thirsty, always a little thirsty. The thin trickle of water that ran near the trail was foul. That morning, Elizabeth had boiled water, but it was late afternoon and the supply of boiled water was low. The last time they had stopped for a rest, Nadya had insisted that Jenny and Elizabeth drink, but had refrained from drinking herself. She could wait until they camped for the night, she thought. She could wait.

Jenny rode on the Indian pony and Elizabeth sat on the wagon seat, gazing out at the dust and the barren hills. When they began traveling down the river, Elizabeth had talked often about the Great Meadows, the place where the river spread out to cover the desert. There they could rest and the oxen could graze. Surely the meadows could not be much farther, she had said, day after day. But there were no meadows. Just the gray endless river and the gray endless land. A few days before, she had stopped talking about the meadows.

The trail turned away from the river, leading up a small rise. Nadya urged the oxen up the gentle slope. The animals strained at their yokes, struggling up the hill. They would have to stop for the night soon. If only she could find a spot where there was more than a few mouthfuls of grass for the oxen. The animals were slowly starving.

From the crest of the hill, Nadya saw a swirling cloud of black on the horizon. Birds, she realized, an enormous flock of blackbirds, taking to the air. Beneath the birds was a patch of green. Fagin lifted his head, as if catching a scent on the wind, then stretched out his neck and bellowed.

"Look," Nadya called to Elizabeth. "It's the meadows."

"The meadows?" Elizabeth looked up, startled, as if she had forgotten that the meadows existed.

"We're almost there! Giddap!" Nadya cried, but the oxen had already quickened their pace, catching the scent of grass on the breeze.

Mary's River, that unfortunate trickle, ended in a burst of glory. Its water spread out over the desert and created a marsh where grass grew thick and California-bound travelers could linger and prepare for the next leg of their journey, the trip across the desert.

Nadya made camp beside a shallow pool, where red-winged

blackbirds sang in the rushes and herons hunted for minnows in the shallows. The pond was spring-fed, clear and cold even in the late afternoon. Nadya and Jenny stripped off their dusty clothes and went wading in the clear water. They tried, without success, to scoop the tiny fish from the water with tin cups. But the fish darted away, flashing silver in the late afternoon sun.

Elizabeth sat on the bank. She had taken off her shoes and was soaking her feet in the cold water. She could see her reflection in the pool: a gaunt woman, her face brown from the sun, her eyes weary with squinting against the light. Her friends in Springfield would not recognize her. She didn't recognize herself.

She gazed across the pond at Jenny and Nadya, laughing and playing in the water. The sun glistened on their wet bodies. Naked as savages.

She bowed her head, examining her hands. They looked clean now, washed in the water of the pool. She had scrubbed them with lye soap until the skin was reddened and rough. There was no visible sign of the Indian's blood. But she knew it was there. She could feel it—a stain on her hands, a stain on her soul.

She heard splashing and Nadya clambered from the water onto the bank beside her. "Why don't you come swimming?" Nadya said. "You'll feel better for it." She sat on the grassy bank, the sun glistening on her naked skin.

Elizabeth did not look at her. "Not just now," she said.

"What's wrong?" Nadya said. "Are you feeling poorly?"

Elizabeth shook her head. "I'm tired," she murmured. She rubbed her eyes.

"We can rest for a few days," Nadya said. "Let the oxen graze, drink all the water we want. I'll go hunting in a bit. I saw a few fat ducks that would make a fine supper. The moon is almost full. After the full moon, we'll cross the desert to California."

Elizabeth had been reading about the desert. "They say that the desert is worse than anything we've seen so far. And even if we cross it, then there are the mountains." She shook her head. "It's so far, so very far."

"That's so," Nadya agreed. "But you knew that before."

"I knew it. But I didn't understand it." She closed her eyes against the sun.

She felt Nadya's hand, still cold from the water, touch hers. "It'll be all right," she said. "We'll get across the desert; we'll get over the mountains. I promise."

A few days later, they set out early in the morning to cross the desert. The trail left the meadows and circled the edge of Humboldt Lake, a pool of brackish water unfit for drinking. A layer of white scum floated on the lake's surface. It took the better part of a day to travel around the edge of the lake.

The oxen were rested and well fed from their time in the Great Meadow, but a few days' rest could not make up for weeks of labor and hardship. When Nadya reached over to slap Fagin's side, she could feel the bone beneath the skin, the ridges of his ribs. Up ahead, on the low land beside the lake, Nadya saw the scattered bones of an ox that had died last season. The skull had been bleached in the sun. As Nadya approached, a small brown snake slipped through the tough grass with a whispering sound and fled into the right eye socket of the skull.

Nadya could smell fresh-cut grass—the wagon was loaded with it. Three kegs of water sloshed in the wagonbed. They were as prepared for the desert as they could be.

For a few miles beyond the lake, they followed a sluggish, alkaline stream. The tough grasses and reeds that grew along its banks were encrusted with salt. A salt crust crunched beneath the wheels of the wagon. At last the river disappeared, seeping away into the dry soil.

Not even sage grew in this desolate landscape. Here and there, clumps of greasewood clung to a precarious existence. Each bush formed the center of a dune formed by windblown sand. The trail wound between the hillocks, heading for a set of low hills in the distance.

In the dim light of dusk, they set out across the desert. The trail was sandy, and the wagon wheels sank, making the wagon more difficult to pull. The land ahead was bleak and forbidding. Barren sands and smooth stone hills. The hills were nothing compared with what they had already crossed. But they had fewer oxen now, and the animals were tired. The animals shuffled forward, heads low.

The sky grew dark, and the first stars appeared, brilliant points of light on a field of deep blue. As the air cooled, the wind took on a bitter edge. It caught the sand and flung it at them. Nadya could hear the sand grains hissing against her trouser legs, against the canvas of the wagon.

The desert was silent except for the whispering of the sand. No crickets, no birds. They were alone, and the only sounds were the ones they made. The wheels creaked and groaned as the wagon moved ponderously forward.

Elizabeth and Jenny walked at Nadya's side for a time, but Jenny kept lagging behind. After an hour, Nadya insisted that she lie down in the wagon. Five minutes after she lay down, she was asleep, exhausted from the day's journey. After that, Elizabeth walked beside Nadya, her head bowed.

The moon rose. Crystals of salt and sand reflected the silver light, and the desert glistened. In the moonlight, Nadya could see evidence of other travelers who had passed this way: the skeleton of an ox, bleached white in the sun; a trunk, cast aside to lighten the load, now half filled with drifting sand. The moonlight glittered on something inside: a silver frame; a square of glass. Someone's silver-framed looking glass, carried all the way from the States. Beside the looking glass was a black leather-bound book, its pages rustling in the wind. A family Bible, left to the desert.

Perhaps, Nadya thought, those earlier travelers had planned to come back for their treasures. "As soon as we find water," they might have said. "As soon as we are revived." But they had never returned and the names that had been lovingly inscribed on the Bible's flyleaf had faded in the sun.

Nadya did not know how long they had been traveling when they reached Boiling Springs, the hot springs located halfway across the desert. Moonlight illuminated a plume of steam rising from pools of brackish water, too hot to drink.

Elizabeth held back the thirsty oxen while Nadya filled buckets and pans with the steaming water. The moonlight revealed the well-boiled skeleton of an ox at the bottom of the largest pool. Some unfortunate traveler had not managed to restrain his animals, and had lost one to the scalding waters.

When the water cooled, they let the thirsty animals drink.

Nadya woke Jenny and unloaded grass from the back of the wagon, giving each animal a ration.

While the animals ate, Elizabeth made a meal of cold pork and johnnycake, served with tea made with hot water from the steaming pool. The water was brackish, but not so bad that they couldn't drink it. Nadya was glad to wet her lips and soothe her dry throat.

After a short rest, they set forth again. "Maybe you should ride for a while," Nadya suggested to Elizabeth. "You need to rest."

"I'll walk," Elizabeth said. "The wagon is too heavy as it is."

Not far from Boiling Springs, the trail grew sandy. The wheels sank in the loose sand and the oxen had to work even harder, leaning into their yokes and struggling with each step. They trudged on, moving slowly.

The moon was high in the sky when Nadya saw the silhouette of a wagon on the trail ahead. Unlike the other wagons they had passed, this one was in the center of the trail. For a moment, Nadya thought that they were overtaking another company. But the wagon had been abandoned; the oxen, long since dead, lay in the yokes where they had fallen.

The wagon blocked the trail, and Nadya turned the team to one side, circling around the obstacle. The wagon dipped down into a dry gully and the right rear wheel slid up to its hub into a pocket of loose sand. "Giddap," Nadya cried, her voice cracking. The oxen pulled, but the wagon did not move. She raised her hand and snapped the whip, and the animals leaned into their yokes. "Giddap!" She heard another crack, much louder than the whip, and the wagon tilted to the right, the bed dropping closer to the sand.

"Whoa! Whoa there."

Nadya inspected the damage. The rear axle, dried in the desert air and weakened over months of travel, had snapped, breaking cleanly.

Elizabeth sat on the sand beside the wagon. Her bonnet was pushed back on her head; wisps of hair that had escaped her braids were in tangles by her face.

"The axle's broken," Nadya said.

"We don't have another axle," Elizabeth murmured.

Nadya nodded. "That's right." She sat in the sand beside Elizabeth.

Elizabeth glanced at the wagon that blocked the trail. "Maybe we could take an axle from that wagon and replace our axle," she suggested. Her voice had an edge of desperation.

"Maybe," Nadya said. "If it's sound. If it fits our wagon."

"We can try."

"If we're lucky, it will take us half a day to get the axle on our wagon. If we can keep working so long without water. By that time, the sun will be up." Nadya looked at the oxen. They stood quietly in their yokes, their heads drooping low. "But when we've fixed the wagon, will the oxen be able to pull it from the gully? And if they do, can they pull it all the way to Carson River? With no water and just a little grass to keep them going?"

Elizabeth looked down at her hands and said nothing.

"We can leave the wagon," Nadya said softly. "Pack what we need on the oxen and leave the rest."

Elizabeth did not look up. In the moonlight, her face was pale. "You want to leave the wagon," she said. Her voice was low, little better than a whisper. "Leave it all behind?"

"We have to," Nadya said. "We have no choice."

Elizabeth looked down at the sand, but did not reply.

Nadya took the oxen from their yokes and gave each animal an armful of grass. She tended to the horses as well. Using wood from the abandoned wagon, she built a fire and made a pot of tea with their last few cups of water. Elizabeth was still sitting beside the wagon, and Nadya went to her and brought her to the fire. Nadya got a shawl from the wagon and wrapped it around Elizabeth's shoulders. She woke Jenny and led the sleepy child to the fire, where she would be warm.

"Why are we stopping here?" Jenny asked sleepily.

"The wagon broke an axle," Nadya said. "You'll have to ride your pony from here."

Jenny blinked owlishly at the emptiness around them. "How far is it to the river?"

"Not so far," Nadya said, trying to reassure herself as well as the others. She had no way of knowing how far it was to water. The breeze smelled only of dust and desert. But they had been traveling so long. Surely the river must be near. "It can't be far."

She touched Elizabeth on the arm. "We have to pack what we can. Will you help?" Elizabeth did not move. She was watching flames flicker along a board. "I'll get started," Nadya said.

Nadya went to the wagon alone. Laying a quilt on the wagon floor, she began packing: flour, coffee, their last few pounds of cured bacon, all the black powder and lead, a frying pan, a pot. She carried the things out of the wagon and laid them on the sand. She was making up a pack of food and another of equipment, when Elizabeth stood from her seat by the fire.

"We must take all of Papa's books," she said. Her voice was soft, the voice of a sleepy child. When she climbed into the wagon, Nadya followed. Elizabeth opened one of the big trunks and looked down at the books.

"We can take a few," Nadya said. "Just a few."

Elizabeth looked up, her eyes confused. "Oh, no," she said brightly. "We must take them all. We must." She began to take the books from the trunk.

Elizabeth handled the books carefully. The leather bindings were cool to the touch, smooth beneath her hands.

Her hands were chapped and callused from handling the whip. Her mouth was dry again; the hot tea had helped only while she was drinking it. She could have drunk another pot of tea and still asked for more. Tea or lemonade or water. She thought about water, and remembered the muddy water of the Platte River. She had scorned that water, complaining about its muddy taste, the grit that ended up in her tea, her johnnycake, everywhere. She had been a fool to complain about that water. If someone gave her a cup now, she would drink it and ask for more—never mind the grit, the taste of mud, the tiny wiggling creatures that squirmed in the bottom.

Her feet ached, a dull distant pain. How long had she been walking? For days, she thought. Somehow, it was still night, even though she had been walking for days. That didn't seem right. She shook her head. How could it still be night? Her mind was fuzzy and she could not think clearly.

She deserved a rest, she thought. For a moment, she considered taking one of Papa's books and curling up by the fire. She would read about the Pickwicks, and she would laugh as she had laughed when Papa read the book aloud to her, many years ago. She looked down at the book in her hand and started to turn away from the trunk.

Someone had been rummaging in the food boxes. Everything was out of place—a quilt was gone, and all the blankets. The wagonbed tilted backward. Something was very wrong, she thought.

She heard Nadya's voice outside and she remembered: Nadya wanted to leave Papa's books behind. She returned to the books and gathered an armful. Walking carefully, she carried them outside.

Nadya was tying a load on Fagin's back. A sack of flour, a bundle of food wrapped in a tarp, a pot dangling off to one side. The ox stood beside the wagon, its head drooping. Clothing and blankets lay in heaps around them. Jenny was wrapping a blanket around an awkward bundle.

Nadya looked up when Elizabeth set the books beside the ox. "I'll pack these," Nadya said. "And then we'll be going."

"Oh, no," Elizabeth said. "It will take some time to get all the books. There are so many of them."

Leaving the pack, Nadya came to Elizabeth and put her arms around her. "We can't take all the books," she said carefully. "The animals are exhausted. We have no more water. We'll die in the desert with all your papa's books."

Elizabeth shook her head stubbornly. "We can't leave them."

"We can't take them all."

Elizabeth pulled away and went back to the wagon. She picked up more books: a thin volume of collected poetry by Mrs. Felicia Hemans, William Alcott's *Young Man's Guide,* Henry Ward Beecher's *Lectures to Young Men,* a book of essays by Ralph Waldo Emerson, *Voices of the Night* by Henry Wadsworth Longfellow. She climbed down from the wagon, clutching the books. Nadya was tying a pack on the horse's back. The pile of books was no longer on the ground. Clothing was still scattered about.

"We're leaving now," Nadya said. "It's time to go."

Elizabeth shook her head. "The books," she said, but her voice was weak.

"Giddap!" Nadya cried to the oxen. Fagin was lying on the ground, and Nadya went to his head and tugged on his lead. "Giddap there, Fagin." Nadya tugged and he stumbled to his feet. "Giddap there, Oliver." When Oliver didn't move in response to her tugging, she twisted his tail and beat his flank with the butt end of the whip. "Giddap, you flea-bitten bastard. Giddap." Finally, with a snort of protest, he heaved himself to his feet.

Elizabeth watched Nadya tug the animals to their feet, beat them, swear at them. It was no way to act, she thought. She held the books that she had gathered and wondered vaguely how she had come to be traveling with this person.

No matter how Nadya poked and prodded and shouted, Artful Dodger and Sweet Nancy would not get up. They lay on the sand, their heads low. At last, Nadya stopped trying, and with Jenny's help she untied the pack that had been on the animals' backs, sorting out things to leave behind and loading the rest onto her horse. At last, all the animals except the Artful Dodger and Sweet Nancy were standing. Elizabeth's mare was limping, but unwilling to be left behind.

Nadya hoisted Jenny onto the back of the Indian pony. Half asleep, the child clung to the pony's mane, swaying a little but keeping her seat.

"Giddap!" Nadya shouted, her voice hoarse. She was stooped beneath the weight of her pack. "Giddap now!" She tugged on the lead, and Oliver shambled forward. "Elizabeth!" Nadya called. "Come along. We have to go."

Elizabeth hesitated for a moment. She glanced back at the fire. The coals still burned, a welcoming patch of warmth. Nadya was leading them into the desert, where it was cold and empty.

"Please, Elizabeth. Come along, love. Come with me, darling. Please come along." Nadya's voice was pleading. She spoke softly, as if to a child. Elizabeth took a step forward, still carrying her books. Slowly, she followed Nadya out into the wasteland.

One step, another step, another step. Ahead of her, the sand glistened in the light of the setting moon. The windblown ripples shifted and flowed like water. Like a lake, she thought, a beautiful lake. She thought about sitting down beside the lake and waiting for the sun to rise. Such a pleasant place it would be, if only it were not so cold. "Come along," Nadya called. "Keep walking."

Elizabeth stumbled and dropped one of the books that she clutched in her arms. It opened to the title page as it fell. She stood for a moment, looking down at the book on the sand. *Voices of the Night,* a collection of poems by Henry Wadsworth Longfellow. The wind turned the pages as she watched. She should pick it up again, she thought.

"Don't stop, Elizabeth," Nadya called. "Come on."

She left the book in the sand and stumbled forward. The wind was cold, very cold, and she tried to clutch her shawl more tightly around her shoulders. Her hands, stiff in the cold, fumbled and another book fell. A collection of essays by Emerson. She left it where it fell.

Nadya and the animals moved steadily toward the setting moon. Another book fell. She did not even stop to note the title. Perhaps she could come back and get it later, she thought. But she knew that she wouldn't. She was letting go of her old life. Leaving it behind. Bits and pieces scattered by the trail. Her papa. Her cast-iron stove. The printing press. The books that meant so much to her. Leaving them all behind.

She'd walk for one hundred more steps, she decided, and then she would lie down and rest. One hundred steps. She tried to count them, but she kept losing track, forgetting what number she had reached. Surely she had reached one hundred by now, she thought. It must have been one hundred.

She called to Nadya. "Wait." Her voice was hoarse and her throat ached. The wind caught her words and blew them away. "Wait, Nadya." Two more books fell, and she clutched only one slim volume.

Nadya kept walking, moving steadily away with the oxen. Elizabeth struggled to catch up with her, but her feet sank in the loose sand and her efforts to hurry brought her no closer. Up ahead, Fagin lifted his head and bellowed plaintively. "Water ahead," Nadya called back to her. "I can smell it." The other ox looked up and quickened his pace. "Come on."

Elizabeth tried to walk faster, but she stumbled and fell. This time, she did not get up. There was nothing ahead but darkness and stars, she thought. She sat on the sand, pulling her shawl closer around her and clutching the last book. She could hear the lonely tolling of Fagin's bell, moving away in the darkness. She was alone now, just as she had been after Papa's death. Alone. She pulled her knees to her chest, trying to conserve her body heat.

Overhead, the stars were bright and terrible. Not angels watching to keep her safe. Big balls of fire, far, far away. They didn't care about her. The sound of the bell faded in the distance.

She was so cold. She could not stop the shaking in her arms. Why did preachers always say that Hell was hot? Hell was cold, bitter cold, with no way to get warm. No wood to burn, no other people near. Bitter cold and raging thirst.

She was afraid. She was afraid of the desert—the heat, the thirst, the sun. She was afraid of the cold, the wind that pelted her with sand, the indifferent stars above her, the emptiness all around. That was the worst of it: the emptiness, the great nothingness. She felt her very soul being drawn away from her body, her life pulled from her to fill the void.

Sitting alone in the desert, she realized that she feared the wilderness and all that was in it. The Indians, the wolves, even the soldiers in the fort, so far from civilization. She feared the wild creatures that made tiny noises just beyond the circle of firelight. "Just mice," Nadya had told her. "Nothing to be afraid of." But Nadya was a part of the wilderness.

Nadya was not afraid. She loved the empty spaces, the wild beasts, the dirty Indians. Nadya was a part of the wilderness, and Elizabeth feared her. Loved her and feared her, but the fear was stronger now. She was afraid of this wild woman who spoke to Indians and rode like a man. Not afraid that Nadya would harm her, but afraid that she, Elizabeth, might become somehow like Nadya, a woman outside the protection of civilization, a woman who belonged nowhere.

In the desert, Elizabeth acknowledged her fear. She accepted it, and held it close. Frozen fear, held close to her heart. It would never thaw, she knew that.

She sat in the desert with her head on her knees, praying for deliverance. She did not know how long she prayed. But when she lifted her head, a bright line rimmed the horizon in the east.

In the west, she could see a low dark line on the horizon. She squinted at it, thinking it might be a cloud that would evaporate as the sun rose higher. But the dark line stayed—a ragged line of trees just a few miles distant. As she watched, she could see a figure leading a horse, moving slowly across the barren land.

27

Nadya found Elizabeth huddled in the scant shade of a greasewood bush. Her eyes were closed. Nadya tried to rouse her. "Wake up," Nadya urged. "I'll take you to the river. Wake up." Elizabeth muttered something unintelligible and turned away, pillowing her head on her arm.

Nadya untied the kerchief that she wore around her neck, wet it with water from the canteen, and used it to wipe Elizabeth's face, trying to cool her. She could feel the heat of Elizabeth's skin through the thin fabric. She splashed water on Elizabeth's wrists and temples, wet her lips.

Nadya's horse stood nearby, his head drooping. The water of the river had revived the beast, but she had given him no time to graze before turning back to find Elizabeth. The horse was still worn out from the long night of work, and she would have to head back for the river soon, or risk losing the animal to exhaustion.

"Elizabeth," Nadya said. "You must wake up." She shook Elizabeth's shoulders.

Elizabeth did not respond.

"Wake up," Nadya said, almost in tears. "You can't leave me."

Elizabeth muttered in her sleep. It might have been a prayer.

Nadya left Elizabeth where she lay and led the horse along the trail to a wagon that had been abandoned a little farther along. Once it had been the property of a large and prosperous family. The desert sun had weakened the canvas top and the wind had tattered it. Sand had blown in through the opening at the back of the wagon, through the gaps in the canvas. The boards of the wagon had warped and dried in the desert heat.

With a hatchet that she found in a trunk of tools, Nadya pried loose one of the wagonbed's side boards. It had cracked down the center and she split it to form two long poles. She found buffalo robes in the wagon and lashed them to the poles, making a sort of travois, like the ones the Cheyenne dragged behind their ponies. She used rope from the wagon to tie one end of each pole to the saddle, and the horse dragged the travois back to where Elizabeth lay. With the remaining rope, she tied Elizabeth to the makeshift stretcher, padding her with buffalo robes and making her as comfortable as possible. Elizabeth shifted and moaned when Nadya moved her, but did not wake.

A few miles to the Carson River. She tied Elizabeth's bonnet so that it shaded her face, but she could not keep the sun off her body. The poles of the travois slid over the sand, but Nadya's feet sank. Her eyes burned, dazzled by the sun.

Once, Elizabeth cried out and Nadya went to her side. Elizabeth's eyes were wide and fearful. When Nadya wet her kerchief and reached out to wipe Elizabeth's face, Elizabeth flinched, as if Nadya had tried to strike her. Her lips moved as if she were speaking, but she made no sound.

She was feverish, Nadya thought. Driven mad by the sun. She would be better when she reached the cool shade by the Carson River. She would come to her senses there.

"You'll be better when we get to the river," Nadya assured her. "You'll feel better then."

Elizabeth's eyes closed and she muttered again, but the words were unintelligible.

Jenny was waiting with the oxen when they reached the river. Cool water, cool shade. "Elizabeth is ill," Nadya managed to say. Then she stumbled and fell in the grass by the river. The grass was cool against her face; the ground was damp beneath her. She could hear Jenny talking, somewhere far away, but she could not respond. She slept then, her face in the cool grass, the sound of the river in her ears.

They spent the week resting by the river. Nadya made a shelter of tarps, and hunted along the river for rabbits. Elizabeth lay on a pallet of pine branches, covered with buffalo hides.

Jenny and Nadya took turns sitting with Elizabeth—giving her water and tea and rabbit broth. In her fever, Elizabeth did not recognize them. Nadya sat beside her in the pine-scented shelter, listening to her talk to people who weren't there. Her face was flushed, and her eyes were wild. She looked at Nadya and shook her head. "You would not believe it, Sarah," she said. "You would not believe." And she shook her head again, tossing to and fro on her pallet, refusing to believe. "I learned to shoot a rifle. And I shot an Indian. A boy really. It was terrible out there, dreadful. It's not an adventure, like it is in the books. Oh, I'm so happy to be back in civilization."

"There," Nadya soothed her. "There now. Sleep a bit."

"That is kind of you," she said. "So kind." She shivered then, and Nadya tucked the quilt more closely around her. "Do you know," Elizabeth murmured, "it's dark in the desert at night. It's dark and there are no angels, just balls of fire in the heavens above. And I'm all alone, all alone. And Papa's books—they're gone now. All gone. Everything gone."

"You're safe here," Nadya said. "You're not in the desert now."

Elizabeth blinked at Nadya, but her eyes remained unfocused. She turned her head and looked out at the camp: smoke rising from their small fire, oxen and horses grazing, regaining their strength for the trip over the mountains. "Not safe," she said, her voice bleak and desperate. "Not safe." She said nothing more. At last, she slept.

When she slept, Nadya watched over her. By her expression, Nadya guessed that her dreams were uneasy.

Nadya woke from a deep sleep to the sound of Elizabeth's terrified voice. "Nadya? Nadya! Where are you?"

"I'm here," Nadya murmured, rolling over to take Elizabeth in her arms. Through the tangle of blankets, she could feel the woman's heart beating, a rapid pounding rhythm. "Hush now. I'm here."

She could smell Elizabeth's fear, a heavy scent that made her want to leap from the blankets and do something, anything. But she could see no reason for Elizabeth's panic. The only sounds were Jenny's soft breathing and the babble of the river outside. Everything was as it should be.

"Where are we?" Elizabeth whispered fearfully.

"By the river," Nadya said. "We've crossed the desert." She stroked Elizabeth's hair, trying to soothe her.

"I had such a frightening dream," Elizabeth murmured. "I dreamed I was in the desert alone. The sky was enormous and filled with stars and I was all alone. I saw you walk away from me and you didn't come back when I called."

Nadya frowned in the darkness, remembering the moment when she had looked back and discovered that Elizabeth had fallen behind. "I didn't hear you call. I thought you were following. And when I looked back and saw you were gone, I had to get Jenny to the river. If I had stopped, we all might have died there." She hugged Elizabeth close. "As soon as I reached the river, I went back." In the dawn light, she had followed their trail back across the desert, picking her way through the barren land.

"All alone," Elizabeth said, her voice bleak with the memory. "All alone in the desert. It was cold, so cold. And the wind was blowing. . . ." Her voice trailed off.

"I came back to get you," Nadya said. "And now you're safe, with Jenny and me."

"Safe," Elizabeth repeated softly. "I don't know if I'll ever feel safe again."

Nadya kissed her cheek. "I'll keep you safe."

"It's not so far to go now," Elizabeth said, her voice stronger. Her heartbeat had slowed, and the scent of fear was fading. "Just over the mountains to California."

"Not so far," Nadya agreed, though the blacksmith at Fort Hall had made it clear that the journey over the mountains was as hard as any trail they had traveled so far. "Not very far at all."

Nadya kissed the soft skin of Elizabeth's neck. It had been so long since they had made love. They had been too tired, too dirty, too thirsty. Nadya kissed her again. Soft skin beneath her lips. Nadya fumbled in the blankets, finding her way through the rough wool to Elizabeth's warm body.

Elizabeth was naked—her nightgown had been abandoned in the desert with so many other things. Nadya gently cupped Elizabeth's breast, feeling the nipple crinkle against the palm of her hand. Elizabeth's breath caught in her throat. "We'll wake Jenny," she murmured.

"Jenny could sleep through a stampede." Nadya pushed aside the blankets and pulled Elizabeth against her. When she kissed Elizabeth's throat, she could feel the warm pulsing of blood beneath the skin.

Elizabeth's scent changed. Nadya did not know the words to describe the scent of Elizabeth when she was aroused. As inviting as the scent of buffalo on the breeze; as rich and intriguing as the spoor of an unknown animal. Nadya breathed deeply, inhaling the musky aroma.

"We shouldn't," Elizabeth murmured.

"Hush," Nadya said.

She ran her hand down between Elizabeth's thighs to find the wetness between them. She stroked the folds of slippery flesh. Elizabeth's breathing took on an urgent rhythm and she moaned softly. The sound vibrated against Nadya's lips as she kissed Elizabeth's neck.

Nadya remembered the last Change, when she had caught a jackrabbit in a grassy meadow. The dying rabbit had screamed as her jaws closed over its throat, a sound that she felt at the same time as she heard it.

Nadya moved her hand in time with Elizabeth's rhythm. Elizabeth's body jerked, pressing upward into Nadya's hand. She moaned again, and Nadya kissed her lips, muffling the sound. The rhythm quickened. She stiffened in Nadya's arms, pushing harder against her fingers. A sudden tension, a sharp inhalation, almost like a sob. Her thighs clamped hard on Nadya's hand. After a moment, she relaxed in Nadya's arms.

In the dim moonlight, Nadya could see Elizabeth's face. She was gazing up at the stars. The tent was filled with the warm smell of sex. "And why shouldn't we?" Nadya said softly, smiling down at Elizabeth.

Elizabeth shook her head, frowning a little.

"Remember the first time we made love," Nadya said. "On the bluff by the river. Afterward, you told me that the stars were angels, watching over us. You were so beautiful, lying naked in the grass."

"Hush," Elizabeth murmured. "Don't talk."

Nadya knew that she didn't want to talk about making love. That was all right. She knew, by Elizabeth's scent in the darkness, by the soft rhythm of her breathing, that she was happy. They did not need to talk.

They made their way up the river, following a trail that repeatedly crossed and recrossed the water. Jenny kept count and announced that they had forded the river twenty-seven times by the end of the first day. After the long haul down Mary's River and across the desert, it was a relief to have plenty of water to drink and grazing for the livestock. But the trail was hard—climbing steadily uphill—and the oxen were weary. At noon each day, the animals grazed on the grass that grew by the river, making up for the days of meager grazing along Mary's River.

Nadya led the pack train with Jenny at her side. Elizabeth rode Nadya's gelding—her sore leg pained her and she could not keep up with the others on foot. With rest, she had recovered somewhat from her fatigue and illness, but Nadya worried about her. She was thin, so painfully thin. But she sang with Nadya and Jenny as they walked and talked brightly about how happy she was to be in California at last.

Seven days' travel took them to a place where the trail left the river. The next few days were easier—a pleasant trail and a gradual climb up a broad valley.

They went as fast as they could, but that was not as fast as Nadya wanted. The mountains rose up like a wall before them. It was early November by Nadya's reckoning, and the air was cold and crisp. Each morning, Nadya studied the sky, wondering if the clouds that hung over the peaks ahead would bring snow. But each day, the clouds burned away, and Elizabeth chided her for worrying so.

Late one afternoon, high in the mountains, the trail passed a campsite of sorts, long since abandoned. Nadya saw the crude shelters in the distance—improvised lean-tos constructed of pine branches, draped with buffalo robes and scraps of clothing. She started to pass without stopping, but Elizabeth saw an iron pot lying beside one of the shelters and insisted on stopping. In Nadya's haste to escape the desert, she had packed only one pot.

"It would make cooking easier to have two," she said.

"There's nothing for us here," Nadya said. The wind that blew from the shelters reeked of death and decay. "This isn't a good place." But Elizabeth had already dismounted and started in the direction of the shelters.

The ground was strewn with debris that marked this as an emigrant's camp. Nadya could see the rusting hardware from a wagon, the decaying remnants of a bridle, hanging from a tree. The lean-tos were draped with rotting buffalo robes and scraps of faded clothing.

Around the camp, trees had been cut down—for firewood, Nadya guessed. It seemed strange: the stumps were taller than Nadya, maybe twelve feet tall, some of them. Staring up at them, Nadya realized that the height of the stumps marked the depth of the snow when the trees were cut down.

Nadya took a few steps after Elizabeth, then stopped. At the foot of a stump not far from the trail was a pile of bones: human bones, Nadya suspected, jumbled with the bones of oxen and horses.

"We must move on," Nadya said. The smell turned her stomach. Not just the stink of death, but the stench of despair, of pain and suffering and hunger without end. There was no good to be had here.

Jenny stood by the oxen, but Elizabeth was approaching one of the shelters. She stooped beside the gap in the branches that served as the doorway to one lean-to and examined the pot that lay on the ground. "Look," she said, picking something up from the ground near the pot. "I've found a book."

"Come away from there," Nadya called. "There's no good to be had lingering here."

Elizabeth walked slowly back to them, limping a little on her injured leg, holding a small, leather-bound volume. "It's someone's diary. It's not too badly damaged," she said, "even though I think it's been out in the snow." She opened the book. Looking over her shoulder, Nadya could read the inscription on the flyleaf. Black ink on a water-stained page, written in a fine, careful hand: "Tamsen Donner."

"What is it?" Jenny asked, frowning up at Elizabeth. "What's wrong?"

"It's Tamsen Donner's diary." Elizabeth's voice trembled. She stared at the camp. "The blacksmith at Fort Hall told us about them. This is where they camped when they were trapped in the snow."

"Put it back," Nadya said softly. "Let it be."

"They were so happy when they set out," Elizabeth said. "I remember. They had a beautiful wagon, strong oxen." Her voice faltered, and she looked at the bits of hardware in the yard, the bones by the stump. Her hands were trembling as she opened the book to the last page. Black ink still, but the handwriting was shaky and uneven. "There is snow," the words read. "Snow and cold and pain and hunger. George is dead and the children are gone—to safety, I pray. I am here alone, and I'm cold, so cold."

"George was her husband," Elizabeth said softly. She looked at the shelters, her eyes wide and frightened. "They died here."

"Leave it be," Nadya said roughly, taking the diary from Elizabeth's hand and tossing it to the ground. "Let the book stay here, with Tamsen and her husband. Let them rest in peace. Come along now."

She took Elizabeth's arm and moved her toward the horse. "Help me here, Jenny," Nadya said, and together they got Elizabeth on the horse.

Nadya hurried away from the place of death. Far ahead she could see the pass that they had to climb, the ascent that had stopped the Donners and the rest of their party. She could see no sign of a trail up the boulder-strewn granite slope, but that was where the trail had to be.

"Are we going to die in the mountains?" Jenny asked.

"No." Nadya rested her hand on Jenny's shoulder, looking down at the girl. "The weather's fair and we're strong. We'll cross the pass tomorrow."

Jenny nodded, looking worried.

Farther on, the trail passed three more cabins, ramshackle dwellings hastily constructed of logs, situated in a dense grove of fir trees. The roofs had fallen in. Here too the ground was littered with debris, but Elizabeth did not suggest that they stop.

Nadya hurried on past, skirting the edge of Truckee Lake and heading toward the formidable pass. They camped just before sunset, in a clearing where the livestock could graze. Elizabeth's mare was failing. The animal's hooves had softened in the water of the Truckee River, during their many crossings, and one had cracked badly. Though Nadya rubbed it with salve each morning and evening, the injury did not heal. The mare needed rest, but that was a luxury they could not afford.

The evening was cold and clear, with a biting wind from the north. Nadya pitched their tent by a granite boulder that provided a windbreak and built a roaring fire to warm them and raise their spirits. Hunting had been poor for the past few days; the deer had moved to lower ground. Their supplies were meager, but Elizabeth made a meal of johnnycake and dried beef.

After dinner, Jenny went to sleep, wrapping herself in blankets and curling up in the tent. Nadya and Elizabeth sat up for a time, gazing across the lake. The moon had risen—a quarter moon on its way to full—and the moonlight reflected from the ripples in the water, painting a path of silver across the lake. The granite slope of the pass rose above the lake, glittering in the moonlight. It was beautiful, Nadya thought, so pure and cold.

"What a frightening place," Elizabeth said. She was looking back toward the cabins and the camp they had passed. She glanced up at the granite slope that lay ahead of them. "Do you think we'll make it over the pass? After all our troubles, will this stop us?"

"Don't worry," Nadya said. "We've left our wagons behind and the weather has held. We'll be fine."

They went to bed in the tent, slipping in beside Jenny. Nadya fell asleep with Elizabeth in her arms. And in the night, it began to snow.

In the morning, the trees were dusted with white. Snow glittered between the boulders on the jagged granite slope that led to the pass. More than a foot of the powdery white stuff. When Nadya looked up at the pass, she shivered.

Fagin and Oliver stood in the shelter of a grove of pine trees. Jenny's pony and Nadya's gelding stood with them. A short distance away, Elizabeth's mare lay in the snow, her brown coat dusted with white. Through the dusting of snow, Nadya could see the horse's ribs.

The animal had died in the night—of exhaustion, starvation, and cold. Standing in the snow, Nadya touched the animal's head, brushing snow from her mane, from her ears, a gesture of thanks for the mare's good service.

That morning, Nadya packed their belongings, redistributing the load that the mare had carried into packs for the oxen and other horses. There was little enough to pack: food, blankets, tent, hatchet, cooking pot, what little clothing they weren't wearing, a sack filled with Elizabeth's books.

Nadya hesitated for a moment, holding the sack of books. The sack was heavy and the animals were tired. The books would not feed them, would not keep them warm. The most sensible course would be to leave the books behind in the snow.

She glanced at Elizabeth, who was tying a strip of wool cloth, cut from a blanket, over Jenny's head and ears. "You must keep your head warm," she was saying. "And then the rest of you will stay warmer."

Her face was so thin. Nadya remembered her first sight of Elizabeth, out on the prairies. She had stood tall and proud, her head high. Now she looked worn and ragged. She had left so much behind. Nadya could not ask her to abandon these books as well.

Nadya turned back to her task, hoisting the sack of books onto Fagin's back and tying it in place. Her hands ached with the cold as she tugged on the knots, pulling them tight.

When they started up the trail to the pass, Nadya tried to make Fagin break trail. But the ox was unwilling, turning aside despite Nadya's best efforts, eager to return to the lake where the going was easier. Nadya was forced to lead the way up the pass, one hand on Fagin's rope, the other clutching a walking stick that she had cut some days before.

The snow was soft and powdery, and breaking trail was difficult. With each step, she sank deep into the snow. In some places, the wind had blown the white powder into drifts that reached to mid-thigh. More than once, she nearly fell, slipping on uneven ground that the snow had hidden, catching herself with her walking stick.

Ice crystals clung to her boots, to her trouser legs, to her wool socks. She had tucked the legs of her trousers into her wool socks, but after less than an hour of hiking, she could feel the cold trickle of ice water penetrating the fabric.

The trail—if you could call the suggestion of a path that she followed between the boulders a trail—led upward, always upward. Nadya paused by a boulder that blocked the wind and looked back at Elizabeth and Jenny.

Oliver and the gelding followed Fagin, and Elizabeth and Jenny came after. Jenny was riding her pony. She was wrapped in a buffalo robe, and her shoulders were hunched against the cold. When Elizabeth and Nadya had rescued her from her family's wagon, they had not thought to search the trunks for warm clothing. In the heat of the prairie, who would have imagined that they would need it? Elizabeth walked with her head down, her hair hidden beneath the scrap of red blanket that served as her scarf.

When the others reached Nadya, they crouched for a time in the shelter of the boulder and ate biscuits left over from breakfast, cold and dry now, but better than nothing. "We must thank God for what we have," Elizabeth murmured, and Nadya knew that she was thinking of the Donners, camped in the snow without even dry biscuits to eat.

Nadya quenched her thirst with snow, though it chilled her lips and made her throat ache. And then they walked again, making their way up the mountain.

It was hard, so hard. When she was climbing, she would sweat and when she stopped to wait for Elizabeth and Jenny, the wind would chill her to the bone. Her feet were wet now, with snow melted by her own body heat. Her feet ached with the cold, and each step was painful.

When she looked back, the lake seemed so close. It was tempting, so tempting, to suggest returning to the lake. They could wait there for a time, and perhaps the snow would stop falling. Perhaps tomorrow would be a better day to travel. But she thought of the Donners and she kept walking. She stopped looking back at the lake, looking forward instead, studying the granite slope, the distant summit. It was closer now, surely it was closer.

One foot in front of the other, each step an agony. Tugging on Fagin's lead. Stopping, now and again, to wait for Elizabeth and Jenny, to help them up a difficult patch, to say something, anything, that might encourage them.

The sun was high in the sky when they reached a granite slope that rose like a wall, leveling out some ten feet above them. Nadya paused beside the obstacle and looked back at the others. The lake was far below them now, a distant expanse of blue. Elizabeth and Jenny toiled up the slope, following Nadya's trail. Elizabeth was limping now.

Nadya wandered along the rock wall, searching for a path that led upward. There had to be a path; others had come this way. At last, some distance from where the trail had led her, she found a narrow rift in the rock, a crevice up which an oxen might climb. Not far away, she found the marks of chains on the slope of granite. Examining the marks, she guessed that earlier emigrants had driven their oxen, one by one, up the narrow gap. Then they had let down chains and the oxen, standing securely above the wall, had dragged the wagons up the impossible slope.

While she waited for the others, Nadya broke branches from the twisted bushes that clung tenaciously among the boulders. By the time Elizabeth and Jenny reached her, she had a small blaze.

"Sit here and warm yourselves," Nadya said. "We'll have tea. And then we'll climb the rest of the way." She rummaged in the packs and dug out a pot in which she could melt snow.

Elizabeth sat on a rock by the fire, silent. She extended her feet toward the fire so that her boots might dry.

"Are we almost to the top?" Jenny asked. She was livelier than Elizabeth.

"I think so."

"I'm glad the wind stopped," Jenny said. "And the sun's come out."

Nadya squatted by Elizabeth, putting her hand on her knee. "There are marks on the rocks that show that other wagons have passed this way. We're on the trail. Soon we'll be over the top."

Elizabeth nodded. "Perhaps it will be easier on the other side," she said softly.

"Maybe so," Nadya agreed eagerly.

Later, as she sipped her tea, Elizabeth revived a bit. "At least we aren't thirsty," she said. "I would have given anything for all this snow when we were in the desert."

After they rested, Nadya led the oxen to the cleft in the rock wall. Jenny climbed up first, clutching Oliver's lead rope in one hand and using the other to help her clamber over the rocks. Then she pulled from above while Nadya drove the ox from below. Oliver was reluctant to attempt the climb, bellowing his protests. "Pull, Jenny," Nadya called, and she twisted Oliver's tail, forcing the beast to move forward. Eventually, they got him to the top of the cleft. From there, Nadya could see the crest of the pass, still distant but no longer unattainable.

While Elizabeth rested by the fire, they drove the other animals up the cleft, with much shouting. The effort warmed them, and Nadya was encouraged by the sight of the summit. Then they pressed onward, over the granite slopes, toward the top, the summit, beyond which the way might be easier.

In late afternoon, they reached the top of the pass. Elizabeth stood at the crest, looking down. Behind them, the lake lay far below and beyond it were broken hills dusted with white. And on the far side of the pass was a world of mountains and fir trees. The afternoon sun glittered on the snow that filled the ravines and dusted the trees—as brilliant as diamonds. A few lakes, clear and blue, were scattered in the fields of white. And beyond them, far, far below, Elizabeth could see a valley where the green grass was not covered with snow, a slash of emerald in the white, with a stream running through it, running downhill toward the Sacramento Valley, where the air would be warm and no snow fell.

Her heart sank to see how far away they were from that strip of green. Too far. She glanced at the oxen. Oliver stood with his head hanging low; Fagin was sniffing the bare rocks, searching for something to eat. The animals were worn out from their long months of travel. Her leg ached and she felt as if she could not take another step.

She could see Nadya and Jenny, standing on a granite slope. How shabby they looked: Nadya in her worn deerskin coat, Jenny with a buffalo robe, thrown like a shawl over her shoulders, a scrap of blanket around her neck. Over the weeks, all their clothing had become a uniform shade of gray-brown, as bright colors faded and light ones acquired a layer of grime. They looked like tramps, worse than tramps for she had never seen a traveler with such ragged attire in Springfield.

As she watched, Nadya turned to look back at her. "Isn't it a beautiful view?" she called. She was smiling, a flash of white teeth in a face burnt brown by the prairie sun. Her eyes were bright in the sunshine. She was happy to be at the summit, undaunted by the distance yet to travel.

"It's so far to go," Elizabeth said softly.

Nadya shrugged, still grinning. "Compared to how far we have come, it's no distance at all. We'll be there in no time."

They traveled down the far side of the pass to the first of the lakes, where they camped in the snow. The oxen wandered by the side of the lake, foraging for leaves or grass.

That night, Elizabeth heard wolves howling in the distance as she shivered in their tent. Nadya stirred in her sleep; Jenny did not even move, her breathing steady and even. Elizabeth was alone in her fear of the wolves, of the snow, of the great wilderness that surrounded them. She lay in the darkness, thinking of the dangers that surrounded them. They could freeze in the snow; they could run out of food, like the Donners, and starve; they could fall down one of the steep slopes—she'd come close enough to that, more than once. They could be attacked by wolves—though Nadya told her not to worry about that, she could not push the thought from her mind, as she listened to the beasts howling. So many ways to die.

The wolves howled again, and Nadya's breathing changed.

"There are wolves," Elizabeth whispered.

"They're hunting," Nadya said, her voice dreamy. "What a wonderful place to be hunting." She fell asleep again quickly, the wolves singing her a lullaby. And Elizabeth lay awake, frightened and alone.

They traveled down Summit Valley, a broad valley that was fair in other seasons. Elizabeth knew from other travelers' accounts that this was reckoned to be a place to rest, where the oxen could graze and regain their strength. Now the grass lay beneath a blanket of snow, and the oxen made do with what little they could find beneath the whiteness.

They came to a river that Elizabeth guessed was the South Yuba and they followed the river downward, day after day, always in snow and cold. She was always cold and always a little afraid. Each day, she considered their food supplies: half a sack of flour, just a few pounds of dried beef. Not nearly enough, she thought. She tried to eat less, to ration the supplies, and she was always a little hungry. Once, Nadya shot a small animal that looked like a fat squirrel and they had a stew, warm and sustaining. Otherwise, they lived on biscuits and dried beef, eking out a meager existence.

On the fourth day after the pass, Oliver died in the night. Poor Oliver, Elizabeth thought. He had worked so hard to die in the mountains.

They ate beef that morning and carried a sack of meat that could sustain them over the next few days. What they could not carry, they left in the snow for the wolves.

So cold, so hard. She trudged through the snow, day after day. A good day was one when the sun came out and no snow fell and her leg did not ache too much. A bad day was one where more snow fell and the wind blew and they made little distance toward their goal, their impossible goal. It seemed to her that she would never reach the end of the journey.

Nadya led the way through the mountains, down great granite slopes, past tumbles of boulders with rocks as big as oxen, as big as wagons. Each night, the moon waxed fatter, rising earlier in the evening. They made camp early on the day of the full moon. Beside a small lake, in a grove of trees, the land was clear of snow. There were even a few patches of grass where the livestock could graze.

At Nadya's insistence, Elizabeth spread a buffalo robe by the side of the lake in the thin sunshine of late afternoon and rested, while Nadya put up the tent and tethered the livestock. The air was still and Elizabeth lay back on the robe with her face turned to the sun, catching the last of its warmth.

Nadya came and sat beside Elizabeth on the robe. "How does your leg feel?" she asked.

"It aches. But I'll make it. We're almost there," Elizabeth said. "Soon we'll reach the settlements, we'll see other people." She managed a smile. "The long journey will be over."

"I reckon that's so," Nadya said. She lay back on the robe, supporting herself on one elbow and gazing at Elizabeth.

"Where's Jenny?" Elizabeth asked.

"Off with my rifle, looking for game. She might find a squirrel or some such."

Elizabeth nodded.

"Tonight, I'll go hunting," Nadya said softly. "But before I go, we have some time for ourselves." She leaned over and kissed Elizabeth gently on the lips.

Elizabeth lay very still, feeling the touch of Nadya's lips on hers, the warmth of Nadya's body beside hers. That warmth could not reach the chill that lay at her heart. In the desert, as she huddled alone beneath the indifferent stars, she had realized that she was afraid—afraid of the wilderness, afraid of Nadya and the wildness within her. She could push that fear back, ignore it for a time, but it was always with her.

The last time they made love had been in the camp by the river. She had protested; she had said that they shouldn't. But Nadya had persisted and her body had betrayed her. Her body, touched by lust and desire, had responded to Nadya's touch. But even then, the fear had been with her.

"Don't," Elizabeth said softly. "Jenny will be back."

Nadya pulled back, frowning down at her. "What of it?"

"We're coming back into civilization, Nadya," Elizabeth said firmly. "We have to think about the proper way to behave." She bit her lip, staring up at Nadya's golden eyes and knowing that Nadya did not understand. She hesitated, struggling for words. "Out here, in broad daylight, where anyone could see. . . . It just isn't civilized. Don't you see?"

Nadya shook her head. "You've changed," she said. "I don't understand."

"Changed? I don't know what you mean."

"You seem cold now," she said. "Distant. I don't know what I've done wrong."

Elizabeth stared past her at the snow-covered peaks from which they had descended. "You haven't done anything wrong," she said. "It's just that I don't feel safe here. I'm frightened, always frightened."

"What frightens you?"

Elizabeth laughed, a brittle sound without humor. "Things that would frighten any woman," she said. "Savages in war paint, primitive dances where men cut themselves and bleed, the barren desert where we could die of thirst, that dreadful camp where the Donners died, the knowledge that we could die in the snow, the wolves that howl every night around the camp. I'm not like you." She was crying then, and Nadya held her in her arms. "I'm not a coward. I'm just scared, so scared."

Nadya held her tightly, but she did not feel safe. There was no safety here.

It was almost sunset when Nadya left camp. She had done her best to comfort Elizabeth, murmuring that they would be out of the snow soon, that everything would be all right. After a time, Elizabeth had stopped weeping, making an effort to pull herself together. "I'm all right now," she had said, but Nadya knew that was not so. She was fearful and unhappy and Nadya did not know why.

Jenny had returned to camp with a jackrabbit, shot neatly through the head, and Nadya had built a fire so that Elizabeth could cook the meat. "You'll be fine here," she assured Elizabeth. Though Elizabeth nodded, Nadya knew that she did not believe Nadya. "You take care of Elizabeth," she told Jenny.

A short time before the moon rose, Nadya walked back along the trail. The wind blew cold, but she could feel the warmth of the rising moon. By a tumble of rocks, where a leaning pine tree created a natural shelter from the wind, she stopped and took off her clothes, hanging them from the stub of a branch and covering them with her deerskin jacket.

She stood barefoot on the carpet of pine needles. The wind shook flakes of snow from the tree branches and they drifted down to kiss her skin. She could feel each one as it melted, a tiny point of cold, an icicle pinprick. Her nipples hardened, responding to the touch of the cold breeze and to the rising moon. She lifted a hand and touched her breast, skin soft beneath her callused fingers, and she shivered in anticipation of the Change.

Nadya stood barefoot in the snow, thinking of Elizabeth. Her body was eager, ready for the Change. She could not see the moon rising behind the clouds, but she could feel it. Her blood beat in her veins, a tropical tide like the surge of arousal, warming her from within. She closed her eyes and let the tide take her, carrying her away from the camp with its smell of wood smoke and its memories of frustration. She stepped out from under the tree, the snow cold against her bare feet. She lifted her arms to the sky and she Changed, but the sense of arousal did not fade with the Change. Instead, it intensified, filling her with eagerness and anticipation.

A gray wolf sat back on her haunches in the snow and howled, raising her voice to the gray sky. From somewhere, not so far away, she heard an answering howl. The day before, Nadya had seen the tracks of a wolf in the snow, crossing the trail they followed. Not a pack, just a single animal, traveling alone. The wolf that was Nadya howled again, her voice rising in a call of loneliness that was answered from the distance.

She trotted in the direction of the call.

Nadya met the solitary wolf, a broad-chested male with gray fur and black markings, and greeted him with a display of cautious acceptance. She laid her ears back and grinned, whining low in her throat and wagging her tail—all indications that she was friendly, not looking for a fight. She sniffed at his muzzle and the ruff of his neck. He smelled of the forest, of the snow, and of himself, a wild aroma that touched old memories of Rufus. Rufus standing beside her at the spring, his hand on her breast, teasing her nipple through the thin fabric of her dress. Rufus at the river, his hand sliding between her thighs. But in her memory, Rufus smelled of the forest as well as of lust.

She lowered her head as the male licked her face, then opened his jaws and gently grabbed her muzzle in a gesture of greeting. His breath was warm as he buried his nose in the ruff of her neck, inhaling deeply of her scent. She laid her head over his shoulders, feeling the fur of his ruff tickle her face and closing her eyes for a moment. They circled each other, sniffing, licking, getting to know each other.

After a time, the male trotted away, looking back over his shoulder to see if she followed. She did, easily keeping pace with him. The snow was packed, and she sank only a few inches with each step, staying on top of the packed snow.

In a valley, they startled four deer and gave chase. The deer bounded away, sinking deep in the snow, and the wolves pursued an older doe, the slowest of the group. She was injured—one of her eyes was inflamed, infected, and the injury had weakened her.

The doe struggled to turn and lash at the wolves with her hooves, but she sank deep into the snow with each bound, while the wolves ran on the surface without breaking through. Nadya attacked from the deer's blind side, slashing at the doe's shoulder and tasting fresh blood.

The other wolf attacked the animal's opposite flank, driving her back toward Nadya. Blood, black in the moonlight, stained the white snow. Its smell filled the air, rich and warm and inviting. The doe bounded forward, weakening but desperate, and Nadya paced her, leaping at her shoulder to slash again. She tore at the white fur at the deer's throat, ripping the skin. Then she leaped again, catching the deer's throat in her teeth and holding tight. The doe's pulse beat beneath Nadya's teeth; the warm blood flowed across her muzzle, splashing her face, filling her with joy.

Together, Nadya and the male wolf tore at the deer's carcass. Nadya could feel herself growing stronger as she ate. Moonlight on snow, the scent of blood in the air. She felt strong and sure and happy.

After Nadya was satisfied, she lay down in the snow beside the carcass, resting as the other wolf continued to feed. She cleaned herself, licking her paws to clean away the blood, biting at the snow that had caught between the pads of her feet. After a time, the other wolf came and stood beside her, then began to clean her, licking blood from her face where her tongue could not reach. His tongue was warm and soothing, stroking her fur gently and persistently. She licked at his face, tasting deer blood.

She stood, getting to her feet so that she could clean him more efficiently, but he did not stay still to be cleaned. He was circling her now, sniffing deeply of her scent. As he moved in front of her, she rubbed her muzzle beneath his chin, stroking him and moaning deep in her throat. His breath was warm on her face and it felt right to lick his muzzle and hear his answering whine. The feeling of lust and desire that had been with her when she Changed was with her still.

When he moved behind her, she felt the warmth of his breath on her cunt as he sniffed her. She moaned low in her throat, a whimpering howl of entreaty, of need and desire.

She remembered making love to Elizabeth on the river bluff, the tall prairie grass whispering around them, Elizabeth's nipple hardening under her tongue, her fingers stroking Elizabeth's cunt, the scent of Elizabeth's desire, so much like her own scent, perfuming the air. And in the wagon after the dance at the Cheyenne camp, Elizabeth's cool fingers on her skin, eager fingers caressing her.

She had no words now. Ape grunts like love and desire and "not now" and "we mustn't" were gone, fading with the excitement of the hunt, the taste of fresh blood. Words had no place here. With words, Nadya would have said that she loved Elizabeth. But Elizabeth did not want her; Elizabeth stank of fear; Elizabeth pushed her away.

Words could lie. But her body told the truth. Her body wanted, her body needed. She could feel the warmth of arousal between her legs, and her scent carried a message of desire and anticipation.

The wolf mounted her from behind, pushing deep into her cunt. She moaned again: no words, just desire and its fulfillment.

Jenny woke in the night from a beautiful dream. She and Nadya had been hunting together in the snow. They were wolves, sleek and gray, and they ran over the snow, light and fast. Jenny was happy, happier than she had ever been.

She woke to moonlight and wolves howling in the distance. Sitting up in the tangle of blankets, she peered from the tent. The full moon was low in the western sky, its light glistening on the powdery snow. It was beautiful, just as beautiful as it had been in her dream. She could see Nadya's boot prints, softened by the recent snowfall, leading away into the distance.

Elizabeth was sleeping, her breathing soft and steady. Jenny pulled her boots on over her wool socks and wrapped herself in the buffalo robe that served as her cloak. It was cold, very cold, but she warmed herself by walking, following Nadya's boot prints away from the camp. She reached the leaning tree, where

Nadya had left her clothes. Boot prints led to the tree; the paw prints of a wolf led away.

Jenny hesitated, shivering in the cold. Nadya did not want her to follow—Jenny knew that. But the memory of the dream held her. And she could see the trail of paw prints; the moonlight showed the way.

Nadya, in her wolf form, had run lightly over the packed snow. When Jenny followed, she sank in the snow up to her knees with each step. Each step was a struggle—she could barely pull her foot from the snow before taking the next step. But she did not want to go back to the tent alone. She wanted to find Nadya. She wanted to run with the wolves.

Standing in the snow, she tipped back her head and howled as Nadya had taught her. A small howl at first, growing louder, powered by her need. The moon was almost at the horizon now, its lower edge just about to touch. The sky in the east was beginning to brighten with the first light of dawn. An uncertain time—neither day nor night, but on the edge of each. She closed her eyes and howled again.

She opened her eyes to see two wolves, running across the snow: a big dog wolf bounding toward her, followed by a smaller gray wolf. Real wolves, not dream wolves. By the light of the brightening sky, she could see blood on the muzzle of the big wolf.

In that moment, the dream that had held her released its hold. She panicked and tried to run, managing one desperate leaping step. Then her boot caught in the crusted snow, and she fell, her leg twisting beneath her with a sudden, sharp pain.

As she struggled to free her leg, she saw the smaller wolf—Nadya, she thought, it must be Nadya—overtake the larger animal and impose her body between Jenny and the wolf. The two wolves wrestled in the snow. Jenny could hear them growling fiercely.

The wolf that was Nadya was so much smaller than the other. She hadn't a chance, and Jenny could not help her. She turned away and floundered through the snow toward the leaning tree, with some vague notion that she might find protection there. When she looked back, the larger wolf was retreating and the small gray wolf stood in the snow, watching him go.

Jenny crawled into the shelter of the leaning tree and lay in the damp pine needles. Her face was wet with tears—from the pain in her leg, from the sudden fear that had touched her when she saw the wolves in the snow. Shivering uncontrollably, she pulled her buffalo robe around her, trying to get warm.

As she lay beneath the tree, the sky grew lighter. The sun rose; the moon set.

Nadya, human once again, stood in the snow, watching the wolf trot toward a line of distant trees. She shivered, suddenly cold, and looked down at her naked body. Was this her body? In that moment, it seemed strange, unfamiliar. Surely she did not belong here, in this weak soft flesh.

"Nadya!" She heard Jenny's voice, calling to her from the shelter of the tree. "Nadya!"

Her name. She remembered it now. And she remembered the name of the young one who had fallen in the snow. Jenny, who walked with her each day and slept beside her, curled up like a puppy each night. Jenny, the one she had sworn to keep safe.

"I've hurt my leg, Nadya! Help me!"

Words. She remembered those, too. Grunts that carried meaning, but that meaning was always incomplete, half-formed. Words left out too much.

"Nadya!" Jenny called to her. Jenny was hurt and needed her help. Nadya turned away from the retreating wolf and went to her side.

28

Three days later—with Jenny riding her pony and wearing a splint made of pine wood that still oozed sap—they left the snow behind. As the trail led down from the mountains, the forest changed. Oaks mingled with the pines and cedars, and the trees were spaced widely, with grassy clearings opening between them. Granite slopes gave way to gently rolling land where the grass was lush and green.

They had eaten well for the past few days. While Elizabeth

cared for Jenny, Nadya had returned to the carcass of the deer and taken a share of the meat. She did not see the wolf, though she caught his scent on the breeze and knew he was nearby.

Elizabeth did not ask many questions. Jenny told her the basic facts: she had followed Nadya and fallen when a wolf attacked her; Nadya had protected her. That was all.

On the third day, late in the afternoon, Nadya caught the scent of wood smoke and roasting beef on the breeze. Tobacco and bear grease, corn bread and coffee. "There's a settlement ahead," she told Elizabeth.

Elizabeth stood in the trail, holding the lead to Jenny's horse. She had been limping for the past hour, but had not wanted to stop, though Nadya had suggested it. She peered ahead. "I can't see anything."

"It's not far," Nadya said. She glanced at Jenny. The girl's face was pale and her lips were pressed together, as if to stop a cry of pain. Traveling had been hard on her, but they had no choice. "Not far at all."

They climbed a small rise and looked down into a valley. There were three cabins, constructed of adobe and timber. Between the cabins, Nadya could see a garden plot, a corral in which horses were milling. A woman in a calico dress and a white apron stood near one of the houses, taking clothes off the line.

"We've made it," Elizabeth breathed, her voice choked. Her eyes were shining. "We're safe."

Nadya glanced behind them, where the wild mountains rose above the oak trees, majestic in the distance. They seemed so far away.

"Hello!" Elizabeth called. "Hello, the house!"

The woman looked up from the line, startled by the appearance of such bedraggled travelers from the snowy mountains.

The tiny settlement was called Johnson's Ranch, after the man in whose cabin they spent the night. It was the first outpost of Californian civilization. Two white women and their husbands lived there, along with an assortment of bachelors and Indians.

Elizabeth, Jenny, and Nadya spent that night under Johnson's roof, cared for by his wife Mary Murphy, a young woman who had been rescued, the year before, from the cabins by Truckee Lake. She had been with the Donners, caught in the snow and starving.

But they did not talk of that. They sat by the fire in the rude cabin, and the crude wooden benches on which they sat seemed luxurious after so many weeks of squatting on the ground. There was beef to eat and wheat bread rather than corn bread, and Mary made them a pie from dried apples.

Johnson marveled at their successful journey. Nadya answered his questions about the route they had followed, but otherwise she said little. The women seemed wary of her. She had made no pretense of being a man, introducing herself as Nadya, and the women—properly dressed despite their frontier life—seemed taken aback by her trousers.

But they fussed over Jenny, combing out her hair and braiding it, making her a comfortable bed by the fire, where she could be warm. And Elizabeth chatted with them easily, asking about the trail to Sutter's Fort, about the distance from the fort to Yerba Buena, where her uncle lived. Mary asked about fashions in the East, and Elizabeth talked about the latest styles in skirts. A lovely, companionable time, but now and again Nadya caught the women glancing at her, at her trousers, and then glancing away.

That night, Mary made them a bed near the fire. Jenny had fallen asleep some time before, but Nadya sat up for a bit. "Isn't it wonderful?" Elizabeth murmured. She was brushing her hair and she wore a nightgown that Mary had loaned her. "Sleeping under a roof again—at last!"

Nadya stared into the flames. The room was stuffy. She preferred sleeping in the open. "I didn't mind the tent," she said softly.

"It's only two days' ride to Sutter's Fort," Elizabeth went on. "We can buy another horse there." She smiled, her face ruddy in the firelight. "And then on to Yerba Buena, where my uncle lives."

Nadya hesitated. She looked at her hands, not wanting to see

Elizabeth's face. "I'm afraid," she said softly.

"Afraid?" Elizabeth's voice was startled. "Afraid of what? I can't believe you're afraid of anything."

Nadya could not name the uneasiness that had come upon her in the tiny cabin, listening to talk of East Coast fashions. She shook her head, unable to find words to describe the dread that she felt.

"Oh, Nadya, just think of how nice it will be at my uncle's house," Elizabeth murmured. "Real beds. With clean sheets and blankets that don't smell of buffalo. Imagine that. Are you afraid of clean sheets?"

Nadya shook her head.

"Lie down and go to sleep," Elizabeth said. "There's nothing to be afraid of now. We're safe. We're almost home." She lay down by the fire and Nadya lay beside her. Eventually, Elizabeth's breathing became even again as she slipped back into sleep. But Nadya lay awake, listening to the crackling of the fire.

On a cool autumn day, they reached the town of Yerba Buena, a cluster of wood frame buildings that huddled on the shore.

Some of the men from Johnson's Ranch had accompanied them to Sutter's Fort. Jenny had ridden in an ox-drawn cart, on loan from Johnson. Her leg was still jarred as the cart jolted over the trail, but riding in the cart was easier than riding her pony. At Sutter's Fort, Elizabeth sold Jenny's pony and bought an ox-cart for Fagin to pull. Jenny and Elizabeth rode in the cart, and Nadya rode alongside. The trip from Sutter's Fort to Yerba Buena was uneventful. The weather was fair and traveling seemed so easy, now that they had left the wilderness behind.

Elizabeth stared around her as she rode along the dirt track that served as the main street. So many buildings. She had not seen so many people and so many buildings since she had left Independence. A farm wagon, loaded with bags of wheat, rolled past them.

"Do you know where Mr. Joseph Metcalf lives?" she called to the driver.

He shook his head. "You'd best ask at the store," he shouted back. "Hiram will know."

Hiram, the storekeeper, directed them to Elizabeth's uncle's house, a two-story building at the edge of town. Elizabeth stopped the cart in front of the house, looking uneasily up at the white-washed façade. She waited while Nadya helped Jenny from the back of the cart. The girl looked pale and tired, but she managed to walk up to the front door, using a crutch that one of the soldiers at the fort had fashioned for her.

Elizabeth hesitated at the front door, glancing back at Nadya and Jenny. Uncle Joseph had built a city house, complete with a polished brass knocker on the door. It was so fine looking. For a moment, it seemed to her that she did not belong here. But they'd come too far to turn back. Elizabeth lifted the knocker and let it drop.

The woman who opened the door looked at Elizabeth for a moment without recognition. She was a tall, straight-backed woman, wearing a dark blue dress of an elegant cut. The air around her carried the delicate scent of rose water. She frowned at Elizabeth. "Yes?"

"Aunt Kate?" Elizabeth said hesitantly.

The woman's eyes widened and she put her hands on Elizabeth's shoulders, studying her face. "Elizabeth!" She shouted back over her shoulder. "Bridget! Alice! Come quickly. Elizabeth is here." She pulled Elizabeth into a genteel embrace. "Why, we have been worried sick about you and your father."

"Cousin Elizabeth!" Bridget cried, running from the back of the house. Alice, Bridget's older sister, followed close behind. Bridget hugged Elizabeth ferociously, squeezing her with youthful enthusiasm. "We thought you'd been lost," she said. "We thought we'd never see you again. We got Uncle William's letter and then we waited and waited. And you look so thin and tired." She hugged Elizabeth again.

"You be careful until we fatten her up. She's so frail you'll break her right in half," Alice admonished her younger sister, laughing as she spoke. "And she's the only cousin we've got. Oh, now don't cry!"

Elizabeth reached up and wiped away her tears. Her cousins would take care of her. The trail was behind her now. "Papa's dead," she managed to say. "Died of a fever." Her cousin Bridget hugged her again and Alice pressed a handkerchief into her hand, a square of clean linen embroidered around the edges with flowers.

"These are my friends, Nadya and Jenny," Elizabeth said through her tears. "We traveled together across the prairies to California." Nadya stood by Jenny's side, looking uncomfortable. "Nadya rescued me after Papa died. I would have died on the prairie without her help. And Jenny's family was killed by Pawnees."

And then the tears came again. She could not stop them. Aunt Kate took charge, summoning a Mexican man who led the horses to the stable, leading them all into the house. In the foyer, Elizabeth caught a glimpse of her face in a looking glass, the first she had seen in months. She was thin, haggard, red-eyed from weeping. Tears had left streaks in the dust on her face.

"Now don't you worry about a thing," Bridget said, putting her arm around Elizabeth's waist. "You'll have a hot bath, first thing. And I'm sure my dresses will fit you. We'll take care of you. You're home now, cousin."

As Elizabeth turned away, she caught a glimpse of Jenny's face. The girl had turned pale beneath her tan. The last few days had been hard on her. As Elizabeth watched, she swayed, and then collapsed in a faint. Nadya caught her as she fell.

Elizabeth's aunt put Jenny to bed and sent the Mexican servant to fetch a doctor. Nadya and Elizabeth stood beside the bed and watched as he examined Jenny's leg. He spoke with them, ignoring Jenny.

"A fine job of bone setting," he complimented Elizabeth. "All she needs now is plenty of rest and good food."

Jenny looked lost in the big featherbed. Elizabeth had dressed her in one of Bridget's nightgowns, and the sleeves fell down over her hands.

"She'll be fine," the doctor said. "Keep her warm and let her rest and she'll be fine."

The high collar of the dress constricted Nadya's throat; the lace cuffs felt tight around her wrists. Elizabeth had borrowed the dress from Alice, who was about Nadya's size. Under Elizabeth's urging, Nadya had taken off her traveling clothes and bathed in a tub of warm water, fetched by a Mexican serving woman.

That was fine: it was pleasant to be clean, even though the scented soap that Elizabeth had given her made her sneeze. She washed her hair clean, removing all the dust of the trail. The warm water had relaxed her, made her think that perhaps this place wasn't all bad. But then Elizabeth brought in the dress and suggested that she put it on.

"You look lovely," Elizabeth said.

"I feel like a fool," Nadya said. When she walked across the room to look in the mirror, the heavy skirt flapped about her legs, forcing her to shorten her stride. She stared at the stranger in the glass. The face was hers: golden eyes, skin burned brown by the sun. But the body was someone else's, someone who walked with tiny steps, someone who did not mind being hampered by tight cuffs and a lace collar, someone who would never have to run or fight.

"Here, let me comb back your hair," Elizabeth said, coming up behind her. Over the past few months, Nadya's hair had grown long enough to curl about her ears. Elizabeth brushed it back, away from her face. "The dress fits very well," Elizabeth said. "You and Alice are the same size."

"I don't understand why you want me to wear this," Nadya said, her voice low.

"You can't go to dinner in trousers," Elizabeth said. "It would bother Aunt Kate."

"What ever I do, it will bother Aunt Kate. She doesn't approve of me."

"You've only just met Aunt Kate. She doesn't know you," Elizabeth said. "And you don't know her. How do you know she doesn't like you?"

Nadya studied Elizabeth's face in the glass. Her expression was cool and distant. She was brushing back Nadya's hair with her hand, toying with the strands that were beginning to curl. Her touch reminded Nadya of the day by the Platte, when she cut Nadya's hair. That was when they were still uncertain of each other. It seemed to Nadya that they had gone backward in time. She did not know this quiet woman. For all the time that they had spent together, they were strangers now.

"I don't much care what Aunt Kate thinks of me," Nadya said

softly. "But I reckon that you don't approve of me anymore."

Elizabeth kept brushing Nadya's hair, but did not look up to meet her eyes. "We're back in civilization," Elizabeth said, in a voice barely louder than a whisper. "I want you to dress like a civilized woman. Just for tonight."

"I'm not a civilized woman," Nadya said. She turned from the mirror. Elizabeth's blue eyes were troubled, bright with the promise of tears.

"Please," she said, "try wearing the dress." She held the hairbrush in both hands, clutching it so tightly that her knuckles were white.

"Just for tonight," Nadya agreed reluctantly.

They ate dinner in the dining room. The room was grander than any Nadya had ever seen. Elizabeth's uncle worked for a trading company, and was quite well-to-do. An Oriental carpet covered the wooden floor; each chair had its own needlepoint cushion. The windows were draped in curtains of white lace. A needlepoint sampler on the wall declared this to be "Home, Sweet Home." Hanging beside the sampler were two framed watercolors: one of a bouquet of flowers and the other of a basket of fruit.

"It's difficult to keep a proper house here," Aunt Kate was saying to Elizabeth. "But we do what we can. Bridget has taken up watercolors. And Alice has a fine hand with needlepoint."

Nadya listened while Elizabeth praised both the painting and the needlework. Then Elizabeth's uncle, a burly man with a loud voice, said grace, a rambling prayer in which he thanked the Lord at length for delivering Elizabeth and her companions from peril.

After the prayer, Nadya watched the others to see what they did with the square of cloth that she had found sitting on her plate, studying the maidservant who brought in the platter of roast beef, examining the fine china off which they ate.

"You have to tell us all about your adventures on the journey," Bridget said. "Wild animals and Indians." She shuddered. "You must be very glad to be back in civilization again."

Nadya shook her head. "I don't mind wild animals," she said quietly.

"But you must have been frightened," Alice said, glancing at Elizabeth. "Alone out there. Without any men to protect you."

"I learned to shoot from my papa, and I do all right protecting myself," Nadya said easily. "And Jenny and Elizabeth have gotten to be handy with a rifle."

Alice stared at Elizabeth. "You learned to shoot?" she asked in amazement.

Elizabeth nodded. "Nadya taught us. For our own protection."

"That was very brave of you," Aunt Kate said. "In the wilderness, a woman must do extraordinary things. Thank the Lord you're back in civilization now."

Bridget leaned forward eagerly. "Tell us about the Indians. Elizabeth said you spent a week in an Indian camp. That must have been frightening."

Nadya shrugged. "We camped for a time with the Cheyenne," she said.

"You're lucky you escaped with the shirt on your back," Elizabeth's uncle rumbled, his first contribution to the conversation. "Terrible thieves, those savages."

"Not if you're a friend," Nadya said. "The Cheyenne are generous with their friends. A medicine man named Painted Wolf saved Elizabeth's life after a rattlesnake bit her. And the chief of the tribe was kind to us. If we hadn't been able to stay there and fatten our oxen, we might never have made it to California."

Elizabeth's uncle waved a hand, dismissing her words. "You're lucky they didn't take your scalps. We do business with them and I'll tell you: you can dress them up in proper clothes, but you can't change their savage minds. You can't trust them for a minute."

"I doubt that your company does business with the Cheyenne," Nadya said evenly. "Perhaps some other tribe."

"One red man is much like another. You do your best and explain the way things are, but they just stay primitive and backward."

Nadya studied Elizabeth's uncle. He had a round, beef-fed face, pale from working indoors. He did not hunt, he did not trap. She wondered what he could have been explaining to an Indian.

"I would have been terrified to stay in an Indian camp," Alice said. "I've heard that they torture their prisoners." She hunched her shoulders and shivered. "You and Elizabeth are so brave."

"The Pawnee torture prisoners," Nadya said. "Not the Cheyenne. The tribes are very different."

"Now, now," Elizabeth's uncle said, in the tone of someone who knows better. "In the end, both tribes attack wagon trains for no reason at all. The U.S. Cavalry will have to deal with both. Teach them a lesson or two."

Nadya stared at Elizabeth's uncle, remembering Chief Slim Face and his thoughtful conversations about the white men. "The Indians have reasons. Army men slaughter their buffalo and shoot them without asking questions. Wagon trains cross Indian land without making peace with the tribes; they drive away the game."

Elizabeth's uncle smiled understandingly, in the way that a grown-up smiles at a child. "Perhaps you met a few good Indians. I understand they exist. But in the long run, the Indians will have to adapt to civilization. It's for their own good and the good of the country."

"Civilization?" Nadya said, shaking her head in amazement. "You mean drunken soldiers and trigger-happy Christians? Any fool can see that the Cheyenne are better off as they are."

Elizabeth's uncle sat upright in his chair, staring at Nadya. "I am not accustomed to being called a fool at my own table."

Nadya shook her head again. "Then you shouldn't talk about things that you don't understand," she began angrily. "The Indians—"

"Of course, Nadya didn't mean that as it sounded," Elizabeth interrupted. "Did you, Nadya?"

"Would anyone like another helping of roast beef?" Aunt Kate interrupted. "I, for one, have had enough talk of dirty redskins. Let's just celebrate Elizabeth's safe return and talk of more pleasant things. I thought Elizabeth might join us tomorrow for choir practice. If I remember right, you have a voice like an angel. Besides, I'm sure you want to give thanks for your safe deliverance from the wilderness."

"That would be lovely," Elizabeth said.

"Will you join us, Nadya?" Aunt Kate asked.

Nadya shook her head. "I reckon not. I don't have much use for preaching."

Aunt Kate frowned.

"Perhaps you could just come along and see the church," Elizabeth said. "There won't be a service tomorrow, but we could give thanks for our deliverance from the wilderness. We really must go."

It was not an invitation, Nadya realized, but a command that Aunt Kate had phrased as a polite suggestion. Nadya shook her head slowly. "No, I don't reckon I will." She addressed Elizabeth's family, all of whom were staring at her in amazement. "You know, it was a group of good Christians who left Elizabeth to die on the prairie. Good Christians killed my mama and papa, back in Missouri. I just don't have much use for church and good Christians."

Elizabeth blamed Nadya for the argument with her uncle. After dinner, on the pretense of going for a walk, Elizabeth took Nadya aside.

"You must behave yourself," she said. "You mustn't antagonize Uncle Joseph. He's a kind man, but he has his limits."

Nadya frowned at her. They walked along a wooden sidewalk, heading toward the harbor. "I don't understand. He was talking about things he knew nothing about."

"You implied that he's a fool," Elizabeth said.

"But he is a fool, if he persists in talking of Indians when he knows nothing about them."

"Uncle Joseph is a very knowledgeable man," Elizabeth said. Her tone was uneasy.

Nadya said nothing. She was looking out toward the rolling hills across the bay. Empty land, with none of the muck of civilization. Ever since they reached Johnson's Ranch, she had felt confined, trapped.

"You need to learn when to hold your tongue," Elizabeth was saying. "You don't have to say everything that you know."

Nadya studied Elizabeth's face. "I don't belong here," she said softly.

"Oh, you've just gotten off on the wrong foot," Elizabeth said brightly. "If you apologize to Uncle Joseph, he—"

"I'm not sorry. I did nothing wrong."

"Oh, Nadya. If you're going to be happy here, you need to—"

"I'm not going to be happy here," Nadya interrupted.

"What do you mean?"

"I mean that I have no place here. I'm going to be moving on."

Elizabeth stopped walking and stood very still on the sidewalk. "Moving on? Where are you going?"

"North, I expect." She jerked her head in the direction of the harbor, keeping her eyes on Elizabeth's face. "I'll find a ship going up to Astoria. I understand there's wild country north of there."

"Why?" Elizabeth sounded like a child, bewildered by a world she didn't understand. "I wish . . ." she began. "I thought. . . ." But she could not articulate whatever it was she wished or thought. Her sentences trailed off, unfinished.

"I don't want to behave in the proper way," Nadya said softly. "I'm not a civilized woman. You have to understand that." She hesitated, studying Elizabeth's face. "You could come with me," she said slowly. "You and Jenny both."

"No," Elizabeth said. The word came quickly, without hesitation. "I can't go. But you could stay; I don't see why you couldn't."

"Stay here and dress like a civilized woman and go to church and listen quietly while fools hold forth." Nadya looked out toward the harbor, avoiding Elizabeth's eyes. "And when the moon is full, where will I go?" She turned to look at Elizabeth again. "You'll be all right here," she said. "You're safe, where you always wanted to be."

Elizabeth nodded, her eyes bright with tears. "Thanks to you, I'm safe. Without you, I wouldn't have made it."

Nadya shrugged, remembering her lonely nights alone, before she met Elizabeth. "And I wouldn't have made it without you and Jenny. I needed you as much as you needed me."

Elizabeth bowed her head, looking down at her hands. "I'll take good care of Jenny," she said. "I'll make sure she's brought up right."

Nadya frowned. She had the money to book passage for Jenny; she had intended to ask the girl if she wanted to go to the Oregon Territory. "Don't you think Jenny should make up her own mind?"

Elizabeth looked up then. "Who will take care of her, when you run off into the night?" she asked, her voice steady. "Who will hold her when she wakes with nightmares, and you're not there? You promised to keep her safe, but you can't keep that promise. Let her stay with me."

Nadya nodded reluctantly, remembering Jenny's broken leg. Perhaps Elizabeth was right; perhaps she should travel alone.

"When will you go?" Elizabeth asked.

"As soon as I can find a ship," Nadya said. She looked out toward the harbor. "As soon as I can arrange passage."

Drink this down," Alice told her. "It will help you sleep."

Jenny drank the glass that Alice held out: warm milk with a bitter aftertaste from the sleeping medicine that the doctor had prescribed to keep her calm and help her rest.

"You have a good nap," Alice said, slipping out the door quietly.

Jenny lay back in the big featherbed, thinking about how wonderful it was to be warm and dry, about how glad she was not to have to move that day. Her leg still ached, but it was better now that it was not being jarred by each step her pony took.

She remembered the last few weeks in bits and pieces, like fragments of a dream. Snow and cold; days on horseback, nights by the fire. Strangers—at Johnson's Ranch, at Sutter's Fort—all of them exclaiming over her and Elizabeth and Nadya, amazed at their story, astounded that they had made it.

"Hello, Jenny." Nadya stood in the door to the room. "How are you feeling?" She closed the door quietly behind her, crossed the room, and sat on the edge of the bed.

Jenny smiled, noticing that Nadya was wearing her traveling clothes again—trousers, a loose shirt, her black hat with the hole where Jenny had shot it. Golden eyes in a suntanned face. Jenny reached out to take her hand, wanting to make sure that she was really there. Sometimes, after she drank the medication, she had dreams so vivid that she was sure they were real.

"Not so bad," Jenny said. "My leg feels better."

"That's good," she said. She squeezed Jenny's hand. "Tell me: do you like it here? Are you happy?"

Jenny nodded. The sleeping draught had left her dreamy and content. "It's nice," she said sleepily. Alice and Bridget took care of her; she was warm and well fed. Of course she was happy.

Light shone from the window behind Nadya, surrounding her with a halo of sunlight. In Elizabeth's Bible, the angels were surrounded by light, just like Nadya. She wondered vaguely if Nadya was an angel, come to earth to help her.

"I guess you'll be safe here," Nadya was saying quietly. "You don't have to worry about Pawnees. Or about dying in the desert or freezing in the snow. Elizabeth will take care of you."

Jenny nodded again, drifting in a place where nothing was real except Nadya's hand. There were flowers in the room—Bridget had brought her a bouquet and put it in a vase by the window. Their scent reminded her of something. "Remember," she said softly, "remember when we gathered flowers by the river. Black-eyed Susans and daisies and all the flowers. And we brought them back to Elizabeth." She smiled, remembering the warm days in the sunshine, when traveling was easy.

"I remember," Nadya said. Her voice came to Jenny as if from a great distance. So far away, fading as Jenny drifted away into sleep. "Don't forget me," Nadya said. "Don't forget."

Jenny dreamed of running through the snow, following a gray wolf with golden eyes.

Nadya sat on the bed, shuffling the cards. Elizabeth sat on the bed beside her. Nadya did not look up at Elizabeth. Her eyes were on the cards in her hand; she shuffled the deck, not looking up.

"I guess that you'd best give that back to Alice. I have no use for it." Nadya jerked her head at the dress that hung from a peg in the wall. She gathered the cards from the bed and stacked them, then shuffled the deck again. "I don't reckon I'll be going back to choir practice."

"I wish you would," Elizabeth said. "You could still change your mind."

Nadya could smell her nervous sweat through the scent of rose water. "The ship sails in a few hours," she said. "But I won't be changing my mind." She glanced up at Elizabeth. "Here: I'll read the cards for you. I'll tell you your future." She flipped through the cards to find the Queen of Cups, the card that signified Elizabeth.

"My aunt wouldn't approve." Elizabeth glanced over her shoulder.

Nadya said nothing. She laid the queen on the bed and shuffled the deck again. "Cut the cards," she said.

Elizabeth did as she was told.

Nadya laid out the familiar pattern, reciting the words for each position, as her mother always had. "This is behind you; this is before you. This is above you; this is your foundation. This is yourself, your future, your hopes and dreams, the ultimate outcome." In the past was a card that showed a man in a boat, paddling toward a distant shore. There were two people in the boat, huddled in blankets. "In your past, there is a long journey."

"Of course," Elizabeth said. "A long, difficult journey."

"Surely it wasn't always so difficult," Nadya said. "Do you remember the sunny days by the Platte River? Remember the prairie dogs barking as we passed and the wolves singing in the night? The sun shone on the grass and the wind carried the scent of buffalo."

Elizabeth's hands were knotted in her lap. "I also remember being tired and dirty and cold. We were bitten by vermin and frightened by Indians."

Nadya fingered the card that showed Elizabeth's foundation. A man stood on the tilting deck of a ship, legs spread wide apart as he tried to balance on the unsteady surface. He held two large pentacles, one in each hand. "Pentacles are cards of wealth and comfort," Nadya said. "They provide your foundation, but your footing is unsteady. Above you. . . ." She tapped a finger on a card that pictured a blindfolded woman. Her arms were crossed in front of her chest and in each hand she held a sword. But though she was armed, she was not ready to fight. Her thoughts were turned inward; the swords were dead weight in her hand. "Again, you wish to find a balance, but that balance is elusive. In the future. . . ." She pointed to the eight of cups. A man was turning away from eight golden cups, walking out into a desolate landscape. "The cups signify emotion. You are turning away from feeling."

Nadya glanced up. Elizabeth was not looking at her. Her lips were tight, not smiling. Her eyes were focused on the blank wall above Nadya's head.

"This is yourself. Temperance." A solemn-faced winged woman poured water from one jug into another. "Sobriety. Caution. And the strengths that accompany those virtues."

"I don't see why you can't just settle down," Elizabeth said, as if that was what they had been talking about all along. "It doesn't seem like so much to wear a dress, to be polite, to behave properly. Not so much to ask."

"This shows your hopes and fears," Nadya said. The card pictured a woman subduing a wild beast with her bare hands. Strength. "And this shows the outcome."

"I don't think I care to know any more," Elizabeth said. Her voice was brittle. "It's all quite clear enough, don't you think? You have to go and I have to stay."

Nadya looked up from the cards. Elizabeth's face was set and pale. "If you think it clear, then it is," Nadya said mildly.

Looking at her, Nadya knew that Elizabeth did not belong in this house, not really. She was afraid of the wilderness, but already she found civilization confining. But she was willing to submit to those restraints for the safety it provided.

"I'll take care of Jenny," Elizabeth said. She stood suddenly and took the dress down from the peg. "I'd best take this back to Alice."

Nadya did not speak for a moment. "Goodbye," she said softly.

Elizabeth hesitated in the doorway. "Goodbye. Good luck." Then she stepped out into the kitchen, closing the door firmly behind her.

Nadya studied the last card, the final outcome, the six of cups. Two young children were playing in a garden under a brilliant blue sky. The cups were filled with flowers and the children were smiling. It was a card of remembrance and nostalgia, a card of looking back, rather than forward. In the future, Elizabeth would look back on her journey with fondness, remembering how happy she had been. Always looking back, at a time to which she could not return.

It did not take Nadya long to pack her belongings. Her mother's cards, her father's journal, a few shirts, her knife, her rifle, her pistol, her bedroll. In the foyer, she met Elizabeth's uncle. She nodded a greeting, but did not smile. "I'll be heading on now. I'm much obliged to you and your wife for your hospitality. But I think it would be best if I left."

Elizabeth's uncle looked uncomfortable, as he always did around Nadya. "Why, yes," he murmured. "Of course. I'm sure you know your own mind." He hesitated, then continued. "I do thank you for conducting my niece safely through the mountains. We are all very grateful."

Nadya nodded. "You take good care of her," she said.

"Of course," he said. "Of course we will."

Elizabeth stayed in San Francisco and founded a school for girls. Jenny attended, but she was never a very good student. She didn't forget Nadya. And when she was eighteen, she ran away and became an outlaw, a woman desperado riding wild across the West. But that's another story.

In 1847, Nadya Rybak walked away, heading for the harbor, for Oregon, for the wilderness. She did not look back.

THREE

■

The Northwest Coast

29

■

When Jacob Lowell was a little boy, his mother told him that the beating wings of the Thunderbird made the thunder that rocked the sky on stormy nights. She explained that the creaking and rattling that he sometimes heard at night came from *memelose tillicums,* the spirits of the dead who wished that the living would join them in their new home. She told him about Coyote—teacher, trickster, and hero—who taught the people the proper way to catch and eat salmon.

Jacob's uncle, his mother's brother, came to visit between his trading and trapping expeditions. Jacob's uncle taught Jacob the proper songs to sing before he hunted deer. When wolves howled outside the fort at night, his uncle told Jacob that the wolves were his brothers. Someday, he said, Jacob would join the Wolf society and learn their secrets.

Jacob's father told him about Jesus Christ, who had died to save Christian people everywhere. He talked about the angels in heaven who protected Jacob and his family from harm. He taught Jacob how to make black marks that other people could read and how to read the black marks in the books that were kept in the manor house library. He showed him how to shoot a rifle and judge the value of a fur.

There were some things that Jacob's father knew nothing about: he did not understand that the wolves were Jacob's brothers; he did not know the songs to sing to the deer before going hunting.

And there were other things that his mother and uncle did not know. To them, the black marks in the books meant less than the patterns the rain made in the mud.

Jacob had a varied and sometimes confusing education. He listened to his mother and uncle and he listened to his father and he formed his own view of the world, one in which the beating wings of angels made the thunder and Jesus Christ led the dead spirits on their journeys through the forest. He sang songs to the deer with his uncle and hymns that praised God with his father.

Jacob's father was a clerk with Hudson's Bay Company, a "King George man," in the talk of the Indians of the area. His mother and his uncle were Indian. Their people lived on the Pacific coast, some distance north of the mouth of the Columbia River.

During winter and fall, Jacob lived with his mother and father in Fort Vancouver, the Hudson's Bay Company outpost on the great Columbia River. Fort Vancouver was a grand place, with a tall stockade wall enclosing some forty buildings. There were many people there: King George men like his father; French Canadian trappers or Kanakas; Sandwich Islanders who came from a distant island country where the weather was always warm; Indians of many different tribes; Russian sailors and American emigrants. New people were always coming and going—setting out on trading expeditions, bringing trade goods by ship from distant places, traveling, exploring, always very busy.

The men of the fort treated him with rough kindness. He was James Lowell's son—a half-breed to be sure, but a bright lad for all of that. From the men at the fort, he learned to bargain to his best advantage, to climb in the rigging of a ship at harbor, to spot a man who was cheating at poker. One year, a sailing ship from England brought a steam engine and a paddle wheel to the fort, and the sailors labored to convert the ship to steam power. Jacob watched and cheered when the paddlewheeler, the first ever on the Pacific coast of America, made its way down the Columbia.

Every spring, Jacob left the fort. When his father went off on trading expeditions, Jacob's mother and uncle took Jacob to live in his mother's village by the ocean. There he learned to handle a canoe in the ocean breakers, to hunt for sea otter and seal, to harpoon salmon and sturgeon from a riverbank or a canoe. He listened to sacred stories and, on the dark night of the ceremony that renewed the world, watched the shaman, a man of great power, conjure spirits that flew around the room.

When Jacob was ten, he took part in *Klukwalle,* the ceremony that made him part of his mother's clan. His uncle had prepared him for the ritual. "You must eat nothing," his uncle said three days before the *Klukwalle.* "Drink only clear water."

Jacob nodded. He had been helping his cousin, a woodworker, shape red cedar planks into bentwood storage boxes, and his mind was still occupied with the task. They had used boiling water to soften the wood so that it would bend easily, and Jacob was struck by how the character of the wood had changed under the influence of the water. What was hard and stiff had become soft and pliable.

"When you fast, you become empty. That leaves room for the spirit that will come to you," his uncle said. "The spirit of the wolf will fill you."

Jacob fasted for three days. On the day of *Klukwalle,* he and the other boys who were coming of age sat by a fire in the lodge. Jacob felt light and hollow, as empty as the bentwood boxes that his cousin had made. The lodge was empty except for his uncle and the other boys. His uncle fed wood to the smoking fire and sang softly to himself, a rhythmic song with words that meant nothing to Jacob.

It was mid-afternoon when Jacob's uncle lifted his head and said softly, "They're coming."

Jacob heard them then: the howling of wolves, the beating of drums. Distant at first, then coming closer. Dancing feet outside the lodge, circling the building and looking for an opening. The creatures outside were howling and barking and growling. The room was filled with shadows and one of the younger boys was whimpering, hungry and fearful. Then the dancing creatures burst into the lodge, filling it with noise and confusion. They had bodies like men, but their heads were blocky and strange, with great glaring eyes and white teeth that gleamed in the darkness.

Jacob's uncle took his hand and whispered, "Be brave, like the wolf. Let the wolf spirit come to you." Then he cut Jacob's arms with the sharp edge of a mussel shell. The firelight flickered on his uncle's face, and Jacob felt the blood run down his arms, warm and wet. As the blood flowed, he felt his head grow light, as light as the bits of eagle down that the dancing creatures scattered. He felt as soft and pliable as the wood immersed in boiling water.

The creatures were surrounding him and the other boys now, and their noise had become musical, a wild song. His uncle was gone; only the boys lay on the cedar mats by the fire, and the strange spirits circled them, singing and growling.

Jacob was not afraid. In all the smoke and the noise and the confusion, he felt very still and quiet. He was waiting for something, but he did not know what it might be.

The creatures reached the end of their song and howled. The sound filled Jacob, finding the hollow places within him and filling them with sound. He lifted his voice to howl with them, one voice among many.

He stood slowly, and it was as if the sound that rushed from his throat lifted him to his feet. He howled and the blood ran freely down his arms as he danced with the creatures of the *Klukwalle,* becoming one of them, filled with the spirit of the wolf, the spirit of the forest, the strength of the clan.

There was dancing and feasting and Jacob fell asleep that night by the fire as the wolf dancers leaped and danced, the light glistening on their skin, the smoke curling around their masks. It was not until after the ceremony that his uncle taught him the steps to the wolf dance, his cousin helped him carve a wooden mask with glaring eyes and gleaming teeth.

That fall, when Jacob returned to the fort, the soft skin on the underside of his wrists was marked with thin white lines, scars from the cuts of the mussel shell. When the men at the fort asked about the scars, he just shook his head, a quiet boy who did not want to tell them about the mysterious power that had come to him and lifted him up, howling. He went on, just as he had before, but when the wolves howled at night he stopped and listened and smiled to himself, knowing that the beasts were his brothers.

Life went on as it had before. Jacob grew from a quiet dark-haired boy to a quiet dark-haired young man. Sometimes, he went with his father on trading expeditions to the interior. He was at ease with the trappers and the mountain men, more so than his father. Jacob spoke French, having learned it from the

Kanakas, as well as English, the language of his mother's tribe, and the Chinook jargon used by traders up and down the river. Sometimes, he went hunting with his uncle and he grew expert with rifle and bow.

The fort changed over the years. In the early years, there were white men only—trappers and traders. In 1836, when Jacob was twelve, he saw white women for the first time: Narcissa Whitman and Eliza Spaulding who had traveled with their husbands overland to the West. Whitman and Spaulding came as missionaries, hoping to convert the heathen Indians to Christianity. Other white women followed: more women missionaries at first, and then women traveling with their families to settle in the Willamette Valley. Farmers came to clear the land and plant their crops and change the place to suit them.

Jacob was bewildered by the emigrant women. Such exotic creatures: soft, pale skin; calico skirts that almost dragged on the ground. They spoke in high, twittering voices, like the little birds that flitted in the bushes, and they watched him with wide eyes, as if he were a wild creature that had somehow strayed into the stockade walls. When he smiled at them, they shied away, frightened and confused.

Late in the summer that Jacob turned nineteen, a smallpox epidemic swept through the fort. Whites and Indians were both struck by the disease. Most of the Indians died and most of the whites recovered. Jacob and his mother both fell ill. Jacob lay in bed for a week, tossing and turning beneath blankets drenched in sweat.

He woke one morning from fever dreams to see his father sitting in the corner of the room, weeping. His mother was dead of the fever, like so many Indians. The week after his mother's death, he learned that his uncle had also succumbed to the disease and that his mother's village had been struck by the pox.

Jacob recovered slowly, regaining his strength enough to sit in the doorway in the sun, to walk to his mother's grave in the small cemetery just outside the stockade walls. Sometimes, he sat by the grave, resting and thinking of his mother. His father had buried her in the earth in the white fashion. His mother's tribe would have placed the body in a canoe with the things that the person might need in their new life.

Jacob wondered if his father had remembered to bury all the things that his mother might need; he wondered if her spirit could escape from beneath the soil and walk free in the forest. He could not ask his father about these things, any more than he could ask his father about the Thunderbird or Coyote. His father would not understand the questions.

It seemed to Jacob that the entire world changed with his mother's death. His father seemed smaller, as if he had collapsed in upon himself in his grief. The rooms that they shared seemed empty—the two of them alone could not fill up the space. And the fort itself seemed different. There were more emigrants passing through, always more white faces, more wagons, more travelers, weary from the trail.

One sunny afternoon, he heard two women talking about him, as if he couldn't hear. "He looks so savage," one of them said. "Like he'd scalp you in a minute."

"I hear there are cannibals on the coast," the other said. "Wild Indians that eat human flesh."

Jacob turned and smiled at them savagely, showing all his teeth. "You look very tasty," he said in English, and the women shrieked and fled to their wagons and the protection of their men.

It was not so long after that incident that his father met Widow Campbell, a Boston woman whose husband had died on the trail west. She had come to dine in the manor house, at the invitation of the chief factor, Dr. McLaughlin, and had lingered to chat with Jacob's father. Not long after that, she moved into a small cabin in the village that had grown up outside the walls of the fort. Jacob's father spent many evenings in her company.

"You spend a lot of time with the widow," Jacob said to his father one night, on a rare evening when they sat by the fire together.

"It seems to me that she needs me," his father said. "And I need her."

"She makes you happy," Jacob said softly.

"That she does."

"And you'll be marrying her," Jacob continued.

His father hesitated, then nodded. "I believe I will."

Jacob watched the flames of the fire. He had been well for more than a month, but he had not ventured farther than a few days from the fort. It was as if he were waiting for a signal that would let him leave. He no longer felt that he belonged in this place. He had no role in the fort.

"I've been thinking about going out to the coast," he said. "The winter here will be too lonely."

His father nodded. "As you like."

But it seemed to Jacob that his father looked relieved. The widow was friendly enough, but she was nervous around Jacob, she watched him too carefully. Once, when he brought her a wild duck he had shot by the river, she had praised his hunting skills too enthusiastically. She seemed surprised that he could read, but not at all surprised that he was expert with a canoe. And surely it would be awkward for her to move into his father's quarters with Jacob there.

A week later, Jacob left the fort and headed downstream. He traveled alone to his mother's village on the coast, and when he reached the village he was still alone. All the lodges were empty; the people were gone. Raccoons had been climbing in the rafters of his uncle's lodge, gnawing the dried salmon. Mice had invaded the food stores, leaving their turds on the dirt floor. The ashes in the fire pit had been scattered by the wind, drifting into the corners and cracks. In the forest near the village, there were canoes filled with the dead. At night, Jacob guessed, the *memelose tillicums* would wander among the lodges, looking for company.

Jacob did not linger. That afternoon, he traveled down the coast to a cluster of lodges. The people there were friendly enough. Two of his cousins, young men who had survived the sickness, told him what had happened. It was simple. The sickness had come and the people had died. It was a white man's sickness, they told him, and they looked at him strangely when they said that, for his father was a white man. The shaman could do nothing against it. The survivors had scattered, leaving the lonely haunted lodges and finding refuge in other villages, with neighboring tribes.

Jacob left his cousins and traveled south, retracing his journey. The nights were growing longer and colder as late summer became autumn. He arrived at Fort Astoria, built at the shore of the Columbia River, not far from the river's mouth.

A village had grown up around the fort. Jacob paddled his canoe between two brigs and landed at the riverbank where he found a place to haul it high and dry and make it secure. Then he made his way along the dirt path to the village. Astoria was a thriving community, a settlement of some six hundred inhabitants, with a custom house, a post office, several sawmills and gristmills, and a trading house. Jacob made his way across town to Bolin's tavern and hotel.

In the tavern's common room, Jacob found a few clerks and trappers he knew, men who had worked at Fort Vancouver in earlier years. They welcomed him to Astoria, and that night, he sat up by the fire, drinking with the men.

"You can find work at the fort, if you like," one man suggested. "We need another hand."

Jacob shook his head. "I'm looking for a different sort of place."

"A place with a woman in it, I'd reckon," the man said, grinning.

Jacob shrugged. He had, a year before, courted a young woman in his mother's village. But there was no use thinking of her, no use thinking of any of the laughing women who used to live in the village. "I reckon I'm looking for a place to settle for a time," he said softly.

The other men offered him another drink and slapped him on the back and tried their best to cheer him. But though he drank with them and smiled at their jokes, he could not shake the feeling of emptiness.

One by one, the men went to bed, wrapping themselves in blankets and lying on the benches and the floor of the common room. At last, Jacob sat by the fire with a man named Lono. A native of the Sandwich Islands, Lono had left his home as a young man, traveling to the Oregon Territory with an American ship that had stopped at the islands to trade for supplies.

Jacob had known him in Fort Vancouver. He had always been an affable man, but he had never seemed happy at the fort. When he left the fort a few years before, Jacob had assumed that he had booked passage to return to his homeland.

"I thought you must have left for the Sandwich Islands," Jacob said.

Lono shook his head. "It's a fine thing to remember the islands. But I don't think I belong there anymore."

They sipped their whiskey. Around them, men snored softly.

"Why did you leave the fort, then?" Jacob asked.

"Not so long ago, I felt like you do," Lono said softly. "Sick of the fort, sick of the white farmers who come to the land and take away the trees. But now I've found a place on Shoalwater Bay." He nodded, studying Jacob's face. "Tomorrow, you come with me and see what you think of it."

"What kind of place?" Jacob asked.

"A place where it's good to live," Lono said.

Sitting by the fire, Lono told Jacob about Shoalwater Bay. The shallow waters of the bay were rich with oysters and other sealife; there were elk and deer in the forests bordering on the bay. Lono had married an Indian woman, and they lived at the mouth of a creek, a beautiful place. A few other people lived nearby—enough to lend a hand when it was needed, but not so many as to feel crowded.

The next day, Lono took Jacob to his home on Shoalwater Bay. Lono's family—his wife and their two children—welcomed him to their lodge at the mouth of the creek. Lono's wife, Myeena, a smiling, round-faced young woman, baked a blackberry pie. Lono's daughter, a laughing three-year-old, pulled on Jacob's hair and climbed on his back while he sat by the fire. Everyone called her Cheechee, the Chinook jargon word for the little birds that flitted among the bushes. Lono's two-year-old son, Kekoa, sat by his side, solemnly sharing his blackberry pie.

Over the next few days, Jacob met the others who lived nearby. It was a community of outcasts, made up of Indians, foreigners, freed slaves—people who belonged nowhere else. "This is a good place," Lono said as he and Jacob walked on the beach. Jacob nodded in agreement. He felt more at home in Lono's lodge than he had anywhere since his mother's death. "It's a good place," he agreed.

"I will help you build a lodge, if you like."

Jacob nodded. He would stay here for a time.

30

Jacob Lowell pushed open the door and stepped into Bolin's tavern and hotel. Lono followed close behind him. It was a chilly, damp afternoon. The rain had let up, but the sky was still overcast. They had come to town to trade sea otter pelts for hard currency and the supplies that they needed to get through the winter: coffee, tobacco, flour, and other necessities. Jacob had been settled in Shoalwater Bay for more than a year, and he and Lono went to town to trade for supplies once every few months.

"Too much rain," Lono grumbled. "Too much cold." After three decades on the Northwest coast, he still found the weather barbaric.

"We can sit by the fire," Jacob said. "I'll buy you a drink."

Bolin's common room was noisy with drunken talk. A group of sailors off the brig that was anchored in the harbor sat at a wooden table by the window, playing cards by the dim light that filtered through the dirty glass. The ship had arrived from San Francisco that afternoon. Since their arrival, the men had occupied themselves with drinking and gambling and smoking.

Jacob made his way to the fire. One young man sat alone on a bench, watching the flames, his boots propped up before the fire. Jacob set his pack against the wall and shrugged out of his damp buckskin coat. He hung the coat on a peg where it could dry and sat down on the bench beside the young man. Lono squatted on his heels a little closer to the fire, holding his hands out to warm them.

"Afternoon," Jacob said to the young man. "You just come up from San Francisco?"

The stranger looked up. Skin dark from the sun. Features that might be called feminine. "That's right." The voice was high and lilting, more like a woman's than a man's. But the stranger was dressed in masculine clothing: trousers, boots, a flannel shirt. Jacob squinted at the stranger's face in the firelight. Was this a woman or a man? "And you?" the stranger said. "Where are you from?"

"I live up the coast a ways. Just came down to trade some furs. My name's Jacob Lowell. This is my friend Lono." Jacob held out his hand. "Pleased to meet you."

"Nadya Rybak," the stranger said.

A woman. Her hand was small, but hard with calluses. She didn't look or act like any white woman he had ever seen.

"Why are you staring at me?" she asked.

Jacob shrugged. "Not many white women in these parts. Even fewer who wear trousers."

"I reckon that's so."

Jacob glanced around the common room, searching for the woman's traveling companions. He had never heard of a white woman traveling alone; they were always in the company of protective white men.

One of the sailors at the card game, a man who wore a bandage on his right hand, noticed Jacob looking in his direction and stared back at him. "Watch yourself, Injun," the man called across the room. "She bites." He grinned fiercely, and the firelight reflected from a gold front tooth. The other sailors laughed. The woman returned the sailor's glare.

"What's he talking about?" Jacob said softly.

Nadya shook her head. "He's not a friend of mine," she said slowly. "That's all."

Jacob frowned, still watching the man. "He doesn't seem like a friendly sort. What did he do to you?"

"On the boat, he tried. . . ." She hesitated, then continued. "He climbed into my bunk one night. I didn't care for it and I let him know." She met his eyes and grinned humorlessly. "With my teeth."

Jacob nodded slowly. Outside, the rain began rattling against the window, an irregular rhythm. He leaned forward and put another log on the fire. The sailors at the table laughed again. Not pleasant laughter, but amusement that was pointed and aimed in their direction.

"Didn't know they let darkies eat with the white folks here," the sailor with the gold tooth was saying loudly. He was looking at Lono. The Sandwich Islander looked up from the fire and studied the sailor.

"Drunken fools," he commented to Jacob. "Too bad Bolin lets them in."

Jacob nodded. "All Bostonmen are fools, right enough," he said, loudly enough to be overheard. "And these seem stupider than most."

The gold-toothed sailor was on his feet and heading for Lono, with three of his friends behind him. Jacob stood and stepped to one side so that his back was to the wall. He found the woman beside him grinning widely.

There was a fight. Not a neat, clean, fair fight—no, not at all. In a dark tavern when the rain is falling and men have been drinking, any fight is a confused melee of fists and feet and flying bottles, rich with the smell of spilled blood and spilled whiskey, noisy with cursing and breaking glass.

The sailors had the advantage of numbers, but they had been drinking for most of the afternoon. And numbers can be a disadvantage as well. Jacob, Nadya, and Lono stood with their backs to the wall, meeting the sailors as they came. The sailors stumbled and got in each other's way. The sailor with the gold tooth swung at Jacob and hit a sailor wearing a red bandana. The second sailor swore and pushed the first—just in time for Nadya to trip him. He went down hard, his forward momentum carrying him into the wall.

Lono chanted as he fought, great rolling syllables of his native language echoing over the shouting of the sailors. Nadya growled softly, an animal noise deep in her throat. Jacob fought with a fierce silent joy.

A sailor came at Jacob, swinging wild with a bottle that he held like a club. Jacob stepped to one side and caught the bottle as it came toward his head, deflecting it and guiding it so that it slammed into the sailor's own knee. The man crumpled forward with a grunt of pain. Jacob lifted his knee to meet the sailor's face, smashing the man's nose.

As Jacob turned to meet the next enemy, someone, somewhere, shouted, "Stop! Stop all this!"

A gunshot echoed through the tavern. Jacob looked up to see Bolin standing atop the bar, holding his repeating pistol ready. He had fired a shot at the ceiling to get their attention. "Stop all this," he said in a conversational tone. "There'll be no trouble here. Maybe you'd better go on back to your ship."

Jacob stood where he was. He glanced at Lono. He was smiling defiantly, watching as the sailors got to their feet, grumbling and groaning. The sailor with the gold tooth had his hand to his face. His nose was bleeding profusely, maybe broken. Another man was clutching his knee. Jacob glanced at Nadya, who stood at his side. She was grinning still, her teeth glittering in the firelight. "Ah," she said. "I'm glad to be off that ship."

Much later, Jacob and Lono sat by the fire, watching the flames and chatting in Chinook jargon. "Don't tell Myeena about the fight," Lono was telling Jacob. "She doesn't like to hear about such things."

Jacob nodded, thinking of the woman who had fought with them. Bolin, in deference to her gender, had shown her to a small storage room off the common room. She had made her bed beneath the shelves of dried salmon and between the sacks and crates.

After the fight, they had shared a few drinks and a meal of fish stew, but the woman had not been very talkative. Lono had carried the conversation, asking her questions about where she was coming from, where she was going. Coming from San Francisco, most recently; going north. No firm destination; just north.

Jacob had found himself watching her eyes as they talked. Wary eyes, like the eyes of a wild creature caught indoors. She sat still, very still, but he felt a tension in her. Though she sat quietly, she was ready to run, ready to leap from the wooden bench and escape the cabin, fleeing from Lono and his questions.

"You are thinking of the woman," Lono said.

Jacob looked up, startled. Lono had been talking of something or other—of Myeena and how she didn't appreciate a good fight, maybe—and Jacob had stopped listening.

"She's a wild one," Lono said softly. "Difficult to tame." He used the Chinook word for tame, *kwan,* which also meant "glad."

Jacob shrugged uneasily. "She's wild, but I think she has a good heart."

"A good heart and a good hand in a fight," Lono said, watching Jacob's face and smiling. "Not a bad combination."

Jacob nodded, remembering how the woman smiled as she fought, baring her teeth with a fierce glee. A wild one, true enough.

They slept by the fire, wrapped in blankets from Bolin's storeroom. The blankets stank of smoked salmon and the wooden floor was hard beneath Jacob's back. He lay awake for a time, thinking of the woman in the storeroom, curled among the sacks and the crates. While they were talking by the fire, he had wanted to touch her, to brush a strand of hair back from her face, to lay a hand on hers and feel her skin beneath his. At last, he fell asleep.

He woke to the sound of Lono's voice. The Sandwich Islander stood by the door, talking with Nadya. His English was laced with words from the jargon. "First you go across the *cooley chuck*, across the river," Lono was saying. "And across Shoalwater Bay. Then you go walking."

The woman's pack and bedroll were on the floor at her feet. While Lono talked, she gazed out the window into the drizzle. The storm clouds had given way to a gray haze—a damp, chilly morning.

"My friend and I—we are going in my canoe," Lono said. "You come with us if you like. *Klatawa cooley*. We go quickly."

Jacob sat up and pushed his hair back. The woman glanced at him uneasily.

"If you're heading north, you'll need to cross the river somehow," he said. "You might as well ride with us."

"I don't have much money," Nadya said. "I. . . ."

Lono waved his hand, dismissing the idea of payment. "Don't worry," Jacob said. "We're going that way. You might as well come along."

Later that morning, Nadya walked down to the bank of the Columbia, following Jacob and Lono. The air was thick with mist and the ground was muddy underfoot—a dismal gray day.

The passage across the Columbia was uneventful. The wind was in their favor and they made good time. Jacob and Lono paddled the canoe, a craft built of cedar in the Indian fashion. Nadya clung to the side and kept looking ahead, hoping to see the far shore through the fog. It took them better than two hours to cross; the river was enormous, bigger than the Missouri at flood, and she did not like to be so far from land.

Jacob was in the front of the canoe and she watched him out of the corner of her eye. When she had climbed into the canoe, he had smiled at her. "You don't like boats, do you?"

"Not much."

"It will be all right," he had said softly. "Don't worry. We'll be back to dry land soon enough."

He was interested in her, she knew that. The night before, when Lono was asking questions, Jacob had sat quietly by the fire and watched her, as if memorizing her face. But she had ignored his attention, answered Lono's questions as briefly as possible.

"Where are you going?" Lono had asked her. She had said she was going north, but truly she didn't know. When she left Missouri, she headed for Oregon, the place her father had chosen for their destination. But now that she had reached Oregon, she did not know what to do next. She did not belong in Astoria; she knew that she had to leave the settlements behind. Otherwise she had no plan. She would go north, farther from civilization, farther from people, deep into the wild lands where she might be able to find a place of her own.

"When we reach shore, we'll have to portage," Jacob said, interrupting her thoughts. As he paddled, he explained the route that they would take to Shoalwater Bay. A narrow peninsula separated the Columbia River from the bay. It was possible to sail out the mouth of the Columbia, travel many miles to the north, then enter the bay. But the seas were rough at the mouth of the Columbia. Brigs had been wrecked and canoes lost in the swirling currents where the river flowed into the sea. And the peninsula that separated the river from the bay extended some twenty miles to the north, making the ocean journey a long one. To avoid the hazards of the rough water and to shorten their journey, travelers in the area crossed the peninsula.

While Jacob described this to Nadya, Lono piloted the canoe to the mouth of the Wallicut River, a narrow winding stream that fed into the larger river. They made their way up the Wallicut, passing many small clearings and cabins. Cattle grazed in one clearing by the river's shore, lifting their heads to watch the canoe pass.

At the point where the Wallicut became too narrow and shallow to continue by canoe, there was a cabin owned by a man named Feister. Lono arranged with Feister to bring their canoe along by ox-drawn wagon. Lono rode in the wagon, while Nadya and Jacob walked ahead along a dirt track that twisted through the forest.

"There are more settlers along the Wallicut than up on Shoalwater Bay," Jacob told her. "On the bay there are some trappers, some men gathering oysters, some loggers. But they're few and far between."

He seemed quite eager to convince her that Shoalwater Bay was a wonderful spot, Nadya thought. And there, in the bright sun of the autumn afternoon, walking under the red cedar trees, she agreed that it might be. But no matter how wonderful, no matter how fine, she would travel north. She did not belong with people; her last days with Elizabeth had convinced her of that. That night, she would travel north.

"It must be a fine place," she said. "But I reckon I'll be heading north."

"The easiest way to travel is by canoe," Jacob said. "But you don't know how to handle a canoe. If you like, I could take you north a ways."

"No, thanks. I'd rather travel alone."

"I reckon you could hike along the beach."

"I reckon I could."

They reached the end of the track at a swampy channel that Jacob identified as Parker Slough. When the ox-drawn wagon arrived, they resumed their journey by canoe, paddling down the slough into Shoalwater Bay.

It was afternoon when they crossed the bay. The wind blew to the north, and Lono hoisted a sail. The water was placid, protected from the ocean waves by the peninsula that they had crossed. On the shores all around them, there was forest.

As they sailed, Nadya rested in the bottom of the canoe. She was tired, very tired. She had not slept well since she had crossed the mountains into California. In Sutter's Fort and Yerba Buena, unhappiness had made her restless. And on the ship, she had always kept her guard up. The captain had happily accepted her money, but the sailors had disliked her. She was a woman—but she didn't act like a woman or dress like a woman. By their standards, any woman who dressed like a man, who traveled alone on a ship filled with men, any woman like that was a whore, not a proper woman. Yet she wouldn't fuck them, no matter how much they suggested it. And when one man tried to insist, she bit his hand and kneed him in the groin and generally did as much damage as she could before the captain, roused by all the noise, came and broke up the fight.

After that, the sailors left her alone, regarding her as something strange and unnatural. For the entire voyage, she had felt the weight of their disapproval, had smelled their hatred in the air. She had slept lightly, ready to awaken at the slightest sound.

She still felt restless. The moon would be full that night. By sunset, she had to be far from these people, these strangers.

A few hours before sunset, they reached Lono's lodge. Lono's family gathered on the beach, calling and waving to the men in the boat. Lono leaped out of the boat into the shallow water and dragged the canoe up onto the beach. A young woman rushed forward to help him, chattering in some incomprehensible language. A little girl clung to one of Lono's legs, oblivious to the water that dripped from his wet leggings.

Watching them, Nadya felt a wave of loneliness pass over her. Her mother had always welcomed her home from hunting. On the prairies, Elizabeth and Jenny had called out when they saw her coming, happy that she had returned to them. But she was alone now.

"Do you speak the Chinook jargon?" Jacob asked her. He was standing close by her side.

She shook her head.

"I could teach you," he said. "It's not hard. It would make your travels easier."

She shook her head again. The sun would be setting in a few hours. She could already feel the tug of the moon from below the horizon. She had to be far from this place by the time the moon rose. "I'll be heading north tonight," she said.

He frowned at her. "Why the hurry? Stay the night here and set out tomorrow."

"You have been very kind," she said with an edge in her voice. "But I must go."

Even so, she did not leave immediately. Lono's wife, Myeena, insisted that she eat with them, sharing a meal of boiled clams and roasted cammass root, a tuber that tasted like a sweet potato. Myeena asked Nadya repeatedly to stay the night, and Lono translated her pleas and added his own. As often as she was asked, Nadya refused.

"You won't be able to travel far before dark," Lono said.

"The moon is full tonight," she said. "I can travel by moonlight."

He shook his head, looking distressed. "Stay tonight. Tomorrow, you go north."

She shook her head, knowing that she could not stay and that she could not explain why. "I have to go tonight."

Lono glanced at Jacob, as if perhaps he could persuade her. Jacob sat at her side, silent. He had stopped asking her to stay, and for that she was grateful.

At last, after thanking Lono and Jacob for their generosity, she shouldered her bedroll and headed north along the beach. Jacob walked with her as far as his own lodge, a small cabin located just a quarter mile or so north of Lono's. Then she walked on alone.

The next morning, after a restless night, Jacob was up early. He was standing by his cabin, chopping logs and adding to his woodpile, when three white men passed by, heading south. Jacob knew one of them, a oysterman from Bruceport, a tiny settlement to the south, and the man greeted him with excitement.

"Best watch yourself," he called to Jacob. "There's a wounded wolf prowling about in the forest."

"That wolf is dead by now," one of the other men said. "I got him clean in the shoulder, I'm sure of that."

"That's why he ran away so fast," the third man said, laughing at his companion. "A bullet in the shoulder always makes wolves run better."

Jacob got the story from the man he knew, while the others continued to joke about how well wounded wolves could run. Apparently the men had spent the previous night camping a short distance to the north. Not long before dawn, one of them had gotten up to pee and saw a gray wolf prowling along the edge of the shore. He had snatched up his rifle and squeezed off a shot, wounding the wolf and waking his companions.

"We tracked it a ways," the man told Jacob, "but lost it in the forest. It'll die soon enough, I expect. He's not as bad a shot as we like to make out."

"Did you see anyone else?" Jacob asked.

The man shook his head. "Not a soul. Why do you ask?"

Jacob shrugged and turned away, as if he were returning to his task at the woodpile. For some reason he couldn't explain, it seemed wrong to tell these men about Nadya. They might offer to help him look for her, and he did not want their help. "No reason," he muttered.

The men headed south, still joking about their friend's poor aim and the wounded wolf. Jacob put his hatchet aside, took his rifle, and headed north.

If Nadya had walked along the beach, the waves had washed away her footprints. The only marks on the clean sand were the footprints left by the group of men. He found their camp easily enough: a rough tumble of rocks where they had built a large fire; flattened vegetation where they had slept.

Casting about in a circle from the camp, he found a splash of blood in a trampled patch of ferns. By the tracks, he guessed that all three men had followed the wounded animal.

He could imagine the scene in the early morning. One man clutching a rifle, the other two barely awake, having been roused by the gunshot. The moon would have been close to setting, that time of day when the world seems half-formed, when the trees are vague shapes and anything is possible. The men wandered through the low mist that filled the forest before daybreak, tracking the injured animal by the splashes of blood it left behind.

He imagined they had laughed and shouted to each other,

careless in their domination over this wilderness. They had shot the wolf—of course, they had shot the wolf. They were white men in the wilderness, and it was their prerogative to shoot any beast, burn any tree, do whatever they pleased.

The wolf had run up into the forest, away from the beach. The men had followed it for less than a mile, then turned back, saying, no doubt, that they didn't need to follow any farther. The beast would die from loss of blood, soon enough.

The men had turned back, but Jacob continued to follow the track of the wolf, peering at scuff marks on the forest floor, noting broken ferns and bloodstains where the animal had passed. It seemed cruel to let the animal die slowly and alone, wounded and bleeding in the forest. And it was dangerous to leave a wounded wolf so close to Lono's lodge.

Those were some reasons for following the wolf. But there was a deeper reason, one that he could not articulate, even to himself. It had something to do with the shifting light at dawn, when the moon sets and the sun rises. It had something to do with Nadya's departure, so late in the day. It had something to do with an uneasy feeling that he couldn't shake.

He followed the wolf up into the trees and back in the direction of his own cabin, climbing to the top of a small ridge, still following the trail. From the ridge crest, he looked down a slope covered with sorrel, a low-growing plant with delicate heart-shaped leaves. He could see something partway down the hill—a pale white shape half hidden by a fallen tree. He approached cautiously, his rifle ready in his hand.

Nadya lay just behind the fallen tree. She was naked, and her skin was pale in the morning light. She curled against the log, as if for warmth. She had lifted a hand to her eyes, protecting them from the light and hiding her face. Her shoulder and side were streaked with dark dried blood. But he could see no wound, no fresh blood.

Jacob hurried to her side, calling her name. She did not move. Her skin was cold, very cold, but a pulse still fluttered in her throat. He could feel it there, beating weakly beneath the skin.

She did not respond when he touched her, when he wrapped her in his deerskin jacket and lifted her, not wanting to jar her but unwilling to leave her so that he could get help. He hurried south, taking her to Keco and Bena, two Indian women who had skill with herbs and healing. Indians from villages to the north and south came to them for spiritual counseling and medical treatment. Keco and Bena would know what to do.

31

Bena sat in the sun, repairing a fishing net. From inside the lodge, she could hear the rustle of playing cards as her wife, Kecomenepeca, practiced her sleight of hand—palming a card and slipping it back into the deck when she shuffled, surreptitiously notching a card with a thumbnail so that she would recognize it in someone else's hand. Keco liked to gamble and liked to win. Bena insisted that if Keco were going to go to Astoria to cheat the sailors, she had to practice regularly and keep her skills up.

"Hello!" called a man's voice. "Keco! Bena! I need your help!"

Bena looked up from her work and squinted into the morning sun. Jacob was coming along the path from the north. He carried a large bundle—no, she corrected herself, not a bundle, but a person. Bena stood up as Keco came to the door of the lodge.

The two women ran to Jacob, hurrying to find out who had been hurt, whom he carried so carefully along the path.

"I found her in the woods," Jacob said. "We have to help her. I don't know. . . ." His words trailed off. He didn't know what to do, he didn't know how to help. "She came with us from Astoria, then headed north. She wouldn't stay. I don't know. . . ."

Bena stopped listening and turned her attention to the woman he carried. She was pale, very pale, even for a white woman. Bena touched the woman's hand and it was cold. "Hurry up quick," she told Jacob. "We must warm her by the fire."

Bena made the woman a bed on a cedar mat. Bena had always been a large woman, and she had grown fat in the year that they had lived by Shoalwater Bay. She cradled the woman in her arms and her lap, warming the pale woman with her own body heat while Keco built up the fire and Jacob tried to explain where the woman had come from.

"A wolf," he was saying. "They said they had shot a wolf and left it to die." He was shaking his head. "I had a bad feeling about it, so I went to where they had camped. I tracked the wolf and found her, lying naked in the woods."

"They shot the wolf?" Bena asked.

"That's right," Jacob said. "But I didn't find the wolf. I—"

Bena waved her hand, dismissing the rest of the sentence. "You found the wolf," she said impatiently. She liked Jacob—he was a sweet young man—but sometimes he overlooked the obvious. "She's lost a lot of blood. But she's strong, she may survive."

Jacob was shaking his head. "How can she have lost blood? There is no wound, no cut."

Bena sighed. Jacob had been raised among the whites which excused some of his ignorance. But she knew that he had heard the tales of people who changed into animals and animals who changed into people. Surely he knew that the world was a shifting and unpredictable place. Sometimes he seemed willfully foolish, in the manner of white men. "She was the wolf," Bena said patiently, as if to a small child. "I will do what I can to help her."

Bena rubbed the woman's skin with warming salves and burned aromatic herbs to perfume the air and keep the woman's wandering spirit nearby. She wrapped the woman in blankets and kept her close by the fire. She put a stew on the hearth—when the woman woke, she would feed her strong broth and meat, strengthening foods for the body and spirit.

While Bena worked, Jacob sat beside the woman. Bena gave him a task, knowing that he wanted to do something, that he would be in the way if she didn't give him something to do. She asked him to hold the woman's hand and rub it gently with warming salve. "Your touch will remind her spirit to stay with her body," Bena said. "She needs to remember that, just now."

In the Chinook trade jargon, there were two different words for remembering. One meant "not to forget," and the other meant "to remember after having forgotten." Bena used the phrase for the second kind of remembering—*klip tumtum*. Translated into English literally, the words referred to something sunk deep in the heart, a memory that was buried so deep that the heart remembered it, even when the mind had forgotten.

"Her name is Nadya," Jacob told Bena. "She came up from San Francisco by ship and she was heading north. She seemed lost. . . ." Again, his words trailed off.

It had always seemed to Bena that Jacob was a little lost. She patted him on the shoulder. "Hold her hand so that she knows you are here. If she wants to, she'll find her way back."

Nadya dreamed she was running away, running from the men with loud voices, running from the smell of black powder. Trying to run from the pain in her shoulder, from the smell of her own blood. Running and falling. Into the river? No, that was the other time, the time her parents died. Long ago.

No, this time she fell onto cold ground. This time, she could run no farther. This time she curled up beside a fallen log, her face in the rich-smelling humus of the forest floor. She stopped running and waited to die in the cold.

She was waiting to die, alone in the cold, but she heard voices speaking in a foreign language. The smell of stew and healing herbs, the cracking of a wood fire, the warmth of wool blankets against her skin. That did not seem right. Where had these blankets come from?

"Easy now," someone said. "You're safe here." Someone was holding her hand.

She opened her eyes. Jacob, the man who had helped her in Astoria, sat cross-legged on the mat beside her. He held her hand. Behind him, an Indian woman was ladling stew into a bowl. "You were having bad dreams," he said.

Nadya blinked at him. "Where . . . ?" she started to ask, but her voice was weak.

The Indian woman said something that Nadya didn't understand. "Don't bother to ask questions," Jacob said. "Bena says you need to eat. You need to build up your strength."

He held the bowl of stew and fed her, one spoonful after another. While he fed her, he talked softly, telling her about where she was. "This cabin belongs to Bena and Keco. Bena is good at taking care of people, so I brought you here when I found you in the forest."

She had many questions. Found her where? Did he know

how she had been hurt? Did he know what she was?

"Eat," he said, holding the spoon to her lips. She ate and then she was tired, so tired. This place smelled like home, but she didn't belong here. She knew that. She didn't belong among people. She turned her head away from the fire, and the room blurred around her, and she tumbled into sleep, into restless dreams.

She was standing in the street in Yerba Buena near Elizabeth's uncle's house. Elizabeth stood on the street not far away, her arm around Jenny's shoulders. Elizabeth's uncle stood between her and Jenny. His face was contorted with anger and he was shouting at her. "You don't belong here," he was shouting. "You don't belong among civilized people. Get away from here. Go away."

She looked behind him, looked to Elizabeth for support, but Elizabeth was afraid. She held Jenny tight, though the girl struggled to escape. Elizabeth was afraid of her uncle, Nadya thought for a moment, then realized she was wrong. Elizabeth was cowering behind her uncle, trying to hide. She was afraid of Nadya, afraid to look her in the face. "Elizabeth," Nadya called to her. "It's only me." But Elizabeth did not look up.

"Go back to the wilderness where you belong," Elizabeth's uncle shouted. "And we'll hunt you down like the animal you are."

Suddenly, there were other people standing with Elizabeth's uncle. She saw William Cooper, the preacher, and the hunters who had shot her, and the sailors, and, right next to Elizabeth's uncle, Rufus, alive and well. While she watched, Rufus stooped, picked up a stone, and hefted it in his hand, grinning. "Rufus," she called, thinking that maybe he didn't recognize her. Then he threw the stone at her. All the people were throwing stones and she was running away on four legs rather than two, running away. She could hear the people shouting behind her.

Nadya woke with her heart pounding and her skin cold with sweat. She could hear the rustle of playing cards. She opened her eyes. By the light that shone through the open door, it was late afternoon. Was it the same day as before or a new day? She didn't know.

An Indian sat on a woven reed mat nearby, shuffling a deck of cards. Dressed like a man, but by the smell, Nadya knew she was a woman. As Nadya watched, she turned the card on the top of the deck. Ace of hearts. She smiled in satisfaction, then replaced the card and shuffled again.

Nadya remembered sleeping and waking and sleeping and waking—though never waking for very long. Just long enough to eat a bowl of stew, then sleep again. The brief times when she was awake seemed as much like dreams as the dreams themselves. Jacob had been there, and an Indian woman named Bena. The cabin belonged to Keco and Bena, Jacob had said.

"Keco," Nadya said tentatively.

The woman looked up. "Ah, you are awake now."

Nadya nodded. She struggled to a sitting position. She was wearing a man's shirt that draped loosely around her. "How long have I been sleeping?"

"Three days, maybe." Keco shuffled the deck again. "Bena and Jacob have been taking care of you. But Jacob is off hunting and Bena is getting plants for medicine." She waved at the herbs drying in the rafters overhead. "So I am taking care of you now." She fanned the cards in her hand and held them out to Nadya. "Take one card, but don't show me."

Nadya obediently reached out and choose a card. The jack of diamonds.

"Put it back," Keco demanded, and Nadya slipped it back into the deck. Keco shuffled the cards—once, twice, three times—mixing them thoroughly. "Your card lost," she said, tapping the deck. "Right?"

Nadya nodded. Certainly, her card was lost in the deck.

Keco cut the cards and stacked them, then held out the deck. "That first card. Yours."

Nadya turned over the top card. It was the jack of diamonds. Keco grinned. "How did you do that?" Nadya asked.

Keco just kept grinning. "*Tahmahnawis,*" she said. Then, when Nadya looked puzzled, she added in English, "Magic." She took the jack of diamonds, returned it to the deck, then resumed shuffling.

Nadya felt at ease with this card-playing woman. Keco, it seemed, wanted nothing from her other than her ability to pick a card and marvel at the resulting trick.

"What was that other word? *Tahmahnawis?*" Nadya asked.

"That's the trade talk. Everyone talks that talk. Only some Indians speak like the white men."

"How did you learn English?" Nadya asked.

"I talk many kinds of talk," Keco said. "Bena and I, we travel around with the white men, with the Indians. Go many places, see many things. Then we come here and we rest. This is a fine place to rest." She looked up from her cards and grinned. "You best learn trade talk, if you going to stay here. *Mika ticky muckamuck?* That means 'do you want some food?' "

Nadya nodded, not bothering to argue about whether she'd be staying in Shoalwater Bay or not. She was hungry again, and that was enough.

While she ate a bowl of stew—feeding herself this time, rather than being fed like a baby—Keco taught her words from the trade talk. It seemed to be a mix of English, French, and Indian words. *Muckamuck* was "food." *Pasese* was "blanket." *Ah-ha* was "yes" and *halo* was "no." After teaching her a few basic words, Keco tapped her own chest. *"Burdash,"* she said. "Woman who dresses like man."

"Burdash," Nadya repeated obediently.

Keco reached over and touched Nadya's shoulder. *"Leloo,"* she said.

"Leloo," Nadya repeated. "What does that mean? Woman?"

Keco laughed. "Not woman. It means 'wolf.' Big gray wolf, that lives in the forest."

Nadya frowned. Keco did not seem upset that she was a wolf. If anything, the woman seemed amused. "I am not always a wolf," Nadya said slowly.

"You are *sitkum lello*—half wolf."

Nadya nodded, still frowning.

Keco put her hand gently on Nadya's shoulder. "Why are you so worried? I am *burdash;* Jacob is *sitkum siwash*—half Indian, half King George man; Lono is *Owyhee*. In Astoria town, they would throw us all out. We don't belong there. But this is our own place. Here, we all belong."

Nadya nodded slowly. She had finished her stew and she was tired now, very tired. They knew that she was woman and wolf, and it was too much to think now.

"Mika moosum alta?" Keco asked. "You sleep now?"

Nadya nodded and lay down again. She felt Keco cover her with the blanket, tucking it up around her chin. And she fell asleep to the rustle of cards.

Chérie," her mother said. They sat at the table in the cabin in Missouri, and the air was perfumed with the scent of healing herbs. Her mother was shuffling the cards. "I will read your fortune for you."

"Mama," Nadya said. "I am afraid. Since Elizabeth sent me away, I've been so lonely and afraid."

"Elizabeth." Her mother's tone made the name an insult. "That whey-faced coward. She was not the right mate for you. You need a mate that's wild at heart."

"I don't belong with people," Nadya continued. "Elizabeth showed me that. I—"

"Don't pay any mind to Elizabeth," her mother said softly. She shuffled the cards—once, twice, three times. "Listen to me. Listen to your heart." She held out the cards and Nadya cut the deck. "Here now, don't cry," she said softly. "Look at the cards."

Nadya lifted her hand to wipe away the tears. She hadn't realized that she was weeping until her mother told her not to cry.

"Look," her mother said.

Nadya looked down at the cards spread on the silk scarf. The card that indicated her past showed a heart pierced with swords: heartbreak and pain.

"Don't look to the past," her mother murmured. "Look at the present. Here now. . . ." She tapped the ten of pentacles, a card that pictured a family—mother, father, children, all touching each other, protecting each other. "This could be yours. But here. . . ." She tapped another card, the four of cups. The picture showed a hand emerging from a cloud to offer a golden goblet to a man who was turning his head away. "A gift is being offered to you, but you refuse to take it. You turn away in fear."

"And look here." Her mother tapped her finger on the card that indicated the immediate future: a figure on horseback rode in a victory procession. "Triumph and success can be yours." Her finger tapped another card: a man sitting up in a bed, clutching his head in the panic that comes from night terrors. "If you don't let your fear take control. You must be brave a little longer, *chérie.* And in the end . . ." She touched another card: *Le Monde,* The World. A woman danced in the center of a wreath of flowers. She was smiling and spreading her arms to embrace the world. A card of joy and completion and reward. ". . . this could be yours."

"Mama, I want to stay here with you." Nadya was crying again. Her mother was dead; she remembered that now.

Her mother shook her head and took Nadya's hand. "It's not your time yet, *chérie.* You must be brave a little longer. But you don't have to be brave alone. Look for help and you will find it."

"Mama . . . ?"

The cabin was empty, and she could smell the acrid tang of burnt powder in the air. An empty cup was on the table in front of her. She had been drinking tea. She was cold, cold to the heart, and the door of the cabin swung open in the wind.

She knew what was outside. A riderless horse and a body lying in the dust; two wolfskins tied to a saddle and the smell of death in the air.

"Mama!" she cried out. "Oh, don't leave me here alone. Mama!"

"Hush," a voice said. A man's voice; Jacob's voice. A warm touch on her hand. "You're safe here. Easy now."

She opened her eyes. Jacob sat on the mat beside her, holding her hand.

"You cried out," he said.

"A dream," she said unsteadily. "A bad dream."

"What did you dream?"

"Just a bad dream," she said softly.

It was late afternoon and the cabin was filled with shadows.

"Keco said you were doing better," he said easily. "She said you talked for a while."

"She did tricks with cards," Nadya said unsteadily.

"Keco used to make her living playing cards," Jacob said. He hesitated. "She wins a bit more often than is natural."

Nadya nodded. "I'd expect as much."

In the dim, late afternoon light that shone through the open door, Nadya studied Jacob. Dark eyes, dark hair, ruddy skin with high cheekbones that betrayed his Indian ancestry. He was still holding her hand. He had big hands, callused from hard work. He had pushed back the sleeves of his shirt and she noticed that the skin on the underside of his wrist was crisscrossed with thin white lines.

Still holding his hand, she reached out with her other hand and ran her fingers over the lines. She felt tiny ridges, scars from wounds, long since healed. "What are these?"

"Among my mother's people, there was a ceremony, a ritual." He hesitated. "I was just a boy when the wolves came to me." His words trailed off.

"The wolves?" she prompted. "Wolves from the forest?"

"Men of the village who had been touched with the wolf spirit," he said. "They wore wooden masks and howled outside the lodges. The wolf had come to them."

"What happened then?" she asked. He was not a man who talked easily, she thought.

He met her eyes. "With the sharp edge of a mussel shell, my uncle cut me so that the wolf spirit could enter. And then the wolf came to me."

She nodded, watching his face. "Were you frightened?"

He shrugged. "Not so much. My uncle was there with me. It was good. It made me one of the people, marked by the people."

His hand was warm in hers. His face was stolid, a mask hiding pain. "Where is your uncle now?" she asked slowly.

"He's dead."

"And your mother?"

"My mother is dead. The village is dead. The people are scattered."

"And where is your father? Is he dead, too?"

Jacob shook his head. "He's at Fort Vancouver. He's a King George man. He belongs at the fort."

"Keco said you were. . . ." She hesitated, remembering the words. "*Sitkum siwash*. Half Indian."

He was studying her face. "Half Indian. Half King George man. And you—you are half white woman, half wolf." His voice was quiet and steady, stating a fact, nothing more. "My mother told me of people who changed. People who were sometimes bears or wolves or ravens. It was a young man from the wolf people who taught the village to dance the sacred dances and sing the sacred songs. But that was long ago. I thought those people were gone."

He sat silent for a moment and then spoke softly. "Tell me—what's it like to be a wolf? It always seemed to me that it would be a wonderful thing."

She held his hand. "Sometimes it is wonderful." Her voice was dreamy. "It can be much simpler than being a woman . . . and much more complicated. There are smells, the most wonderful smells. I can hear the rustling of mice in the underbrush, the shifting of sleeping birds in the trees."

"How does it feel?"

"It feels right. I belong in the forest, and no one can tell me I don't." Her voice was stronger. "It's like coming home at last."

"Ah," he said, a sound of wonder and envy.

"But then, when the moon sets, I change back into a woman. And that's hard, very hard. I change back and I don't belong anymore. I come back, and I'm alone."

"You don't belong in the forest anymore. But you belong with people."

"Do I?" she asked.

"I think you do."

They sat in silence for a moment. He still held her hand. She liked the feeling of skin against skin, warm and comforting. She closed her eyes and drifted off to sleep.

32

Nadya stayed for a time in the cabin that belonged to Keco and Bena. Keco taught her trade talk and did card tricks and told stories, many stories, about her adventurous youth with Bena. Bena made her eat stew and herbal tea and regain her strength. Jacob went hunting and brought back game and stopped by to visit.

Bena and Keco took it for granted that she would stay until she was better. After a time, Nadya came to accept that assumption. As she recovered her strength, she went walking sometimes with Jacob—along the beach where the air held the tang of salt, through the forest where the rain whispered through the branches of the great trees, dripping from branch to branch until the drops that fell on the forest floor were scented with resin. The weather was wet—sometimes storming and sometimes drizzling, but always raining and damp. But her old deerskin jacket kept her dry enough and Bena promised to make her another if she would hunt for the deer and that was fine.

On their walks, Jacob took her to meet the others who lived in the small community. There was Ivan, a Russian trader who had fallen in love with an Indian woman and left his ship. He lived with Elakha, a sweet-faced woman who was too shy to talk to Nadya, even when she tried her best trade talk. Ivan spoke English with an accent that reminded Nadya of her father.

A short distance to the south lived two Japanese men everyone called Tick and Tack. A decade before, their small fishing boat had washed up on the beach. Caught in a typhoon, they had been carried across the ocean to this foreign land. They had built a neat cabin and planted a tidy garden. Though they were excellent fishermen, Jacob said they would never take their canoe outside the safety of Shoalwater Bay, for fear of being swept to sea again.

And there were Sam and Mattie. They were free blacks, and according to the law of the Oregon Territory, they shouldn't be there at all. Not wanting to be a slave state or a free state, the government in Oregon City had legally forbidden residence to Negroes and mulattoes. Jacob called them *klale siwash,* which meant "black Indians," and they lived in a well-tended cabin sheltered by trees.

Nadya grew used to spending time with Jacob. Sometimes, he took her out in his canoe to explore the bay, showing her the best oyster beds, the rocks where he collected mussels, the river where the salmon ran. He took her to gather cattail root for Bena, and they walked in the marsh where the air stank of mud and decay, rich intriguing smells. He took her with him and demanded nothing of her.

Just when the cabin she shared with Bena and Keco started to feel too small for the three of them, Jacob took her to see an Indian lodge that had been abandoned some years before. As they walked along the beach, the sun broke through the clouds. It had not rained since the day before, and the breeze felt unseasonably warm.

The cabin was small, a house that an Indian family might use as a temporary shelter while fishing in the summer. The structure was among the trees, but the open door faced the beach.

"Lono says that no one has come here for years now," Jacob told her..

Moss grew thick on the wooden walls, but the interior was dry enough, an empty room waiting to be filled. Nadya stepped in through the open door, leaving Jacob outside. It had been a long time since anyone had visited this place. She liked the smell of it: no human scents, just moss and cedar and wood mice.

She could be at home here, she thought. It was small, just the right size for one woman. She could hear the waves lapping at the beach. Through the open door, she could see water and sand.

For the past few days, she had been wondering when she should leave. She had recovered from her injuries. Perhaps it was time to go north, away from people and civilization. But she was no longer eager to move on. The pressure that had driven her to escape San Francisco and Astoria had eased. She felt at home in this small community.

She stepped out into the sunshine. Jacob sat on the edge of the beach, not far away. She sat on the sand beside him.

"It needs repairs, of course," he said. "But that would be easy."

"I'm not sure," she said. "I wonder if I should go north."

He put his hand lightly on her shoulder. Through her shirt, she could feel the warmth of his hand. Despite the sunshine, the beach was chilly.

"Why would you leave?"

She closed her eyes. "I reckon I don't belong among civilized people," she said.

He laughed then, a sound so unexpected that she opened her eyes. He was grinning. "Well, that's all right, then," he said. He held up his scarred wrist. "Is that the mark of a civilized man?" He shook his head, still grinning, and took both her hands in his. "Listen. There are no civilized people out here. Ask the folks in Astoria, if you don't believe me. We don't belong in Astoria; we don't belong anywhere." He laughed again. "Don't you worry about civilized people in these parts. You'll fit right in."

She frowned, overwhelmed by his rush of words.

"You belong here," he said simply. "You belong with me."

His hands were warm against hers. He wanted her. In the cool air, she could smell subtle changes in his sweat that told her he wanted her. She had known that since they met in Astoria, but she had chosen to ignore that knowledge. It wasn't time.

But now she could feel her body responding to his scent. She was aware of the steady pounding of her pulse, perhaps a little faster than before; the rough fabric of her shirt rubbing against her nipples; a warmth and a wetness in her crotch.

She lay back on the sand, still holding his hands and pulling him down beside her. She pressed herself against his body. He was warm and solid.

"You belong here," he said again. He put his arms around her and she could feel his hands on her back, strong hands pulling her close.

Not far away, the waves washed against the beach, blending with the sound of his breath, coming and going, coming and going. It was not civilized to make love outdoors. Elizabeth had told her that. It was barbaric. She grinned fiercely, feeling the cool breeze on her breasts as he unbuttoned her shirt.

His mouth was on her breast, licking and sucking and teasing her. She did not feel the cold air. She was warm, so warm, and his hand was between her legs, pressing against her in a rhythm that made her heart pound faster. She unbuttoned her trousers and then unbuttoned his and reached inside to stroke his cock, its soft skin smooth against her hand.

Her cunt was wet and hot. She rolled on top of him. It was barbaric to make love in the sand of the beach, beneath the open sky. It was barbaric to open your legs to your lover's tongue, to moan low in your throat like a cat in heat. It was barbaric to kick off your trousers and wrap your legs around your lover, pulling him into you, feeling a pleasure that was close to pain. It was barbaric to feel the urgency that came with the Change, the heat and the need and the desire that demanded fulfillment, out of control, beyond control, beyond all bounds, a pulsing wave that took her and left her limp and shaken. It was barbaric to fuck like animals, not caring who saw. It was barbaric.

It was wonderful. They lay together in the sand, their bodies pressed close together. The breeze was cool and their clothes were tangled around them. He kissed her neck and his lips left a spot of warmth behind. Her shoulder ached and she was cold, but none of that mattered, it didn't matter at all.

She laughed then, a low chuckle that rose from deep inside her. "I'm glad," she said. "I'm so glad you're not civilized here."

Two days later, Jacob helped her move her things into the abandoned cabin.

She had thought she had little enough to move—just her bedroll and the things in her pack. But then Jacob brought her a bentwood food storage box made of red cedar. When she opened it, she found he had filled it with provisions from his own winter stores: potatoes, smoked salmon, and loaves made of baked cammass root. Bena gave her three mats, woven of cedar bark and fragrant with the smell of the tree, to cover the dirt floor. Keco gave her a bottle of brandy she had won from a trapper in Astoria. And Bena, muttering about the cold nights, insisted that she take another blanket. And medicinal herbs to make strengthening tea, and a pot to brew the tea in, and a cup to drink the tea from.

"Enough!" Nadya said, waving her hands and laughing at the Indian woman's generosity.

"In trade talk," Keco admonished Nadya sternly. Keco had taken to insisting that Nadya practice trade talk at every opportunity, scolding her when she lapsed into English.

"*Kopet hiyu!*" Nadya managed. "That's plenty. *Mahsie.* Thank you very much."

Bena shook her head, frowning at Nadya's things, obviously considering them far too meager. But they set off down the beach loaded down with mats and blankets and such. Along the way, Keco started telling Nadya about another time when she and Bena had had too much to carry.

Keco and Bena had grown up in a village beside the Mississippi River. As young women, they had left their tribe and had traveled across the country, masquerading as man and wife. They had lived as adventurers—cheating the whites and Indians alike, sometimes trapping or working for a time, but more often getting by without honest work.

Some twenty years ago, back when white men were first building the fort at Astoria, Keco had obtained a letter that was written in English. She and Bena had traveled up the Columbia River, and showed the letter to Indians in the villages along the way.

"We told them that it was from the great white chief. We told them it said he would be sending them great gifts very soon."

"What did it say?" Nadya asked.

Keco shrugged. "I don't know. It might have been from the great white chief. Who knows?"

Happy with the news of coming good fortune, the Indians showered gifts on Keco and Bena.

"It was very good. *Nika hiyu iktas*. We were very rich." Keco smiled. "But we couldn't go back there for a while."

Nadya nodded. "I imagine not."

"You can see why I don't think you should play cards with this one," Jacob said to Nadya.

Keco pretended to be affronted. "I am always honest when playing with friends," she said.

"None of her friends will play with her," Jacob said. "So her honesty doesn't really matter."

Bena laughed and Keco pretended she was outraged. They talked and laughed and strolled along the beach. Nadya thought it was strange to walk along the beach with a group of chattering friends. She had laughed and joked like this with Lottie—but that was long ago. She thought about how long and realized that it had been less than a year since her parents had died. They had died in the spring, just eight months ago. But she had been much younger then.

"Hello!" Lono was hurrying down the beach toward them. Jacob had told him that Nadya was moving to the cabin, and Myeena had sent him to meet them with a basket filled with cakes made from dried sallal berries from Myeena's winter stores.

"Myeena always thinks of food," Lono said. "She said you would be hungry, living by yourself."

"I won't be hungry. I'll go hunting," Nadya said. She smiled at Lono. "But you can tell Myeena that I'm very glad to have sallal cakes."

They came to the cabin. Bena frowned when she saw the floor. She gathered handfuls of rushes at the nearby creek and set to sweeping the hard-packed dirt surface. The fire pit in the center of the cabin was a tumble of stones. As Bena swept, Nadya rebuilt the hearth, arranging the stones so that she could balance the pot that Bena had given her on two stones and push burning coals beneath it. Lono and Jacob gathered wood from the forest, accumulating a respectable pile of fallen branches and tinder. Keco, always inclined toward the duty that required the least physical effort, burned herbs to cleanse the place of any spiritual residue left by its former inhabitants.

The sky grew cloudy. The past few days had been fine, but the wind was changing and the weather was growing colder. A fine drizzle began to fall. Nadya put a pot of water on to boil and they all had tea, passing Nadya's single cup from hand to hand.

Nadya sat by the fire, looking out through the open door at the cold world outside. This was her cabin, she thought. These were her friends. It was cold outside, but she was warm. How strange it was to sit by the fire with friends, drinking tea. How very strange.

When the others left, Jacob stayed after. "I can help you build some stools, a table," he said. He looked around the small room, at the mats and the fire. Already, the cabin looked more like a home. "If you like."

"I think so," she said. She sat on a cedar mat by the fire, staring into the flames. He sat down beside her and waited. He was a patient man, willing to wait. She was wild, he knew that. But he loved wild things.

When she looked up at him, her face was calm—not frightened, not fierce. "This is a wonderful place."

That night, they made love in her cabin and he slept beside her on the reed mat. When he woke in the night, he pressed close to her, reassuring himself that she was still there. He had worried, all those nights that she slept at Bena and Keco's. She could have vanished, as quickly as she had appeared. She was a magical creature—a white woman who was touched by Indian legend.

She reached up and touched his cheek. "You're afraid of

something," she murmured. "I can smell it. What are you afraid of?"

"I'm not afraid."

She ran her hand along the line of his jaw, down his throat. "What are you afraid of?" she repeated. "What is it?"

He could see only her eyes, reflecting the dim light from the fire's last embers. He closed his eyes and pulled her closer, so that she could not see his face. "Afraid that you aren't real. Afraid that I'll open my eyes and you'll be gone. I just wanted to feel you near." He hesitated. "I wish I could spend every night like this."

"The Cheyenne tell a story about a man who marries a buffalo wife," she said softly. "When she comes to his village, she's a woman. But after a time, she becomes a buffalo and returns to her people."

"If I had a buffalo wife, I would follow her," he said. "I would follow her back to the buffalo."

"Suppose you couldn't follow. What would you do then?"

"I'd wait until she came back." Her body was warm and tense against his.

"You sound very sure. A buffalo wife is very different from a human woman. Maybe she wouldn't come back. Maybe you couldn't wait."

Jacob thought of his mother and father. Very different, but they had loved one another. "If I loved her and she loved me, she'd come back. I would wait. That's how love works. There are differences, but what matters is something deeper. Under the skin, we're the same."

"Tomorrow night, the moon is full," she said softly. "Tomorrow night, I'll Change. And you won't know who I am."

"You'll change. But then you'll come back. You'll come home."

"I'll come home when the moon sets," she said.

She kissed him, and they made love on the mat by the fire, warm beneath the blankets. Afterward, as they lay together, Jacob felt Nadya shiver in his arms.

"What is it?" he asked.

"Listen."

He listened. In the distance, he heard a faint sound: a dog barking? No, a wolf, he realized, as the barking gave way to a howl. Another animal joined in, and then, after a pause, another.

"Sounds lonely," he said.

"No, not lonely," Nadya murmured. "They've been hunting. And they've made the kill. Now the leader is calling them together. They'll eat well tonight. Not lonely at all."

Jacob listened to the thin, lonely howling. Nadya hugged him closer. He could feel her hot breath on his neck. "Are you lonely?" he asked her.

"Not now," she said. "Not at all."

33

■

On the day of the Change, she woke with Jacob beside her. It was a cold morning—the wind was blowing from the north, bringing the scent of snow. Before Jacob left the cabin, he insisted on chopping wood, until she had a pile of firewood that would last her for days.

"We're in for a cold spell," he said, frowning. "Maybe you'll need another blanket."

"I'll be fine," she said, smiling at him.

Later that afternoon, after Jacob had reluctantly left for his cabin, Nadya went hunting along the creek. Some distance from the bay, the creek spread out to form a marshy area where ducks were plentiful. In the reeds on the edge of the marsh, she shot a plump duck.

On her way back, she found paw prints in the mud beside the creek, evidence of the pack she had heard the night before. She examined the prints. They were old; their sharp edges had been softened by the previous day's drizzle. The scents had been washed away, but by the tracks she guessed that the pack included one large male and a few younger animals.

She sat on her heels, remembering the howling she had heard the night before. Such a sweet sound. It was both a call and a warning. To those who belonged to the pack, it meant "Come to me. Hurry and come to me now." And she had longed to go. But she didn't belong to the pack, and she remembered the pack that had pursued her on the plains. For strangers, the howl meant "This is our place, our land. Keep your distance."

Nadya stood and headed back to the cabin, carrying the duck she had shot. The day was misty, and the wind blew cold. It would be a cold night.

She stewed the duck in the pot that Bena had given her, with a few of Jacob's potatoes. She ate well before sunset. Though she was alone in the cabin, she was comforted by the gifts that people had left her: the mats on the floor, the food, the blankets. This was her place.

When the edge of the setting sun just touched the water of the bay, she stripped and stood outside the cabin door. The wind was cold, very cold, and she shivered, waiting for the moon. She could feel it below the eastern horizon, a point of heat in a chilly world. She hunched her shoulders against the wind, feeling small and weak in the cold.

The moon rose and she was warm, she was strong and confident. The moon rose and she Changed.

The gray wolf lifted her head and breathed deeply, sampling the scents on the wind. The cabin behind her was filled with human smells: tea and stew and wood smoke and Bena's scent on the mats and the lingering scent of sex in the blankets where she and Jacob had made love. Warm, comfortable smells.

From the forest, the wind blew cold, ruffling her fur. She caught the scent of deer, not far off. She wasn't hungry, but the smell was intriguing.

The forest floor was cold beneath the pads of her feet. She had no destination; she was wandering north, investigating the scents she encountered. She paused to sniff a place in the ferns where a deer had rested, then moved on, still heading north.

She was about a mile from the cabin when she found the scent marking of the wolf pack: a bush where the pack's leader had left his mark, the weaker scents of the younger animals. She sniffed the bush, then curled her lips back into a snarl and sniffed again, caught by conflicting emotions.

The hair on the back of her neck bristled at the scent of these strangers on her land, her territory. This was her place and she would protect it. But at the same time, the scent of the other wolves attracted her, gave her a sense of kinship. She had been alone so long and these wolves, strangers or not, were her own kind.

She followed the pack's trail. It had not been long since the animals had passed that way, and the scent was strong. In a sheltered valley, where a ridge blocked the north wind, she found where the wolves had startled three deer. They had given chase to one of the three.

The deer had bounded away through the bracken fern, heading up the ridge, harried by four wolves. Even in the cold, Nadya could smell the heavy, dark scent of blood on the ground.

After making the kill, the pack would linger near the carcass, feeding and resting and protecting their food from other predators. Nadya slowed as she approached the crest of the ridge. The wind carried the scent of the wolves, and she was caught by desire and fear. She could still run away, leaving this pack and the danger it presented. But she continued up the slope, her head high to scent the wind.

At the top of the ridge, she flattened her belly to the ground and looked down into a clearing where three young wolves were playing in the snow. They were upwind of her, and they had not scented her yet.

Three young wolves—older than pups, but not full grown, siblings from the same litter, born last spring. As Nadya watched, one of the females pounced on her brother, bowling him over. The two wrestled, and she could hear their growls—mock fighting, nothing serious. The third wolf, another female, trotted around the wrestling animals, making eager whimpering sounds in her throat. Then the wrestling female broke free and ran, her brother in pursuit and her sister running alongside, charging down the slope through the trees in helter-skelter play. A distance down the hill, the male caught up with the female and they wrestled again, growling and yipping in excitement. Then they broke off and ran again, heading downward.

Nadya found herself on her feet, ready to follow and join in the play. She took a few steps forward.

In a sheltered place beside the clearing, a black wolf got to his feet. He was an imposing animal, deep-chested and powerful, and he stared intently in her direction. She stopped where she was, the hair at her neck bristling. This was the wolf she had heard howling the night before, the leader of the pack, the father of these pups.

She returned his gaze and took a few, careful steps forward. Her attitude was not threatening, but she did not tuck her tail between her legs and flatten her ears and drop her gaze as a submissive wolf would. Her head was up, her ears were erect, she met his gaze as an equal.

He stalked toward her slowly, his head extended to sniff at her neck. She held her ground, allowing him to approach, to sniff the bristling fur of her neck. She could feel his breath through her fur. She breathed deeply, taking in his scent: a warm smell that reminded her of Missouri and wild nights running with her mother and father. And she found herself whimpering deep in her throat, a sound of entreaty. She narrowed her eyes and let her ears flatten a little as she pushed her muzzle toward his, sniffing his face in the greeting of a wolf to a pack mate. As he circled, she turned, keeping her head toward him, keeping her eyes on him.

The big male was not antagonistic, but curious about this lone female who had wandered out of the woods. Nadya relaxed a little, confident that he would not attack. They had met and accepted each other—not as equals quite, because he was clearly the leader, but he had recognized her strengths, had not attempted to establish his absolute dominance.

She whimpered again in her throat, a low expressive whine of acceptance. Still facing him, she crouched suddenly in the posture of a wolf ready to pounce in play, her tail wagging, her head cocked to one side. He wagged his tail and she sprang, a playful leap with no threat behind it.

When the younger wolves returned, they found Nadya and their father rolling and playing in the clearing.

The moon was low over the bay when Nadya came down the ridge and headed for her cabin. She was bruised from the rough play with the other wolves, but happy, at ease with herself.

On the path to her cabin, she paused, smelling a familiar scent in the air. A man had passed this way. She hesitated on the edge of the forest, listening to the small sounds that came from within the cabin. The snap of twigs, the scratch of steel on flint. Then she smelled wood smoke and heard the crackle of fire. A liquid sound—water pouring into a pot.

The moon set and the sun rose and Nadya Changed. Colors returned to the world and smells became less intense. The breeze was suddenly cold on her naked skin. She shivered in the cold, remembering how comfortable she had been with the wolves. She was alone and filled with longing.

Words came to her, and with them came names. Jacob—that was the name of the man in the cabin. She took a step toward the cabin. "Jacob," she said softly, testing the name, listening to her own voice. Then louder. "Jacob."

The cabin door opened and she ran into his arms, naked and cold from her night in the forest. The cabin was warm, and johnnycake was baking in a pan by the fire. He wrapped her in a blanket and gave her hot tea to drink. While the johnnycake baked, he asked her about her night in the forest.

So strange, to talk about the Change. With her parents, there had been no need to talk. And Elizabeth had not wanted to hear. But Jacob asked her where she had gone, what she had done.

When she told him about the other wolves, he nodded. "Late last spring, I found a wolf den in the hills. There was a pup crouched just inside the opening, growling at me." He smiled. "Tiny baby growls. Two other pups watched me curiously from inside. Parents were probably out hunting."

"What did you do?"

"I put out my hand, and the pup sniffed it. He was curious, that's all. Then I went up the hill and kept watch for a while. Saw two wolves come back to the den: big black wolf and smaller gray one. They sniffed around where I had been and the black one glared up the hill at me, letting me know that I wasn't welcome there." He shrugged. "I went back in a month and the den was empty."

"You left them alone?"

He shrugged again. "Had no reason to disturb them."

"I wonder what happened to the pups' mother."

"I'd reckon she was shot. Maybe by the oystermen up the coast, maybe by the farmers down south. There's a bounty on wolves."

Nadya stared into the fire, remembering romping with the black wolf, with the young wolves. "Out in the plains, I met a pack of wolves. They chased me away. Wanted me out of their territory. But that black wolf—he didn't chase me."

Jacob nodded. "This is your territory, too. Besides, I'd reckon he was lonely." He put his arm around her shoulders. "I know what that's like."

She turned to study his face. "Does it bother you?" she asked him suddenly. "Does it worry you to know that I'm running with the wolves?"

"When you're a wolf, you run with the wolves," he said softly. "And when you're not a wolf, you come back to me." He shrugged. "Seems to me that's how it should be."

She sat by the fire and held his hand. With her other hand, she traced the scars that marked him as a brother to the wolf.

With Rufus and Elizabeth, falling in love had been like tumbling off a cliff. With Jacob, it was like finding a solid place to land. She had her cabin, but more often than not she spent the night at his lodge or he slept at hers. They hunted together for deer and small game. Jacob sat by the fire and chatted with Bena while Keco taught Nadya card tricks. They visited Lono and Myeena, spending the night in the crowded lodge among friends.

Jacob took Nadya out in his canoe, and she learned to paddle the small craft, to hoist the sail and control the boat's movement over the smooth water of the bay. They sailed south to visit Sam and Mattie, Ivan and Elakha, and Tick and Tack.

Sometimes, sitting by the fire at night or lying under the blankets in his bed or hers, he told her about the tricks that trappers used to conceal their deadly, steel-jawed traps. He told her of pitfalls and deadfalls and rawhide snares. He warned her of settlers who laced meat with strychnine. She listened, knowing that he was trying to keep her safe.

Less than a month after she moved into her cabin, Jacob helped her move her possessions into the lodge where he lived. Late in the day, as the sun was setting, they walked together to a clearing on a hill, not far from Jacob's cabin. Nadya sat on a fallen log, with Jacob at her side, to watch the moon rise. That evening was clear and bright, and the moon was one day from full. She could feel the warmth of its light on her skin.

"Ah, listen," she said. From the north, she heard a wolf howl—the black male that she had romped with in the woods. Other voices—the younger wolves—joined in. Sweet sound, calling to her. Jacob's arm was warm around her.

She wanted to respond, to let the pack know she was there, but she hesitated, remembering how Elizabeth had chastised her for singing with the wolves. In that moment, Jacob tipped back his head and joined the chorus, howling on a low note that blended with the wolves. She smiled and joined in, singing to the wolves, to the rising moon, to the success of the hunt to come.

The next night, she walked to the clearing alone. Jacob had hugged her goodbye and let her go. The wolves were howling as the full moon rose. After she Changed, she headed north, following the sound of their call, running through the forest that she knew so well.

When she found the wolves, they greeted her as wolves greet a pack mate who has strayed and returned, with wagging tails and much sniffing. They hunted for deer under the full moon. With the others, Nadya gave chase to a young doe, tearing at the animal's flanks and tasting blood. They brought her down in a clearing and feasted on fresh meat.

34

■

For the first time in months, the weather was warm and dry. Lono and Jacob had gone out fishing for herring, while Nadya and Myeena went up to the hills to cut the first shoots of the wild raspberry plant. Keco and Bena had spent the morning foraging along the beach, and they had brought baskets of clams and mussels to Myeena's door.

It was early in the afternoon, and Myeena had spread cedar mats on the ground outside the door of her lodge. The women sat together in the sunshine, peeling the raspberry stalks. Stripped of their tough outer skin, these shoots were crisp and tender. Eaten raw, like cucumbers, they had a delicious tart flavor.

Cheechee, Myeena's daughter, sat beside her mother, industriously chewing on a peeled stalk. Myeena's son lay in the shade, napping.

Nadya paused in her work and rested a hand on the curve of her belly. She was pregnant and she marveled every day at the ways her body was changing.

"*Hyas kloshe,*" Bena said to Nadya, touching the hem of her dress. Very good. For the past week, Nadya had been wearing a calico dress that Bena had made for her. Nadya's trousers were no longer comfortable; the waistband did not ride comfortably over her swelling stomach. Noticing the difficulty, Bena had dug through her stores, found a length of calico, and stitched Nadya a simple dress.

Nadya smiled at Bena. When Bena had learned of Nadya's pregnancy, she had begun bringing her herbs to brew into strengthening teas. Nadya felt fine and healthy, but she enjoyed Bena's attention and concern.

"You need another dress," Keco told Nadya. "Might as well recognize that you won't be wearing pants for a time."

"I reckon I could use another one," Nadya admitted.

"I help you make it," Myeena said cheerfully. Over the winter, Nadya and Myeena had become friends. On rainy afternoons, Nadya and Jacob had come visiting the big lodge. While Jacob and Lono whittled, making wooden spoons and bowls and other useful objects, Myeena had shown Nadya how to do domestic chores the way they were done by the Indians of the area: weaving baskets from cedar bark and spruce root, twisting nettle fibers to make twine and knotting the twine to make fishing nets, making mats from rushes to serve as rain capes and canoe coverings. Nadya had learned to speak passable trade talk; Myeena's command of English had improved.

"I reckon that would be good," Nadya said, placing the raspberry stalk she had peeled in a basket and reaching for another stalk.

"Hello," called an unfamiliar voice in the distance. "Hello, the house!"

Nadya looked up, startled. Three white men were leading a packhorse along the beach.

Visitors were unusual. The settlers who lived to the south

rarely traveled north. The oystermen who lived to the north journeyed to Astoria on occasion, but they preferred to travel by canoe, rather than by foot.

"Hello!" called another man. He waved to Nadya and she lifted her hand and waved back.

The three men—a father and his two grown sons—were emigrants to the territory from Saint Louis, Missouri. Like Nadya, they had crossed the plains the previous summer, but then they had wintered in Oregon City, in the Willamette Valley.

"Beautiful land there," James Russell, the older man, told Nadya over a cup of tea. Myeena had brewed a pot to offer the men, serving the hot beverage in tin cups and offering them raspberry stalks. The men had tied their horse to a nearby tree and had made themselves comfortable on the mats. "But I reckon I hadn't come so far to stop short of the ocean. At the first warm weather, we packed up and headed west. We left the womenfolk in Astoria, and we're scouting a place to settle."

Nadya nodded, frowning a little. The younger men had wandered away. Last week, Myeena had begun tilling the soil to plant potatoes. The men were walking along the edge of the patch of tilled land. As Nadya watched, one of them stooped and scooped up a handful of soil.

"No farmers in these parts," she said uneasily. "We live by fishing and hunting. Grow a few potatoes, but not much more."

"I'm fond of potatoes," James Russell allowed. He addressed his words to Nadya, ignoring the Indian women. "And I could do without farming for a bit. This land looks ripe for logging, and I reckon that the new sawmill that they're building down by Astoria could mill the lumber." He smiled, looking out toward the forest. "You and your husband live here alone?"

Nadya's frown deepened. She glanced at the other women. Keco sat at her side, but Bena and Myeena had drawn away. They were quietly peeling raspberry stalks at the far end of the mats.

"I don't understand," she said. "This is Myeena's lodge. She and her husband, Lono, live here. Keco and Bena—"

Russell laughed, waving a hand to dismiss her words. "I meant white folks," he said easily. "Not Injuns. Is this Lono fellow an Injun?"

"Lono is a Sandwich Islander," Nadya began.

"I met one of them up at Fort Vancouver," Russell said. "Good swimmers, they say, but not much use on land."

"There are other lodges down south," Nadya continued. "You must have passed them on your way. Sam and Mattie live down that way, and so do Tick and Tack."

Russell nodded. "Niggers and foreigners," he said. "But you and your husband are the only white folks."

"Hey, Pa," one of his sons called, before Nadya could speak again. The two younger men sat down on the mat beside their father. One was about Nadya's age—no more than twenty; the other looked a bit older. "That pastureland looks fine for cattle."

"Fine timber," the other man said. "We could log over this area and make a good profit."

"Maybe your husband could tell me a bit more about the land around here," Russell said. "This looks like the sort of place we wanted to settle."

"I don't think you'd like this area," Nadya said, her voice touched with a desperate edge. "The soil is bad and the land floods in the winter." She glanced at Keco for support.

"Too many Injuns in these parts," Keco said. Her face was an impassive mask; her voice was deep and matter-of-fact. "You wouldn't like it."

But Russell and his sons weren't listening. They had spotted Lono's canoe coming in and they were standing and walking down to the beach to greet the men. Nadya sat for a moment with the women.

"Bad luck," Bena said quietly in the trade talk. "Very bad luck."

The strangers stayed to eat fish and mussels and raspberry stalks and potatoes from Myeena's stores, all cooked over an open fire on the beach. It was awkward and strange, but Lono had invited them, as he would have invited anyone who came strolling down the beach.

As Nadya listened to James Russell and his sons, Edmund and Jack, she grew more uneasy. They spoke with Jacob about the hunting and fishing, about the forest and the pastureland. Jacob, having spoken briefly with Nadya after he and Lono landed, did his best to discourage them. "I hear the pasture is better down to the south a ways," he said. "Besides, that's closer to Astoria. Better for trading and such."

In the afternoon, the men left, heading south to return to Astoria. They would camp by the shore, they said. Nadya was glad to see them go. She noticed that Lono did not urge them to stay the night.

After they left, the group sat in silence for a moment. Then Keco spat in the fire. "I told them that it flooded here every winter," she said. "No matter where you built your lodge, you'd be wet."

Lono nodded. "I said the hunting was bad. And the fishing was much better farther north."

Everyone, it seemed, had told the men that this spot of coast was not a good place to live. They had talked of mosquitoes and sickness and bad soil and bad weather. They laughed as they talked, the atmosphere lightening as the afternoon wore on. The men were gone.

"It'll be all right," Jacob said, touching Nadya's shoulder. She sat at the edge of the group, silent and thoughtful. "Out of all the places along the coast, surely they won't come here."

She nodded slowly. Of course, he had to be right.

He was wrong. A week later, the men returned with their wives and possessions. Nadya heard about it from Myeena, who came to visit her the next day. They were staying in an old fishing lodge, just south of Myeena's lodge.

"I don't like them," Myeena said simply. "The women are pale and tired. The men are always frowning." She scowled, demonstrating the expression.

Nadya patted her friend's arm. Myeena liked everyone; it was odd for her to take such a sudden dislike to people. "Did they say something mean to you?"

"They talk about dirty Injuns," Myeena said. Then she shrugged. "I don't like them."

Nadya and Jacob paid a neighborly call on the newcomers the next day. The two young men had brought their wives along: Anna, a pale blond woman who looked very tired, and Virginia, a sharp-faced brunette who showed too many teeth when she smiled.

Nadya sat with the women and had tea while Jacob chatted with the men. They had set up housekeeping in an abandoned fishing lodge, a ramshackle structure with holes in the roof and gaps in the walls where the cedar boards had separated. One corner was piled with boxes and bags. On top of a pile of boxes, Nadya noticed a stack of animal traps, twin crescents of steel with sharp teeth.

Virginia boiled water over the open fire and made tea in a bone china pot. They sat on blankets spread on the dirt floor and drank from china cups that had somehow survived the westward journey.

"Edmund will build us a proper cabin soon," Virginia was saying. "We're just camping here until it's done." She shook her head, looking around the cabin.

"It's terrible, living here like filthy Injuns," Anna said softly.

"How long have you been settled here?" Virginia asked Nadya, not giving her time to react to Anna's comment.

"Since November," Nadya said. "Through the winter."

"Must have been lonely, out here with no one for company." Virginia shook her head.

"I had company," Nadya protested. "I thought you had met Myeena and Lono."

"Myeena? Was that the Injun woman who came here begging yesterday?" Virginia asked Anna. "I think so."

Nadya was shocked. "She wasn't begging. Myeena is a wonderful person. And Keco and Bena live not far away."

"Those are other Injuns that Jack told us about," Virginia told Anna.

"They're good friends of mine," Nadya said sharply.

"Of course," Anna said, her soft voice understanding. "Living out here by yourself, you had to find what friends you could. I can't imagine it myself. Out here, with the wolves howling at night." She shuddered delicately. "It was bad enough on the plains, listening to the beasts wailing all night. But here, in our own home. . . ."

Virginia patted Anna's hand. "Don't worry. Edmund and

Jack are going hunting for wolves. And they'll set out the traps, soon enough."

Nadya sat stiffly upright, holding her teacup in both hands. "I like the sound of the wolves," she said, her voice strained. "Why do you want to kill them?"

Virginia laughed, as if Nadya had made a joke, and exchanged a glance with Anna. Her expression suggested that Nadya was touched in the head; she had been living with Indians too long. "Oh, let's talk about nicer subjects," she said. "Jack tells me that you served him the most interesting food when he was here. Some kind of wild plant that you peel and eat."

Nadya left as soon as she could, interrupting Jacob's conversation with the men. Together, they headed north along the shore. Nadya found herself walking quickly, her arms folded protectively across her chest.

"They're going to hunt wolves," she told Jacob. "That's what the women said."

She was afraid. She felt the fear as a chill, deep in her bones where the spring sunshine could not warm her. She was afraid of the hunters who would come for her in the night, chasing her with dogs and guns. She was afraid of shouting men and barking dogs and the burnt aroma of black powder and sudden pain. It was better to run now, she thought, to find a new place where she could be safe.

"I can't stay here," she said. "I have to go."

"Go where?" Jacob asked.

She bit her lip, worrying the flesh in her teeth. "North," she said at last. "There are fewer people to the north, I hear."

"Eventually, the people will come." His voice was soft. "You can't keep running forever. You've got to stand and fight."

Nadya kept walking, watching her shadow rippling across the ground before her. She remembered her father's shadow stories, where the wolf fought and won. And she remembered how her father had told her, not long before his death, that the wolf can't win. The wolf can't win.

"I can't win," she said, her voice thin and weak. "I can't."

"You can't run away," he said.

"You could come with me," she said. "We'll go north, find another place."

"Maybe you can't win if you're alone." Gently, Jacob touched her shoulder. "But you're not alone."

Nadya stopped for a moment, her arms crossed, hugging herself for protection. She would run away; she would find a safe place. But even as she thought that, she knew that no place would be safe forever.

Jacob put his arms around her. "The others will help. Let's talk to Keco and Bena, and Myeena and Lono. You don't have to fight alone."

Bena made Nadya herbal tea and wrapped a blanket around her shoulders. She sat on the mat where she had slept while recovering from her injuries. It seemed long ago that she had rested by the fire, watching Keco do card tricks and learning the basics of trade talk.

Jacob fetched Myeena and Lono. Nadya huddled in her blanket and listened to the others discuss what to do.

Calling the discussion a council of war would have been an overstatement. It was a group of friends, discussing how to solve a problem. There was no overall organization. Just the understanding that they could not allow these people to shoot and trap wolves, to log the forest, to chase away the community who lived there.

"We kill them," Myeena said fiercely. She glanced at Nadya, her face set in an uncharacteristically grim expression. "They are bad people and we kill them."

Keco nodded, calmly agreeing with Myeena. "We could kill them easily enough. No one would come looking for them."

Bena shook her head. "You don't know that. And even if we kill them, others will come along. If we want to keep this place as our own, we need to make them go away saying that this is a bad place, a place no one wants to live. They will tell others and no more white folks come here."

Nadya pulled the blanket more closely around her. She was cold, despite the heat of the fire. Virginia had spoken so casually, saying, "They'll set out the traps, soon enough." She remembered the preacher who had come to Wolf Crossing and told the men to kill the wolves and drive out the Devil. There was nowhere that she could be safe. She shivered, and Jacob put an arm around her shoulders.

"We can't let them hunt wolves," Myeena said, still fierce, more passionate than Nadya had ever seen her. "We can't let them set traps."

"I'll spring any traps they set," Lono said, touching his wife on the arm. "Any trap they can set, I can find and spring."

"That's not enough," Bena said in a patient tone. "They must leave this place. But they have to think that leaving is their idea. They must believe that they are moving on because this place is no good."

"We can't change the way they think," Nadya said, her voice low and trembling. "They will not listen, they will not learn, they will not understand. They look at the trees and they see lumber. They listen to the wolves howling and they hear nothing of the joy of the hunt. They don't understand. And because they don't understand, they are afraid. They are afraid of the wolves, they are afraid of the wilderness. So they kill the wolves and chop down the trees, leaving nothing behind."

Jacob tightened his arm around her shoulders, but she could not stop trembling.

"They are afraid of what they don't understand," Bena said thoughtfully. "*Delate wawa.*" That is true.

"There are many things white people do not understand," Keco said slowly. "There are many things that scare them."

"What kinds of things?" Jacob asked.

"Indian things," Keco said. "*Tahmahnawis*. Indian magic." She leaned forward. "Did you know—the lodge where they are living is the house of the *memelose tillicums*." *Memelose tillicums*, the trade talk words for dead people. Keco was saying that the lodge was haunted.

Jacob was shaking his head. "They won't believe that."

Keco raised her eyebrows. "But it is true. I passed by there near sunset one day, and I heard the voices. No one was there, but I heard the people talking." Her voice was soft, almost hypnotic in tone. "I heard them walking around, inside the lodge, their feet moving on cedar mats."

Nadya heard a faint rustling sound off to one side, away from where everyone was sitting. A rustle of the mats, a pause, another rustle, another pause. Footsteps, moving stealthily across the mats—but no one was there. Maybe a mouse, searching for fallen bits of food, but Nadya could not smell a mouse.

"I came closer and I listened to the voices," Keco continued, her voice low. The room was quiet except for the rustling, and it seemed darker than it had before. Myeena had pulled her knees to her chest, curling up like a frightened child. Jacob's hand was tense on Nadya's shoulder. Bena held a hand to her face, half covering her mouth. "They spoke to me." Keco lifted her hands suddenly, and the movement drew Nadya's eyes.

"Kecomenepeca," a voice whispered. It came from the doorway to the cabin, from a place where no one stood. Nadya shivered. It was a knowing voice, a voice from beyond death. "Kecomenepeca, *kopet wawa. Mika mamook kwass* Myeena." You must stop this. You are frightening Myeena.

Myeena yelped, terrified that the voice knew her name, and Lono put his arms around her. Keco laughed then, shaking her head at Bena. Bena opened the hand that she had been holding to her mouth, revealing a speaking tube, fashioned from the stipe of a kelp frond. Keco held up her hand. She was holding a string that ran under the mats to the corner of the hut. By tugging on it, she could make the mats rustle.

Nadya stared at Keco, understanding why the Indians that came to her for counsel were so convinced of her powers. Though they had settled down, Keco and Bena had not given up their old ways.

"We will fool them," Bena said, her voice solemn. "We will fool them with things that they do not understand. And they will be afraid and they will go away."

Nadya leaned against Jacob, still afraid, but willing to hope.

And so the community on Shoalwater Bay welcomed the new settlers.

Myeena took them a basket of fresh caught herring, an oily fish that the Indians always ate with raspberry stalks. Without the tempering effect of the acidic raspberry, feasting on the fish often gave people bellyaches and disorders of the bowels. She brought them no raspberry stalks.

Ivan brought them a blanket as a gift, but of course he let his dog sleep on it for a few days first. In the warmth of the settlers' lodge, the flea eggs hatched and the lively insects infested the settlers' bodies and clothes.

Edmund and Jack set traps for the wolves, but they were not skilled trappers, and it was easy enough for Lono to find their traps. He sprang the traps and stole the bait and made marks in the dirt that an unskilled eye might mistake for animal tracks. Day after day, the traps came up empty.

And Nadya and Jacob went visiting. Nadya sat with the women and had tea while Jacob chatted with the men. As they were sipping tea, Anna complained that she had been feeling poorly. Virginia dismissed her complaint. "You just had too many of those fish to eat," she said. "It's no wonder you're unhappy."

Nadya stared at Anna, frowning.

"What's wrong?" Anna said, watching her. "You look worried."

Nadya wet her lips, still frowning, then shook her head again. Keco had coached her carefully and had made her rehearse her role. "Don't tell them," Keco had said. "Make them ask you."

"I shouldn't tell you," Nadya said. Her voice was fearful. That was easy. She did not have to feign fear. In this house, surrounded by her enemies, she was afraid. She hesitated, then continued. "It's nothing."

"What's nothing?" Anna demanded. "What shouldn't you tell us?"

Nadya kept her eyes on her tea, refusing to look at Anna. "It would only worry you." When she looked up, both women were watching her. "Perhaps a little peppermint tea would make you feel better," she said. "I know where some wild mint grows. I'll gather some."

"What's wrong?" Anna said, her voice peevish and worried.

"Really, Nadya," Virginia said. "You mustn't be so mysterious. You must tell us what you're talking about." When Nadya remained silent, Virginia continued. "You'll worry us much more by remaining silent."

Keco had said that the best way to tell a convincing lie was to tell the truth as far as you could. And when you came to the part that was a lie, you did your best to believe what you were saying, to convince yourself that your story was true.

Nadya glanced at Virginia and then at Anna. "You won't believe it," she said softly. "And I don't blame you. But I can't help but worry." All that was true. She held her teacup tighter and bit her lip. "This land, this cabin . . . You might wonder why no one lives here. People have tried to live here before, but they always leave."

"Why do they leave?" Virginia said, frowning.

Nadya kept her voice low. "The Indians say that a shaman lived here years ago, a very strong medicine man. He built this place and he lived here for many years. This medicine man—he was not just a man, he was a wolf, too. The Indians say that some people change into animals, and he was part man, part wolf. They say that the wolves that live here—the ones you hear howling at night—were his friends. At night, he would run through the forest with the wolves."

Anna was listening eagerly, like a child hearing a ghost story. Virginia was still frowning.

Nadya drew her shawl closer around her shoulders. Bena had given her the shawl to wear, saying it would make her look like a respectable white woman. "Then the smallpox came. The Indians got very sick. They came to the medicine man for help, but he couldn't help them. They died; so many died that the beaches were crowded with bodies. Then the medicine man caught the pox. He blamed the white men for his sickness, for the disease that was killing his people." She hesitated, biting her lip.

"Then what?" Anna asked. "What more?"

Nadya hugged her shawl more tightly around herself. "As he lay on his deathbed, he cursed this place, this cabin, this patch of land. He cursed any white man who came here, vowing that they would sicken and die, just as he was sickening. They would have no luck in this place, no joy. When he died, the Indians say that only the man died. The wolf part of him is still alive, still running through the forest at night, looking for revenge."

Nadya looked up at the women. Anna had clasped her hands beneath her chin; her eyes were bright and fearful. She was, Nadya thought, the sort of woman who enjoyed being a little afraid. Virginia was shaking her head.

"That's why Edmund and Jack can't trap the wolves," Anna whispered breathlessly. "They've set the traps so many times—and they always come up empty."

"Superstitious nonsense," Virginia said. "Ghost stories to frighten children."

"But Virginia," Anna began.

"Hush," Virginia said. "You'll just make yourself sicker, worrying about this nonsense."

"I should never have mentioned it," Nadya said. "But when Anna said she was ill, I started to worry." She patted Anna's hand. "I'll make you an herb tea that will settle your stomach. I'm sure it will help."

The next day, Nadya brought a pot of herbs for tea. They were, as she told Anna and Virginia, mostly mints of one kind or another, all good for the stomach. Of course one plant, mixed in with the strong-smelling peppermint, was a powerful diarrhetic, liable to exacerbate any stomach problems Anna might be having. While she was visiting, Nadya inquired about their success in trapping wolves and looked concerned when she learned that the traps were still empty.

A week went by like this. Each day, Nadya visited the women and showed her concern. After she left their cabin, she prowled the forest, checking the traps that the men had set. Lono sprung them, but Nadya could not help but check.

At night, Nadya's pack howled in the hills, and Nadya listened to their song—glad to hear each voice join in, but wishing that they would stay clear of the cabin, move away for a time.

Once, Lono took the men hunting for wolves, following an old trail up and down the ridges. He led them through brambles and swamps, up steep grades and down. After they made their way through the swamp, getting wet and muddy and chilled, he produced a flask of whiskey from his jacket pocket and they warmed themselves a bit. He ended the expedition at the remains of a kill, a deer carcass that had been stripped and abandoned several days before.

At the carcass, looking up at the empty hillside, Lono shouted that he saw a wolf and fired at nothing. Up on the hill, he found no sign of the animal—which was not surprising, since there had been no wolf when he shot. "He's gone," Lono said solemnly. "Vanished like a ghost."

Jack and Edmund returned to their cabin, weary and disgusted with the country in which they found themselves. They had accepted Lono as a capital fellow after he produced the whiskey flask, and they were both convinced that they had seen the wolf on the hill. "A big black fellow," Jack told his father. "Grinning like Satan."

Anna grew wan and frightened. She confided to Nadya, when Virginia had stepped outside to fetch wood for the fire, that a medium had told that she was very sensitive to spirits. She had attended several table-rapping séances before she met Jack. And the medium had said that the spirits were drawn to her. "I wish Madame was here," Anna said wistfully of the medium. "Maybe she would be able to chase this spirit away."

Nadya looked thoughtful. Anna's interest in spiritual guidance presented an opportunity. "Well, you could—" she began, and then stopped herself. "No, I suppose not."

'What?" Anna said eagerly. "What could we do?"

"There's a medicine man who lives near here." Keco had suggested that she pose as a medicine man and have a little ceremony for the settlers. This seemed like the perfect opportunity to offer the medicine man's services. "He did a ceremony to clear our cabin of spirits. And after that, we weren't bothered at all." Nadya looked down at her hands, avoiding the woman's eyes. "But I'm sure that Virginia would have no interest in that." She looked up and found Anna gazing at her with rapt attention.

"Would he come here?" Anna asked. "That would be wonderful."

"I don't think Virginia would care for that," Nadya said softly. "And Jack and Edmund might not—"

"I'll take care of all that," Anna said resolutely. Nadya had no doubt she would. Beneath that air of sweet femininity, Nadya suspected she was as stubborn as they came, more than a match for Virginia.

"It'll cost you," Nadya said. "When he came to us, he demanded three blankets and a pouch of tobacco."

"You talk to the medicine man," Anna said. "I'll take care of the rest."

A few days later, as the sun was setting, Kecomenepeca came to the settlers' cabin, led by Nadya and Jacob. Jack, Edmund, Anna, and Virginia were there; James had gone to meet with the oystermen who lived some distance to the north, wanting to confer with them about lumbering the area and transporting the wood to sawmills in Astoria.

Virginia, determined to be a good hostess, made tea and offered everyone a cup. The men looked grim and uncomfortable. "If it'll make Anna happy," Jack muttered to Jacob, "it's all right with me." But he didn't look happy to have Keco and Bena in his house. He gave Jacob a pouch of tobacco for Keco, which the Indian accepted after examining it closely.

Anna stayed at Keco's elbow as the Indian woman prowled the cabin, shaking her rattle and muttering chants under her breath. The cooking fire and a lantern that hung from the center of the cabin cast a flickering light.

Kecomenepeca was dressed in an amazing assortment of ceremonial clothing, gathered from the many tribes that she and Bena had visited on their travels. When she moved, the strands of shell beads and bear claws that hung around her neck rattled together. She wore a loose tunic, beaded with elaborate designs in the fashion of the Cheyenne, and her face was painted like a raiding Pawnee. She carried a rattle made from the shell of a desert tortoise from a tribe far to the south.

Nadya had worried that Jack and Edmund would recognize Keco, but Keco had assured her that they wouldn't. "All Injuns look alike to them," she had said. Even if Keco's assessment of the men had been wrong, they were safe. Nadya herself wouldn't have recognized her friend in her ceremonial garb.

"What's he doing?" Anna asked Nadya softly.

In trade jargon, Nadya asked Keco what she was doing. Then she translated the gruff answer. "He's looking for spirits," she said.

Virginia was pouring a cup of tea for Anna when Keco called

out, an inarticulate shout of alarm. She snatched the cup from Anna's hand, as Jack moved in protectively. Keco was chanting in some language Nadya couldn't identify and passing her hand over the cup, her face set in grim lines. Then she looked into the cup and grunted in satisfaction, then held out the cup so that Anna and Nadya could examine the contents.

In the bottom of the cup, submerged in tea, Nadya could see five white beads, each the size of a pea. With a spoon, Anna fished the beads from the tea. When she saw them clearly, she gave a little scream and nearly dropped the cup. Five small skulls with staring eyes, carved from bone.

"There is a very strong spirit here," Keco said in the trade talk, her voice low. "Very strong."

Jack took Anna in his arms to comfort her, while Jacob and Edmund examined the beads. "I've seen these before," Jacob said. "Indians use them." Nadya stood at his elbow, listening.

"What for?" Edmund asked.

Jacob hesitated. "To curse their enemies, I reckon," he muttered.

"Where'd they come from?" Edmund said. "I reckon he put them in the cup." He glared at Keco, who returned his stare impassively.

"I was watching, Edmund," Virginia said. "There wasn't anything in the cup before. And he didn't have anything in his hands when he took it."

Edmund moved to pour the beads from the spoon into his hand and Keco shouted again. "Don't touch them," Jacob said, putting his hand on Edmund's. "He says they're dangerous."

Keco took the spoon from Edmund's hand and issued a series of peremptory commands that Jacob and Nadya translated. Bena moved the teapot and built up the fire. Jacob and Nadya arranged the settlers in a circle with the fire near the center. "We must all sit in a circle," Jacob translated Keco's commands. "That way, we will be protected from the spirits."

Keco still held the beads in the spoon. As Nadya watched, she addressed the beads loudly, speaking in a commanding tone. "What's he doing?" Anna asked, her voice fearful.

"He's trying to remove the curse," Nadya whispered. "He's arguing with the old medicine man." She glanced at Anna.

The woman's face was flushed with excitement.

Keco was listening and glaring at the beads. Then she spoke again, shouting in an angry tone. The circle of watching people were silent as she listened again. Glancing at the fire, Keco spoke to Bena and she opened Keco's pack and placed three bundles of herbs on the burning logs. The herbs burned smokily with a pungent smell.

Keco tipped her head back and howled, like the leader of a pack calling the others to his side. From outside the hut, off in the distance, Nadya heard answering howls. She recognized Lono's voice and Myeena's. Anna shivered and Jack put a comforting hand on her shoulder.

As the air filled with smoke from the herbs, Keco lifted her hands high. With another howling cry, she cast the beads into the flames. She was moving now, her feet shuffling in time to the rhythm of her howls.

There was an explosion, as sharp as a gunshot, and Keco cried out as if in pain. The fire flared with a yellow flame. Then another explosion. Then three in rapid succession, each accompanied by a flash of fire.

"What the hell. . . ?" Nadya heard Jack say, but Anna had a hand on the man's shoulder.

"It's dangerous to leave the circle," she said. "Don't go."

Keco was howling like an animal in pain, waving her hands in the air and beating at the smoke. As she lifted her hands high, something leaped at her from the fire. In the smoke and confusion, Nadya could not see it clearly: it looked like a great black snake that tried to coil around the Indian. Keco wrestled the creature and howled. The wolves outside howled louder. Anna was in tears in Jack's arms and Virginia clung to Edmund.

Keco had fallen and Nadya lost sight of her in the smoke. But she heard the woman cry out—a shout that was almost a scream, a wail of agony. And another shout, weaker this time, but with words that Nadya could understand. "Go away," Keco called in the trade talk. "Go away from this place."

The wolves outside retreated. Nadya could hear their footsteps, moving away. The smoke began to clear and Nadya could see Bena kneeling over Keco's body. Keco's face was smeared with blood, and a trickle of red flowed from the woman's mouth.

The black snake, if there had been one, was gone.

"Is Keco all right?" Nadya asked Bena, moving forward in the circle, honestly alarmed. Bena warned her back with a glance. Keco murmured something, and Bena repeated it for Jacob to translate.

"Not good," Jacob told the settlers. Anna's face was streaked with tears, and Virginia looked frightened. The men were frowning, uncertain. "The spirit is very strong. He chased it away, but it will be back."

Bena spoke again, her voice steady. "She says you can't live here," Jacob said. "It isn't safe." He glanced at the door where the wolves had been howling. "They'll be back."

After a time, when the smoke had cleared, Bena gathered the things that she and Keco had brought to the cabin and left quietly, taking Keco with her. Keco seemed weak, and she leaned on Bena as they made their way along the path and out of sight.

Nadya lingered for a time, talking with Anna and Virginia. Anna was certain that the spirits were responsible for her illness. Nadya and Jacob left soon after.

"Do you think that they will leave?" Nadya asked Jacob.

He shrugged, frowning. "It's hard to say. Edmund asked me again about the lumbering down south of here. He may be losing heart."

They went to Keco's cabin, where the Indian woman was resting on the mat by the fire. She had washed her face clean of paint and changed into her usual clothing.

"Battling the spirits is very hard work," she said, when Nadya commented on how tired she looked.

"I saw a snake spring from the fire toward you," Nadya said. "What was that?"

"The Sisiutl," Keco said solemnly. "Snake spirit. Very powerful."

"Some medicine men make Sisiutl from wooden tubes," Jacob said. "They collapse together." He brought his hands together, showing how the tubes could collapse.

Keco nodded. "Some do," she acknowledged.

Nadya patted the woman on the hand, knowing that she

would say no more about her illusions. Keco had, Nadya thought, slipped the beads into the cup with sleight of hand. The explosions could have been gunpowder, packed into the beads.

It didn't matter. The ceremony or the performance, whichever you decided it was, had been convincing. It was just a week until the full moon. Nadya could only hope that the settlers would leave before they shot any of the very real wolves who inhabited the hills, before the moon was full and the Change came.

35

■

A few days later, when Nadya and Jacob went to visit the family, they found Edmund sitting by the cabin door, sharpening his knife on a whetstone. He said nothing of leaving, nothing of the spirits that haunted their cabin. "My father's back," he said to Jacob. "And we're going hunting for wolves. Maybe you'd like to come along?"

Nadya held Jacob's hand, listening to the men talk. The conversation was punctuated by the scrape, scrape, scrape of Edmund's knife on the whetstone.

"You can't kill them," Jacob said, a desperate edge in his voice. "You've tried for yourself. Your traps have come up empty. And the medicine man told you—"

"Hocus-pocus," Edmund scoffed. "I never believed in it. He took in Anna and Virginia, but I wasn't fooled." His knife continued its rhythmic scraping. Sharp steel on cold stone.

"It was strange how the wolves started howling," Jacob commented. He shook his head, looking doubtful and uncomfortable. Nadya knew that he was uncomfortable to be lying, but his hesitation could be interpreted as a practical man's discomfort with mystical matters. "It bothers me, though—I've never been able to trap one of those wolves. And I worked for years as a trapper."

"Well, I'll bring one back for you," Edmund said, his voice filled with bravado. "I wonder how much the fur of a spirit wolf sells for in Astoria."

"The same as the fur of any wolf," his father said. The older man stood in the door of the cabin. Nadya could see Anna and Virginia in the shadows behind him. "No different." He studied Nadya and Jacob, frowning. "I reckon we'll kill those wolves and bring you a fur to show you there ain't nothing supernatural about them at all." He glared at Jacob. "But that's not news to you. You figured you'd scare us away with your medicine man and your hocus-pocus. You want to keep this for yourself." He waved a hand at the timber, at the bay. "But you figured wrong. I'll be logging this land and killing every wolf along this coast—and maybe all the Injun medicine men, too. This place is mine and I don't plan to leave it."

He was staring at Jacob, ignoring Nadya. "Why?" she said suddenly. "Why do you hate us?" The words came out before she thought. She was suddenly angry, warmed from within by a startling passion.

James Russell glanced at her, as if startled to realize she was there. "Hate you? Miss Nadya, I don't know what you're talking about. This is men's business. That's all." His tone was dismissive. "I don't reckon I hate anyone. I'm just claiming the land that's rightfully mine—and I got to kill a few wolves and a few Injuns to do it."

"You hate the wolves and you hate the forest," she said. Her voice was passionate. "You hate the Indians and you hate anyone who is not like you. And we're not like you."

"I'd say you aren't like me—that's true enough." He shifted his gaze back to Jacob, his expression contemptuous. "You and your Indian medicine man. Well, driving us out just ain't going to work. We're bringing civilization to this place."

"Civilization?" she said, her voice fierce and angry. "I've seen your kind of civilization. It means death and it means pain. I have no place in your civilization. I can't be civilized." She bared her teeth at him. "Listen: when the moon is full, I am a wolf. I run through the forest and howl at the moon. If you were my friend, you would have nothing to fear from me. But you are no one's friend."

James glanced at Jacob, shaking his head and frowning a little. "Your wife isn't well," he said.

"She is fine." Jacob slipped his arm around her shoulders. "And she is right. We have no place in your civilization."

* * *

That night, the moon would be full. Late in the afternoon, Jacob stayed near Nadya as she prepared supper. He watched her hands as she stirred the corn-bread batter, added wood to the fire. She moved with a heavy grace, carrying herself with careful dignity.

"Maybe you could stay here," he suggested as they sat down to eat. When she frowned at him, he tried to explain. "In the cabin, I mean. After you change. Just stay here with me."

She laughed then, an abrupt painful sound. "Spend the night of the Change within four walls?" She shook her head. "Can't do that."

"Then stay far away from their cabin," he said. "Head north. And you'll be all right."

She nodded as if she understood, but she did not speak and her eyes were unreadable, the eyes of a wild creature.

"We can leave," he said suddenly, reaching across the table to take her hand. "We'll go north, like you wanted before. We'll find a place where there's no one who will bother us."

She shook her head slowly. "No. We can't run away."

That evening, she insisted that he stay in the cabin. "What can you do?" she said to him. "Follow a wolf through the forest? Lock me up so I'm safe?" She shook her head.

When he hugged her goodbye, he did not want to let her go. Warm body against his, so solid and real. It seemed impossible that she should Change. "I've got to go," she said softly. "I can feel the moon." He released her reluctantly.

He watched her walk away, and he fought the urge to run after her.

She walked slowly toward the clearing on the hill, following the trail she had worn over the past months. Late afternoon. The shadows were thick around her and a cool breeze blew. Though she wore only her thin calico dress, she was not cold. Knowledge of the coming Change and the lingering anger that had touched her that afternoon warmed her.

She did not know what would happen that night. That afternoon, she had read the cards, and the card that appeared in her immediate future was *La Mort,* Death, a skeleton striding across a battlefield littered with corpses. Behind the skeleton, the sun was rising; a new day was dawning. A great change was coming. The cards told of change, but that was all. No clarity.

She untied the leather cord that held her hair back and shook her hair loose. She folded her dress and set it on a fallen log. She took off her boots and stood naked and barefoot in the grass of the clearing. She lifted her arms to feel the warmth of the rising moon caress her like the hand of a lover, bringing a rosy blush to her nipples, her face.

She Changed. A gray wolf stood in the clearing, her head lifted to sample the breeze. She did not think about the death that the cards had foretold; she did not plan for the night ahead. The only time was now, this moment and no other. No past. No future. Only now.

She barked once and then tipped back her head to howl, calling to the other members of her pack. A chorus of howls answered her from the south, and she recognized the voice of her mate, of the other wolves of the pack. At ease in her body, pregnant but graceful even in her pregnancy, she trotted toward the sound.

She met the pack a few miles to the south, in a clearing by a creek. The wolves surrounded her, wagging their tails and licking at her face, welcoming her back. She returned their greetings, making low noises in her throat and moving among them, pushing her muzzle against the muzzle of one wolf, then another. She lingered beside her mate, burying her nose deep in the fur of his ruff and inhaling his scent.

But even among her pack mates, she could not relax. There was something bothering her, a lingering uneasiness, a touch of passion that made her restless and agitated. She trotted with them alongside the creek, and they found a metal thing that smelled of dried blood and fear and men. On the ground was a piece of venison that had been in the jaws of the metal thing. One of the younger wolves snatched up the meat and swallowed it in a gulp. The others sniffed around, looking for other scraps of meat.

The trap had been sprung; it was harmless. But the smells that surrounded it stirred her uneasiness. It wasn't just the smell of men that disturbed her, but these particular men in this particular place.

The wind carried other scents: wood smoke and cattle and humans. She whimpered low in her throat and then growled. This man smell touched an anger that lay deep within her, deeper than conscious thought.

Her restlessness was contagious. Her mate sniffed the wind and growled with her. The younger wolves circled them, lifting their heads and breathing deeply of the scent.

Nadya shook herself, trying to shake off the anger, the uneasiness. But the feelings persisted; the human smell drew her. She trotted in the direction of the wind, heading toward the cabin that was the source of these smells. There was something she could not remember, a feeling that she should not go near that cabin, that she should run away, up into the hills. But the anger would not let her go. She went toward the cabin and the rest of the pack followed.

She saw the cattle in their corral, pale-faced beasts staring over the split-rail fence. Easy prey—slow-footed and too stupid to fight. But she did not turn aside to chase the cattle. It was not hunger that drove her. Wolves are territorial animals. A pack ranges over a large area, but they know their land, their territory. They mark their territory with their scent, and they chase out intruders, taking back what is theirs. The humans in this cabin did not belong in her territory. Nadya had no words—words were gone—but she knew, with a deep certainty, that these people were a threat to her pack, a threat to the pups that she carried.

She slowed her pace from a trot to a walk, approaching cautiously. The moon was overhead now, casting a pale silver light. Here, not far from the cabin, the trees had been felled and the air was sharp with the scent of newly cut cedar. The cabin was a dark blocky shape against the moonlit sky.

The wind shifted, carrying the wolves' scent to the cattle, and the animals snorted and spooked, backing away from the railing. Nadya hesitated on the edge of the forest, still standing in the shadow of the trees. Then she crept closer, moving from the shadow of one cedar stump to another. She did not know why she felt the need to approach the cabin. The fur on her neck bristled, prickling with fear and the knowledge of danger. There was something that had to happen here. A conversation about power. About territory. About wolves and men. The smells drew her: the scent of anger that lingered by the cabin door, the scent of fear—her own fear, mixed with a human scent.

Behind her, the cattle snorted again, and the cow bellowed in alarm. One of the young wolves had her paws up on the split-rail fence and was staring between the rails at the cattle. At the far side of the corral, the cow stood between the wolf and her calf.

From inside the cabin, Nadya heard the rustle of mats and blankets. Someone was getting up. There was a strong scent of black powder, the clack of metal on metal as a rifle was loaded. She flattened herself into the shadow of the woodpile, seeking the safety of darkness.

The door creaked open. James Russell wore a pale nightshirt that flapped in the wind from the bay. Under his arm, he carried his rifle, primed and loaded. His bare feet quiet, he stepped into the yard, staring in the direction of the cattle.

The cattle returned his stare. The wolves were gone, they had melted into the shadows of the forest. "Goddamn varmints," Russell muttered. He stank of anger. Still staring toward the corral, he walked away from the cabin, scanning the shadows for the varmints that had startled the cattle.

He was just a few feet from Nadya when she heard him exhale suddenly, a sigh of satisfaction. She followed his gaze. The black wolf had stepped from the shadows to stare toward the cabin, looking for Nadya, waiting for her to return. Russell raised his rifle, sighting on the wolf. At this distance, he would not miss.

In that moment, Nadya leaped from the shadows, throwing herself against the man. He staggered and the shot went wild. He fell beneath her. The air was thick with the smoke of burnt powder, but through the acrid smoke she could smell his fear. He struggled to push her away with one hand, his other hand still clutching his rifle. The rifle was useless now—he would have to reload before firing again—but he would not let it go.

Nadya snapped at the hand that was at her throat, catching the wrist in her teeth and clamping down. The skin broke beneath her teeth—such delicate skin, unprotected by fur—and the taste of fear and blood filled her mouth. She released his wrist, startled at the ease with which she had drawn blood. He snatched his hand away from her, curling himself around the injury, protecting his belly, his throat.

Standing above him, she hesitated for a moment. He lay still, as submissive as a wolf who acknowledges defeat. She had established her dominance, and that was enough. She could let him live. But he shifted beneath her suddenly, attacking her again, clubbing at her with his useless rifle. She went for his throat, tearing at the thin skin to let the blood flow, black in the moonlight, tasting of hate. She heard his breath catch in his throat, a scream that stopped before it began.

A gunshot from the cabin, men shouting, and she was running, heading for the shadow of the forest. She ran with the pack—away from the acrid reek of burnt powder, the tang of fear, the warm smell of blood. Not her blood. A heavier scent, cloying and sweet. Human blood.

She followed the pack to the stream where she drank, trying to wash the taste of blood from her mouth. Then the black wolf led the pack to the north, toward her own cabin. The young wolves stayed close beside her, gathering around whenever she stopped, licking at her muzzle and face and cleaning the blood from her fur.

When they stopped, the moon was low over the ocean. Nadya could feel its warmth in her blood, but it was starting to fade. She was sore where James Russell had struck her, weary from running. But despite her pains, she felt good.

On the beach, not far from the cabin she shared with Jacob, the big male wolf sat back on his haunches. Nadya could smell the smoke of the fire, could catch a whiff of Jacob's scent. This was a good place to be.

The male lifted his head to stare at the moon. He howled, a pure note that started low and held steady. The young wolves joined in, each on a different note to form a chorus. Nadya tipped back her head and added her voice to theirs, a song of triumph and challenge. This is our land, this is our place. We belong here and you can't chase us away.

The moon set and she Changed. Where there had been a gray wolf, there was a young woman, sitting naked on the sand.

What does it feel like to return to your body after a night in the wild? What does it feel like to awaken with the lingering taste of your enemy's blood in your mouth, on a misty beach surrounded by wolves?

Words come back to you, words like "home" and "love" and "friends." Sometimes words are false—people can shape them to make lies—but sometimes they are good and true and they let you remember the past with its pains and joys, they let you consider the future, when you will live in a cabin with your children beside you, happy in this land that is your own.

As the moon sets, the smells fade. You accept that. You know that there will be other nights to run in the forest beneath the tall trees. And you accept who you are.

You are a woman.

You are a wolf.

You have found your place and you have defended it from those who would do you harm. You belong in this place. You have conquered your enemy and discovered yourself.

Nadya sat for a moment on the cool sand, her knees pulled up against her chest, staring out over the bay. A line of pelicans was flying north, one following the other in an uneven line. The sun was rising and the birds were starting to sing, defending their territories with song.

The wolves sniffed her cautiously. She smelled the same as before: wolfish, but a little strange. She lifted a hand slowly and stroked one wolf's soft ears, touched another's muzzle.

She stood, stretching in the sun. The settlers would leave—she was confident of that. Without James Russell, they would go south, where they would find others of their kind—loggers and farmers and trappers.

As she stood, she felt the child within her shift and kick, a solid thump inside her belly. She laughed at the strange sensation, happy to feel the life inside her.

The wolves drifted away, heading up into the forest, away from the beach and the cabin and the smell of smoke. Nadya went home, striding along the beach toward the cabin. "Jacob," she called as she approached. "Jacob! I'm home!"

Epilogue

You are driving north on Highway 1, heading from San Francisco to Seattle. You have left things behind in San Francisco—a job, a lover, a life—and you are going to Seattle to start again. Somewhere, north of Astoria, along the coast and beside a bay, you camp for the night. The moon is full and you are camping under tall trees, second-growth forest. The moonlight glistens on the placid water of the bay. Willapa Bay, it's called now. Early settlers called it Shoalwater Bay.

You wake in the night to the howling of wolves. You lie awake in your tent—moonlight shining down through the blue nylon—and pull your sleeping bag more tightly around you. Not wolves, you think. Coyotes, maybe. There are no wild wolves on the Washington coast, not anymore. Or maybe it's a dream.

You sleep again. In the morning, you pack up your camp and drive a few miles to a gas station, just a few miles north. No town to speak of, just a wide spot in the road, a ramshackle building with a pair of gas pumps, halfway between nowhere in particular and nowhere at all.

The young woman who comes out to pump your gas can't be much more than twenty: a lean muscular brunette dressed in grease-stained jeans and a red tank top that shows off the tattoos on her arms. One arm is fire and light: a phoenix rising from the flames of a dragon that holds the world in its coils. The other arm is shadow and darkness: trees rise in complex swirls of abstract foliage; from the forest, a gray wolf stares with golden eyes. The woman's hair is tied back in a braid. Her eyes are an unusual color, golden brown like the eyes of a wild animal.

"I camped out not far from here," you tell her. "And I thought I heard wolves howling last night. Are there any wolves around here?"

She smiles a crooked smile, upturned lips with a touch of a sneer. "Not just now," she says easily. "Maybe you heard coyotes."

"It makes a much better story with wolves," you say, a little wistfully. "It sounds so much more adventurous."

The woman shrugs again, still grinning. "Well, when my great-great-great-grandmother settled here, back in 1848, the Indians told stories about ghost wolves that no one could trap, no hunter could kill. People heard them howling on the night of the full moon."

"The moon was full," you remember.

The woman nods. "Then maybe you heard the ghosts."

You nod. "Ghost wolves," you murmur. "That'll make a great story when I get home."

"Glad to help out," the woman says easily.

You drive up the wild coast, through fog that rises from the bay, thinking of the young woman at the service station and the ghost wolves that run through the forest on the night of the full moon. Somehow, in a way that makes no sense, the two seem to go together.